Jill,
Congratulat
May you alw e in.
Tamar
June 2015

initial conditions

a novel

T. K. FLOR

ISBN-10: 150752420X

ISBN-13: 978-1507524206

For Alon and Ori

CONTENTS

1

THE HUNGRY BOSON

It was a fine morning - the sky was azure, birds chirped from treetops, and a stream on the edge of the lawn glinted in sunlight. In a living room of a two-bedroom brick house nestled between the stream and Chadwick Drive, Danielle Meller was sitting with her back turned to a pair of large windows, unpacking yet another cardboard box. From a TV set that she had absent-mindedly turned on, an insistent feminine voice carried on.

"Nowadays, a woman must have a profession. Not merely a day job, but a rock-solid career that empowers and sets up her own social circle. Dependable income secures a woman's independence."

Danielle raised her head above the box and glanced at the TV. The woman on the screen was rather young and immaculately groomed, but nevertheless she reminded Danielle of Mrs. Lerner, her mother-in-law-to-be. Too strongly, Danielle decided. She felt no regret ruffling Sarah Lerner's feathers. If Jonathan's mother could not accept that they had agreed on a long-distance relationship, that was not Danielle's problem.

Danielle turned off the TV, pulled up the blinds and opened the windows. Daylight burst inside, bounced off bright creamy walls and half-filled bookshelves, dappled the lovely fireplace and the polished hardwood floor cluttered with kitchenware, books and clothes. She breathed the fragrant air, surveyed the garden and the sparkling stream. The morning was too bright for reflections, too pretty for organizing her belongings in her new home. It was, after all, one of the last days of her well-earned vacation before starting a new job.

Dressed in a light summer dress and sandals, Danielle left the rented house and ambled along Chadwick Drive. Small patches of wood interposed with tidy lawns. Shiny minivans, carelessly tossed bicycles, and scattered toys indicated that people lived there peacefully and comfortably.

The sun rose higher, dissipating the morning's freshness. What had started as a pleasant walk became a monotonous stroll along nearly-identical leafy streets. Unable to distinguish one nice neighborhood from another - they all looked like hundreds of other well-to-do neighborhoods sprawling across small mid-Atlantic towns - Danielle decided to go back to unpacking.

"Rats," she muttered, realizing she did not have the slightest idea where she was or where Chadwick Drive was. She lifted her head, narrowed her eyes and looked around. In the middle of the town, towering over the two-story brick and wooden houses, was a group of massive buildings, collectively known as King Solomon University.

Envisioning a glass of icy lemonade, Danielle headed straight towards the tallest edifice. The sun was nearly above her head when she reached a street bordering the university's campus. She turned to the left, in the direction of the Main Street and its cafés. To her right, a narrow lane branched into the campus - a shady lane that stretched like an invitation to hide from the glaring sun. Going into the alley, she half expected to see a "private" or "no trespassing" sign posted on one of the trees, not a huge marble arch rising high over the paved lane. It looked incongruous and forbidding, like a gigantic guardian, erected to deter those who had no business going in. Danielle hesitated. A swift sensation of foreboding made her take a few steps back. There was no commemorative plaque, but near the top of the arch was an inscription. It read:

"King Solomon University. Since 1822. Truth We Pursue."

"A nice motto," she murmured. But there was something creepy about the arch. Feeling slightly unnerved, she returned to the street she came from and started to look for a nice café to relax in.

The buildings facing Stateside Street were law firms and real estate offices, boutiques and an upscale barbershop. Parched and annoyed at not being able to find her way in a small town,

Danielle was slow to distinguish a new scent wafting in the warm air, an elusive aroma that intensified as she walked down the street. A whiff of the tantalizing mixture brought to Danielle's mind freshly baked cakes, summer berries, and melted chocolate.

"A fantasy," she dismissed the thought, but quickened her pace. A bakery shop would have cold bottled water and fresh muffins and brownies, maybe a few tables.

Danielle's nose twitched when she reached a single-story house. Her mouth watered, so seductive was the scent engulfing her. On a sign above the door, she read "The Hungry Boson."

A strange name for a café or a bakery, Danielle thought. For a while, she just stood there and inhaled the smells that floated around, tickled her nostrils. Then she stepped inside.

Shaded from bright light, Danielle saw lace curtains drawn on windows, wooden round tables, and wide flowery chairs that belonged to an old-fashioned teashop. Buttery scents, fruity scents, and heavier chocolaty aromas swirled and glided all over. She inched forward; her eyes grew bigger and bigger as her stare shifted from an espresso machine to trays laid on refrigerated shelves. No muffins. No brownies. She gaped at neatly arranged éclairs, pies and tarts.

"A lovely day, isn't it?" a woman's voice came from the back of the shop. Glancing in that direction, Danielle glimpsed an elderly woman put a book aside and walk to the counter.

"How can I help you?" the woman asked. Her voice was friendly, its light accent matching the teashop ambiance.

"It's so beautiful here," Danielle said. "Can I get a cappuccino and a glass of water?" She turned her head towards a distant tray. "And one of these éclairs, please?"

Danielle gulped the water while drops of coffee slowly dripped into a cup. Her curious stare flitted from object to object, until it paused on a couple of newspapers at the edge of the counter.

"The *King's Monkey?*" Danielle read aloud. "Is it a local newspaper?"

"The *Monkey* is a satirical students' paper," the woman replied.

"*Hopeville Herald?*" Danielle read another title.

"Plenty of gossip, and some university news." The woman put the coffee on the counter. "Drink carefully when you are reading," she advised.

The coffee and the chocolate éclair were excellent. Reading about a professor in a Martian barbershop, Danielle felt at peace with herself and the world. She did not notice other customers walking in.

"Crawford will have to resign." Danielle heard a man's voice nearby. "Even he won't get away so simply."

She darted a sideways glance at the speaker. He was blond, somewhere in his late forties, well dressed, and fairly agitated. Of his companion, Danielle saw only the back of a blue polo shirt and bright ginger hair. She speculated that both men were affiliated with the university.

"So simply?" the redhead scoffed. "He has been apologizing in every possible forum ever since he let that remark slip."

Gathering that the men were talking about Crawford's scandal, Danielle pricked up her ears. Crawford's messy slip, as to why female scientists lagged behind their male colleagues, had received unprecedented nationwide coverage, and was met with wide disapproval. She was curious to hear what these men thought about it. Since they made no attempt to speak quietly, she had no qualms about eavesdropping on their conversation.

"And he will continue to do so," the blond said darkly, "maybe even after his resignation."

"Come on," the redhead objected. "At some point he'll kindly explain that he has other obligations and ignore further taunts. For how long is he expected to pay for a single misguided remark?"

The blond shook his head. "The criticism won't subside if he tries to ignore it. He simply cannot appear condescending to women scientists."

"I see no point in fretting about it," the redhead said. "Crawford has a nice faculty position to fall back on, and nobody is interested in an ordinary professor's views."

The conversation paused while the men drank their coffees and privately lamented, or so Danielle assumed, the lack of public interest in ordinary professors. Enjoying the free entertainment, she speculated about which department the men belonged to, if they were indeed university professors. When the blond lowered his cup and sighed, Danielle put guesses aside. She listened attentively.

"Yet, there is something in his remark. For years women avoided physics, and nobody could figure out why."

"You don't attribute their lesser aptitude to biological differences, a la Crawford?" the redhead chuckled. "What about women in astronomy, in biophysics, even a few headstrong, like Susan, in theoretical physics?"

"What about them?" the blond grumbled.

"How would you explain their success without suggesting that they're freaks?"

Danielle itched to enlighten the chauvinist crackpots that intelligent women were not nature's accidents, but decided that as a new post-doc, it was not a good way to introduce herself to the members of faculty.

"Don't gloat, Isaac," the blond gruffly advised. "The media has already taken care of that. The uproar has nothing to do with the outstanding ones who are sought by top universities. It's about the entire pool of female researchers."

Danielle glowered at her empty plate.

"What I recall and most people seem to overlook is that Crawford was speaking of a biological bias that shifts the odds, and not about general laws." The blond went on, "Just look at the statistics in physics. Despite all the encouragement, the special grants and scholarships they have been getting, only precious few go beyond the graduate level. The women to men ratio among tenured researchers is embarrassingly small."

"Have you considered that women might be too rational to pursue a career with such unfavorable odds?" Isaac asked. "Or that most female students might discover that they dislike quantum mechanics?"

"You treat this as a joke because you couldn't care less why it is so. What if women are less apt to understand quantum mechanics?"

"Does anyone understand it?" Isaac quipped.

While the blond drained his cup and grumbled something inaudible, Danielle made a mental note to introduce herself to Isaac when he would not be in the company of the stuffy bore.

"We know that male students do not shy away from making a living from abstractions they don't understand," Isaac said. "But what allows us to assume that most women have similar inclination?"

A thud behind the counter startled Danielle. The men rose, the blond headed straight to the door, Isaac approached the woman.

"Are you hurt, Anne?"

"My book fell," Anne said firmly. Isaac whispered something and went to join the blond.

Denied the rest of the conversation, Danielle picked up the *King's Monkey* and *Hopeville Herald*, and put them back on the counter.

"My name is Danielle," she introduced herself to the woman.

"Anne," said Anne. She slightly bowed her head. "How do you do?"

"Great. I'd have never imagined, but I'm really happy to find a teashop so close to the university."

"Working there?" Anne asked politely.

"I'm going to in a few days." Danielle smiled. She wanted to know more about Isaac, but Anne's elegant looks did not encourage a chummy approach. "I thought interest in Crawford's remark was ebbing," Danielle commented offhandedly, "but I see it is still making waves."

"I suppose you could not help overhearing them," Anne said rebukingly.

"I normally wouldn't listen uninvited, but Isaac's words reminded me of a guy I had dated." Seeing interest flicker over Anne's face, Danielle went on. "Paul Zeeman was a very bright and unbearably arrogant graduate student. He showed contempt for anyone less quick and bright than himself."

"People mellow when they become older. They often learn to treat others with some respect."

Danielle shook her head, to show that she doubted anything could cure Zeeman.

They sat quietly for a few minutes, each woman immersed in her own recollections and thoughts. When Anne rose to collect the dirty dishes, Danielle continued to sit uninterrupted, until new customers came in.

2

FIRST IMPRESSIONS

The dawn of the first of September was unusually chilly, or so it seemed to Danielle, who woke up shivering. She was alone, without Jonathan to cuddle up with under the blanket, to snuggle against while he was sleeping. Through the open blinds a pale morning light rose above silhouettes of trees, pushed its way upward through solid gloom. Danielle curled up and wrapped herself tightly. Feeling warmer and more comfortable, she wished for the day to start with a good omen, then sank back into a slumber.

The new day had already begun when Danielle heard the next-door neighbor's Rhodesian Ridgeback barking, and distant barks joining it as a choir. Along the street someone started a car. Her phone rang persistently.

"Good morning," Danielle yawned into the receiver.

"Good morning, dear," her mother's voice greeted. "How do you feel?"

"Sleepy." Danielle sat up, adjusted her pillow, and tried to stifle another yawn. "I'm still in the bed. How are you and Dad?"

"Just fine," her mother said curtly, her voice worried and tired.

A suspicion that something was wrong woke Danielle up. "Has anything happened?"

"Nothing unusual, just an early call from the hospital. Joe asked me to give you his best wishes before he left."

Pleased that her father had remembered it was her first day at work, Danielle smiled. Having grown up with a surgeon father, she was accustomed to ignoring medical emergencies as long as all was well with her family.

"Thanks, Mom, and don't worry," she said lightly. "Dad is too happy to mend and sew to mind these early calls."

Although Michelle made no reply, Danielle could bet that she smiled. Her mother may prefer understatements over flippancy, but at the core they were alike.

"Do you teach the first period today?" asked Danielle.

"Honors Physics for Sophomores and Juniors. I'd be going. Take care and good luck for your meeting with the professor."

"Thanks, Mom. I'm pretty sure I'll be fine, especially as I won't see Green until October. Besides meeting with the department's secretary, I'm free to do what I want."

The conversation ended, and Danielle went to dress. Soon clothes were scattered all over the bed; little tubes and bottles – the discreet providers of unblemished complexion – vied for a place under the mirror. Sounds of screaming and yelling children interrupted the good-looks routine. She hurried to the living-room, where the shrieks were even louder, and peered from a window. Children were reveling on her neighbor's lawn, a few playing tag, and others cycling carelessly or showing off on skateboards. Adults formed a chattering circle, paying no attention to the commotion. Danielle looked on as a school bus came roaring through Chadwick Drive. Bicycles and skateboards were tossed aside, and backpacks and lunchboxes were picked up. After a few hugs and kisses, cameras documented the children forming a line and getting into the bus. Three minutes later it drove away. Chadwick Drive was empty again.

Only the very old, babies and stay-at-home moms are not in a hurry to be somewhere else, Danielle thought, walking to the kitchen. She made instant coffee, buttered a piece of toast and spread jam on it. Alternating between crunchy sweetness and scalding coffee, Danielle was contemplating her hopes and worries when the phone rang.

"Yes," she snapped.

"Good morning, Doctor Meller," said a drowsy male voice.

She grinned to hear Jon's voice. "Good morning, Doctor Lerner. Who woke you up so early?"

"A sense of duty. Who else would hurry you up or suggest

you leave part of your wardrobe untried?"

"Too late. I'm already dressed..."

A soft whistle came through the receiver. Ignoring it, Danielle said, "... in a pair of jeans, a gray T-shirt and a new pair of sneakers."

"Not exactly exciting," he groaned.

"I want to make a good first impression."

For an answer, Jonathan yawned so deeply that Danielle decided it would be worthless to banter with a sleepy man.

"I'll change into something more seductive when you come," she offered.

"I'm looking forward to it." Jonathan yawned. "Sorry, I had a nearly sleepless night."

"Why did you have a sleepless night when I'm not around?"

"Remember that tricky algorithm I had trouble with?"

"Hmm. Sort of."

"Well, last night I cracked it. Changed a few lines in the code and it runs with a whooping speed."

"Great! Did you fall asleep happily hugging your computer?"

"Not quite. I still could distinguish between the keyboard and the pillow, and happened to prefer the latter. I vaguely remember having crawled to bed, even though it wasn't so long ago."

"I know." Danielle's voice warmed. "Go to sleep. I'll email you later."

"Have fun, and good luck!"

Outdoors, Danielle felt she had both. Chadwick Drive was bathed in sunlight, and lawns sparkled so vividly they might have been strewn with emeralds. She wanted to skip and twirl, but, believing she would look silly acting like a child, she walked lightheartedly towards King Solomon University.

Turquoise and gold, the colors of the university, glittered from shop windows and shimmered from ribbons and balloons tied to wrought-iron bars fencing off the campus. High above the open gates of the main entrance a huge banner was stretched, welcoming the students to a new academic year. Walking through the gates, Danielle joined other young men and women who flocked to a cobbled half-circle separating the entrance from a lawn. For a moment, her eyes scanned the imposing buildings and trees tended by generations of dedicated gardeners. She soaked up their dignity, wealth and tradition.

Reminding herself that there would be plenty of time to tour the campus, Danielle navigated her way through a network of paths. After passing by a small building that looked like a Gothic chapel, the stream of people thinned. She stopped, turned around in search of a gray edifice, and sighted the pediment of Fitzgerald Hall.

From a distance, there was nothing welcoming about it. Coming closer, she stared at a grandiose façade, enormous stone stairs and massive columns. Gray without a speck of color, Fitzgerald Hall looked overbearing even on a sunny day.

Not every pomposity should be preserved in stone, Danielle thought, eyeing the stony grandeur with disdain. She ascended the stairs and pushed the oversized wooden door. It did not budge. Applying both hands, Danielle pulled and tugged until the door opened. She slipped into a small lobby before the door closed. To the left and right extended a modern labyrinth of doors and corridors, illuminated by fluorescent lights and covered with grayish carpets. On the second floor, Danielle sauntered into another labyrinth of corridors, which looked vaguely familiar – she had been there for an interview a few months ago. She met no one as she wandered about, looking at photos and posters on the walls. Most doors were closed. The place was unusually deserted for the first day of the fall term.

Danielle hesitated before a door standing ajar, but before she could make up her mind, a guy swung it open from within and scanned her with an amused glance.

"You got lost?" he asked. "This is the theoretical physics building. All the lectures are given at Lawrence Hall, over the parking lot. Not here."

"Good." Danielle looked straight ahead, but the guy's tall frame blocked the room from her view. Striving to sound cheerful, she added lightly, "Who would like to hear math or physics this early in the morning?"

"You are not a physics student?" The guy managed to sound even more patronizing than before. "What are you studying then? Materials science? Chemistry? History of art?"

"None. I'm not a student."

"Looking for your boyfriend?" There was a glimmer of

interest in his glance. "Have no boyfriend and need assistance?"

"Not quite." She smiled. "My name is Danielle and I'm on my way to meet Mrs. Klein. I'm a new post-doc in professor Green's group."

As it sank in on him that she was a post-doctoral fellow, the stupid expression on his face was a pure pleasure to look at, even though it did not last long.

"George mentioned a new post-doc, but..." The guy shook his head and smiled broadly. "I'm Ben. Marjory's office is farther along the hallway."

Danielle took her time to survey the locked doors of professors Lisitsin's, Green's, and Cobs' offices. She looked at photos of exploding stars, images of colliding galaxies and illustrations of black hole halos hung on the walls. At a notice board she stopped and drew a breath. Next door was the secretaries' office, and it was wide open.

A woman in her fifties sat behind a large desk, looking at a newspaper. Her suit was very well-tailored and her earrings looked expensive. She raised her head at Danielle's knock and said "come in" in a businesslike tone. Perceiving that Mrs. Klein would rather continue reading than speak to her, Danielle quickly introduced herself.

Mrs. Klein put the newspaper aside, said "How are you?" and motioned for Danielle to sit down. She completed the paperwork in ten minutes, and handed the forms to Danielle to sign.

"That finishes the administrative part." Mrs. Klein smiled cordially and gave Danielle a key. "213 is along the hall. You will share the office with Chi Wang, another post-doc of Dr. Green."

"Thank you."

"If you have any problems or questions, don't hesitate to ask me or Amanda." Mrs. Klein gestured to a smaller desk standing vacant by the other wall.

"I will," Danielle said as Mrs. Klein rose and went to the filing cabinet. Curious about what she found so interesting in *King's Monkey*, Danielle sneaked a glance at the open page. At its bottom was a caricature of a man standing inside a whale. A bubble above the whale said: "Please professor, let me take you to the beach." A bubble over the man's head said, "Not yet... Not until my Great Theory of Everything is completed."

"That's funny," Danielle murmured when Mrs. Klein was back at her desk, holding a thick folder. Mrs. Klein gave the drawing a cursory glance, then looked at Danielle.

"Do you find the professor amusing?"

"No. He and the whale look quite miserable."

"What is so funny then?"

"Who has ever heard about a professor choosing a cramped hideout over the comfort of the academic life? The idea is ludicrous."

"Dr. Green has asked me to give you this," Marjory said a tad too politely, and handed the folder to Danielle. Her face softened seeing Danielle's bafflement. "These are papers and reviews George wanted you to read before his return."

Danielle looked perplexed. Pitying her, Marjory asked, "Didn't George tell you he'd leave you papers to read?"

"Yes," Danielle murmured, unable to shift her eyes from the folder. "A few papers. I did not realize it would be hundreds of pages."

Marjory's pleasant expression did not betray the amusement she felt. She nodded when Danielle thanked her, then shook her head as Danielle took her possessions and left. Danielle was still close to the secretary's office when Marjory answered the phone.

"Yes, Isaac, I know about the *Monkey*." Danielle heard her saying. "I was looking at the caricature when you called."

The door to room 213 was closed but not locked. The office was very narrow. The combination of two desks, three chairs, two shelves over each desk, and a blackboard gave it a crammed look. On the desk closest to the door was an old monitor. Otherwise, it was empty, and so were the shelves. Beaming with gratification that she had half an office at the physics department of King Solomon University, Danielle put Green's folder on the edge of the desk's worn surface. To her surprise, Chi, who sat by the desk near the window, did not turn his eyes away from his monitor.

"Hi. I'm Danielle." She waited for Chi to turn his head. "We met when I came for the interview with George and later at a conference."

"Chi." He bobbed his head in greeting. "Dr. Green wrote me you will come today."

"I should write him. Does he communicate a lot through emails?"

Chi flashed a shy smile and returned to stare at the screen.

Not a friendly type, Danielle thought. Reckoning that he was not interested in conversation, she began setting up her computer.

It took a couple of hours, several phone calls, and eventually Chi's help, before Danielle was able to write emails using her brand new university address. Satisfied with the achievement, she leafed through papers in Green's folder, read random bits, then emailed Green. A sideways glance at Chi found him immersed in whatever was on his screen. Neither passers-by on a nearby sidewalk, nor cars coming and going to the parking lot distracted him. Not even a pair passionately kissing near the window. Jon, Danielle thought, envying the kissers.

"Do you want to go for a lunch?" Danielle asked Chi. Even if he was reticent, he had helped her, doing so in a nice, pleasant way.

"Not today," Chi said without moving his head.

"Do you have group lunches occasionally?"

"I usually bring food from home, and Ben eats out with other graduate students. We have pizza seminars when Dr. Green is here."

"Is Ben tall and blond?"

"Yes."

Recalling Ben's patronizing attitude, Danielle opted to go and eat alone. She had a copy of the *King's Monkey* when she came back.

"How do you fine-tune the cosmological constant?" a male voice carried from the office.

She must have misheard, Danielle thought, letting go of the knob. No one did anything with the cosmological constant. That term had been obsolete for decades.

"I don't," Chi said. "I assume it's a flat universe."

Chi's reply reassured Danielle that nothing was wrong with her hearing. "Flat" referred to a universe with a regular three dimensional Euclidean space that stretched endlessly. She opened the door and saw Ben and Chi huddled in front of Chi's monitor, their noses almost touching the screen. She laid the newspaper on her desk and stepped closer to take a look.

On the monitor, shiny specks drifted through a backdrop of black voids, bright spots merged into even brighter islands. Excited to see a computer simulation of the universe (that was why she came to Green's group), Danielle asked, "Does each island represent a galaxy?"

Chi nodded and moved a bit, so she could see better. They watched the coalescence of lights form local patterns, then the emergence of a distinctive network. The universe rolling on the screen was billions of years younger than ours. Millions of years of evolution took about a minute.

"It's amazing!" Danielle told Chi when the simulation ended.

"Can I have the *Monkey* for a moment?" Ben asked from Danielle's desk.

"Sure."

"That guy has guts." Ben showed Chi the page with the caricature. "Don't you think so?"

Chi's expression was blank. Ben, on the other hand, seemed to know exactly what the caricature was about.

"Do you know who is the professor?" Danielle asked.

Ben eyed her, not exactly mocking, yet wordlessly asserting that he knew more than she did. Seeing that she bore with his stare without flinching, Ben addressed Chi with, "You haven't said anything."

"It's tasteless."

"Of course it is. But isn't it on the mark, considering whom they picked on?"

"He is a professor from the fourth floor, or someone from another department," Chi said indifferently. He looked at Danielle. "Why do you ask who he is?"

"I'm curious about the physics department. Who is on the fourth floor?"

"High-energy physics," Chi replied.

Danielle darted a dubious glance at Ben. "Is there anyone you know as a reclusive hermit?"

Assessing that Chi, despite his usual reluctance to speak ill about the department's faculty, was also interested, Ben said, "I think it was aimed at Cobs. His first name is Jonah."

That got Chi's and Danielle's attention.

"Cobs is credited with bringing cosmology and astrophysics to the physics department. He was pretty famous twenty or thirty years ago, but..." Ben sniffed. "He has no students and he hasn't published anything for five or maybe even ten years."

With so many brilliant young physicists vying for every opening for a tenured position, Danielle had little sympathy for a self-indulgent professor who desperately stuck to his chair.

"If he is burned out," she said, "can't the department find an excuse for an early retirement?"

"I suppose they have sent Cobs a couple of hints, but no one would ever dare to do more than that." Ben cast a meaningful glance at the post-docs. "It boils down to having excellent connections at top universities and research facilities."

At this point Chi turned back to the monitor, but Danielle could not shrug it off that quickly.

"Maybe Cobs is working on a new theory?" she asked.

"If he is," Ben sneered, "no wonder it was premiered in the *Monkey*." He turned to Chi. "Can we go back to your program?"

They delved into the details of the simulation. Trying to ignore Ben's rising voice and Chi's calm responses, Danielle started to read the first paper from Green's folder. Her thoughts, however, meandered from science to the caricature. Wondering whether it depicted a professor she might encounter in the hallway, she browsed the physics department's website, looking for a link to Cobs' homepage.

In a small photo, Cobs looked about fifty. There were no dates along the names of distinguished universities Cobs had attended as a student and as a postdoctoral fellow; the first date was the year he had started as an assistant professor at the physics department of King Solomon University.

Unless he had been a prodigy preteen, the photo was fifteen or twenty years old, Danielle reflected. If Cobs was promoted to associate professor around thirty-five, or even thirty, he should be in his late sixties.

She read with growing interest that Cobs was for several years an editor of one of the most prestigious physics journals, and drooled over the names of the professional societies he was a member of. The awards Cobs had received evoked her respect.

Looking at the middle-aged man in the photo, a remark

attributed to a great physicist sprang in Danielle's mind: "One will never accomplish what he has not done by the age of thirty."

Her thoughts shifted from Cobs' declining career to her aspiration to become the first female professor at the physics department of her alma mater. Deeming that this was achievable if her post-doctorate went really well, Danielle began to read in earnest the first paper from Green's folder.

3

CANDLES IN THE SKY

Observations demand assiduous effort, Danielle mused as she struggled with a lengthy astrophysics paper. After working insanely for half a year, no one wants the results to appear hastily or easily achieved, so the authors cram the pages with copious details. Reading such a paper was like eating a piece of triple-chocolate cheesecake - anticipation builds up after a first bite, but satiation comes quickly.

Other articles from Green's folder were strewn over her desk, together with newly borrowed library books and notes scribbled with calculations and comments. Like most of the papers she had read so far, the paper was comprehensive, rich with minute details about observations and with formulas used for their analysis. Did Green usually choose such papers? Danielle wondered. What kind of boss would he be? She darted a furtive glance at the other desk, where Chi was cocooned from anything that might impinge his unflagging concentration; his desk was tidy.

How can he go on without intermissions, Danielle thought, marveling at Chi's tenacious dedication to his monitor and keyboard. She could muster concentration and grapple with the papers from Green's folder, but her mind frazzled after a big serving of dryly-articulated, densely-printed data (meticulously amassed from stars exploding in different galaxies, mysterious outbursts of radiation, and cataclysmic events that had happened billions of years ago). Stumbling on an especially tedious section, she often sped up the reading by skimming through it, but after freely galloping to "conclusions," she had to retrace and cull the evidence for new data. To make the reading more interesting, she wrote down every shred of information that challenged the Cosmological Standard Model.

The model was based on and supported by numerous observations, but in nutshell it relied on three pillars. The first was that the universe has been expanding and cooling uniformly from a much denser and hotter state. The second was that elements were first created when the universe was only few minutes old. The third was that primordial photons, known as Cosmic Microwave Background Radiation (CMBR), have freely streamed throughout the universe since it was about 400,000 years old.

By the end of her first week at work, Danielle found nothing in the papers to shatter these pillars. The theory of general relativity supplied a framework for astrophysicists to analyze data coming from distant, unrelated sources. All of the data snugly fit into a blueprint of the universe's early history. Some questions, however, remained unanswered.

The distribution of Cosmic Microwave Background Radiation pointed towards a flat, eternally expanding universe. General relativity required that such universe had a certain, "critical" value of energy density to sustain itself. What forged the energy density was open to speculations, yet most cosmologists considered massive matter in its various forms as the most straightforward source.

Recalling a paper she had already read, Danielle rummaged in the mess on her desk. She found it under her most recent reads. The paper argued that all the mass gathered in stars, globular clusters and dust, amounted to few percent of the critical energy density. That was not surprising, for it had been shown long ago that regular matter could not account for galactic gravitational pull. Dark matter, a form of matter never encountered on Earth nor directly observed, was necessary to fill up local shortages in matter.

Yet, the paper's conclusions pointed to a bigger shortage. Even with dark matter tossed in, matter accounted only for about a quarter of the energy density required to sustain the observed universe. Finally understanding why Green had assigned her to read these papers, Danielle turned towards Chi.

"What values of matter density do you use in simulations?"

she asked.

Chi's inscrutable expression did not give away whether he was annoyed at the interruption.

"Four or five percent for regular matter," he replied after a short pause. "I vary the values for dark matter between different runs."

"Do different values change significantly how galaxies are formed?" Danielle asked. She deemed that they should.

"You should ask Ben. He knows more about dark matter, and he works on fitting matter density and interaction strength on galactic scale."

"So Ben works with WIMPs?" Danielle asked, expecting Chi to smile (in some theoretical models, dark matter was composed of hypothetical Weakly Interacting Massive Particles).

Chi shrugged and turned to scrutinize his monitor. Disappointed that discrepancies in universe's mass and energy density did not evoke a stronger reaction in Chi, Danielle decided it was about time to update Green. She frowned, twiddled a stray lock of hair and rubbed her ear, and after eleven trials composed four short sentences that conveyed her tenacity without groveling or resorting to phony enthusiasm. After clicking on send, she unscrupulously left the office to reap her reward at the Hungry Boson.

In the following days, Danielle studied more papers from Green's folder. The only change in the routine was an invitation, which said:

> *You are cordially invited to a physics colloquium to be held on Thursday, September 9th, at 4pm in the auditorium (room 11a) at Fitzgerald Hall. Geoffrey Pierce, from Birchwood University, will talk about:*
>
> *The standard model: milestones and setbacks.*
>
> *Teas and light refreshment will be served in the Lounge (room 10) at 3:30pm.*

Teas and light refreshment sounded like an invitation to a tea party, Danielle reflected. At physics colloquiums she had attended, physicists tried to tear each others' research to pieces while stuffing their mouths with chocolate-chip cookies and holding plastic cups with cooling coffee. Yet, the phrase "teas and light refreshments" suggested that scientists in old universities had a more refined attitude, that they nibbled refreshments while making snide remarks, and that they showed better manners while gloating over others' mistakes. Envisioning bite-size savory sandwiches and fruit tarts, Danielle glanced at Chi to check whether she might talk to him; he was typing industriously, showing no inclination to chat about pastries. No one would complain if they catered from the Hungry Boson, she reflected.

Ben peeped in from behind the door. "You'd better hurry," he said. "The best cookies disappear first."

This was a strong argument, which fully convinced even Chi. They quickly strode along the corridors to the main staircase, descended to the first floor and joined a steady stream of people heading to the Lounge.

"Where are they all coming from?" Danielle whispered to Chi.

"Lawrence Hall," he murmured back. "Condensed matter, plasma, low temperatures, everything except astrophysics and high-energy are at Lawrence Hall."

Danielle wanted to point out that only those who could not or chose not to pretend that they were doing something useful were left at Fitzgerald Hall. Considering Chi's reluctance to criticize anything involving the department, she said, "There must be better lecture halls at the newer building. Why aren't they having the colloquiums there?"

"The auditorium in Lawrence Hall has cushioned seats, three screens, and it's connected to the communications center," Ben said from behind. "But it doesn't have over a hundred years of tea sipping tradition. Chocolate chip cookies are called a snack at Lawrence Hall and 'light refreshment' at Fitzgerald Hall."

"Really?" Danielle asked.

"Didn't you know that the physics department at King Solomon is over a hundred years old?" Ben teased. "Generations of physicists have gathered at the Lounge since the dawn of something."

"Over teas and pastry," Danielle continued in the same tone. "Does the department's determination to keep up with its noble traditions extend to using china and real cutlery?"

"You'll see," Ben said solemnly. After another turn, they

stopped in front of oversized, widely opened wooden doors. "Here it is."

"It" was an impressive room, with a high plastered ceiling and heavy green drapes hung over unusually large windows. The butter-colored walls were adorned with portraits of men of different ages dressed in the high fashion of the late nineteenth century. The decor was dignified and elaborate but not overbearingly fastidious. Unlike Fitzgerald Hall's façade, the Lounge looks hospitable rather than grand, Danielle thought. If they'd get rid of that old green blackboard, it could as well be a nineteenth century drawing room.

Only one man in the room wore a suit. He was talking to those around him, quite at ease despite the inevitable plastic cup clutched in his hand. The speaker, Danielle observed, looked as if he knew what to expect.

Real china, Danielle sniggered wordlessly when she came closer to a long wooden table, where an assortment of cheap cookies was piled on a few white plastic plates. She cocked an eye at the gentlemen solemnly gazing from the walls, as if asking them, "Do you have any idea what is happening here these days?"

Chi and Ben were already in the queue for a plastic cup, a tea bag, or a teaspoonful of instant coffee. The less patient, Danielle noticed, avoided the queue altogether and hung around the "refreshments" table.

Why can physicists spend billions on accelerators and space telescopes, but cannot afford anything edible at their seminars? The question was always beyond Danielle's understanding. Narrowly eying the "light refreshments," she doubted that bacteria would bother with this revolting mixture of sugars and fats. The Lounge was impressive, but the plastic cups and the questionable cookies were not an iota better than what they had had at similar gatherings at TIST (her alma mater, Thorboro Institute of Science and Technology). At TIST, she could chat and joke with fellow graduate students, and whine about the faculty. Here, she was a newcomer. Having no wish to schmooze with strangers, she went to the least crowded corner, to while away the time in forming impressions about the people of King Solomon University's physics department.

Tall, lanky professor Lisitsin, caught Danielle's eyes. She remembered him from the job interview, as a faculty who worked with Green. The man Lisitsin was talking to was noticeably younger, yet looked too old to be a grad student or even post-doc.

An assistant professor fawning a senior member of the faculty, Danielle speculated, watching with some compassion how the younger man gesticulated, a plastic cup in one hand and a fistful of cookies in another. Pity they weren't close enough to be overheard.

"It's time," someone called. Discarding cups and leftovers, physicists flocked into a spacious and modern auditorium. Professors descended from the topmost steps to the first rows, while students and post-docs took seats farther back. A young professor introduced the guest speaker, and then left the lectern to professor Geoffrey Pierce.

Pierce started his presentation with quarks and leptons – the most basic units of matter.

"The crowning achievement of the standard model is explaining how quarks and leptons interact to constitute the known particles."

Danielle smiled thinly at the conceit omission. When speaking about "the standard model," Pierce, like most high-energy physicists, meant the High-Energy Standard Model, not the Cosmological one.

He skimmed through constraints and conservation rules that determined which particles were feasible, and explained how short-lived heavy particles decayed into lighter ones. For leptons, the situation was straightforward: every lepton was an independent particle, and only the electron and its neutrino were stable. Single quarks, on the other hand, never formed a particle.

"Baryons like protons and neutrons are formed by three quarks." Pierce flickered a slide. "A proton is composed of two up quarks and one down quark, and it is stable. A neutron is composed of two down quarks and one up quark, and it is slightly heavier than a proton. A neutron decays into a proton, an electron, and its anti-neutrino."

Deciding that the audience was warmed up, Pierce moved on to more exotic particles. A colorful bubble, showing the year of discovery, was assigned to each particle. The number of bubbles grew quickly, creating a colorful chaos on the screen behind him.

"With the rising of energies accessible in accelerators, the number of new and unsought for particles was pushed up. In a few years, we were facing an overcrowded zoo." Pierce paused for a moment. All of the bubbles disappeared after he clicked on his laptop, and only quarks and leptons were left, this time divided into three groups.

"Three families," Pierce said. The up and down quarks were grouped with the electron and its neutrino into a first family; the rest of the quarks and leptons were divided between the other two families. Pierce pointed out the inherent order discovered underneath the apparent chaos. Then the lecture became more technical.

"Photon." With a click, Pierce added the particle mediating the electromagnetic interaction.

"And massive vector bosons that mediate the electroweak forces," he said, adding three more particles to the picture.

Pierce complicated the standard model further with the addition of gluons - particles carrying the strong interaction. He recounted the rudiments of the Standard Model and stressed its mathematical elegance. Danielle listened attentively as Pierce discussed the unification of electroweak interaction, the role of the Higgs boson, and the standard model's predictive power. He did not mention gravity, for the fourth fundamental interaction was not part of the high-energy standard model.

Although it was a bit jittery when encountering inconvenient infinities, the presentation was succinct. Pierce continued through the triumphs of the standard model without interruption, outlined the quest for further unification, and reached the end with, "Finding the particles predicted by the standard model is not sufficient to fully attest it, not until the most important prediction, the Higgs boson, could be verified."

What about dark matter? Danielle thought. Even if it was not detected, dark matter constituted most of the matter in universe.

There was applause. The faculty who introduced Pierce came back to thank him. As soon as questions were allowed, someone from behind asked, "Have you considered the possibility that the Higgs might never be discovered?"

"Who didn't?" Pierce chuckled. Ignoring a buzz stirred by his reply, he added, "I gather that someone from CERN is coming here in a few weeks."

"Armand Brochard will come in December," came a voice from a second row.

Pierce nodded. "I'd ask him about the likelihood of detection," he advised.

"Those who have been betting on Higgs's mass for the last twenty years," a voice from far left rumbled, "would appreciate an educated guess from a fellow in the Birchwood group."

"In short, give us numbers, Geoffrey," someone translated. "How much energy will it take?"

"A lot of money is being invested to show that the Higgs is just around the corner. I hope and pray that its mass would be in the range accessible by the planned Large Hadron Collider."

Laughing snorts from those who were amused by the laconic humor mixed with sporadic boos from those who were not.

The high-energy jerks are having a good time, Danielle concluded, recalling similar behavior from TIST. Considering the colossal cost of the new accelerator, she could not imagine the ramifications of not detecting the Higgs boson. From accelerators her thoughts flitted to Friday. She was wondering when Jonathan would come, when a loud voice asked, "What about the dark energy?"

The noisy background subsided into an expectant silence.

"I'm not sure I follow your meaning," Pierce said. His eyes searched the audience.

"I'm speaking about the recently observed cosmological constant," the same voice replied. "If it is a zero-point-energy, can you explain why it is not zero?"

"No," Pierce said after a moment. The audience hummed again.

"There is some confusion about the terms," someone pointed out. "Can you explain what is 'dark energy,' how it is related to zero-point-energy, and whether it's a new incarnation of the infamous 'cosmological constant'?"

Expectation permeated the sudden silence. Danielle wondered what they were talking about.

"I wish I could answer what 'dark energy' is," Pierce said.

"The term 'dark energy' is used interchangeably with the energy of the vacuum, aka zero-point-energy."

"Why it is not zero then?"

"There is no reasonable answer that I'm aware of from the high-energy perspective." Pierce looked at the front rows. "I think that Susan can give a better explanation from the astrophysical perspective."

"Dark energy is a form of energy which does not arise from matter or radiation," said a blonde woman in the center of the third row. "For those of you who vaguely remember of having heard the term, cosmological constant was first introduced by Einstein in his theory of general relativity."

"Wasn't it his most famous blunder?" someone quipped.

"Einstein introduced the cosmological constant to balance galaxies' gravitational pull," Susan replied. "After Hubble discovered that the universe is expanding, Einstein discarded the cosmological constant as superfluous."

So? Danielle thought. Historical anecdotes usually were not relevant to modern physics.

"Recent supernovae data strongly favor a non-zero cosmological constant. Right now, I'd call Einstein's brainchild a very far-reaching blunder."

The words pounded in Danielle's head, stirring up confusion. It was inconceivable that they were treating the cosmological constant as an observational fact.

"If the cosmological constant is indeed vacuum energy, do you have any comments about its value?" the professor who introduced Pierce asked.

Pierce spread his arms in a gesture of hopelessness. "Any value aside from zero would be orders of magnitude too high to agree with the reported observations."

"By 'orders of magnitude' do you mean a hundred and twenty orders of magnitude?" the person who first asked about dark energy inquired.

A hundred and twenty ORDERS of magnitude? Danielle pinched her arm. The number was unfathomable.

"The potential energy of the Higgs field contributes to the vacuum energy and so do the zero-point vacuum fluctuations of the fields of the standard model. We can't tell to what extent these contributions cancel each other, since we are unsure about their signs."

Gaining precious little understanding, Danielle felt even more confused. Energies in high-energy models tended to soar, but she had never heard about anything coming close to this mismatch.

"If the total vacuum energy is of the same order of magnitude as the largest contribution," Pierce continued, "we expect it to be about Plank's mass to the power of four. That is a hundred and twenty orders of magnitude higher than the observed value."

"A discrepancy that requires further consideration," the professor who introduced Pierce added cryptically. He crossed his hands, thus signaling that the time allotted for questions was over.

Most of the audience, including Danielle, burst into laughter. Pierce hesitated a moment, then smiled. A discrepancy by a hundred and twenty orders of magnitude did not imply a need for additional study. It demonstrated that something pivotal was completely wrong.

Back from the colloquium, Danielle shoved aside a review she was plowing through, and searched for the papers she had not read yet. A title, "Observational Evidence from Supernovae for an Accelerating Universe and a Cosmological Constant," drew her attention.

Accelerating Universe. The words raised question marks in her mind. After a very violent start, the universe was cooling and expanding, expanding and cooling. It was dotted with supernovae (cataclysmic explosions of stars), but at large, it was undergoing a long stretch of repose. Could there be a repulsive force that accelerated its expansion? Was it really pushed apart?

She began to read the authors' account of how astronomers collated data from distant supernovae. Photons emitted at a star's explosion streamed in space, their wavelengths elongated (redshifted) as universe expanded. "Observational evidence" summarized intricate techniques used for measuring fluxes of photons, the photons' redshifts, and supernovae luminosities. The account of how data was calibrated, extracted, and later used in a multifaceted analysis was not particularly interesting. All she needed to know was how distances to supernovae were derived from supernovae luminosity and from the flux of detected photons.

These distances, Danielle read, were also calculated independently for every redshift, using cosmological parameters such as mass density. To test the cosmological picture, the calculated and the observed distances were compared. If the distances were close - the cosmological parameters were considered reliable. Otherwise, computer software adjusted the values and then calculated the distances. The best fit for a flat universe had a cosmological constant.

For Danielle, this was incredible. She reread the section about distances and examined figures illustrating various combinations of cosmological parameters used for the best fit. The authors considered possible sources of error, but she could not see whether there were flaws in underlying assumptions or in interpretation.

She glanced at Chi, suddenly irritated by his monotonous clicking on the keyboard. He was at the colloquium, but he did not look impressed, bothered, or affected at all by what he had heard. Chi probably read it months ago, Danielle reflected, feeling a little ashamed that she had not.

Although it was a recent paper, Danielle looked for a newer preprint that would refute or cast a doubt on the paper's findings. She skimmed through Green's folder, pausing every time her eyes glimpsed the word "supernova." Only one paper, published in *Nature* by another group, seemed to be of any relevance. It was titled, "Discovery of a Supernova Explosion at Half the Age of the Universe and Its Cosmological Implications."

The data came from a different supernovae survey, but Danielle found the conclusions to be the same. The universe's evolution, inferred from faraway supernovae, was dominated by something omnipresent and unknown, which accelerated universe's expansion.

"What went wrong?" Jonathan asked, when he called that night.

"Nothing."

"You sound frazzled."

"I'm trying to reconcile what I heard and read today with the cosmological picture ingrained in my brain."

"Everything you have studied is wrong?"

Danielle recounted the papers' conclusions, then asked, "What do you think?"

"I'm impressed," Jonathan said, "even though I have only a nebulous idea what is a supernova."

"Why didn't you ask? The type Ia supernovae originate in white dwarfs. These stars are much denser than our Sun, so they have an enormous gravitational pull."

"Do they explode?" Jonathan asked hopefully.

"No, a white dwarf balances its gigantic gravitational pull inwards with a similarly huge pressure outwards. Supernova occurs when a white-dwarf is paired with a sun-like star. The white dwarf's gravitational pull is much stronger, so it rips the other star's outer layers and sucks them like a vacuum cleaner."

"Sounds like a typical take-over."

"Much worse," Danielle promised. "As the white dwarf pulls chunks of the other star, it gains more and more matter, which, in turn, increases its monstrous gravitational pull. The white dwarf's growth reaches a tipping point when its gravitational pull inward becomes too high to balance the outward pressure. That destroys the equilibrium that held it intact."

"A blundered take-over," Jonathan acerbically pointed out.

"Photons emitted when white-dwarf explodes are detectable after billions of years. The supernovae always have similar imprints."

"Is there anything else I should know about them?" Jonathan's voice implied that he already had had enough.

"Never mind how it happened. Just think of supernovae as candles in the sky. The dimmer they appear, the farther they are from us."

"Nice," Jonathan said. "Candles in the sky sounds quite romantic."

She laughed. "You don't care at all about supernovae."

"Not if they are far enough," Jonathan admitted. "I care when you are too far."

"I won't be far tomorrow," Danielle whispered meaningfully.

4

LUCAS LODGE

Next morning, Danielle cast away any thought about candles in the sky, and set herself to finish reading the review paper before leaving for the weekend. She almost completed the task when Chi returned to their office, carrying a warmed lunch. Homey, yet unfamiliar spicy scents wafted from his bowl; their aroma percolated through the crammed office. Danielle sniffed, and her thoughts raced to the evening, when she would be with Jonathan. Done with the reading, she sorted scattered papers, went over her notes, and tossed the unimportant ones. Then she checked the mailbox; Green had not responded to her second email.

"See you on Monday," she said to Chi. He nodded.

At a quarter-to-five on Friday, every table in the Hungry Boson was occupied, and the teashop hummed with conversation. Relaxing as the line progressed, Danielle imagined Jonathan's surprise at getting fresh tarts. She sensed the fruity taste that would linger on his lips.

"How can I help?" Anne asked, offering Danielle a warm, welcoming smile.

Still focused on an image of herself and Jon licking the filling of a chocolaty éclair, Danielle pointed at golden tarts, devilishly sinful éclairs, and other tempting pastries she had not sampled yet. Ending up buying too much, she ambled home. In the driveway was an unfamiliar car. On the stairs, propped against the locked front-door, his head bent over an opened laptop, sat Jonathan Lerner. Bursting with joy, Danielle ran into his arms.

* * *

"Well?" she asked after they moved apart and were capable of talking.

Jonathan rolled to look at the bedroom he had just made love in. "A perfect dollhouse for a physicist." His stare shifted from a big poster of the Milky Way stretching its spiraling arms to a crumpled flowery quilt on the floor. "Where did you get that from?"

"Aunt Sophie." Danielle giggled. "Isn't it cute?"

"Sickeningly so. At least we don't have to look at it till tomorrow. We are going out tonight."

"Yeah?" Danielle purred contentedly. "How far out do you mean by 'out'?"

"About fifty minutes of reasonably fast driving. I made reservations for a dinner."

"It's a long drive back," she pointed out the obvious.

"We're staying there overnight." Jonathan planted a light kiss on Danielle's forehead. "I've booked us a cabin in an adjoining inn."

"You are not serious?"

"We have a car and everything is arranged. Just slip into that sexy dress we bought in Italy and pack whatever you need."

Danielle draped a sheet round her breasts, rose up and went to the cupboard. She returned with a burgundy-red dress spread over her shoulders and waistline. Jonathan's eyes twinkled, suggesting she come closer.

"I can't go out wearing it."

"It will spoil the view but you can put on underwear."

Danielle locked stares with Jonathan.

"Why not?" he asked. "You liked it in Italy."

"I still like it, but Hopeville isn't Florence or Rome." Danielle rolled her eyes. "I might meet someone belonging to the physics department."

"Afraid to set tongues wagging?" Jonathan whistled softly, and drew closer. "Will sleazy murmurs follow you in the physics department's corridors?"

Danielle shook her head and stepped out of Jonathan's reaching hands.

"Green might treat me differently if he gets a wrong impression before I have a chance to prove myself." Seeing Jonathan's puzzlement, she added, "Someone might see me and tell him."

"You assume that your boss is an idiot."

"I know he isn't, but professors can be condescendingly polite or arrogantly insolent. Most of them look askance at women without even noticing how prejudiced they are."

"You should not let chauvinists like Crawford oppress you."

"It's easy to say that I shouldn't, but being a male, you will never understand the tiptoeing I have to do to be treated the same."

"The world is changing faster than ever, and even physics departments will have to change their attitude. Dress anyway you like and don't pay attention to schmucks. If you are competent, they are the ones who should be on the defense."

Danielle neither bothered to argue, nor cover her rear as she went to the cupboard. Jonathan watched her go to the bathroom and return wearing the tightly fitted crepe-de-chine dress. Her chin went up, her shoulders straightened, her posture changed.

"Do I look like a physicist?"

Jonathan's hands extended to hold the proud figure. Danielle quivered as his fingers slid on the silky material and explored her uncovered skin.

"For your eyes only," she whispered.

Jonathan's hands slid below her waistline.

"Or in front of strangers I won't ever see again." Her mouth brushed his lips and she pulled away.

"You are paranoid," Jonathan rasped.

"Just because I don't want to take chances that can damage my work?"

"That place is way too expensive for students, and the probability that you might bump into an unidentified physics professor in a small restaurant over sixty miles away from Hopeville is..." Jonathan finished the sentence with a shrug.

"Negligible," Danielle agreed, letting him pull her back. "What is this tiny restaurant called?"

"Lucas Lodge."

"Sounds familiar, although I can't recall where I've heard the name before."

"What about George Lucas and Star Wars?" Jonathan suggested.

She patted Jonathan's cheek. "Jane Austen's *Pride and Prejudice* would be closer. I have a copy somewhere in the living room if you're interested."

When Jonathan said "another time," Danielle laughed.

"You'd better get packing," he said unperturbed. "I liked the squashed éclairs, but I'm starving."

Danielle was soon ready. Jonathan drove fast, juggling through the suburban traffic, then racing through the open countryside. Too used to his driving to worry or protest, Danielle looked around. The farther we get away, the happier we are, she reflected, reminiscing about how she and Jonathan had recklessly roamed through Italy. Freedom, she thought and smiled, was many times more thrilling than a telltale diamond ring.

"Where are we?" Danielle asked when the car turned abruptly. They left the road for a paved lane in the woods.

"You will see in a few minutes."

Lucas Lodge was built in a clearing. Despite its unassuming façade, the two-story house bore an unmistakable mark of expensive simplicity. Jonathan parked the rented car between a Land Rover and a Jaguar and gallantly opened Danielle's door.

"Nice car," he commented about a slick silver Saab. Danielle's eyes followed his stare.

"Jon," she squealed, pointing at a sticker with King Solomon University's parking permit.

"I doubt it's within the budget of a physics professor," he said. The parked cars showed off a different sort of financial wellness.

They went inside, into a lobby decorated with oak paneling and furnished with dark leather sofas and armchairs. A demure receptionist welcomed them and gave Jonathan a key to their cabin. From the lobby a hostess glided forward, to accompany them into a dining room.

The spacious dining room brought to Danielle's mind an old-fashioned country manor whose family portraits and useless gadgets had been removed. The room's unpretentious elegance was enchanting, its opulent décor was restrained and understated, commanding and offering respect without snobbery. Graceful and stylish in her burgundy-red silk-dress, Danielle followed the hostess walking between widely spaced tables. Merry yet muffled voices enlivened the genteel atmosphere, without merging into unpleasant hum. Passing a table with elderly couples, decorously dressed and apparently in very good mood, Danielle reflected that they knew how to make a good use of their money. She smiled at the thought.

"Hello, Danielle," Marjory Klein greeted her from the table.

Danielle's smile froze as she stopped and turned her face. Mrs. Klein's tailored clothes looked too dressy for Fitzgerald Hall; her evening dress was too elegant and expensive to wear anywhere. Drawn by glitter, she stared at Marjory's bejeweled neck. If the necklace was genuine, what the heck was Marjory doing in a physics department?

"How do you do?"

Danielle jerked at the familiar voice. Anne from the Hungry Boson was sitting one seat from Marjory, at the other side of an older man who looked vaguely familiar. She looked ladylike in a plain evening gown (everything seemed plain in the vicinity of Marjory's attire). Danielle wanted to say something polite and introduce Jonathan, but stood transfixed, her lips fixed in an idiotic smile. The hostess smiled apologetically, Jonathan nodded to the elderly couples, then wordlessly took Danielle's hand and led her away. At their table, Jonathan helped her with the seat.

"What happened?" he asked after the hostess left.

"The bejeweled woman is Marjory Klein, a senior secretary whose office is a few doors away from Green's. Rats, she saw me in that dress gawking at them."

Jonathan cupped her hands."Who was the other woman?"

"Anne from the Hungry Boson."

"It could have been much worse," he said soothingly.

"How can it be more awkward?"

"Meeting a physics professor from the university. As it is, Green is away, and I don't see any reason why Marjory would blabber about you to other people."

"She was already talking," Danielle muttered. "Haven't you seen her whispering to an old man who sat between her and Anne?"

"She probably told her husband who you were," Jonathan

said sensibly. Seeing that Danielle's face brightened, he added mischievously, "And to Anne."

"Rats."

"Speaking about Anne and the éclairs..." Jonathan said, his eyes dancing with laughter. Recalling how they ate the pastry she had squashed when she had clung to Jon, color rose on Danielle's face, deepening from red to burgundy, until it perfectly matched her dress. Yearning stirred again. She darted a forbidding glance at Jonathan, he chuckled and squeezed her hands. Danielle shook her head, Jonathan smiled. The charm was back, elusive yet tangible. The air around vibrated. Magic, they both felt, was still there, unspent.

They took their time to enjoy the entrees and the red Burgundy wine Jonathan ordered. The food was superb, the ambiance accommodating and uplifting. Jonathan's comments and Danielle's irreverent observations spiced up their conversation, recollections made them grin. Engrossed in the present, Danielle did not think about Marjory and Anne.

"Did you like it?" Jonathan asked over a coffee and a dessert they shared. His voice was earnest, his eyes keenly watched Danielle. The air around shimmered with anticipation.

"Every calorie." Danielle laughed, her eyes sparkling from the wine, her complexion pink under Jonathan's expressive look.

The sky was cloudless when they left the house. The crisp air carried little noises from the nightly woods.

"Look at the stars," Jonathan whispered.

Away from lights, the sky was strewn with bright, twinkling objects; entire worlds flickered like celestial candles. Feeling rapture, they hugged and looked at the firmament. Then, beaming with lust and happiness, Danielle and Jonathan went to find their cabin.

5

A MATTER OF BOOKKEEPING

The weekend with Jonathan was over, and life went on, swirling sweet recollections into lonely breakfasts, and piling up information for the rest of each day. At the astrophysics lunch Danielle met Michael Axelrod, an assistant professor she correctly pegged when she had seen him talk to Lisitsin. She exchanged a few polite words with Susan Brophy, the professor who had spoken about the cosmological constant at the physics colloquium. Aside from going to the astrophysics lunch and the physics colloquium, Danielle kept to her office. She did not want to bump into Marjory Klein, and it took time to trawl through lengthy articles reporting and analyzing observations, to decipher theoretical papers sprinkled with forbidding mathematics, to study other groups' reports about computer-generated universes. Each paper focused on its authors' contribution, but Danielle reasoned that Green expected her to do more than glean a plethora of disconnected results. In a group specializing in simulations of structure formation in universe, one had to be able to construct the simulation using both theoretical insights and data from observations.

The title "Modeling Large-Scale Perturbations in Flat Universe" suggested that the paper would overview how galaxies, clusters of galaxies, super clusters, and voids observed nowadays had been formed. The problem, Danielle remembered from an introductory cosmology course, was whether galaxies dotted the universe before they gathered into clusters, which eventually formed super-clusters and voids, or was it the other way around: super-structures emerged first, then split into smaller, denser structures?

It was a long paper, and Danielle took it home to read in the evening. Over a steaming cup of tea, she followed equations summarizing how matter clumped together. It started from almost homogeneous distribution in space, and continued as lumps of matter coalesced to seed the universe with progenitors of galaxies or of larger structures. Equations describing the structure formation at later times gave little insight about the underlying physics. Before long, rows of monstrous integrals, solvable only by computer programs, swam in front of Danielle's eyes. She waded through cumbersome derivations, her thinking confounded and her head aching, until late at night she fell asleep.

In a dream, inky, starless skies stretched all over. A translucent blue apparition shimmered in the darkness and gradually materialized into a badly-shaped giant. It strode ahead, each enormous foot undulating whatever it stepped on. Waves rippled in its wake, creating loose structures interspersed between dark voids. The giant faded, and another shimmering apparition materialized into a smaller giant. It trod between tenuous structures and voids, its shorter footsteps imprinting finer wavelets. The wavelets, trapped in the first sprawling structures, forged smaller, more intricate structures. A third shimmering giant appeared in place of its evanescent predecessor, a little bluish figure that scampered through structures like a drunkard searching for a coin. Its steps wiggled little patches, shaping single, gleaming galaxies.

Danielle remembered the dream when she woke up. Amused with her version of structure formation, she recounted the dream to her mother over the phone.

"I don't see what giants' strides had to do with how clusters of galaxies were formed," Michelle said when Danielle was done.

"Deviations in the matter density are sorted according to their length-scale," Danielle started explaining. "If we look at this down-scaled to Earth, the crests of the largest wavelets would interpose between continents and oceans. Smaller wavelets correspond to crisscrossing between major cities on the same continent. The smallest ones..." Danielle's voice trailed off as she looked for a good analogy for the smallest cosmological unit.

"Yes?" Michelle prompted.

"You can think of a galaxy as a city. Its bright part is the downtown. Galactic halos are the suburbs."

"I understand that you want to be prepared before you meet your boss." Michelle paused diplomatically. "But wouldn't it be better to read something lighter before sleep?"

Regretting that her mother could not see her smile, Danielle asked, "Have you forgotten? You used to tell me about an apple falling on Newton's head for a bedtime story."

Refraining from voicing any comments, Michelle asked Danielle when she planned to come to Thorboro.

"I don't know. I have many more papers to read before I can form a picture of what I'm going to do during the post."

"Have you discussed with Green his research interests?"

"He mentioned a few things, but nothing concrete. Anyway, deducing from the papers he had left me, I'll simulate galaxies and clusters of galaxies with different proportions of regular and dark matter. That's what his graduate student does, and it is a hot topic."

"See if you can come," Michelle said, "and don't overwork yourself."

Thinking that she needed more concrete career advice, Danielle decided to ask Ben about his simulations. When she walked into the grad students' office (a room, similar in size to the secretaries' office, partitioned into six cubicles), Ben was leisurely scanning winter conferences on the screen.

Not overly busy, Danielle noted contentedly. Physics and computer textbooks were stacked on shelves over Ben's desk. Photos pinned to the lowest shelf were more unusual: a pristine tropical beach, azure water lapping on a sandy cove. In the foreground was a willowy model posing in a skimpy bikini, her eyes green, her legs endless. Appreciating Ben's taste and nerve, Danielle cleared her throat, added "ahem."

Ben turned his head, then closed the conferences list.

"Hi," Danielle said. Taking Ben's cocked head as an invitation, she asked about his work.

"I focus on dark matter," he said. "Mostly how it is distributed in galaxies and clusters of galaxies."

Seeing no second chair in Ben's cubicle, Danielle sat on the edge of his desk, and looked expectantly at the monitor.

"I have a course at Lawrence Hall in ten minutes," Ben added. Rising up, he locked the screen.

Danielle got up and looked pointedly at Ben, but that was all the explanation she got.

At her office, Danielle shrugged off Ben's behavior, and shifted her thoughts to dark matter. Despite all her recent reading, she knew precious little about it.

But who does? she thought. Dark matter was never detected, and except for high-energy theorists who put forward exotic candidates, no one could tell what it was. Its existence was inferred from the strength of gravitational pull at the distant fringes of visible galaxies. Observations indicated that in galactic halos there was much more matter than could be attributed to regular matter found in stars and dust. Since this matter was "invisible," astronomers concluded that galactic halos are mostly composed of dark matter.

Danielle thumbed through Green's folder, looking for papers studying the distribution of dark matter in space. She found a recent one and skimmed its abstract. Dark matter, the paper claimed, was by far more abundant than regular matter, but not abundant enough to sustain a flat universe.

Bearing in mind the supernovae papers (and the cosmological constant they reintroduced), Danielle began to read the rest of the paper. Like many other papers from Green's folder, she found it to be an insightful, albeit wearisome, read. The authors made a thorough analysis of observations of massive clusters of galaxies and estimated the amount of invisible dark matter lurking within super-clusters. Using computer simulations, they probed how much dark matter was cloaked in the surrounding voids.

Skipping graphs and details, Danielle proceeded to the conclusions. There, she did not find clear-cut answers, only a summary that restated the inconsistencies found in dark matter's bookkeeping, followed by the ubiquitous note about the need for further research. A proposition in the end suggested to include dark energy in calculations. A good idea, Danielle thought, ready to bet that it was already implemented in Green's group.

She glanced sideways; Chi's expression indicated he was in

his own universe, and would not be disposed to talk. She went over the universe's inventory. Radiation (particles moving at or close to the speed of light) made a negligible contribution to the overall energy density. The regular, "baryonic" matter contributed four or five percent of the critical energy density. The other ninety-five percent were divided between dark matter and dark energy. Was it all dark matter? Was it half-and-half? Were the supernovae papers correct and most of the energy in the universe came in the form of dark energy?

Skipping the details of the universe's bookkeeping, Danielle tried to picture mind-boggling swaths of space governed by two opposing forces. Gravity attracted, binding matter together; dark energy repelled, pushing matter apart. The existence of galaxies proved that dark energy exerted a rather weak force. Apparently, it was too weak to sunder clusters of galaxies. Did dark energy counter gravity in the sparse super-clusters? Could it prevent their growth?

Why is it so weak? A niggling question sneaked into Danielle's contemplation. She looked for an answer in the papers on her desk. Finding none, she turned to her monitor to search the preprints archive. It did not take long before Danielle stumbled on an intriguing paper. In the early universe, it argued, dark energy was much stronger. Quintessence, a field that generated dark energy, decayed over time. A figure on the screen illustrated quintessence as rolling downhill. Could that be a key to the dark energy's mystery? Danielle closed her eyes and tried to envision a field ebbing away. If quintessence diminished with time, could it someday become zero? Had it had once the expected value of vacuum energy?

Immersed in wondering, she was suddenly aware that someone stood behind her, craning forward.

"Interested in dark energy?" Ben asked. His stare slid from the monitor down to papers strewn on Danielle's desk.

"I'm interested in many things," she replied, a little appalled.

"Aren't we all?" Ben skimmed the titles, then moved to stand between Danielle's and Chi's desks. "What if it turns out that dark energy does not exist?"

"From a quick search I did, dark energy is taken seriously. Do you have any reason to think that it shouldn't?"

Simpering, Ben walked to the window.

"How then would you explain the results of supernovae papers?" Danielle persisted.

Unconcerned, Ben said, "It's a waste of time."

"Don't you use dark energy density in your programs?" Danielle asked.

"Yes, among many other parameters. It's a number. Don't expect to eke out a post by fine-tuning it."

At a loss as to what he meant, Danielle stared blankly at Ben.

"You might do that after getting a tenure at some obscure college," Ben elaborated, grinning maliciously. "But don't expect it'd work with George."

"In simulations of large-scale structures," Chi said before Danielle could repay Ben's little dig with her own, "it doesn't matter what dark energy is. Its density is a constant, fixed at the start of each run."

"But what if dark energy evolves over time?" she asked. "How do you take that into account?"

Oozing amusement, Ben turned to Chi, wordlessly inviting him to poke fun at Danielle's ignorance. Seeing no change in Chi's deadpan expression, Ben said to Danielle, "Have you considered how many interrelated parameters are involved in simulation of large-scale structures?"

Danielle said nothing. She hoped she was not blushing.

"You'll find out that it's hard enough to fix everything else simultaneously without tinkering with the unaccounted for time-dependency."

Ben turned to Chi, and asked about his program. After Chi answered, Ben brought up an algorithm he was struggling with. Danielle listened attentively, tried to glean what they were discussing. Before she could get the gist, Chi and Ben huddled in front of Chi's monitor, looking for open-source software components on the web. Annoyed, she randomly picked another paper from Green's folder.

From that day on, Danielle was aware that Ben took a quick peek at what she was reading whenever he came to ask Chi about some feature in his program. When Ben's voice rose to inconsiderately loud levels and she had to reread the same sentence over and over, she would listen covertly. Gradually, she began to draw conclusions. Writing code for large-scale structure evolution was by far more complicated and time-consuming than what she had imagined. Chi and Ben ran endless simulations with different parameters, aiming to pinpoint the ones that generated the most compelling universes. Chi worked frantically; Ben worked hard, compensating for the rest by goading Chi into helping him. Even though Chi seemed happy to spend his post-doc this way, Danielle doubted that she also would.

Green's reply to Danielle's email straightened out her wondering. His email instructed her to familiarize herself with the group's simulations while continuing her reading. Since Ben had evaded her questions about dark matter, Danielle deemed that Chi would be a better choice. Chi knew what he was doing, and he always responded nicely to Ben's interruptions. Yet, lacking Ben's easy impudence, she did not feel comfortable imposing herself on Chi when he was engrossed in work. Lunch, it seemed, would be the right time. Going to and from the kitchenette at the end of the hallway, Chi usually lost that meditative, detached look.

In the late afternoon, even before Chi returned from the kitchenette, Danielle's nose twitched in anticipation. Chi's lunches, whether fried shrimps, crab legs, or pieces of pork and vegetables sparking with sauce, always wafted pungent yet comforting scents of homemade food. The tantalizing aroma floating in the air diverted Danielle's thoughts from simulations to a rustic country inn offering homey soups and serving perfectly roasted lamb with freshly baked bread loaves.

Waiting for an opening, she watched out of the corner of her eye the progress of Chi's meal. He gorged steamed rice, bolting down the contents of his bowl at a speed that showed little appreciation for his wife's efforts. Apparently, Chi was not aware of what he was eating, nor of his blinking screen-saver. She was readying herself to politely accost Chi the moment his intent stare would shift away from a framed photo, from which a small boy smiled back. To her dismay, Chi did not look anywhere else.

Although Danielle shied away from interrupting Chi, she cried, "It's absurd!" when she read an email notification that "a lab-safety mini-course will take place on September 16 in room 164 at Lawrence Hall. Attendance is mandatory for physics postdoctoral fellows who were not graduate students at King Solomon University." She thought it was one of those administrative blunders.

"Have you ever been required to attend a lab-safety course for post-docs?" she asked Chi.

"I took it a year ago."

"But why? I haven't seen any hazardous materials in Fitzgerald Hall. In fact, I don't recall seeing any laboratories here either."

Chi, who always remained closemouthed when anyone in his hearing criticized a professor, the physics department or King Solomon University, did not reply.

"Rats," Danielle muttered.

* * *

On September 16, slightly before the specified hour, Danielle crossed the lawn between Fitzgerald Hall and Lawrence Hall. The newer, glass-plated building lacked Fitzgerald Hall's frayed Victorian grandeur; it looked unpretentious, modern yet slightly worn. On the first floor were lecture halls, student labs and classrooms. Danielle entered room 164 when the mini-course was about to begin.

The instructor, a good-humored experimentalist, took pity on the bored post-docs unwillingly attending his PowerPoint presentation. He whizzed through what-might-happen if so-and-so went wrong, summarized the different hazards and dangers, and concluded with cautionary remarks.

"Any questions?" he asked, turning on the dimmed lights.

"Can you give a live demonstration?" someone gibed.

The instructor waved his hand in dismissal. "Anyone else?" he barked.

"Yes?" the instructor addressed a bespectacled, slim guy, who seemed to be in his late teens.

"Could any of the situations you've shown occur at Fitzgerald Hall?"

Heads turned, incredulous glances were darted, and murmurs were exchanged.

"Have you noticed any containers with liquid nitrogen there?" the instructor inquired.

The guy shook his head.

"Signs cautioning of radioactive materials?" the instructor pleasantly went on. "Warnings of high magnetic fields?"

Another shake of the head was followed by a quiet "no."

"Any lasers more powerful than a pointer?" the instructor quipped.

Someone discreetly giggled, a few others smirked.

"No," the guy replied more firmly. "At least not on the fourth floor."

The room rippled with laughter, which no one bothered to suppress. Danielle snorted before she could control herself. The fourth floor at Fitzgerald Hall was akin to Mount Olympus, only instead of having Greek gods, it was a stronghold of high-energy theoreticians. Despite his audience's mirth, the instructor kept a straight face.

"Anyone else here from Fitzgerald Hall?" he asked.

Danielle and three men raised their hands.

"Let me summarize the course for you, guys. If you have nothing to do in a laboratory, better stay out of it."

Fully agreeing, Danielle left Lawrence Hall. Bright light and a gust of fresh air made her look at yellowing glints on the ample foliage. She stopped to watch boisterous squirrels scurrying around, climbing on and off oak trees, carrying green acorns. Jittery like students before exams, she reflected, then realized that the same could be said about her. Deciding to stretch her legs before going back to the office, she took a longer path that crossed the parking lot. A silver Saab caught her eyes; it glimmered in sunlight, slick and expensive, reminding Danielle of the Saab she and Jonathan had seen parked by Lucas Lodge. Reflecting that Jonathan would know whether it was the same car, Danielle's thoughts meandered to their future. She wondered when she would return to the apartment she and Jon had shared, and whether she was asking for too much by aspiring to return to TIST as a junior faculty.

After circumventing Fitzgerald Hall and reaching its back entrance, she still felt restless. Needing to walk off her impatience, Danielle turned left to a narrow road flanked by trees. The alley could be a back-road out of the campus, she reasoned, but even if it led nowhere, she did not care. The air was permeated with a serene silence. She ambled forward between towering, gnarled trunks, her lips slightly opened, her head lifted upward. Topmost branches stretched in all directions, arched over the road, merging into a lush green canopy, dappled with yellow, saffron and vermillion. Bright-blue patches of sky peeked through the dome. A kingdom to itself, Danielle thought. Each tree was a fief, a world, or a galaxy, separated yet connected. The yellow and red leaves were stars, the green foliage encasing them was invisible dark matter.

"Could anyone guess the existence of green leaves, by looking at the bright leaves, stems and twigs?" she asked a nearby trunk.

It did not respond, but Danielle took the silence as "yes."

"If stems and sticks connecting the leaves act like gravity, then counting their number in each tree will be like weighting a galaxy. Would that give a fair estimation of the number of leaves?"

Caught up with weighting "dark matter" leaves by subtracting the number of twigs and stems connecting to "star" leaves, Danielle inched forward. No good, she finally laughed, kicking fallen leaves on the ground. That number would have changed with every gust of wind. Her expression sobered at the sight of colorful leaves left to shrivel, wither and slowly rot on the ground.

At the end of the lane was an open sky and a street; in between hovered a gray arch. Realizing that she was within a five minutes' walk from the Hungry Boson, Danielle hesitated. An unplanned espresso and tart would be nice, yet she was uneasy about talking to Anne after that embarrassing encounter at Lucas Lodge.

She stopped, looked at the arch. From the alley, it did not look forbidding, but merely an elaborate opening, a grandiose construction erected to separate the university from the street. On the gray marble were inscribed rows of unintelligible words. Some were Latin, others were Greek letters she was familiar with from countless physics texts.

"A senseless embodiment of nineteenth century's delusions," Danielle muttered. Her finger stroked the weather-battered stone. It was cold, dirty, and slightly-moist.

"Whoever commissioned it might have shown some foresight and ordered the epitaphs to be carved in English," she grumbled. "But some highbrow idiots must have expected people to know dead languages in the future."

"These were written for the educated," a voice behind the arch replied, "in languages that were recognized as classic, not dead."

Danielle's eyes widened as she gaped at the opening. Whoever he was, an educated or at least a civilized person would have pretended he had not heard her ramble, rather than taunt her without provocation.

"Educated in what?" she asked caustically. As far as she could tell, only those who studied humanities had the expertise to explore bygone cultures and read ancient Greek untranslated.

"Educated in general," the voice said, "in arts and sciences and literature."

"All of that?" Danielle asked, forgetting there was an unknown man veiled behind the voice. "Such multifaceted knowledge might reflect the upper crust of the well-educated during the renaissance in Italy, although I doubt it. I'm willing to bet that elsewhere, such a diverse education was as rare in nineteenth century as it is today."

"Will you?" an elderly man asked, stepping from behind the marble. Danielle squinted, positive that she had seen him before, yet unable to place where.

"Yes, I will," she said. "Those who hold their ground with ancient Greek texts usually shy away from the same letters in an equation."

The man's eye twinkled with mischief. He bobbed his head, then pointed at one of the lines.

"A good name is better than precious ointment," he translated.

"What does it mean in English?"

"I believe that using Greek was not the only omission made by the nineteenth-century's well-educated," the man replied. "They miscalculated assuming that future generations would be familiar with proverbs from Ecclesiastes."

Danielle eyed the old fogy, who should have kept going to whatever department he belonged. She was about to excuse herself and walk to the Hungry Boson, when her face suffused with red. The man who had been showing off his Greek, was the same man, only differently dressed, to whom Marjory Klein had talked at Lucas Lodge. Looking at the colorful leaves on the ground, Danielle fervently hoped that the eccentric Mr. Klein did not recognize her, and that he would forget seeing her before speaking to Marjory.

Seeing Danielle's crimson face, the man concluded she was more timid than he expected. "No need to blush," he said kindly, "unless you feel compelled to be uncomfortable about something."

He turned to the inscriptions, waited for a couple of minutes for the young woman to regain her composure, then pointed at another proverb.

"To everything there is a season, and a time to every purpose under the heavens," he translated. "Another timeless proverb from the book of Ecclesiastes, and also excellent advice."

He proffered his hand, and said, "My name is Jonah Cobs."

Danielle's instincts urged her to flee, her first thought was to hide behind the marble. Her second thought dismissed both fleeing and hiding. Cobs had already seen her dressed like a starlet, heard her talking to herself, and chided her for being ignorant and narrow-minded. The last thing she needed was to act cowardly, and expose herself to his scorn.

"Danielle Meller," she said, extending her hand to shake Cobs'.

In the ensuing silence, Danielle raked her brain for a light, noncommittal comment, but came up only with questions. Why had she never seen Cobs at Fitzgerald Hall? Why had he been dining with Marjory that far from Hopeville? Was he really the scientist in *Monkey's* caricature? Was he working on a "great theory of everything"?

"I assume you would rather discuss physics than proverbs attributed to King Solomon," Cobs asked gallantly.

Danielle nodded, mistrusting her voice.

"Good. Can you tell me what question in physics puzzles you most?"

Danielle looked incredulously at the old professor, hardly believing her ears. Space, Time and Forces puzzled and fascinated her since she was a child. Most of what she studied puzzled her until she gave up fruitless attempts to reach understanding and learned how to solve problems. Since she could tell none of that to a physics professor whose office was opposite Green's, Danielle picked the latest puzzle.

"Dark energy," she said. "I'm intrigued about what it might be, whether it's a manifestation of a new fundamental force."

"I had only a vague idea about what it could be," Cobs said, "but experiments conducted over a decade ago practically ruled out the existence of a long-ranged fifth force."

Having a chance to talk about dark energy with a physicist who knew more about it than she did, Danielle allowed curiosity to overtake awkwardness and caution.

"What about quintessence?" she asked. "Do you think it is slowly relaxing to zero?"

Cobs looked ruefully at the arch. "Not so long ago theoretical physics was rooted in experiments. The last few decades have witnessed a proliferation of models whose predictions are not observationally accessible. They are hard to rule out, which nevertheless does not make them correct."

Surprised by such a response, Danielle asked, "Do you mean high-energy models?"

"I mean any model that spawns indiscriminately what is called elemental particles." Cobs said "elemental particles" with evident disgust.

Was he speaking to the arch? Danielle wondered. Cobs seemed to forget she was there.

"Not only have they stopped teaching ancient Greek, but the concepts of its science have also been obliterated. Do you know what was the original quintessence?"

Danielle shook her head.

"Can you name the Greeks' five elements?"

"Five?" Danielle mumbled. She decided it was a slip of tongue. "Air, fire, earth and water."

"That's four," Cobs said irritably. "What about a sublime element that pervaded the skies?"

"I can't recall any such element."

"The aether."

Danielle forced her expression to remain impassive, even

though it was evident that something was not entirely right with his mind. The best she could do, Danielle reasoned, was to tactfully leave Cobs to his own pondering.

"I'm sorry," she said, affecting a smile. "I was on my way to the Hungry Boson."

She half-expected him to look confused or dejected, but Cobs chuckled. "Off you go then," he said, "and I strongly recommend the apple tarts."

6

COINCIDENCES

After a weekend in Thorboro, where Danielle had seen her parents, met friends, and had Jonathan to herself for two mornings and nights, Monday morning and Fitzgerald Hall's grave façade had little effect on her jolly mood. She quickly ascended to the second floor and turned to her hallway.

"Good morning," Danielle said to Ben, who stood by the secretaries' office, examining the notice board.

"Hi," Ben said. "What's up?"

"Nothing special." She stopped to look for workshop announcements and conference posters. "Has Amanda posted anything new?"

"Yeah."

Typically, Ben did not give away any useful tips. (She was learning not to expect any, after he had deflected her questions with "have to run to a lesson," "too busy right now," and "rewriting some essential parts of the program.") She scanned the departmental announcements. A new posting about postdoctoral fellowships was irrelevant for her, as well as changes in schedules of courses and the delay of coursework submission deadlines. A notice framed by the university's gold and turquoise colors caught her attention. Under the university logo was written "Physics Department, King Solomon University." Below was a title: "A tenure position at the physics department of King Solomon University."

Danielle stepped closer, and read it carefully.

The Physics Department invites applications for a tenure track faculty position in cosmology, at an assistant professor level. Successful candidates must have outstanding record of research accomplishments, strong potential to secure external funding and a commitment to teaching at both graduate and undergraduate levels.

Inquiries and applications, including a curriculum vitae, list of publications, research and teaching statements, and three letters of recommendation should be sent to Faculty Recruitment, Department of Physics, King Solomon University, Hopeville.

Application review and interviewing will start as soon as qualified applications are received and will continue until the position is filled.

King Solomon University is an Equal Opportunity Employer and strongly encourages applications from women and minorities.

Danielle barely finished reading when she heard Ben's sniggering voice.

"Strongly encourages applications from women and minorities," he read aloud. "That wouldn't leave much chance for a guy."

For Danielle, whose mother was obliged to leave graduate studies in physics after giving birth, the comment was outrageous. Her anger was so strong, blood pounded in her temples and clouded her vision. For a moment, she saw colorful bubbles floating in darkness. Then the image faded and the notice board reappeared. The door of the secretaries' office was closed, no one was within earshot. She glanced at Ben and saw a sneering smile, derision written over his face. Ben, she thought, wouldn't dare to say that if his words could be overheard. Through his friendly and easygoing persona, she saw a willingness to seize every opportunity and to exploit every weakness. Using every bit of willpower she could muster, Danielle willed herself to smile obnoxiously.

"You would better read the first paragraph," she said, in a mock maternal voice. "They're looking for an outstanding researcher, Ben, not an outstanding schmuck."

The remark hit where it was intended; Ben averted his eyes.

Danielle waited for a retort, but he floundered, gawking awkwardly. Concluding that they were even, she left Ben to console himself with forthcoming conferences and winter-schools around the world. Ready to snap at whoever she would encounter, Danielle went to her office. Chi was already by his desk, tautly watching his program running. She stifled the urge to say something nasty, put her backpack on the floor, and turned on the monitor.

The first paper on the agenda, a forbiddingly long review on "From Primeval Perturbations to Structure Formation" did not bode well, starting with models steeped in high-energy physics.

Still seething with annoyance, Danielle muttered "What the heck?" Who cared what was the universe's energy at its very beginning? The temperature at the very beginning had plummeted so rapidly that a mere second after the Big Bang, it was below the realm of high energy. For the first few hundred thousand years, photons and other rapidly moving particles, collectively dubbed as radiation, had carried most of the energy in the universe.

In her mind's eye she saw opaque skies swarmed by darting, colliding particles. As the universe expanded, the temperature dropped, the distances stretched. Particles bumped into each other less often, their energy fell off. Massive particles cooled and slowed down.

Since photons' energy decreases as their wavelength grows, radiation's energy density fell faster than that of cold massive particles, dubbed as matter. That resulted in a gradual shift of balance, until matter's energy density caught up with radiation's energy density. After a brief period of equality, matter dominated the universe's energy budget. When the universe's temperature was about three thousand degrees Kelvin, primeval photons had last scattered from primeval electrons and protons. From then on, these photons freely streamed in space, and the skies looked clear and deceptively empty.

For billions of years thenceforward, matter aggregated, stars formed, and the first galaxies dotted the sky. Several billions of years later, radiation's energy density dwindled and matter's energy density significantly decreased. On the other hand, dark energy density hardly changed.

Fascinated by dark energy's unique ability to withstand universal expansion, Danielle pondered on the "coincidence problem." About the time when Earth was created, dark energy density took over matter's energy density, and started to push space apart. Billions of years later, dark energy density was larger than matter's energy density, but not by a lot. The similarity of numbers could be a coincidence, or there might be a profound reason.

Her stare fell on the name of the review's author, a well-known cosmologist. Respected professors, Danielle reflected, can toy with speculations, and leave the toils of testing the plausibility of their cogitations to post-docs and grad students. With luck and persistence, assiduous studies of structure formation bore publications. But could a post-doctorate dedicated to simulations amount to an "outstanding record of research accomplishments" that physics departments demanded in their calls for candidates? Jon and her parents believed in her abilities, but what were her chances? Having no one to consult on what may be considered as an outstanding post-doc, she turned to the departmental homepage of the person on whom her career depended.

George Green's résumé was an example of a seamless academic career. He had a BSc with honors from Harvard, a PhD from Princeton, and a postdoctoral fellowship at Berkeley. His post-doctorate must have been very successful, Danielle mused. After three years at Berkeley, Green had moved to Edmonton in Alberta, to begin his assistant professorship. She scrolled down the page, but there was very little left to read. Green was a tenured faculty at King Solomon University's physics department for the last eighteen years. Wondering how his advance was related to the number of papers he had written, she clicked on Green's list of publications and counted how many he had per year. He published frantically while he was a post-doc and junior faculty, Danielle concluded. She closed Green's homepage and went back to read the review paper.

The intricacies of gravitational collapse of sub-horizon perturbations occupied Danielle's mind. She was struggling with a set of non-linear equations when Ben barged into their office, passed her desk as if she was not there, and paced restlessly back and forth while telling Chi his troubles.

"I integrated the components we had borrowed from the open source." Ben's irritable voice rose shrilly. "It doesn't run."

Unable to filter out the ranting, Danielle had little comfort in Ben having genuine problems with his program. His lack of consideration added to her difficulty comprehending what she was reading. It also brought back the memory of his taunting in the morning, and the wondering on how he could so easily belittle her. When Ben passed her desk without deigning to glance at her, she looked daggers at him.

Keep believing that we benefit from affirmative favoritism, and that I'm here because every physics professor was so encouraging and keen to help, Danielle told Ben in her mind. And yet, her career was much better off than her mother's. Michelle Wiseman had graduated with honors from TIST's physics department the same year George Green had graduated from Harvard. She had married Joseph Meller right after she had graduated, and had stayed at TIST to pursue a graduate degree. At twenty-four, Michelle gave birth, and that was the end of her studies at TIST. Having the dates from Green's résumé fresh in her mind, it struck Danielle that Green had been appointed an assistant professor when her mother had given birth to Julia and Joyce. Eighteen years ago, Green became professor at King Solomon University, Danielle begrudgingly summed up the differences. Her mother had taught physics at Thorboro high schools for the last seventeen years.

Ben's voice resonated like a compressor. Morose and resentful, Danielle mulled over how her birth had ruined her mother's prospects. She worked herself up until her head throbbed. Then, unable to bear Ben's voice, she snatched the review paper and left the office.

Craving sanctuary, even more than a boost of sugar and caffeine, she headed toward the Hungry Boson. A rapid walk through the pretty alley wore off most of her resentment. A silver Saab parked by the sidewalk in front of the teashop awoke some curiosity. Was it the same Saab she had seen at Fitzgerald Hall's parking lot? Danielle opened the entrance door, and found Marjory Klein a few steps away from her. Something in Marjory's mulberry suit brought back a memory of Marjory dining with Jonah Cobs at Lucas Lodge. Embarrassed, Danielle stood and stared.

"How are you?" Marjory asked, her heels tapping on the hardwood floor.

"Fine," Danielle muttered as Marjory stepped out the door, leaving behind a trail of perfume. She heard a thud of the car's door being closed. Peering at the window, she glimpsed the Saab cruising away.

"Come in," Anne invited, her hand gesturing to a tray with apple tarts.

Reminding herself not to be nosy, Danielle made her order.

"A lot of work?" Anne asked.

Anne's tolerant, pleasant countenance invited Danielle to confide in her. Being in need of a sympathetic listener who was not connected with the physics department, Danielle said, "I have quite a few papers I should go through before my boss returns. It'd be easier if I could speed up the reading, but I can hardly skip anything, not knowing which topics I should concentrate on."

Anne put a steaming mug and a plate with a tart on the counter. "Isn't there something you have a special interest in?"

"Well, finding information about dark energy is way more interesting than reading about yet another simulation. I'd like to track dark energy's origins, but my topic of research must be approved by the professor I work for."

Seeing Anne's puzzled face, Danielle explained, "When it's a professor's grant money, he chooses what the post-docs research. I hope that my work will yield several papers. Without a solid list of publications and a superb letter of recommendation, I won't stand a chance to be considered for a faculty position."

"You speak about research as if it is motivated by a need for quick success." Anne's voice was tinged with disapproval. "Do you value having many publications more than making a lasting contribution to your field?"

Danielle opened her mouth, thought she would better think first, and closed it. She took a few sips from the mug, weighed what she might say without offending Anne, making herself look like a moron, or steering away from the truth.

"When I applied to colleges, I didn't delude myself that I

might one day make a groundbreaking contribution," Danielle said at last. "I liked physics in high school, I was good at it, and I was reckless enough to give it a shot. When I started at Thorboro Institute of Science and Technology, there were no tenured women at the physics department. Ten years later, there still aren't."

This simple, unaffected reply appealed to Anne. "I wish you the best luck finding what you are looking for," she said kindly, before stepping aside to bring more trays.

In the following days, Danielle continued to read, collate information, take notes, and go over calculations. Her improvised schedule allotted days and evenings to papers from Green's folder, and nights and weekends to papers about dark energy she found on her own. One night she must have overdone it, for Jonathan told her she sounded like a zombie.

"Thanks a lot," Danielle retorted to the receiver. She got no reply.

"I thought you'd understand. I must have a clear notion of what I want to research before meeting with Green."

"You'll lose your mind if you keep doing nothing but reading physics papers for weeks. Have you spoken to anyone lately? Did you ask others what they do?"

"Whom exactly? Ben ignores me, and Chi is so closemouthed it's impossible to get him to talk. When Ben blabs about Green or other professors, Chi fiddles with the keyboard, without uttering a single word."

"Did you ask Chi about simulations?"

"He is too polite to brush me off like Ben did, but he is not going to help me. Why would he, if he considers me as a competitor?"

"You didn't shy away from people at TIST," Jonathan commented. "How do you expect to have an academic career if you can't befriend anyone?"

"I think Chi and Ben will come around once Green is back and I'll have my own topic." Danielle hesitated for a moment, decided she should not beat about the bush with Jon. "I definitely will be happier to work on a problem in physics, and not spend my post in programming, which is what Chi mostly does."

"I don't recollect you were bothered about programming during the endless discussions we had before you decided to go to Green," Jonathan said skeptically. "Haven't you said that being able to do high-level simulations should boost your career?"

"I was clueless about how complicated and time consuming they are. And I didn't know about dark energy. Now that I know more, it's natural to have second thoughts about what I'll do."

"Do you?" Jonathan compressed considerable sarcasm into the question. "You haven't even tried simulations."

"Jon, there is a chance that dark energy will be discarded next year, but it also might turn out to be the breakthrough everyone has been waiting for for decades."

"So?"

"I've seen only a trickle of theoretical explanations. One is that dark energy is the vacuum energy, which is the state of minimum energy."

"You can skip the rest of the explanations," Jonathan dryly suggested.

"The point is that there are barely any others. Quintessence is likely to be ruled out."

"Can you spare me the physics?"

"Sure," Danielle said resignedly. Tiredness seeped through her body. She wished she could nestle against Jonathan the way they had done over the weekend. "I miss you."

"Tell me about that," Jonathan suggested, at last expressing interest.

* * *

September was drawing to a close, while Danielle slogged through papers from Green's folder. She had not yet ventured to ask Chi about his simulations.

She was reading a paper on mapping of CMBR (cosmic microwave background radiation), when it started to rain heavily. Alone in the office, she peered through the window – all she saw through the frame was thick, grayish sky and pelting rain. She watched as raindrops sled down, leaving transparent trails on the glass. She yawned and rubbed her forehead. Rainy days made her drowsy.

By noon, it was as dark as if it was late in the evening, a

creepy darkness of sky that turned into a dense, impregnable fluid. Disliking the unvarying gloom that enshrouded even the sidewalk, Danielle tried to focus on what she was reading. The CMBR was the oldest direct evidence from the early universe, and thus a cosmologists' trove. For once, it was easy to envision the opaque skies before primordial photons had last scattered off matter. One got the gist just by looking out the window.

Danielle went again to the window. Straining her eyes, she discerned a pair of quivering beams, probably the headlights of a car from the parking lot. Light, she noted, didn't seem to move through air filled with discrete, falling raindrops, but through a uniform substance that was entirely different from the torrent of water and vapor. In her mind's eye, the universe was filled with a barely perceptible substance, a medium through which galaxies swirled and glided away. Danielle sighed. Long ago, physicists had posited that universe was pervaded with a medium called ether. Nowadays, some physicists argued that it was permeated with dark energy. So far, she had scarcely any information about what dark energy was. Unable to focus on CMBR, she searched for preprints about dark energy's origins and printed the ones whose abstracts were comprehensible.

The eerie day turned into a ghoulish evening. At home, surrounded by a new crop of papers, Danielle jerked when lightning after lightning struck the sky with ghostly white blows, ominously flashing the living-room through closed blinds. She lost her train of thought every time it thundered.

Old Victorians knew how to muffle noises, she reflected, wincing at the thunder's vicious crackle, wishing the little house had Fitzgerald Hall's sturdy walls. Dark energy seemed more real with the Gothic backdrop, and closer than she wanted. To distract her mind, Danielle went to the kitchen. The quiet hum of the refrigerator was reassuring. She started to make tea.

All of a sudden, the kitchen was lit by bright, dazzling glow. A blink later, all lights in the house went off, the refrigerator's hum stopped. Before Danielle's eyes could get used to the darkness, a menacing thunder boomed from above.

The power cut lasted for hours. Danielle found a flashlight and did her best not to think about dark energy seeping through the house undisturbed. Lightning and thunder were creepy enough, without imagining herself engulfed in an arcane, fluid medium.

As soon as electricity was back, she dialed Jonathan's apartment. No answer. Eager to hear his voice, she called the office, but no one picked up the phone. Reasoning that Jon might be on his way home, Danielle made fresh tea and drank it, then made another call to his apartment. Getting the same outcome, she dialed Jonathan's cell phone. An irritating, prissy voice said that the number was not available at the moment and invited her to leave a message in the voicemail. Danielle disconnected. A third call to his apartment bore no response. She left a message.

Waiting for the phone to ring, she paced back and forth across the living room and the kitchen, staved off morbid thoughts about accidents. After half an hour, she called Jonathan's cell phone, and left a message on his voicemail. She left another message on his answering machine before she went to sleep.

The torrential rain abated at night. In the morning, the grubby-grayish sky lost its opaque, impregnable quality, but heavy rain continued pouring. Cars queued on both sides of Chadwick Drive, children and parents huddled together, waiting for the school bus. Morning news showed the rampage a tropical storm made as it progressed along the shoreline: torn roofs, flooded houses, uprooted trees, and debris floating on streets. Danielle watched until the anchorman switched to a report about local politics, which, in face of the storm's havoc, seemed even more meaningless than usual.

In her office, Danielle reassessed her priorities, and made a resolution to ask Chi about his simulations as soon as he would arrive. Meanwhile, she tackled the clutter of papers she had amassed. The papers that she had found on her own were stowed into the lowest drawer. Other papers she had read went back into Green's folder. Papers she should go over by Friday were stacked together. When the phone rang, Danielle picked up the receiver, ready to inform Mrs. Wang that Chi had not come yet. Jonathan's familiar voice politely asked to speak with Danielle.

"Jon?"

"Yeah. What happened?"

"It thundered through the night and is still pouring. I haven't had much sleep."

"Do you have any damage?"

"No, Hopeville was pretty far from the eye of the storm."

"Why didn't you sleep then? Did you wait all night for the roof to leak?"

"You sound very cheerful," Danielle pointed out. "I called you several times last night. Haven't you got any of the messages I left?"

"I checked the answering machine ten minutes ago. You sounded miffed, but didn't mention any emergency. What did you want to say last night?"

Looking at the dour sky on the other side of the window, Danielle noted that Jon sounded too cheerful. He was rarely bearable in the mornings, let alone in bright mood.

"Never mind," she said. "Where were you last night?"

"Oh, that?" A cocky chuckle followed the question.

"What are you so conceited about?" Danielle asked. Knowing pretty well what would make him sound upbeat at any hour, she added, "An algorithm finally runs?"

"No. I was at the Heidrun."

It made sense. The pub was underground, and cell phone reception there ranged between bad and awful. "Were Nickka's brightest celebrating the completion of the demo?" she asked.

"No, we aren't there yet." Jonathan's voice lost a good portion of its cheerfulness. "Amos and I had a long brotherly talk."

"That's surprising," Danielle said coldly.

When she had first met Amos, she disliked his vulgarity. A couple of years at TIST's prestigious MBA program smothered Amos' innate crudeness and provided some polish, but her dislike grew stronger, for Amos began to egg Jonathan into breaking with her and looking for a more suitable girlfriend. With her and Jon no longer living together, Danielle imagined Amos had many morbid things to say about her.

"Are you miffed?" Jonathan's voice cut through Danielle's recollections.

"No, just wondering what you could be talking about."

"And?"

"His affairs are none of my business, as long as he does not interfere with mine."

"It was all about him." Danielle practically could see Jonathan smirking. "And you'll hear about it anyway."

"What did he do?"

"Not over the phone. I want to see your face when you hear it."

That was tantalizing enough to kindle Danielle's curiosity. "I'm alone at the office. I promise to tell you everything that comes into my mind."

"Deal," Jonathan's voice tinkled with laughter, "but you guess first."

"Amos received a lucrative job-offer, and he was bragging under the pretense of asking your advice?"

"Not even close."

"I give up. I can't fathom what goes in his mind."

"So fast?" Jonathan teased. "You hypothesize how universe evolves. How can you be clueless when it comes to discerning human feelings?"

"Cosmology relies on observations," Danielle said. "So far the evidence for a repulsive energy pervading the space is more conclusive than for Amos having any human feeling other than ambition and greed."

"Come on. You can say something positive about my little brother."

"I'll leave that for your mother," Danielle retorted before she stopped to think.

"Or Amy?" Jonathan suggested. "Does that ring a bell?"

"I can hardly believe she is still dating Amos."

"Amos told me he'd proposed last weekend. He wouldn't have mentioned this unless Amy said 'yes'."

"I thought that Amy is too intelligent to tie her future and happiness with Amos," Danielle murmured. On the other hand, Jon had a point. Amos would not have brought the subject up if his proposal might be turned down. Either way, Danielle concluded, Amos and Amy's decisions had nothing to do with her. She stifled curiosity, and tried to infuse a little warmth into her voice.

"Congratulations," she said aloud.

"Thanks. I'll speak to you after work."

"It can't be all you are going to say. How can you leave me wondering for half a day?"

"Not when you need to free your mind for physics," Jonathan poked fun at her fondly. "Okay, shoot."

"How did your mother react?"

"I don't know. I unplugged the phone so she won't tell me at seven a.m."

Danielle was still pondering how Sarah would treat the new addition to her family when Chi came into the office. He put his backpack and lunch bowl in their regular places, said "good morning" and settled before his monitor.

"Good morning," Danielle replied. "Such nasty weather. Did you have a power cut last night?"

After a curt "yes" Chi started typing.

There was no time for an opening, Danielle realized. Bracing herself for Chi's refusal to talk, she said, "George wrote me that I should learn about the group's simulations."

She could hear her heart pounding, as she weighed whether to ask Chi what initial conditions he used, and whether he took into account radiation. Should she fish for other crucial details? A gut feeling prompted Danielle to be as direct as possible.

"Can you explain a bit about your program?" she asked.

Chi did not respond, but neither did he start typing. Was he taking his time to consider her request, or was he looking for a polite way to brush her question aside? Danielle mentally crossed her fingers and willed herself to remain quiet.

"You can go over the program I'm running," Chi said. Danielle's heart pounded faster and louder. "It does not have much documentation, but you can ask me later what you don't understand."

Having had a fraught night, Danielle did not entirely trust her understanding.

"Are you giving me your code?" she asked.

"Write your address," Chi said. Danielle did so, Chi attached his program and sent the email.

The dull sky outdoors looked brighter as relief welled up and washed away Danielle's worries. Her problem with the group's simulations was neatly resolved. Chi, whom she often underestimated, had shown unbelievable generosity. Self-conscious about having thought meanly of him, she was ready with a wide smile and sincerest gratitude. A glance at Chi made it clear he was not interested in hearing any of it.

"Thanks," Danielle said. Chi made a brisk nod and returned to his program.

The smile waned as Danielle skimmed through the code, which was intricate and nothing like the programs she had written at TIST. By the time she scanned most of the program, her relief was long over. It was professional-grade programming, she thought in growing panic. Did Green expect his post-docs to write such simulations? The answer sat by the other desk, oblivious to everything beside his code.

Hours passed as Danielle scrolled back and forth between the main program, its various procedures and subroutines. She felt subdued, but resisted the temptation to ask Chi for help.

Find the redshift the simulation starts at, she told herself. That would pinpoint the age of the universe and its temperature when the simulation began.

Indeed, "z=1100" was easy to find. The redshift corresponded to an epoch when the universe was about four hundred thousand years old and dominated by matter, to times when primeval photons (the CMBR) had last scattered from primeval electrons and protons. Chi's choice of initial conditions became obvious. Measurements of CMBR gave a snapshot of the universe's temperature at the age of four hundred thousand years. Whereas the temperature had been almost uniform at every direction in sky, its tiny fluctuations corresponded to slight variations in matter's distribution.

Feeling a tad more confident, Danielle started to search for other cosmological parameters.

"It's amazing," she informed Jonathan that night, after recounting how she had gotten Chi's program.

"He gave you the entire code?"

Although Danielle had just told him so, she understood Jonathan's disbelief. "Yep," she said.

"Did you ask him?"

"I wouldn't dream about doing such a thing," she righteously protested.

"Hmm, hmm."

"I might have thought about it, but I wouldn't have dared to make such a request. All I asked Chi was to tell me about his simulations."

"And who urged you to do it?" came a triumphant inquiry from Thorboro.

"Someone I expect to spend the weekend with."

"I miss you," Jonathan said.

Danielle noticed tiredness in his voice. Jon's words were followed by a pause, a lingering silence which did not bode well for their plans. "Has anything happened?" she asked.

"Nothing in particular. Paul and I had to listen to Pilcher rattle on about not getting to see Paul's presentation."

Why Pilcher? Danielle wondered. Jonathan usually reported directly to Roy, Nickka's founder and CEO, not to Nickka's administrative director.

"Where is Roy?" she asked.

"Out of town, coaxing investors."

Rats. She stretched on the sofa, ready to hear how Pilcher played the big boss.

"Would you believe the idiot changed something that stacks the demo, and he is clueless about what it was?"

"Who? Pilcher?"

"Paul."

"Don't you have a backup version?" Danielle asked automatically.

"Yeah," Jonathan grunted, "from three days ago."

Danielle itched to remind Jonathan that she said many times that Paul Zeeman should not be at Nickka at all. "What are you going to do?" she asked.

"Paul and I reconstructed the code."

An image of Jonathan and Zeeman hunched over a pair of computers, doggedly perusing line after line formed in Danielle's mind. Jon could be irked by Zeeman's sloppiness, but he would not be able to resist the challenge of fixing it before Pilcher realized what Zeeman had done. "So?" she asked.

"We have a meeting with Pilcher tomorrow," Jonathan said sourly. "At nine a.m."

"Let Pilcher have his petty revenge," Danielle said soothingly. "Whatever it takes, I'm going to finish with Green's papers before Friday night."

"Great, you'll have some time to try Chi's program."

"What about going somewhere this weekend? Get inspired by autumn beauty, catch a breath of fresh air and all that?"

"I can't. We are going to work through the weekend."

"I thought we'd spend the last weekend before Green is back, together."

"By Monday the demo should be waiting for the graphical designer," Jonathan said firmly.

"Can't you leave Zeeman to work through the weekend?" Danielle grumbled. "It's a mess he created. If you don't rush to save his programs, he'll do a better job next time."

A scornful sniff came from Jonathan's end of the line. "That would be an ingenious plan in a big, established firm. We don't do that at Nickka."

"It's not about competition but responsibility. Isn't Zeeman in charge of the demonstration?"

"Officially," Jonathan scoffed. "Pilcher can insist on orderly project delegation, but if Paul's presentation falters, the entire project might sink."

And that was the end of it.

7

GEORGE GREEN

Danielle finished her reading by Friday night, two days before Green's expected return. She looked at stars twinkling and flickering in the clear sky, stretched her arms towards them, took a deep breath of crispy night air, and shut the window. She fell asleep as soon as her head touched the pillow.

It was around noon when she woke up to sounds of muffled burr rising and falling from the closed window. Rays of light slanted through the blinds, leaving bright patches on the bed and the floor. Recalling that she was finally through with the papers, Danielle thought she deserved a break and a celebration. Wanting to bask in sunlight, she decided on a good brunch.

Chadwick Drive was uncharacteristically noisy, with her neighbors blowing leaves on their lawns. The Main Street bustled with couples, with roaming groups of teens, and with leisurely strolling families. Danielle, who was usually at work at this hour, was surprised to see lines before restaurants' doors. Of course, restaurants would be crammed on a bright Saturday around lunchtime. People probably came from neighboring towns to enjoy the variety of food and the upscale atmosphere rendered by the university, she mused. Noticing an ice cream parlor, and kids and grown-ups licking their scoops, she opted for a big ice cream. While waiting in line, she found out that Hopeville's Historical Society was tucked on the second floor of the small wooden house next door. A free campus tour was to commence in less than an hour at the university's main entrance. Joining it seemed like a good idea.

"King Solomon College was founded in 1822 by a group of prominent landowners, who donated the acreage, commissioned the main building, and subscribed to pay a headmaster and two other tutors." The tour guide waved her hand and all eyes turned towards a majestic, overstretched building, whose two rows of Doric columns grandly faced the university's main entrance. "Alexander Hall is the college's oldest building. It had classrooms, a dormitory, and a dining hall."

The guide moved aside, answered questions. "Yes, King Solomon College was established as an all-male college, but female students have been admitted since the 1890s," "No, the only subjects they taught were Classics, Mathematics, Philosophy, Natural Sciences and Literature."

Danielle listened to the buffs of local history, bemused by their minute interest in the university's past. Others, meanwhile, posed and took pictures, documenting distinguished buildings and themselves in the foreground.

"They copied the design from Nassau Hall in Princeton," a man knowledgeably explained to a woman beside him. He wore a regular camera mounted with an enormous telephoto. The woman nodded, smiling apologetically.

The guide moved in front of the group. "Alexander Hall is a fine example of the Greek Revival architectural style."

She herded the group along paved paths, pointing at different buildings, citing various styles and dates. People they passed were mostly young; they looked like university students.

"Do students live in dormitories?" someone asked. Someone else wondered aloud where the old fraternity houses were.

"The undergraduate students live in four colleges on the other side of the campus," the guide replied. "We'll see the South and West colleges on our way back. The new dormitories are near the stadium. To see the old fraternities, stroll along the Faculty road."

"Do grad students live off the campus?" Danielle asked.

"No, there is an apartment complex for them off the University Drive. Here, Harrison Hall," the guide added cheerfully. "As you see it's Greek Revival again. It was a very fashionable style in the first half of the nineteen century."

After a few turns they reached a picturesque old building,

which despite the bright sunlight, had somber medieval airs. "The university's oldest chapel, built in Gothic style," the guide introduced. Cameras documented. "The chapel is renowned for its stained glass."

"Do they do weddings there?" a broadly-smiling woman asked wishfully. Other women in the group craned forward, their eyes gleaming with interest.

"Yes. Students of King Solomon University and others affiliated with one of the colleges may have the ceremony in the chapel. Usually, it is followed by a reception in one's college."

There were resigned murmurs. Seeing nothing special about the old building, Danielle wondered why others admired it.

"The pair of buildings you see on the right are Campbell Hall and Austen Hall. Both are circa 1840s. By then the college's faculty had expanded. There were seven professors and four tutors."

"Is Austen Hall named after Jane Austen, the writer?" a woman asked.

"It's a common misconception, as Austen Hall houses the department of English literature. Austen, Alexander, and Harrison Halls were named after families who provided the means for the college back in the early 1820s. Campbell Hall was named after the college's first president."

Ignoring the parking lot on their right, everyone turned left, then halted to admire the elegant faculty clubhouse.

"It was given to the university in 1919 by the alumni of the Class of 1884," said the guide. They were close to Fitzgerald Hall and the gray marble arch, but the tour proceeded to the right, going straight to the monumental central library and the fabulous Italian Gardens. Evidently, Fitzgerald Hall was not one of the highlights of the campus. When most of the group scrutinized the pond and its fountain, she asked the guide about Fitzgerald Hall.

"It was named after one of the three first tutors," the guide said. "Fitzgerald was a Princeton graduate, who taught mathematics and natural philosophy at the new college. He later became the first chair of Mathematics."

"What about a gray marble arch at the end of an alley? It faces Stateside Street."

The guide looked inquiringly at Danielle. "Have you seen it?" she asked.

"Yes, many times." With a flicker of pride, Danielle added, "I work at Fitzgerald Hall."

"It was commissioned for the main entrance. I can't recollect when it was removed to the other entrance."

"Do you know why it was moved?"

"In the local lore, the arch was deemed as a bad omen. There are conflicting stories about where the superstition had come from, but before it was removed, townies and students alike insisted that it brought back luck."

Bad omen? Danielle echoed in her mind. Her thoughts leaped to Green and dark energy. She felt a frisson of foreboding and ripples of nervousness.

After the tour was over, she went to buy groceries. Back in the house, she did laundry, scrubbed tiles, mopped the floor. It was easy to occupy her hands, but her mind kept dwelling on the forthcoming meeting, looking for what would be best to work on, career-wise. Her gut feeling pointed to dark energy, but reason resisted shaky arguments. Long after the laundry basket was empty and the kitchen appliances gleamed, Danielle debated on how to present her hunch to Green.

Jonathan called on Sunday night to wish her good luck.

"Are you calling from the office?"

"No, no need to. The demo works," Jonathan said contentedly. "Have you made up your mind on what you'll wear tomorrow?"

"Not yet, but I made an important decision." Danielle stopped, shut her eyes for a moment. "I don't want to work on simulations."

"What?"

"I'm not really that good at programming."

"Are you backing away after seeing Chi's code?"

"Partially, yes. It's a sinkhole that drains one's time, and it certainly won't be worthwhile if I won't become really good at it."

"You will, if you do the work," Jonathan stressed.

"Maybe," Danielle said, doubtfully. "But what is the point in a post that focuses on programming rather than physics? For that, I could have stayed at Thorboro and looked for a job."

Silence hovered long enough for Danielle to realize that Jonathan completely disagreed.

"Are you mad with me?" she asked.

"No, just sorry that you can't stick to what you decided."

"Green and I haven't decided upon the subject of my post. Actually, he might be interested in having someone in his group who works on the more theoretical aspects of dark energy."

"Why then have neither Ben nor Chi grabbed it?" Jonathan asked. "From what you said about Ben, he isn't one to pass an opportunity to beef up his résumé."

"Ben doesn't think it's a major discovery. When he realizes that it is, he'll be the first to jump on the bandwagon."

"But you are resolved to pursue it right now. Are you ready to gamble on your career, going boldly where no one else cared to go before?"

"You paraphrased the wrong movie. I'm neither the first nor the only one who seeks the origins of dark energy. A more adept one-liner would be 'trust your feelings'."

"Is that what you are going to tell Green tomorrow?"

"No, that is for your ears only. With Green I'll stick to arguments physicists conventionally use."

"Anything else for my ears only?" Jonathan asked, veering the conversation elsewhere.

Lying in bed, Danielle thought about Jon, and pictured their life together after she'd return to Thorboro. She sank into sleep envisioning the future, but before long she became aware of being surrounded by a swampy green-gray substance that extended as far as she could see. Wondering where she was, she flailed her legs and arms, dived through plums of murky green-gray undercurrents, passed through spinning eddies. Bizarrely, the substance exerted no pressure – her motion didn't meet any resistance, there was no sensation of something brushing against her skin. She noticed circles converge into smaller circles, and plunged towards the smaller ones. Straining to see through the mist, she glimpsed a contour of a submerged solid object large enough to pass for a shipwreck. As she steered closer, the object looked like an enormous stone, and then like a huge marble arch. Gliding around it, Danielle noted that the arch stayed in place even though it was anchored to nothing. The inscriptions on the gray surface were effaced, but otherwise it was the arch from the university's back entrance. Shudders running all over her spine, she woke up. The grayish sky was dappled with inconspicuous looking clouds rather than a thick pall of mist.

Stretching and rubbing her eyes, Danielle mulled over her dream and whether it had any meaning besides her being jittery. She made herself a cup of coffee and toast. She spooned raspberry jam from a jar, licked it, and spooned for more. A few teaspoons later, her looking for omens in a dream seemed pretty stupid.

Green was more likely to ask about what she had read than what she wanted to do, she reflected, deciding to play it by ear. Keen to look determined and capable to do outstanding research, she tried on various shirts, most of her pants, and even a skirt, each time checking the look in front of a mirror. The most flattering combination was a few notches above what she usually wore to work, but it looked casual enough for a regular day. "If I don't meet Amanda or Marjory," Danielle told her reflection, "no one will notice the difference."

Although it was early in the morning, she met Chi in the second floor hallway. They walked together, silently passing Green's locked office. The thud of their steps echoed along the vacant corridor.

The door of Green's office was ajar when Danielle stood before it four hours later. A big poster was pinned to it. "The Dark Elements of the Universe," she read the title, then the date and the location of a conference.

Nice. She liked the idea of spending a week in May in Montreal. The blurb was interesting. The co-chairs of the organizing committee were among a handful of eminent cosmologists who were well-known beyond their field. She scanned the names and affiliations of other members of the organizing committee listed below in an alphabetical order. Seeing "George Green, King Solomon University," Danielle felt a flutter of satisfaction amid growing nervousness. She clasped her hands. They were cold and sweaty. Shoulders straightened, eyes closed, she waited for her mind to clear, for unbidden thoughts and everything she had read to fade into a nondescript background. Then, she checked the watch and knocked. It was eleven thirty-one.

"Come in," a level male voice bade from within.

Danielle stepped into a spacious office, painted in a pale blue-gray color, but stopped a couple of steps from the door and squinted. Daylight filtered through half-opened Venetian blinds, bounced from a huge whiteboard, suffused the room with luminescent, pearly glow. Adjusting to the light, she noted that most of the whiteboard was covered with neatly written equations, except its left-most part, where phone numbers and names were jotted. The cabinets under the window were similar to the ones in the secretaries' office, but in place of photos and gadgets were high piles of papers. Bookshelves filled with hard-covers lined up most of the other two walls. Reassured by the presence of books, Danielle took a few steps forward to stand between two armchairs that faced an enormous, cluttered desk. There she waited, her lips curved into a shy, tentative smile, her gaze lowered, not to stare at a tanned, bespectacled man who was reading from a state-of-the-art monitor.

Seconds stretched, without any response from professor George Green. Nervous and diffident, Danielle warned herself not to perceive his absentmindedness as a slight, and inched closer to the desk. Green's eyes were still on the monitor, when he nodded and gestured Danielle to sit down. She sat in the armchair closest to the window.

Slightly shifting, Green took off his glasses, smiled, welcomed Danielle to King Solomon University, to the physics department and to his group. She thanked him quietly.

"Have you found an accommodation?"

"I rented a small house on Chadwick Drive."

"It's a good neighborhood," Green said. "In all, Hopeville is a pleasant, safe town, and the university offers various cultural activities. The Ross theater has a long-established theatrical tradition."

Not particularly interested in artistic excellence, Danielle smiled politely. Green's recommendations of local eateries received more attention. Bearing in mind Jonathan's future visits, she registered Green's praise for King's Kitchen and that he did not mention the Hungry Boson. At a quarter to twelve Green concluded the small-talk by inquiring about Danielle's

PhD supervisor, Alec Smith.

"Alec is on sabbatical in Geneva. The last I've heard from him was in August, when he forwarded me a referee's response to a paper we had submitted."

"Where to?" Green asked.

Reflecting that it wouldn't harm mentioning that their paper was submitted to the prestigious *Physical Review Letters*, Danielle replied, "PRL."

"How is your reading progressing?"

"I read all the papers in the folder you left me."

Danielle's voice was steady, but her body tautened. She went over notes in the morning and came prepared to describe the Sacks-Wolfe effect, the different modes of primordial perturbations, anisotropies in CMBR, and many other cosmological fine-points referred to in the papers Green had dumped on her. She rubbed her sweaty hands under the table and waited for Green to lunge with questions.

Green reclined on the back of his armchair and folded his arms."Have you looked at simulations?" he asked matter-of-factly.

Simulations? What about the papers? Shouldn't Green inquire about the darned papers, show interest in what she gathered from what she had read? Forget it, Danielle ordered herself. Dithering with response did not make a good impression.

"Chi gave me his code and an overview of what it does. I'm not done with the details yet."

"Why not?" Green's equable voice exuded authority and impatience. His slate-gray eyes scrutinized her forehead, probing and calculating.

Did he want a truthful reply? Danielle thought rebelliously. Believing that he didn't, she raked her mind for an answer that Green would deem acceptable.

Finding none, she looked at books stacked on shelves behind him. There was a behemoth *Gravitation* (a professor at TIST had once recommended using it as a door-holder when it was not needed as a reference book), deep red *Classical Electrodynamics* (a masterpiece renowned for haunting generations of physics grad students), the familiar *General Relativity*, and even *Black Holes, White Dwarfs and Neutron Stars* she had used so much in the course of her graduate studies. Focusing on the books, Green's presence blurred a little, gave way to thoughts about dark energy. For now, it was yet another of nature's mysteries, but one day, its enigma would be cracked, its origins would be understood, and its essence would be distilled into concise, probably elegant, equations. What physicist wouldn't aspire to contribute to finding the solution?

"I searched for papers on dark energy and its origins," Danielle said. She glanced surreptitiously at Green. He reposed in the armchair, his eyes half-closed, as if he was contemplating or bored. "I focused on models that explain dark energy without assuming it's a property of the vacuum itself."

Green's eyes narrowed into slits of opalescent grayness, creases crossed his forehead. "Why?" he asked.

"The main contribution to vacuum energy density is about Plank's mass to the power four," Danielle said. "Comparing with observations, that estimate is off target by a hundred and twenty orders of magnitude. I think that, by itself, it's a good reason to look elsewhere for an explanation. A model like quintessence can give a better estimate."

Green's expression remained inscrutable, his eyes mostly closed. "Observations so far are inconclusive on whether dark energy has changed over time."

"A paper I read attributed it to a slow relaxation into a true vacuum state. I thought that there might be other models explaining dark energy, ones motivated by cosmology."

Green opened his eyes, his lips curved in a way that hinted a smile. "Dark energy is a recent discovery," he said placidly. "There were a few papers predicting it, but by and large it was not expected."

Incredulous that Green could acknowledge the discovery, yet speak so dispassionately about it, Danielle silently stared at him.

"Like any breakthrough, dark energy attracts an extensive interest. It is special," Green stopped to look discontentedly at the eager post-doc in front of him. He had nothing against diligence and ambition, but he preferred his group members to come with tangible results rather than brim with raw enthusiasm.

"Dark energy has been of utmost importance through the evolution of the universe." Green unfolded his arms and leaned forward. "If you are interested in dark energy," he said businesslike, "study its effects on structure formation."

"But I thought..." Danielle's voice sank. Studying structure formation, she wouldn't tackle the roots of dark energy, but work mostly on computer simulations. And as far as simulations were concerned, dark energy was merely a parameter in a program. Had Green just brushed her off?

"It is bound to become a highly competitive field, once theoretical physicists will join forces to explain the discovery," Green continued equably. "Undoubtedly, cosmology and astrophysics will provide important insights, but to come up with a plausible explanation of what dark energy is..." Green's painfully skeptical expression completed the sentence. She did not stand a chance.

Disappointment was written all over Danielle's face. Green considered her silent misery, estimating that she had invested time and effort preparing to work on the dark energy problem.

"Have you any background in string theories?" he asked.

No, Danielle thought, unless dating Zeeman counted. Unfortunately, a few dates at the beginning of their graduate studies had not clued her about string theory's predictions, only about what Zeeman had thought of those unable to grasp more than four dimensions. She shook her head.

"No?" Green looked at his watch, indicating the time allotted for their conversation was nearing its end. "Then you may not be aware that this is a very different milieu than astrophysics and cosmology."

"Can I work on a topic related to dark energy origins?"

"You'll keep an eye on the emerging dark energy models, but at this stage I don't see any theoretical aspect you can work on. In a post-doctorate, you focus on obtaining publishable results, not plunging unprepared into a new field."

Rats. She nodded to show she understood and respected Green's directive.

"Work on simulations and stay updated about the observational data." Green added, looking again at his watch. Realizing that her time was up, Danielle rose from the armchair, smiled at Green and left the office. She did not know what to think of her boss, but it was a relief to be away from him. She emailed Jonathan, then duly perused Chi's code.

8

SPACE OPERA

A week had passed since Green's return, but it felt longer after seven days of incongruous bustle. Hyped-up Ben regularly came into Chi and Danielle's office, stressed Chi went back and forth to Green's. Engulfed in an atmosphere of assiduous code-improving and eagerness to please Green, Danielle engrossed herself in simulations.

Her assignment was to simulate universe inhabited with two types of generic particles. Light and pretty fast particles represented ordinary matter (hydrogen and other light elements). Ultra-heavy and slow particles represented dark matter. This stripped-down-to-the-barest-minimum universe did not consider radiation, as it had a secondary role in real universe's evolution at that epoch. The question Green posed was whether this simplistic model sufficed to create structures similar to ones observed.

By the time primordial photons had decoupled from electrons and protons, the real universe had already been sown with local aggregates of dark matter. Bearing in mind that these aggregates had grown very little before matter and radiation decoupled, Danielle decided to start the simulation with randomly positioned particles.

Astrophysicists inferred from observations that dark matter contributed five times more to the universe's energy density than regular matter did. However, the masses of dark matter particles (and their interactions) were theorists' educated guesses. Green had left it up to Danielle to figure out what values to assign to particles' masses, instructing her to check various values and cream off the ones that yielded best results. The number of particles in the simulation had no cosmological motivation – it was constrained by how much running time one got on the group's cluster of computers.

Having characterized the generic particles, Danielle turned to their interactions. Every particle exerted gravitational pull. Only light particles participated in a made-up interaction devised to keep them at equilibrium. The interaction did not require sophistication, only fixing the rate at which light particles bumped into each other.

Einstein equations, on the other hand, could not be treated lightly. They were the crux of every cosmological scenario – at every moment of time they interrelated the universe's energy content and the way the universe expanded. Reckoning that any code that churned Einstein equations required an intricate piece of programming, Danielle opted to postpone the inevitable headache; the procedure she wrote to calculate the forces acting on particles was based on the Newtonian law of gravity.

* * *

Days slipped away in quick succession while she tried to pin the rate of made-up interaction that would keep the light particles at equilibrium but not the ultra-heavy ones (otherwise, the ultra-heavy particles would not start to aggregate). She had a mental picture of ultra-heavy particles slowly gliding in space, gradually clumping together to form miniature droplets, and of light particles darting in every direction, while bombarding the heavy aggregates. But it took some more time before her program ran on the group's cluster. To check the code, she let the program run without expansion, even though the simulation made no sense. Within a few days dark matter congregated into several lumps, which kept growing by trapping errant light particles. To create a network of structures, she had no choice but to include universal expansion in the code.

That was easier said than done. Struggling with the code, Danielle regretted her complacency during the long days of reading without interruption. It would have been much smarter, if she had heeded to Green's email, and had started to work on simulations before his return. But how could she foresee the extent of his expectations? In fact, she could not fathom how Green managed to squeeze in all the demands on his time. He went to the weekly astrophysics seminars (and also insisted that she, Chi and Ben attended, regardless of the topic). He even listened while Michael Axelrod's graduate student droned about filtering extra-galactic radio sources from the surrounding white-noise. Later, Green asked about the filters Axelrod's group was using, then grilled the unfortunate student about inconsistencies in the analysis. Green also attended departmental meetings, and other, more mysterious ones, for which he wore a jacket. Curious as to what occasions required a professor to wear a jacket, Danielle asked Chi.

"Dr. Green always wears a jacket when he teaches undergrads at Lawrence Hall," Chi replied.

"Hasn't he missed half a semester?"

"No, he teaches Introduction to Astrophysics and Cosmology jointly with Dr. Brophy. She starts the course at the beginning of the term, and Dr. Green teaches from the eighth week to the end of the term."

"Very efficient," Danielle murmured, and stuck her nose back in the code. Efficiency, she told herself, was what Green expected.

She had no flair for programming, but having plenty of stubbornness and determination, she worked conscientiously, stripping her days of anything that was not essential. Her code was devoid of Jonathan's brilliant shortcuts and of Chi's intricate algorithms, but it ran.

Finally having something worth reporting, Danielle relaxed her stiffened shoulders and went to Green's office. He listened to what he deemed as adequate yet not quite impressive progress, then asked, "Did you incorporate repulsive dark energy?"

Green's instruction to include dark energy compelled Danielle to add Einstein equations. She stayed at the office as late as Chi did. Arriving home, her eyes were bleary, and she fell asleep without food or calling Jonathan. She dreamed of a thick soup simmering in a bowl, a loaf of fresh crusty country bread, and a butter dish full with herbal butter. Minutely cut vegetables darted in the bowl, grumbling that it was too dense there and too hot.

"Well, I cannot expand at a whim," the soup bowl replied fretfully.

"You can use some dark energy," scoffed the morsels of meat.

Danielle remembered the dream in the morning, but could only reminisce about fresh bread and herbal butter. The refrigerator was practically empty. She rummaged the kitchen cupboards, without finding anything she wanted to eat. After Green's return her shopping dwindled; it had been almost a week since she had run out of milk.

A prospect of breakfast at one of the cafés on the Main Street cheered up Danielle's unpleasantly rumbling stomach, but every place she peeked into, she saw a line reaching to the entrance door. Hungry and annoyed, she passed the university's main entrance, reached the intersection of Main and Stateside streets. As she turned to the right, her nose started twitching in anticipation of the barely perceptible wafts of baked apples and dough. The scents intensified as she walked, reaching a crescendo at the door of the Hungry Boson. Salivating, Danielle thrust forward. Her eyes noted tarts first, then Anne, who was poring over a book beyond the counter. To Danielle's utmost disbelief, she was the only patron.

"Good morning," Danielle said.

Anne lifted her head and smiled. "Good morning," Anne said, as she put a bookmark in a worn-out paperback. "What would you like to have?"

Danielle wanted to order five different pastries, but she asked for an apple tart and a large cappuccino. The tattered paperback lay closed on the counter. Thinking it was better manners to look at a book than stare at food, she craned her neck to read the upside-down text on the back cover. Her eyebrows rose, as she read about rip-roaring adventures across the galaxy, battles between good guys and baddies. An old sci-fi was not what she would have expected to find Anne reading.

"A dollop of Devonshire cream?" Anne suggested.

"Yes, please." Danielle darted a greedy glance at a golden tart on a plate. After subsisting on snacks from Lawrence Hall's vending machine for several days, an apple tart with Devonshire cream was a luxury bordering on decadence. "I've missed reading a good science fiction," Danielle added, loud enough to mask the noises her stomach made.

"Why don't you borrow one from the library?" Anne flipped the book and put it in front Danielle. "The English department has a very good one in Austen Hall."

Looking at the title, *Galactic Patrol,* printed in bold letters, Danielle thought she'd better not mention that *Programming in C* was the only book she had recently opened. She flipped the book back to read the blurbs.

"Your coffee is ready," Anne said.

The entrance door opened, lively female voices poured in.

"Can I take the book with me for a few minutes?" Danielle whispered. The blurbs promised a space-opera packed with ideas and action, and Danielle craved for both.

Anne nodded and put Danielle's order on a tray.

Buttery and tangy tastes mixed and melted in Danielle's mouth. She licked the froth, took a sip of hot coffee. The breakfast would have been perfect, Danielle reflected, if she could block out three blabbering voices that merged into a persistent prattle.

"I think that a white cake with a black and white soccer ball is a far better option," one of the women suggested a compromise. "We can order it drawn over pink icing."

"Light green icing decorated with pink icing looks better," a higher-pitched voice objected.

Danielle almost snorted into her coffee. Watching the three women from the corner of her eye, she observed nothing unusual in their clothes, haircuts, or make up. They were neither young nor quite middle-aged. Together, they looked like a PTA committee. When the discussion stopped, Anne welcomed the newcomers, and asked, "How can I help you?"

The trio consulted over the question, then ordered three lattes and an apple tart.

"A dollop of Devonshire cream?" Anne offered.

Taken aback, all three promptly declined the cream. Danielle rolled her eyes, and wondered whether these women could contemplate something more serious than icing.

Shouldn't she check the status of the job from last night? What if Green was looking for her? Danielle glanced at the watch. It was only quarter to nine, early enough to indulge in a decent breakfast. Shelving worries about Green and simulations, she sampled the cream. A rich, slightly sweet taste spread in her mouth. Appreciating it slowly, Danielle opened the book, leafed yellowing pages, absentmindedly read random phrases. In spaceship Britannia, *Galactic Patrol's* crew scrambled the ether; in an unnamed spaceship, plundering pirates "darted away, swept the ether." With so much testosterone oozing in two spaceships, Danielle was ready to bet on an imminent battle. Indeed, the spaceship zoomed "towards the enemy at the unimaginable velocity of ninety parsecs an hour."

Zooming faster than light wasn't unimaginable, Danielle retorted in her mind. It was only contradictory to every experiment and observation known to physicists. Yet, unlike physicists, science fiction writers could take ludicrous liberties with nature's laws. They were free to speculate about alien cultures and futuristic technologies. No one required them to be grounded in the reality of the observable universe.

What about physics professors like Tobi? Danielle chuckled. Grounded was a relative term and perhaps a too strong requirement. Ten-dimensional universes might entitle the highest ranking in being unimaginable, yet they prevailed in theoretical high-energy physics enclaves. Compared to these, ether was a ridiculously simple concept: an omnipresent medium hypothesized by mathematicians and physicists to explain how electromagnetic waves propagated in space. It was also anachronistic. The Michelson–Morley experiment had shown that there were neither ether drift nor any motion of ether relative to earth. Einstein's special theory of relativity made the notion of ether-as-medium irrelevant.

She flipped the pages back to check when the book was published. The copyright was dated from 1950; the original story was serialized in 1937. Astounded at such a blatant ignorance, Danielle glared at the pretentious title, which enticed her to while away more time than she could justify. On the page's upper right corner, her eyes noted a name scrawled with faded blue ink. "Gemma Cobs," Danielle read.

Female voices rose as they debated which cake should be ordered for the end-of-fall-season soccer game. Danielle looked at the counter. Anne was weeping a nozzle of the espresso machine, emanating the same poised, ladylike demure she had exuded at the elegant dining room of Lucas Lodge.

Galactic Patrol's crude machismo and battles in ether-filled space could not be Anne's cup of tea, Danielle concluded. Why then was Anne reading it?

A well-honed, curious mind, which was recently denied its exercise, could not resist the temptation to look for a satisfactory explanation. Combining extrapolation with speculation, Danielle deduced that the book was a keepsake from Gemma Cobs, who was not around anymore. If Gemma was professor Cobs' wife and she had passed away, deep grief could explain his declining career and his self-isolation better than a burnout. Professors, she had found out, compensated for diminishing inner drive by pushing their students to produce more.

Maybe she just left him, suggested another thought. Danielle concentrated, but could not recall seeing Jonah Cobs either at seminars or in his office, nor anywhere else in Fitzgerald Hall, except for the secretaries' office, talking with Marjory Klein. Ever since she had seen Marjory and Cobs together at Lucas Lodge, she suspected that they were in some sort of relationship. Following the idea, she noted that their lukewarm affair must have started decades ago, and therefore, it was likely to wreck Cobs' marriage.

She looked again at the name. The faded handwriting taunted Danielle to picture Gemma as a middle-aged woman, a washed-up wife of an unfaithful professor. There was something sparkling, even flaunting about the name, Danielle thought as she stared at it. Gemma Cobs was not a woman who would tolerate her husband looking at anyone but herself.

The paperback was old, but the name had been added no more than ten or fifteen years ago, probably when Gemma had been ailing. Danielle shuffled dates in her mind, and deduced that Jonah's career had crumbled along with Gemma's declining health. She almost regretted that her explanation fitted like a missing piece in a puzzle, for it felt that Gemma Cobs should be alive.

It was twenty minutes past nine, but Danielle could not leave before she found out how Gemma fated. Reasoning that Anne was Gemma's close friend, Danielle waited impatiently for the three women to leave. As soon as their backs disappeared behind the entrance door, she snatched the paperback and hurried to Anne.

"Thank you," Danielle said as she slipped the book on the counter, near Anne's hand.

"Did you like it?"

"Well," Danielle hesitated. *Galactic Patrol* reinstated outdated ideas instead of imaginatively pushing the boundaries of science. Saying that about a cherished keepsake was unthinkable. "I really haven't read much."

"Otherwise you would have said it's interesting or creative," Anne said. "*Galactic Patrol* is considered a classic space-opera, but I could never understand why it was Gemma's favorite when she was in high-school."

A high school friend? The suggestion crossed Danielle's mind and was dismissed promptly. A glance at her watch reminded Danielle that she should be at work.

"Is Gemma Cobs a relation of professor Cobs from the physics department?" she asked.

"Of course," Anne smiled, but her smile waned in response to Danielle's sober face. "Haven't you heard Gemma's name through Fitzgerald Hall's grapevine?"

"No, I haven't. I just saw it written on the book."

Anne looked strangely at Danielle.

"I know nothing about professors' private lives," Danielle muttered.

Anne's face lit, her eyes glinted with mirth. Even more confused, Danielle asked whether Gemma lived in Hopeville.

"Gemma lives near Tintagel." Seeing Danielle's blank expression, Anne added, "It's in Cornwall, England."

"Sounds like a pretty place," Danielle said flatly, not knowing what else to say about Jonah Cobs' estranged wife.

"It is. My brother and sister-in-law have a small farm on a hill overlooking the castle and the Atlantic coast."

Manners forgotten, Danielle stared at Anne's wedding ring. She had a plethora of reasons why it was impossible, yet the last piece of information did not add up, unless Anne was Jonah Cobs' wife.

"I have never," Danielle muttered, her face glowing with a

vermilion shade.

"You've never asked how the Hungry Boson got its name." Anne laughed. "Otherwise, I would have told you that Jonah and Gemma named my teashop."

"I must go," Danielle mumbled.

She left the teashop feeling like an idiot, a meddling idiot who was very late to work. Why had she pried into a stranger's name written on an old book? Danielle chided herself as she strode faster, but not fast enough to escape the awkward scenarios her mind conjured. Anne's delight in recounting the story to Jonah was as evident as their sharing the joke with Marjory Klein.

"Rats," Danielle greeted the marble arch. Behind it stretched an alley padded with writhed brown leaves, and flanked by old, gnarled trees. In a sudden surge of defiance, she raised her head, looked at the canopy of branches. It glowed like a tunnel on fire, in satisfyingly fierce, flamboyant colors. Feeling empowered, Danielle purged her mind of thoughts about the Cobses and went forward.

"Hi," Danielle said to Chi when she entered into their office. "Has George looked for me?"

"No," Chi replied, his eyes focused on the screen.

Relieved of one worry, Danielle checked the status of her program. The job had been aborted shortly after midnight. Gritting her teeth, she began to search what went wrong. The culprit was not where she suspected it to be, nor in other places she thought of. She added controls and sent a short test run. After hours of dogged examination of every piece of code, the morning's escapade slipped from her mind.

"I can look over your code on the weekend," Jonathan volunteered when they talked that night.

A thrill of joy flashed through Danielle. "Are you coming?"

"I'm tied up until Saturday afternoon, before Roy and Paul fly away with the demo. Can you come over? My parents invited us to dine at Chives and Tarragon."

Since Richard and Sarah had never invited her to any of Thorboro's fancy restaurants, Danielle doubted that she understood correctly. "Your parents did what?"

"Invited us to Chives and Tarragon on Saturday. Will you

come?"

"Of course I will," Danielle said, triumphing inwardly. It was not that long ago that Sarah had articulated her opinions about spoiled, ungrateful women who chased after dreams when they should have made a serious effort to find a good position in or around Thorboro. Thinking of Sarah's resentful farewell, Danielle added, "Your mother surprises me. I didn't expect her to mend fences in such a gracious way."

Jonathan harrumphed, thus summing up what Sarah Lerner had actually said before she grudgingly allowed him to invite Danielle to a dinner originally intended for the four Lerners and Amy. Fifteen hours at work did not exhaust him as much as forty minutes on the phone, listening to his mother's misgivings about Danielle.

"I don't think she sees the dinner that way," Jonathan said diplomatically.

"Why would she make such a generous invitation if not for a reconciliation?" Danielle countered.

"The dinner is in honor of Amos and Amy's engagement."

Silence. Danielle had no need to ask questions nor pretend she got the invitation by right of being part of Jon's family.

"Give them my regards," she said very quietly, her voice intimating she preferred to let go of the subject and of the invitation.

"Dad will be happy if you come."

"And I'll be happy to see Richard." Danielle waited for a moment. "Do you really want me to be there?"

"Sure," Jonathan replied.

Having a day and half with Jon to look forward to, she pushed herself with renewed determination. By Wednesday night, she fixed several glitches, but the program still did not run properly. The only remedy she could think of was to rewrite the part that used Einstein equations. On Thursday, she came to work when the sky was still gray and was oblivious of her surroundings until Chi said, "Colloquium in ten minutes."

"Do you know what it's about?" Danielle asked, raising two bleary eyes from the monitor.

"Scale-free networks."

The little Danielle knew about the topic brought to her mind neural networks of the brain, social contacts and networks of the internet, all of which were removed many times from cosmology. Some part of her mind protested against leaving in the midst of writing a subroutine. Suspecting there might be undesirable consequences if she didn't, Danielle chose to play safe. At the Lounge she, Ben and Chi grabbed what was left of the cookies. Green, she observed, talked with Axelrod and Lisitsin, and also nodded to at least half a dozen other professors. Shortly after that observation, the grumpy blond whom Danielle had seen on her first visit to the Hungry Boson summoned everyone to the auditorium.

"Christopher Keller," the professor introduced the speaker, "started his career here as an undergraduate student. Chris proceeded to Penn for graduate studies and then to Los Alamos National Laboratory for postdoctoral research."

After the introduction, Keller got the mike. "Thank you, John," he said. "It's a pleasure to return to King Solomon university."

Danielle listened for a couple of minutes, but when Keller flipped a slide and said, "Similar networks are characterized by the number of connections each of their nodes has," she let the words drift. For the rest of the talk, she daydreamed about the forthcoming weekend.

She came early on Friday, hoping to untangle her code and make it run before the end of day. By the time Ben peeped his head into the office, she itched to hurl the monitor into the nearest wall.

"George wants to see you," Ben said. Danielle jolted, then lowered her head back to *Programming in C.* It was not worth the bother, asking Ben to call Chi without interrupting her.

"Come on," Ben repeated over Danielle's head.

He volunteered no explanations while they walked to Green's office.

"Danielle, Ben." Green waved towards the two armchairs in front of his desk. "How are the simulations progressing?"

Like the Buridan's ass's dinner, Danielle thought. She sat down and looked for a better reply.

"The three runs I have on the cluster," Ben said, "experiment with different temperatures for WIMPS at redshift sixteen hundred."

"Good," Green said. He drew a preprint from a large stack of papers on his desk, showed it to Ben and Danielle.

"Long Range Forces Explain Dark Matter and Dark Energy," Danielle silently read the title.

"I was asked to referee it by one of *Science's* editors." Green's equable voice intimated that he regularly refereed papers for one of the most prominent scientific journals. A slight change in his countenance indicated his gratification at being asked.

Ben squashed an involuntary whistle; Danielle lowered her blushing face, feeling awkward to show how much she was impressed.

"This is a theoretical paper. I'd like you to read it and derive the limits the authors obtained." Green turned to Ben. "Are you taking any courses this semester?"

"Yeah, in parallel computing," Ben said nonchalantly.

Never losing an opportunity to blow your own trumpet, Danielle gruffly noted, miffed that Ben's tactics worked. For once, Green looked pleased.

"Then we'll resume our pizza seminars after the midterms," Green said. "I'll give a talk on Friday after next. Can you present the paper and the main results at the beginning of the seminar?"

Ben and Danielle quickly agreed, as if Green was really asking their assent.

"Hand me a written report with your derivations at the seminar," Green added. He gave Danielle the preprint. "Would you please photocopy it?"

Understanding it was a dismissal, she took the paper and left. Before she closed the door, she heard Ben telling Green about his latest results. Frustrated and tired, Danielle sauntered back to her office.

"Jonathan called you," Chi said.

"Did he leave any message?"

Chi proffered a piece of paper. It read: "Jonathan called at 11:40 from Thorboro's hospital. Tell Danielle he's O.K. He'll be at the airport to meet her."

Danielle reread the note several times. A cold quiver spread through her body, her hands trembled. Could something have happened to Richard or Sarah?

"Did Jonathan tell you what happened?" she asked in a

barely audible voice.

"A colleague of his had a car accident. He asked me to tell you he'll tell you about it when you meet."

Danielle's sight blurred even before tears gathered in her eyes. Jon had pals at Nickka, but she could think of only one whose injury would induce a call to her work from the hospital.

"Did he mention a name? Someone called Paul Zeeman?"

"Yes," Chi said gravely. He averted his eyes and pretended not to hear Danielle's stifled sobs.

9

THE SECTION OF OLD PERIODICALS

It was half past eleven on a beautiful Sunday. The Jeep Cherokee moved slowly, giving Danielle plenty of time to watch Thorboro's outskirts roll into an open countryside. Glorying in the Indian summer, horses grazed behind fenced meadows, whereas cows looked indifferently at the road. Michelle's hands held the steering wheel tightly. She slowed down at every turn and bend of the road, and eyed it suspiciously, as if waiting for a bypassing car, a reckless motorcycle, or wandering deer. Danielle yawned; the Jeep growled in protest. Wishing it was Jonathan at the wheel, she closed her eyes.

"You must be very tired," Michelle said. "I should have insisted on your staying at home and getting some rest while Jonathan is visiting Zeeman."

"Then I wouldn't see you when I'm finally at Thorboro," Danielle said. "I'm sorry I missed Dad."

"I hope Joe will be home before we get there. How is Zeeman doing?"

Here it goes, Danielle told herself. She did not want to think or talk about Zeeman's injuries. But her mother, who should have been hardened by her husband's profession, fretted over any possibly-lethal accident. Projecting her tenderness and compassion onto Danielle, it did not occur to Michelle that her daughter's lousy mood had nothing to do with Zeeman's health.

"He was discharged yesterday, with an arm and hand in cast."

"Discharged so soon after a concussion?" Michelle frowned.

"Neurologists suspected a concussion only because Zeeman had spewed up in his car and all the way to the emergency room." Danielle grimaced. "I suppose that vomited pizza mixed with blood looks spectacularly gross."

Unable to overlook her daughter's insensitivity, Michelle said rebukingly, "Danielle."

"Mom," Danielle countered, "Jon and I had a terrible night when Zeeman was hospitalized for a neurological observation. After dreading that he had damaged his brilliant head, I'm glad he got away with a broken wrist and superficial cuts. I don't pity him for bumping a new Audi into a lamppost."

It seemed to Michelle that for a woman who professed to feel so little, her daughter was protesting too much. Yet, Michelle only said: "I don't like crass talk."

"Then I won't say that neurologists wouldn't conclude that nothing is wrong with Zeeman's head if they conferred with a shrink."

Danielle glanced sideways at her mother, expecting to see her smiling. Michelle looked troubled.

"Promise me you won't bite anything but the food," Michelle said.

"You know that Aunt Sophie can fend for herself. I, on the other hand, exhausted my self-restraint last night."

"I'm sorry you had a bad time," Michelle said. "You and Jonathan deserved to relax and enjoy yourselves after all the stress you have been through."

"Well, I docilely smiled and humored everyone, but even Chives and Tarragon cannot counterbalance Sarah when she is in one of her officious moods."

"You know Sarah." Michelle's voice was calm, even soothing. "She is not a bad person, but you shouldn't let her interfere in your relations with Jonathan."

"Oh, she was too busy for that last evening. She fawned Amy, declared what a delight it was having her as a member of Lerner family, and sweet-talked her into trying various dishes. I could hardly believe it when Sarah showed interest in Amy's studies."

"Did she ask about your post-doctorate?"

"Of course not. Sarah wouldn't acknowledge I'm doing something worthwhile. But she wasted no opportunity to dart sly glances and mocking hints in my direction."

Michelle sighed. Danielle's decision to move out of the apartment she and Jonathan had shared had ruffled Sarah's feathers. Danielle doing so for a post-doctorate in cosmology stirred animosity.

"I've thought about it many times," Michelle said. "I believe that Sarah's antagonism won't last after you show you were right in choosing that particular career path."

"I'm positive it won't. Once I'm on a tenure track, Sarah will recall all the encouragement she has given me to pursue my career. If I'll ever make it and become a professor at TIST, she won't let anyone forget that most of my success is due to her."

Michelle felt growing discomfort, as she listened to Danielle's oozing cynicism. "How is your research?" Michelle asked.

"It'll be an understatement to say so-so. The simulation stalls, and I can't find what went wrong."

"It's less than two months since you've started," Michelle said reassuringly. "Aren't you pushing yourself too hard?"

Danielle shook her head. "There is no other choice in Green's group. I didn't expect this kind of pressure, but comparing my hours to what Jon puts into Nickka, I know I shouldn't complain."

The words reminded Michelle of having similar sentiments when Joe had been a resident at the Thorboro Medical Center. Her heart swelled with emotion and she accidentally stepped on the gas. The jeep joyfully lurched forward.

Seeing that her mother was immersed in thoughts and did not notice, Danielle cheered up.

"Where is this Hungarian Café Aunt Sophia raved about?" she asked after a while. "We seem to be in the middle of nowhere."

"It's in a small mall half the distance between Odinton and Thorboro. We're a bit late, but don't worry. We'll be there in five minutes."

The small mall was a cluster of squat one-story buildings surrounded by a vast parking lot. About twenty cars were scattered around on stained asphalt. The place reeked with gasoline.

"Mom," Danielle squeezed through her teeth. "It's the dingiest mall I've seen in a long time. Any restaurant here would be too shabby and shapeless to offer decent food."

"Don't be a snob," Michelle hissed impatiently as they headed towards a crummy little café jammed between a nail salon and a paint store. Danielle gawked at the see-through windows, white plastic tables, and cheap garden chairs, all crammed in with no regard to patrons' privacy and comfort.

"I know Aunt Sophie doesn't like to splurge on appearances," Danielle whispered, "but that is carrying the principle too far."

"Their catering has an excellent reputation. Look, the café is almost full."

Although she would be hard pressed to call that a café, Danielle grudgingly agreed that the place was packed. Most of the patrons were drably dressed old women, sitting by themselves or in small groups. A more careful inspection discerned several old men and even a few forlorn children.

"The kids look as if they were dragged in or bribed by their great-grandparents," Danielle muttered. She was pleased that neither Amy nor Sarah could see where she was, but also embarrassed for feeling so.

"Shh." Michelle looked around, her stare skipping anyone who might be younger than sixty. "I see Sophia." Michelle nudged her daughter. "She's waving to us."

Sophia Bloom beckoned to her niece and grandniece from a table she had reserved by strategically putting her belongings all over it. When Danielle and Michelle came close, Sophia rose up. She wore a dress she would put on for a brunch at a good restaurant. Her lips glowed with freshly applied cardinal lipstick. She smelled of perfume.

"Michelle, dear." Sophia extended both hands to her niece. They exchanged kisses. "Thank you for coming with Michelle," Sophia said as she embraced Danielle.

Seeing tears suspiciously glitter in Aunt Sophie's hawk-eyes, Danielle felt shame at her own pettiness. She kissed Sophia's creased cheeks.

"Is Joseph still at the hospital?" Sophia asked. Michelle said he was.

"He needs to get a bit of rest now and then," Sophia advised. Michelle readily agreed.

"How are Joyce and Julia doing?"

"They are fine. I think they are overworking, but Julie assures me that they have recuperated from their first midterm at medical school."

Before Sophia could explain to Michelle what the twins should do, a teenage waitress squeezed her way to their table, bringing a nicely printed and surprisingly long menu. Danielle leafed through pages that listed crêpes with dozens of different fillings, pastries, and gateaux with foreign names. There was a section for cream puffs, and two pages listed hot beverages, ranging from exotic coffee blends to an assortment of teas.

It's more extensive than Chives and Tarragon's, Danielle thought. She looked inquiringly at Sophia, who was busily swapping family news with Michelle.

"How is Tali?" Michelle asked about her cousin.

Sophia heaved a deep sigh, to show that she was not one to complain even when there was a reason. Gathering that the matter once again revolved around Natalie's son, Michelle asked, "What did Dorian do?"

"Nothing in particular." Sophia expressively cocked her brows. "Dorian does not do much, and Tali does too much. As always, I'm grateful they are both well."

They paused to order. After the waitress left, Sophia turned to Danielle. "You have been very quiet. How do you do at the new place?"

"Quite well. I rented a nice little house not far from the campus. My boss, professor Green..." Danielle's voice trailed off. Sophia's pursed lips indicated that whatever happened at the physics department was not the information she had in mind.

"How do you find Thorboro?" Sophia asked.

"It hasn't changed since my last visit."

"Did you have a good time dining with the Lerners?"

Surprised that her great-aunt had heard about the dinner, Danielle glanced at Michelle. Her mother smiled innocently.

"We went to Chives and Tarragon. We got a good table. As a matter of fact, everything was fine."

Responding to Sophia's raised eyebrows, Michelle explained in an undertone, "The restaurant has been a great favorite in Thorboro since it opened its doors last year. People make reservations two weeks ahead to eat overpriced pasta with herbs."

"A freshly made pasta," Danielle corrected, imitating Sarah Lerner.

Sophia's eyes were fixed on Danielle. "Did you get on with Jonathan's parents?"

"Richard is a nice person," Danielle said warmly. "He always treats me well."

"What about Sarah?"

"I placated her a bit by duly admiring Amy's diamond ring," Danielle said, her voice momentarily chilled. "And I did not roll my eyes when Sarah coaxed Amy into having a dessert because she was studying so hard."

"Who is Amy?"

Idiot, Danielle chided herself. Any information she volunteered gave Aunt Sophie new ground for probing.

"The dinner was in honor of Amos and Amy's engagement," Danielle said. She trusted Aunt Sophie to remember that Amos was Jonathan's younger brother.

"What is Amy's surname?"

"DeWitt."

"Hm," Sophia succinctly expressed her opinion. "What is she doing?"

"Amy is a graduate student. She studies towards a master's degree in child psychology at one of Boston's universities, I forgot which."

"Harvard?" Sophia suggested the only university in Boston she knew about.

"I wouldn't forget Harvard." Danielle smiled at the idea, and then, knowing what the next few questions would be, she said, "Amy is twenty four, naturally blonde, and very amiable. I don't particularly like her preppy style, but the look suits her."

"What is her father doing?" Sophia asked.

Danielle waited for the approaching waitress to place their crêpes, cakes, and coffees. The service, she noted, was efficient. The plates were clean, albeit slightly chipped. The food, although plainly arranged, smelled good. Even though Sophia tended to skimp on presentation, Danielle could not recall her compromising on quality.

"Amy's father and eldest brother are lawyers; something about white-collar tax loopholes. Amy's other brother is in the

TIST MBA program with Amos."

"And the mother?" Sophia inquired.

"I don't know whether she has any profession. Jon told me she is a homemaker and a volunteer."

"A housewife," Sophia said, looking meaningfully at Michelle.

Reckoning that she had answered enough questions, Danielle pointedly took a few bites of her crêpe. "It's great. These guys are really good, they should be able to branch out to a decent place."

"I'm happy you appreciate good, unpretentious food," Sophia said. "But I'm sorry the dinner yesterday did not help to reconcile you with Jonathan's mother."

Michelle cupped her daughter's hand. "I think Danielle is paying too much attention to Sarah's disapproval."

"I wouldn't mind if it were a mere disapproval," Danielle grumbled, "but regardless of what I do, I get under her skin."

"You are not someone Sarah would want to be," Sophia said. "And you are impractical. She cannot understand how you could leave Jonathan for a temporary job with nebulous prospects."

"I didn't leave Jon. We see each other as much as we can."

"You are also astoundingly naïve." Sophia lowered her voice to a whisper. "Do you remember the time you told me about accelerators? You tried to convince me that our government was spending billions on constructing and operating underground accelerators, for no other reason except to let physicists investigate how the universe was created."

"How can I forget?" Danielle muttered. She had tried to explain what high-energy accelerators did and why they were built, but nothing she had said could shake Sophia's conviction that government would not finance such an endeavor if it could not be used to make and store powerful, very dangerous, ultra-secret weapons. Striving to keep a respectful expression on her face, Danielle looked at her mother. Michelle studiously drank her coffee, keeping her amusement to herself.

"Do you think," Danielle asked, "I made a mistake in temporarily leaving Thorboro for a chance to carve out a career in physics?"

Sophia studied her plate, brought the cup to her lips, and put it back. She was an outspoken woman, but in Danielle's case it was hard to offer any advice. For herself, Sophia strongly believed that ordinary women and men should choose practical and financially stable occupations. She was a librarian, her late Arthur had been a bookkeeper; together they had provided for Mark and Natalie, helped them to acquire respected and financially rewarding professions. Sophia's mind turned to her brother Aaron, who had studied physics. Aaron died very young, before having children. Sophia sighed and shifted her thoughts to Michelle. Her niece was happy teaching physics, but she probably was not as fulfilled as she might have been if she became a researcher like her uncle.

"I'm sure Jonathan does not think like his mother," Michelle broke the silence.

"A good point," Sophia said. "How did he act last night?"

"Before the food came, Jon spoke with Amy and teased Amos. After that, he dug into a plate of lamb chops with Portobello mushrooms, and mostly talked with Richard about restoration of old cars. Thinking of it, I doubt that Jon noticed Sarah's nasty little digs."

"I don't know about pursuing a career," Sophia said, "but if you have any sense, you won't let Jonathan stir until he proposes, and then you will marry him."

Having heard this advice many times, Danielle did not dignify it with a token protest. She looked at her mother. Michelle ate silently. Danielle followed her example.

"Which ones do you like most?" Sophia asked after they sampled all the cakes on their table. Michelle and Danielle named their favorites. "I'll keep them in mind," Sophia said, "to order for late November."

The broad hint about Sophia's forthcoming birthday brightened Danielle up. "How are the preparations going?" she asked.

Aunt Sophie knocked on the table three times. "Everyone I talked to promised to come, and Mark has already made flight reservations. You will come with Jonathan, won't you?"

Danielle gently squeezed Aunt Sophie's wizened hand with her own.

"I won't miss your seventieth birthday," she said, looking

squarely into Sophia's hawkish eyes. "I'll invite Jon, but I can't promise on his behalf."

A tear or two shone in Sophia's eyes. "Don't worry if Sarah thinks poorly of you," Sophia said. "What's important is that Jonathan knows what a treasure he has."

Looking forward to being treasured, Danielle brought two delicious crêpes and a half of an apple strudel back to his apartment. Jonathan was already there, sitting in the living room, with an open laptop on his lap. Danielle hugged him from behind. "A place for me?" she whispered into Jonathan's ear.

* * *

On the following morning, Danielle was drinking her first cup of coffee in the little house on Chadwick Drive, when it occurred to her that she had forgotten to pass Sophia's invitation, and even worse, to show Jon her program. Too late, she thought as she mentally went over a to-do list for the day.

"Rats," Danielle hissed when she realized that she had completely forgotten about the *Science* preprint. She rummaged in her backpack, but it was not there. It was not on the sofa, not on the shelves in the living room, and nowhere else in the house. She cursed frantic Fridays, gulped the rest of her coffee, took her backpack, and rushed to the university.

"Long Range Forces Explain Dark Matter and Dark Energy." Danielle's eyes caught the ambitious title as soon as she reached her desk. A little breathless, she slumped on the chair and pored over the preprint. The authors, of whom she had never heard, posited that regular matter dominated the universe. They argued that phenomena attributed to dark matter and to dark energy, were, in fact, manifestations of regular matter interacting through two new forces.

A pair of new fundamental forces? Moreover, fundamental forces with extremely long yet finite range? Danielle eyed the text suspiciously. Of the four known fundamental forces, the strong and the weak nuclear forces had very short ranges, whereas the electromagnetic and gravitational forces extended indefinitely. Was there any observational evidence to support the claim such new forces could exist?

After reading a few more lines, it became apparent that the

hypothesized forces were motivated by high-energy super-symmetric models. Skeptical yet intrigued, she skipped to the first equation; it described an attractive force which brought regular matter together, and a repulsive force which pushed it apart. The strengths of the forces were chosen so they would account for observations usually attributed to the pull of dark matter and to the repulsion due to dark energy. Not surprisingly, the necessity of complying with astronomical observations required that each of the forces would be strong enough to be detectable on Earth.

How the heck is that possible? Danielle wondered. Extremely precise terrestrial experiments did not trace unaccounted for long-range forces.

The authors, she found, circumvented the apparent inconsistency. They set the repulsive and attractive forces to cancel each other out at terrestrial distances, so the net force was practically zero everywhere within the Solar system. The attractive scalar force was postulated to stretch to the fringes of galactic halo. There it steeply (exponentially) decayed, becoming negligible at farther-than-galactic distances. The decay of the repulsive vector force, on the other hand, was so mild (power-law tail), that it extended beyond super-clusters. On the largest length-scale, the repulsive force was stronger than gravity. It pushed space apart.

Three forces competing with each other at cosmological distances? Danielle found the idea disturbing. In the theory of general relativity (which is the theoretical frame at the core of cosmology), only gravity played a role at these distances. The authors, however, countered this deep-rooted tenet by arguing that gravity was not well tested for distances stretching beyond galactic halos.

It wasn't an entirely new argument, Danielle mused. In some theoretical models gravity undergoes modifications at inaccessibly high energies or in other dimensions. While she ignored any prediction irrelevant to universe's evolution, she could not shrug off a possibility that cast doubt on the mere existence of dark matter and dark energy.

"Hi," Chi said, entering the office.

"Good morning," Danielle replied. To her surprise, there was dark puffiness under Chi's eyes, and his haggard face betrayed a severe lack of sleep. A kinky night with Mrs. Wang? Danielle speculated. Or egregious demands from Green? She waited for Chi to doze off in his chair, but in ten minutes, she heard the familiar, monotonous clicking. It's time to go back to the simulation, Danielle guiltily thought. She and Ben had agreed to work on the preprint on Wednesday, after Ben would have completed his midterm assignment.

She turned to her program, and started tinkering with the code. Anticipating that her turn would come next every time Green summoned Chi to his office, she shuddered at the thought of how awkward it'd be to admit she made no progress. The perceived humiliation spurred her to look at Chi's program again. It simulated a different universe, one with several types of particles and more realistic interactions. The code did not provide a ready-made solution, but Danielle found useful clues on how to code Einstein equations better. She modified parts of her code, then tackled bugs. Engrossed in culling errors, she first noticed that Wednesday was drawing to a close when Chi was about to leave the office late in the evening.

Next morning, she woke up with a nagging feeling that she had overlooked something. The sensation grew stronger when she entered the office, but once she found out that her job had been aborted during the night, she forgot every sensation but urgency. Another round of debugging was unavoidable. Irritated and jumpy, Danielle noted that she was not the only one unnerved. Chi sat tautly in front of his monitor. When Ben came into their office, he fretted about graphs and plots. Seeing that Ben was more agitated and stressed than herself, Danielle felt a tinge of sympathy. The feeling dissolved at the moment she grasped that Ben was ranting about graphs and plots Green wanted for his forthcoming talk.

When Ben grumbled about being summoned thrice a day to Green's office, either to get instructions about new plots or to revise whatever Green did not like, Danielle wondered why Green didn't call her. Was it because he considered her too slow, or because she had not come up yet with workable code?

That was absurd, Danielle reasoned. Whatever her shortcomings in programming, she had done hundreds of presentable plots for Alec during her graduate studies. Moreover, Green wouldn't have given her a challenging theoretical paper to review if he deemed her to be incompetent.

"Have you read the *Science* preprint?" she asked Ben.

"No," he snapped, "I didn't look at it."

Danielle lifted her eyes, fixed her stare somewhere between Ben's towering shoulders and shaved chin, and willed herself to calm down. The office was already permeated with tension, and no one needed more nerves. She reminded herself to be tactful, then she said, "I think you should do it pronto. Something is wrong with what the authors did."

"Is it a hunch?" Ben jeered. "That will be handy when you do the derivation on your own."

Using all the patience she could muster, Danielle asked, "Are you going to backtrack the derivations by yourself?"

"Nope," Ben said from above. "George told me it's all yours."

"Aha?" Danielle fired a piercing glance at Ben. He did not look as if he had just made a lame joke. "What do you mean?"

"You are going to write down the derivations by next Friday. I won't."

"How did you weasel out?" Danielle asked, in a voice that hissed like a snake with a cold.

"I didn't," Ben simpered. "George told me to leave it."

Accustomed to do simple math quickly, Danielle concluded that it made little sense. Green pushed them hard, but he was too pragmatic to assign Ben all these graphs within twenty four hours.

"When did he tell you that?" she asked.

"Last Saturday," Ben said matter-of-factly.

For a moment Danielle could not figure out why Ben enjoyed seeing her stuck with a difficult preprint. Then she envisioned Green's reaction if she would not accomplish the assignment on time.

"And since Saturday you haven't bothered to tell me?" she yelled.

A gleeful smile was the only response she got. Quivering with anger, she snatched the preprint and left the office. Needing a place to sit down and mull over what to do next, she headed to the library.

The physics library was well lit, bright and accommodating. Danielle passed the lobby, the circulation office, and rows of stands stocked with recent issues of leading journals from around the world. Several cozy looking armchairs were scattered around three low wooden tables; all of them were occupied by grim-looking students, who gazed into laptops. Even more irritated, Danielle strode into an area with desks intended for reading and note-taking. On midterm examination week, there were no vacant desks. Turning to the periodicals section, she prowled between lined bookcases stacked with bounded volumes, looking for a place amid rows of desks in between. The library was even more crammed than her office; blurry-eyed, tired students sat, dozed, or slouched on every available chair.

Circling around the book aisles, Danielle reached the most secluded tables. She saw students munching candy bars while leafing through notes and textbooks, students twiddling their hair, and scratching calves or shins. She heard whispers and the distinct crunch of potato chips. But she did not find a single unoccupied chair. Resolute not to give up, she scanned every vacant surface between the inner aisles. When she noted a couple suspiciously snuggled on a single armchair, Danielle stared at them meaningfully (they could go to a dormitory or to the nearest parking lot). Her assertiveness turned into subdued respect as soon as she recognized the heavy tome on their knees as Cohen-Tannoudji's *Quantum Mechanics*. She withdrew to another, shorter aisle, where she stumbled on a narrow spiraling staircase. It looked out of place. Lifting her head, Danielle saw that the upper stairs were shrouded in dimness.

The library archive, she speculated, looking for a sign "employees only." On a faded note taped on a nearby aisle, there was a drawing of an arrow pointing to the staircase. Above it was printed "TO THE SECTION OF OLD PERIODICALS."

Danielle ascended the staircase, then stopped to let her eyes adjust to the cavernous space, which was faintly lit by spotlights on the ceiling. Sectioned by several long rows of aisles, the place was quieter than a graveyard, and more solemn than the catacombs she had seen in Rome. Danielle's hand inadvertently gripped the preprint. She stepped forward, walked slowly along an aisle that stretched up to a window. The old hardwood floor carried the thud of her footsteps. The windows, Danielle found, were shaded by heavy, musty drapes. The place seemed to be larger than the main library; just a staircase away, it was a world in itself.

Away from the drapes, she noticed a fusty smell wafting from old papers. The glow of spotlights sufficed for walking comfortably, but it did not dispel the sensation of stepping uninvited into a netherworld, where spirits were as tangible as specs of dust and dapples of light. Apprehensive of her own thoughts, Danielle browsed the shelves. She saw volumes of the *Philosophical Magazine* and *Nature* from the late nineteenth century; the tomes looked abandoned, like graves too old for friends and relatives to remember, yet too new for rains and winds to deface the tombstones. Decades might have passed since anyone took out any of these tomes. Having never held papers or books printed in another century, Danielle doubted whether doing so was a good idea. She looked left and right before letting her fingers touch the golden letters inscribed on the old binding. There was no one to tell her not to, not even a sign.

The musty smell grew stronger when she took a step closer. Her fingers brushed the binding of volume 55, dated 1897, the oldest *Nature* tome in the row. She put the preprint aside, gently pulled the tome, and opened the binding. She cautiously flipped ocher pages, releasing translucent dust to glimmer in the air. Reassured that the old paper would not crumble in her fingers, Danielle turned the pages faster. She smiled at outdated titles and paused when she saw famous authors. On page 347, the name P. Zeeman drew her attention. She read the title: "The Effect of Magnetization on the Nature of Light Emitted by a Substance." Curious, Danielle's eyes wandered over the lines, stopping to reread:

> *...the thought occurred to me whether the period of the light emitted by a flame might be altered when the flame was acted upon by magnetic force. It has turned out that such action really occurs.*

The archaic, quaint phrasing belonged to Pieter Zeeman. The paper reported about broadening of sodium spectral lines under the influence of a magnetic field.

Goodness, she thought, it's the first account of the Zeeman Effect. She read on, until reaching: "Prof. Lorentz, to whom I communicated my idea, was good enough to show me how..."

A century after the words had been printed, Zeeman's courteous admiration for Lorentz resonated in Danielle's ears. She shook herself. There was not much left to read. The paper that merited a Nobel Prize in physics was only one page long.

Propped against the aisle, she stared at the parchment-colored paper, inhaled the fetid glue of the binding mixed with motes of dust. The heavy drapes obscured the sunlight; the soft lighting brought to mind candles or gas-lights. Danielle's thoughts veered to Victorian pioneers of modern physics, then meandered to the TIST undergraduate physics lab. In her mind's eye, she saw a dark room, where the apparatus of the experiment was already assembled. The sodium lamp warmed up, emitted heat, glowed with a bright orange light. She measured the light's exact wavelength and wrote the number in a lab notebook. Unlike Zeeman, she knew exactly what to expect when she turned on a magnetic field. Two new spectral lines appeared, symmetrically shifted from where the original line had been.

Danielle's next encounter with Zeeman Effect was in an introductory course to Quantum Mechanics, where it was borne in on physics students that nothing was as simple and straightforward as one perceived. "Hidden degeneracies," she had learned, were in fact indistinguishable, "seemingly identical" states. The trick to determine whether they were indeed identical, was to "lift the degeneracy" by interaction.

It's like looking at two similar scoops of ice-cream, Danielle mused, thinking of French vanilla and of white chocolate ice-cream. One cannot tell whether these are different flavors until the ice-cream interacts with taste-buds.

The Zeeman Effect was a textbook example of how the presence of an external field lifted up a degeneracy – an atom's "apparently similar" states were separated by interacting differently with a magnetic field.

Danielle looked again on the title. In her previous encounters with Zeeman Effect, she had never known that a paper behind a Nobel Prize had no equations in it, and that both the experiment and its explanation relied solely on late nineteenth century's classical physics. Evidently, Zeeman had studied the influence of a magnetic field on spectral lines, without suspecting that hidden degeneracies existed. So, how could he and Lorentz come up with a correct explanation years before anyone dreamed about quantum mechanics?

Unable to perceive how geniuses worked, Danielle's thoughts meandered from P. Zeeman, a Nobel Prize laureate, to P. Zeeman, whom she had dated. At the physics department at TIST, even churlish professors had agreed that Paul Zeeman stood out from other graduate students. Recognizing his potential, many had asked whether he was a great-grandson or another descendant of the famous Zeeman. Paul rarely bothered to answer the question, but whenever he responded, it was a scathing denial.

Recollections of more recent, sadder events followed the memories from grad school. As a guy, Zeeman was noisome, but he was the most brilliant physicist Danielle had ever met. What a meaningless waste, she thought, that Zeeman had bartered a chance for a Nobel Prize for a shiny Audi, which he smashed on a sturdy lamppost.

It was high time to go back to the office, but she could not. The endless debugging, the memory of the dread after Zeeman's accident, Ben's backstabbing, all took their toll of Danielle's determination. She eyed the *Science* preprint. It taunted and ridiculed her aspirations to understand dark energy. Stop procrastinating and get going, Danielle told herself. Gawking at "P. Zeeman" printed on an old paper won't sort out whether the proposed long-range forces might replace dark matter and dark energy.

A chill rippled Danielle's back, as her stare shifted between the open *Nature* and the preprint. Unlike Paul Zeeman, she knew practically nothing about super-symmetry and other extensions of the high-energy standard model. Why, then, had she questioned what she read? Why did she feel bound to distinguish between two forces that were tailored to cancel out? Maybe because the way her work was ignored rankled her. After all, she was used to better at TIST. Her research about neutron stars was appreciated, and it was published in good journals.

Waste of time, Danielle thought, as she put volume 55 in its place. Past success brought her to Green's group, but it did not imply she could distinguish between the absence of force and two forces that amounted to zero.

Maybe the place was haunted by ghosts, for something stirred, swirled, and converged in Danielle's mind, while orange sparks flashed in front of her eyes.

"Neutron star!"

She stood motionless, looking at the century-old, half-forgotten volumes again. Not in a hurry anymore, Danielle toyed with a new idea.

10

ANTIGONE

On the morning of the pizza seminar, a first frost lay over lawns. Along Chadwick Drive, plumes of smoke billowed from chimneys. Contemplating the change of seasons and how they mirrored different stages in her post-doctorate, Danielle felt a whiff of optimism: after almost two months in Green's group, her presentation would finally show Green that she had other strengths than programming. Ten minutes before the time specified in Ben's email, she took the *Science* preprint, her report, and a paper she had found, and went to the seminar room. The door was closed but not locked. Inside, Ben twanged something unfamiliar with a stretched rubber band. On an ebony table was laid a large bottle of coke and two boxes of pizza.

"Hi," Danielle said, looking doubtfully at the single bottle. "Who else is coming?" she asked when Ben turned his head.

"Our group and Lisitsin."

"Five people?" Her voice combined relief and disappointment. The room was almost full during the astrophysics seminars.

"Lisitsin doesn't have any grad students or posts."

She knew that. "What about Cobs?"

"He's on the mailing list, but..." Ben's dismissive tone insinuated that no one cared whether the old professor came or not. He made a catapult out of the rubber band and balled the pizza receipt. It flew across the table, hitting a screen pulled over a whiteboard.

"Impressive," Danielle commented. She put her papers on the edge of the table, with the *Science* preprint on top.

Ben gave the first page a cursory glance. "Did you do the derivations?" he asked, noting the absence of marks or scribbles.

"Didn't have to. Their conclusions are wrong."

Unimpressed with Danielle's answer, Ben said, "They wouldn't submit a paper to *Science* without double and triple checking every result." He looked meaningfully at the authors' affiliation. "They wouldn't put their reputation at stake."

"Not if they had any insight," Danielle agreed. "Maybe they didn't figure out what they should have looked at."

"But you did?" Ben jeered, almost involuntarily.

"Some physicists have uncanny hunches," Danielle retorted. Her patronizingly amused voice implied that Ben would not know what a hunch was.

Chi came in exactly on time. He looked slightly baffled by Danielle's and Ben's sparring, but all he said was, "What is the paper about?"

"An attempt to explain both dark energy and dark matter with two new forces," Danielle said.

Chi looked closer at the preprint. "Do they predict a correct large-scale structure?"

"In a high-energy paper?" Ben countered. One had to be joking if he asked whether a high-energy paper took notice of such mundane objects as galaxies.

"May I?" Chi asked Danielle. She gave him the preprint.

Danielle, Chi, and Ben were huddled over the paper when animated voices filtered into the room. Green and Lisitsin came in, continuing their discussion. Green cleared his throat, and the three heads rose in unison.

The professors took the pair of chairs at the top of the table; Chi opened the soda bottle; Ben fetched paper plates, cups, and napkins from a cupboard. While Danielle wondered where to sit, Chi took a chair beside Green, Ben sat on Chi's other side, and everyone but her took a slice of pizza. Green immediately asked Chi and Ben about software for plotting three-dimensional stringy structures. Seeing that Lisitsin had already started to read the preprint, Danielle took a seat next to him. She shifted her papers and took a slice of pizza. Ignoring Danielle, Lisitsin read the first page, flipped over and read on, then snorted and turned to his pizza. Surprised by Lisitsin's manners, Danielle took a bite of her slice. The crust was too soft for her liking, and the cheese was not even a distant cousin of Italian Parmesan. The tomato sauce with traces of garlic and basil was not bad at all.

"Did you track the derivations?" Green asked. His voice was stern, as if he was aware of her intention to impress him with intuitive understanding.

Danielle swallowed the pizza and said "No." Faster than she could have expected, Green's face clouded with disapproval.

"I thought that repeating calculations is a waste of time." Danielle's voice came out distorted by a lump squeezing her throat. "The authors' underlying assumptions are tripe."

Chi looked dumbstruck. Ben leered behind a cup with coke he affectedly sipped. Danielle could not see Green's face, for Lisitsin jutted his head forward, puckering his lips and deprecatingly flaring his nostrils. His expression reminded Danielle of one of Sarah Lerner's pugnacious moods.

"Can you articulate your last statement more scientifically?" Green instructed equably. "Start with their tenets," he pointed to the whiteboard, "and leave the papers where they are."

Feeling a little groggy, Danielle went to the whiteboard, lifted the screen, and took a deep gulp of air.

"It is a salient premise in cosmology that high-energy physics can shed light on insofar unknown forces and constituents of the universe." Danielle stopped before any of the men occupied with splitting what was left of the pizza would comment. The words she wanted to be articulate, sounded like a welter of physics and Jane Austen's most famous opening. Composing herself, she continued.

"In the *Science* preprint George gave me, the authors propose two new interactions. Their main argument is that a combination of an attractive and a repulsive force can account for the gravitational pull found in galactic halos and for dark energy dominance beyond super-clusters' length-scales."

"What is the theoretical motivation for these forces?" Lisitsin asked.

Who cares? Danielle answered in her mind, while racking her brain for a better answer that would gloss over how little she knew.

"Models with higher symmetries than the high-energy

standard model predict additional elementary particles and fundamental forces," she said tentatively. "To be of any relevance for cosmology, these interactions should have a very long range and be at least as strong as gravity."

She paused to take a breath; Lisitsin pointedly sniffled, Green said, "go on."

"The model considered in the preprint assigns a charge associated with an attractive scalar field and another charge associated with a repulsive vector field."

Standing with her back to the cosmology group, their presence blurred into an unobtrusive background for fields and charges, whose strength, range, and interactions Danielle wrote on the whiteboard. Field equations she was unaware of remembering, streamed in her handwriting.

"The model has a single coupling constant," she said after explaining all the symbols in the equations. "It fixes the attractive and repulsive forces to be of the same strength."

"Does that stem from super-symmetry?" Ben interposed. He did not look at Green, but Danielle had no doubt that his question was to show off.

It took several heartbeats to sift through the little she knew about unconstrained degrees of freedom in super-symmetry. Pretty sure that the model did not offer any experimentally accessible predictions, she said, "The strength of the forces is matched ad hoc, to ensure no detectable net force in terrestrial and solar system experiments."

She darted a glance at Green, whose expression remained inscrutable. "I don't remember the exact limits," she continued, "but the existence of any residual force was practically ruled out by Eötvös experiments."

"Fine-tuning," Lisitsin commented loud enough for everyone to hear. Privately agreeing, Danielle caught herself wondering whether Green saw the model's inherent flaw. Three furrows creased his forehead. She hoped he was not growing impatient.

"The model is unlikely to impact on the physics community," Green said to Lisitsin. Turning his head to the whiteboard, he asked, "do you have anything else to add?"

"Yes," Danielle said immediately. Having almost reached the crux of her presentation, she was eager to go through it. "On

Earth and everywhere within the solar system," she pointed at a pair of equations for the charges, "these would remain undetected because the repulsive and attractive forces completely cancel each other. In stars with a very strong gravitational field, the gravitational field affects the star's binding energy, which in turn modifies the hypothesized charges. In neutron stars microscopic charges with equal strength can add up to unequal macroscopic charges. In such a case, the two forces would not cancel out."

She turned to the whiteboard, and wrote a short and simple equation that related between the pair of charges and the binding energy of a star.

"As you can see, the mere existence of stable neutron stars constrains the coupling to baryons to be weaker than gravity." She felt lighthearted. Taking a step away from the whiteboard, she noted Ben's confused and Chi's glazed expressions. Green seemed to be immersed in thoughts, whereas Lisitsin shifted in his seat, swayed hands as if he was making a point in a silent monologue. She stifled a smile. One could not tell whether Chi grasped the attractive force's inability to mimic dark matter, but Ben was clearly clueless, albeit too cocky to ask questions. It was evident that for Green and Lisitsin the equations on the whiteboard were self-explanatory.

"Did you derive these by yourself?" Green asked after a couple of minutes.

"I looked for a field that could lift the degeneracy of the two charges." Danielle paused before paying her tribute to Zeeman's paper, without which she would have never thought about the possibility. Interest flickered in Green's stare, but it looked too feeble to extend to the ghosts of dead physicists. "I came up with neutron stars, since their strong gravitational field seemed as the most relevant option."

Green nodded in agreement, which was the highest praise he ever gave to Danielle.

"Then I searched for papers that considered hypothetical fields in neutron stars. A paper in *Astrophysical Journal* dealt with a similar problem. It studied a combination of gravity and a pair of attractive-repulsive interactions, with an identical coupling constant. The details of the interactions were different, but their proof is quite general. In compact objects like neutron stars and white dwarfs, attractive-repulsive forces do not cancel each other completely."

Lisitsin muttered, Green shut his eyes and reclined. Starting to feel self-conscious, Danielle looked at Ben and Chi, silently asking them to say something. Chi slightly shook his head, Ben ignored her. Concluding that it was the end of the discussion, Danielle returned to her seat.

"Stronger limits might be derived from binary pulsars with a neutron star or white dwarf companion," Green said at last. "What do you think?" he asked Lisitsin.

"Aha," Lisitsin replied, slightly bobbing his head.

Eager to show that she had the answer, Danielle drew a photocopy of the paper from *Astrophysical Journal* from her stack, and put it between the professors. "In the paper I mentioned," she said, "the authors calculated the rate of change of the orbital period of several binary systems with white dwarfs and neutron stars."

Slate-gray and watery-blue eyes stared at her in unison. Danielle stared back.

"Good, email me the reference." Green rose up. "What about five minutes break?"

Danielle's elated mood lasted throughout Green's talk on "Ramifications of Accelerated Expansion." After listing collaborators on two continents, Green summarized an analysis of the Galaxy Redshift Survey, elaborated about equations neatly presented in his slides, and explained the plots. Chi soaked up Green's words; Ben listened carefully, while timing the duration of the talk. Lisitsin looked at Danielle's dreamy face almost as often as he looked at the screen. After Green was done, he asked for input. Lisitsin and Ben made comments, Chi asked a couple of questions. Danielle, still basking in her triumph, silently daydreamed about a very pleasant weekend with Jon.

That night, she recounted to Jonathan what had happened at the pizza seminar. "Only a week is left before Green goes to the conference," she jubilantly concluded, "and then I'll have two Green-free weekends."

"I can't come," Jonathan said. Before Danielle could offer to fly to Thorboro, he added, "I'll be most of the time at work."

"On both weekends? What about being able to work from

anywhere?"

"Not when I'm working with others. We are already past the deadline on the demo."

"The demo?" Danielle creased her nose. "Why do you work on it? Hasn't Zeeman returned yet?"

"He is back, with breaks for physiotherapy." There was no trace of complaint in Jonathan's calm voice. "Paul does some work, but he is still shaky."

"So, you do his job alongside yours. Who appointed you to do that?"

"Appointed?" Dry amusement was carried through the phone. Jonathan's position at Nickka came with the freedom to work as much as he could and even more.

"Never mind. Does Pilcher know what you are doing?"

"He doesn't care as long as Paul comes before nine, attends every meeting and leaves after him. Pilcher's policy is to act as if everything would be achieved if everyone sticks to the schedule."

"What about the big boss?"

"Roy is still in California, working to smooth over our delay."

"Doesn't he know what is happening in Thorboro?"

"Roy hasn't intervened, as far as I know. Throwing his weight around isn't Roy's style, and I don't think there is any point pressing Paul. Right now, he can't wrap up the presentation quickly."

Realizing that Jon did not really mind that most of the workload fell on him, Danielle gave free rein to her disappointment.

"Sounds perfect. Roy negotiates, Pilcher bosses around, Zeeman slacks, and you are left to make the demonstration work."

"Do you have to paraphrase it so nastily?"

"Nasty or pithy depends on your perspective," Danielle retorted, irritated that he willingly accepted the extra work, but not a single remark from her. "Anyway, did I say anything wrong?"

"Everything," Jonathan said emphatically. "Paul's car accident created an unexpected havoc, which I and others are working to fix. Unlike corporations or academia, we can't afford delays."

It was useless, Danielle decided, to tell Jon that he gave too much of himself to Nickka.

"I'll be sorry not being with you until Thanksgiving," she said in a softer tone of voice.

"Actually, well...the presentation is on the twenty-second, but Roy and I will stay in San Francisco until the twenty-sixth."

"A day after Thanksgiving? You will miss my mother's Thanksgiving dinner. What kind of morons are you working with?"

"We'll have a meeting with a potential investor. I'll return early on Saturday."

She could not be hardhearted when Jon was willing to brave the airports on the night after Thanksgiving to be with her. Two days together were not much, but better than none.

"Mom will keep something for you," Danielle said. "And Aunt Sophie will be happy to see us even when we come late."

"Not on Saturday?" Jonathan groaned.

"I know, but we must go. You don't have to do anything, just be without a laptop and bear with the Bloom branch of the family for several hours."

"Does it have to be on the twenty-seventh?

"It has been Aunt Sophie's birthday for 69 years."

She heard Jonathan swearing, although he was not speaking into the phone.

"Jon?"

"Can't she postpone the celebration for a day?"

"Considering the discussions and preparations that occupied Aunt Sophie for months, no one in her right mind would suggest to put back the celebration. My uncle and his wife are going to fly with their two little kids and a baby, from Vancouver. The day is not open for negotiations."

"It's not that simple."

Fed up with Nickka's endless needs, Danielle said, "Skip the excuses. Are you coming or not?"

"The DeWitts are throwing an engagement party on the twenty-seventh. I have to be there. You are invited to come."

"Rats," Danielle squeezed through her teeth. The word was too mild to express her exasperation. Instead of being with Jon, she would be facing the Blooms' unwarranted wisdom alone.

"Can't we visit her on Sunday?" Jonathan suggested, his

voice inappropriately calm.

"No, I can't."

"Just like that?"

In her mind's eye, Danielle saw Aunt Sophie standing upright, her hawkish eyes staring blankly forward, old, painted lips twisted in a strained smile. Sophia would be hurt, but nevertheless she would keep appearances in front of her guests, secreting what she felt from loving and prying eyes alike.

"It's not just like that," she said. "I promised."

"Fine. It is not worth fretting about."

How could Jon be so relaxed? Sarah would raise hell if he'd come without a date.

"You don't mind if I won't be with you at DeWitts'?" Danielle asked.

"I want you to come, but it's okay if you can't. Amos and Amy won't notice, Dad will understand, and mother will call me a swab, but she won't let that spoil her day."

And pigs might fly, Danielle added in her mind. Sarah would not be happy to see her, but if she would not show up, Jonathan's mother would rub it in that he was slighted. Blowing Danielle's offenses out of proportion was something Sarah excelled in.

"Your selflessness is appreciated," Danielle said. "I promise to nurse whatever is left after she skins you alive." Anticipating that Jon would ask her to elaborate about the nursing, she envisioned the possibilities. She did not expect to get a confused "aha?" for a reply, but she had a pretty good idea what it meant.

"Are you working while we speak?"

Jonathan responded with a soft chuckle.

"No wonder you don't mind missing Aunt Sophie's and DeWitts' parties."

"Would anything change if I did not take a look at the screen now and then?"

"Just a look?" Danielle's voice intimated she knew the answer.

"I checked a couple of things, but it requires a few more changes before I send the job overnight."

"You're hopeless," she said lovingly.

* * *

In the following days, Danielle waged a war on the bugs that infiltrated her program. Looking for the sneaky culprits, she wondered how anyone could love writing code. She would rather wash dishes, mop the floor and scrub the bathroom, Danielle raved in her mind, until a more reasonable voice chimed in to remind her that cleaning did not lead to an academic career. Determined to force the universe into expanding and cooling, and make its constituents interact as Green instructed, Danielle battled every subroutine and procedure that refused to follow her bidding. She perused *Programming in C* and even consulted with Jonathan over the phone. The code fought back. For every problem she fixed, more bugs and inexplicable glitches popped up.

Danielle did her utmost to be able to tell Green that the program runs, but on Friday, it became clear that it wouldn't run before he left for the conference. Frustrated and weary, she felt that she had to get out, yet she hardly dared to be away when Green might call her. Allowing herself twenty minutes, she sneaked to the students' cafeteria, where she bought a packed lunch and a new issue of *Hopeville Herald*.

The salad was reasonably fresh. While she munched pieces of stringy chicken, Danielle went over the university news. A drive to install solar panels to heat the water for the campus restrooms met strong opposition from proponents of aesthetics. Disregarding ecological benefits and monetary savings, they signed in droves a petition to preserve the university's oldest Greek Revival and Gothic buildings. She skimmed through the report, darted an absentminded glance at an illustration of Austen Hall coated with solar panels, and skipped to the next page. There, Danielle's eyes stopped on a headline, The Timely Return of Antigone.

"The venerable Ross theater has a long tradition of showcasing Greek plays, but it has been over a decade since the last staging of *Antigone*." Danielle skipped a few lines. "This year, a generous grant from the Art Council enables the Drama department and the Center of Women's Studies to co-host a mini-symposium about the ambivalence of *Antigone's* feminism and its seminal impact on women's integration in corporate culture, politics and academic life."

"A Center of Women's Studies?" Danielle reread. She could not recall ever hearing of such an academic unit at TIST. Under a smaller headline was an interview with Dr. Jessica Pratt, an associate professor affiliated with the center. Pratt brought up gender perceptions in ancient Greece and the evolution of women's entitlements in Western culture. The interviewer asked about the impact of prevailing gender biases in our society, dragging Crawford's name in as an example.

"Crawford resigned from his administrative position and took a sabbatical," Pratt had responded. Despite the guarded reminder, Pratt was not about to let the notorious slip about female researchers to fade into oblivion, for it was "a ready example of the implicit discrimination festering under a politically correct and seemingly enlightened veneer." By the end of the interview, Danielle almost pitied the careless chauvinist, who voiced what many men were thinking.

"Do you want to see *Antigone* at Ross theater?" she asked Chi when he had a break. "It is running for the first three weeks of November, on Thursdays and Saturdays."

Seeing Chi's puzzled face, Danielle showed him the newspaper.

"I didn't hear about the play," he said.

"It's a Greek tragedy. Antigone was Oedipus' daughter." Chi's blank face indicated that her explanation did not clarify anything."Didn't you study Sophocles at high-school?"

Chi shook his head.

"Antigone attempted to bury her brother against the ruler's decree, but was caught and brought before him. I don't remember details, but it ends with Antigone being sentenced to death."

"Is it about politics?"

"It's open to many interpretations," Danielle said, deciding not to mention the feminist angle. "It has a romantic twist, and remotely reminds me of *Romeo and Juliet*. I'm going to see it tomorrow. Maybe your wife would like to come."

A phone call confirmed that Mrs. Wang would be happy to see a play at Ross theater.

* * *

On Saturday afternoon, while professor Green was boarding his flight, and Lei Wang was at an extended play-date, the Wangs met Danielle at the stairs of Ross theater.

The dark, slightly stuffy auditorium made Danielle think of the section of old periodicals, with its musty aisles removed, and its cavernous space furnished with upholstered seats. The auditorium was far from being packed, but the best rows were occupied. The inevitable hum ended when the stage lights focused on two sultry-looking young women, who argued. The redhead invited her blonde sister to come and bury their disgraced brother, the sister cautiously advised against the plan. Their acting was amateurish, yet Danielle thought that the redhead portrayed a stubborn bitch quite convincingly. When the ruler Creon came to the stage, he was smug but hardly vicious, more a caricature of a fractious university professor than a raving despot. Haemon (Creon's son and Antigone's betrothed lover) dutifully said his lines, but it was plain that the actor would readily ditch his crazy fiancée for a more accommodating princess.

Why wouldn't he? Danielle empathized. She also found Antigone's carelessness about the obvious consequences incomprehensible and unconvincing. Women made the ultimate sacrifice in countless stories and movies, but they did so to save someone. In Antigone's sacrifice, Danielle could not see any noble purpose.

The appearance of the old seer Tiresias evoked giggles, which sporadically continued through the rest of the play. At the end, most people clapped. The actors did the curtain twice.

"Did you like the play?" Danielle asked the Wangs after they stepped outdoors.

"Not much," Chi shook his head. Mrs. Wang only smiled. "We should be going," Chi added, before he and his wife went to their car.

Having no one waiting at home, Danielle intended to work on fixing her program. She ambled to Fitzgerald Hall, thinking about Antigone's nonconformity and her own acquiescence in spending her post on simulating Green's model. Was she wrong not to follow that gut feeling about dark energy?

Professional suicide isn't heroic, Danielle reasoned, casting aside glimmers of rebellion. Green was not a bullheaded despot, but a very successful, shrewd professor. It was easy to rant that he was deaf to ideas, but the fact remained that she had not been able to come up with a concrete and promising suggestion.

She reached the Italian gardens, and slowed to watch trees and shrubs lit with hundreds of colorful bulbs. In the dusk, she had an uncomfortable feeling that she was going nowhere despite putting endless hours into her program. She had shown the ability to connect and draw conclusions from seemingly unrelated phenomena, but being able to discard a paper submitted to *Science* was one thing, authoring a *Science* paper was an entirely different feat.

Needing to find something that would entice Green's interest, Danielle reflected that the lonely office was the last place she could look for inspiration. She could not bear to spend the evening there, examining her program again, tinkering with code as incongruous as a mythological creature with wings, paws and hoofs. Craving normalcy, she veered to the main entrance and out of the campus.

On the Main Street streetlights glowed; shop windows glittered with gold, tangerine, and russet holiday decorations. Danielle loitered about, feeling more like herself among people. A wine store's window was decorated with strings of brown paper turkeys and genuine acorns. Two men came out, each carrying self-importantly a bottle of wine. A display of a jewelry store attracted more attention - she envisioned the pale-yellowish beads gleam around her neck, compared a translucent amber pendant to sun-beams trapped in honey, drooled over gems' shiny, polished facets. Reminding herself that nothing in the shop could be within her budget, Danielle moved to the next window, which belonged to a bookstore. She eyed eagerly the books on display, but resisted the temptation to go in. Reading for fun was inexcusable self-indulgence when she had to catch up on concurrent research. Adjacent to the bookstore, a café advertised a pumpkin-flavored latte among other fall specials. Reckoning that she deserved at least that much, Danielle went in.

A very sweet, tepid concoction with a crunchy cookie was a

poor substitute for a homey dinner, as much as a crowded café was for the family atmosphere Danielle suddenly pined for. In her mind's eye she was eating a goulash at Aunt Sophie's kitchen, while a warm-from-the-oven apple strudel was waiting on the counter, to be served at the end of the meal with a freshly brewed tea.

How would Aunt Sophie respond to the play? Danielle wondered. Sophia could not care much about Creon and the seer, but she'd commiserate with Antigone's plight, then advise the defiant princess to move on, get married and start her own family. Idiot, Danielle told herself as another thought struck. She had completely forgotten about Aunt Sophie's birthday present. Having a new topic to mull over, Danielle weighed the options. The gift should be at least somewhat practical, yet lovely and not strictly necessary.

It took legwork and perseverance to browse the merchandize in the stores. Danielle did it despite a growing headache, caused by very persuasive salespeople who knew everything about the hottest trends except of Sophia's abhorrence of them.

Reaching a store filled with woolen scarves and sweaters, Danielle knew she had to get in. She scanned the shelves and racks systematically, pleased that the saleswomen were too busy to notice her. A cerulean afghan, hand-knitted in Scotland, was warm and soft and recklessly expensive. Deciding that Aunt Sophie would enjoy but never buy something like it, Danielle handed a saleswoman her credit card.

11

QUESTIONABLE LEGACY

"It's easier to make progress when Green is away," Danielle told her mother over the phone. "Chi helps me with the code, and Ben is not as nasty as usual."

By Wednesday, her program was running on the group's cluster of computers.

Although Green returned on Sunday, Danielle first heard from him on Tuesday, when Chi handed her the receiver mouthing, "Dr. Green." All Green said was, "please come to my office." He stopped writing when Danielle entered, raised his head and asked about the state of her simulation.

"It's running. It hasn't generated data yet, but I'm halfway through writing code which will analyze it on-the-fly."

"I jotted down a few references." Green handed Danielle a list with names and years. "Could you add papers' titles and the usual bibliographical information?"

Danielle nodded, even though she was told to do a student's work. Green's face was inscrutable. His left hand rested on the keyboard and the fingers of the right tapped on the desk, betraying that he was pressed.

"For older papers," Green gestured towards the door, "ask the circulation desk to direct you to the old periodicals section."

Danielle began the search with the Science Citation Index, copying the relevant information and skimming a paper's abstract whenever there was "vacuum energy" or "cosmological constant" in its title. It was satisfying to see that Green started to pay attention to dark energy. Next time, Danielle cynically thought, she shouldn't lose sleep or look for convincing arguments, only wait until he goes to a conference.

The door of the office opened with a swoosh.

"Collecting references for Academia?" Ben asked behind Danielle's chair. "Nineteen forties and nineteen sixties. You'd have to dig these up from the periodicals' graveyard."

Anticipating sneers (if Green did not deem her time as the least valuable in the group, he would have assigned the references to Ben), Danielle took Green's list, a notebook, and a pen. "George knows I'm interested in dark energy," she said with as much dignity as she could muster, and closed the door behind her.

The tomes of Physics Abstracts, the printed predecessor of online search, were shelved over several aisles; they looked old, heavy and dusty. Secreted in a gap between aisles, Danielle found stately oak tables and outmoded, faded chairs. There were neither monitors nor internet connections. She picked a table and tentatively turned on an old-fashioned lamp. The bright yellowish glow revealed a stack of papers laying on another table.

"A student sent to pad out a grant proposal," Danielle reasoned, unable to think of anyone else who would step into this anachronistic enclave. The place was eerily quiet. Carrying the tomes of Physics Abstracts, she heard only her own footsteps.

Jonah Cobs saw a little circle of light when he walked in one of the passages. Obscured by an aisle, he stopped to look at a young woman poring over old tomes. Recognizing Danielle, he recalled that she was George Green's post-doc and that it was grant-writing season.

There is nothing new under the sun, Cobs cited one of his favorite proverbs from Ecclesiastes. Surmising that Danielle would leave as soon as she had all the references George had asked for, Cobs went back through the gap between aisles.

Unaware of being watched, Danielle tried to figure out whether vacuum energy and the cosmological constant might have subtly different origins. Vacuum energy, the lowest energy state, was a concept rooted in quantum world. The cosmological constant, on the other hand, was a feature of space-time. She skimmed through abstracts. Although she was tempted to read the entire papers, she willed herself to focus on gathering the references.

* * *

Days drew in, as they always did in November. To Danielle, they seemed to slip by while she analyzed data streaming from her simulation of a toy universe's early evolution. She used a graphics software to visualize every snapshot. Regardless of how much she fiddled with the presentation, the toy universe at its beginning resembled sprinkles suspended in inky jello.

"The images I got so far are invariably anticlimactic," she complained to Michelle. "For some unfathomable reason, after a couple hundreds of millions years of evolution, the toy universe resembles a byzantine filigree, with threads woven into a blackened tapestry. I wonder what Green will say when he sees it. My simulations hardly look like Chi's and Ben's."

After a while, Danielle accepted that the snapshots would be rejected by any low-budget science-fiction movie, and stopped tinkering with the graphics software's options. She pinned her hopes on the model's ability to capture the essentials of structure formation.

Nothing unusual happened until Monday before Thanksgiving, when an email from Alec Smith jolted Danielle out of the data analysis routine. It had been months since she had last exchanged emails with her PhD adviser. Last time, Alec, who was the corresponding author of a paper they had submitted to *Physical Review Letters*, had forwarded her a referee's response. Bracing herself for news about their paper, Danielle read. "Hi Danielle, our PRL has been accepted. Attached are the second referee's comments. Please make the required corrections ASAP. Congratulations, Alec."

Accepted!!! The word almost levitated Danielle over the floor. She turned to call Jonathan, but realized that she did not know where he was. Anyway, since Jon was about to present Nickka's demo to investors in a few hours, telling him about the PRL would be a colossal waste of excellent news. Foreseeing how delighted her mother would be, Danielle thought of calling her. But Michelle was still teaching, and she would stay late at school for parent-teacher conferences. Too happy to feel disappointment, Danielle decided to wait until Thanksgiving, and announce her news face to face.

Bearing in mind that by "ASAP" Alec meant "right now," she opened the file attached to his email. It took the anonymous reviewer almost five months to point out a typo in one of the equations, note an omitted reference, and make a few other trifling comments. Shaking her head at such laxity, Danielle reminded herself to be grateful that the reviewer made no serious objections. She read the paper's four pages again and beamed with delight at her own best work. Nothing in the paper hinted at tears she had shed and the frustration she had felt during the years she had forged a crude model from Alec's idea, anchored his hand-waving in calculations and finessed the model until it was publishable (which included several drafts that Alec had made her rewrite). In retrospect, she had thrived doing the work that led to the paper, a period that more or less coincided with the time she dated Jonathan.

Green summoned Danielle after lunch. After she succinctly described the new data from her program, he asked, "Have you looked at different expansion rates?"

"No." Danielle averted her eyes from Green's somber face to his bookshelves. "I'll do it right after I finish with the few corrections a referee required." She smiled unintentionally, a smile that radiated happiness. "It's for a paper just accepted to PRL."

"I expect you to author more PRLs during the post." Green's face brightened. Danielle felt his eye reappraise her potential. "Keep working on your program until it generates data comparable with observations. And," he added as an afterthought, "email me the paper accepted by PRL."

She emailed the corrected version to Alec and to Green on the same evening. On the following day, Danielle added two new runs with different expansion rates. If everything went well, she mused, the program would start generating data shortly after the holiday.

* * *

On Thanksgiving morning, Danielle was awakened by dapples of light slanting through lacy curtains. Squinting, she recognized her old bed, her bookcases, and the desk she had used in high school. In the adjacent room, her sisters were still snuggled under warm blankets, catching up on much needed sleep. A typical Mellers' Thanksgiving forenoon, Danielle reflected, heading straight to the kitchen. Her father would be at the swimming pool while her mother would be preparing the festive dinner.

In a cheery, spacious kitchen, Michelle was trimming the fat from a cut of beef with a chef's knife.

"Good morning," Danielle said. When Michelle put the knife aside, Danielle wrapped her arms around her mother and nestled her chin on Michelle's shoulder. "Are you making roast beef?"

"You know that Joe and the girls don't like turkey. I thought we might have a main course everyone enjoys."

Michelle did not say "this year," but Danielle knew what she meant. With Mark and his family coming for a visit, Aunt Sophie would celebrate Thanksgiving with her children and grandchildren.

"I can see Aunt Sophie's brows move reproachfully to imply that traditions should be upheld in a, ahem, traditional way."

"The three of you are old enough to uphold any traditions you consider worth upholding." Michelle took again the chef's knife. "Get yourself some water. You must be parched after spending half a night over the phone."

"Not my fault. It's the time difference between California and Thorboro."

"How was Jonathan's presentation?"

"Good, as far as I could gather. He thinks the morons on the board were pretty impressed by the demo, but he is unsure about whether it'll translate into giving a green light for the next step."

"Is it for making a commercial version of their software?"

"A beta version. Anyway, Jon is about to start working on a patent." Danielle hesitated, then broached the less pleasant news. "The law firm is based in California."

Michelle sighed, then asked, "When will he return to Thorboro?"

"Tomorrow night."

Michelle turned from the beef, and looked inquiringly at Danielle, wordlessly inviting her to share what she thought.

"Jon sent the happiest Thanksgiving for you and Dad."

"I hope you thanked him and sent our best wishes."

"I did. Frankly, there is no need to pity him, when he is going to have a great time today."

"Is he invited for a dinner?"

"I doubt it. Jon planned to rewrite the code the way it should have been done, after the fuss of the presentation is over."

"On Thanksgiving? Doesn't it bother you?"

"Why should it, if he can't be here anyway?" asked a muffled voice from the recess of the refrigerator. "I'm willing to bet that Green is now polishing the grant proposal in his office, leaving his children, turkey and whatever else is on their agenda to the care of Mrs. Green."

The refrigerator teamed with desserts, cheeses, and cold meats. Danielle rummaged through sealed boxes of various sizes, wondering what was inside. She twitched, grasping that she was thinking about the monetary value of the foods in her parents' refrigerator. It was embarrassing to crave delicacies she could not afford.

"Pick yourself something and close it," Michelle said. "And I'd rather you leave the desserts for after the dinner."

Casting a resigned glance at the most appealing items, Danielle took some feta cheese and a cucumber.

"How did the parent-teacher conferences go?" she asked while cutting a fresh baguette.

"Not bad, aside from having to disillusion a new crop of overachieving parents."

Michelle's comment, pithy without a whiff of resentment, pained Danielle. She surveyed the upscale appliances standing ready on the granite counter, shifted her stare to the pricy pots gleaming on the oven, and turned her eyes again toward the extensive collection of spices her mother used so knowledgeably. Long ago, the kitchen was "Mom's office," a place where Michelle cooked and baked, checked students' papers and prepared new lessons, all while keeping a watchful eye on the twins. Joseph Meller spent most of the time at the hospital. He was a supportive father who did not interfere with the daily responsibilities of parenthood.

As a child, Danielle had not questioned why their well-being and upbringing were left under the care of her mother. That changed when she discovered that Michelle had been a graduate student in the TIST physics department before she, Danielle, was born. Curious and uncomfortable, Danielle bombarded her mother with questions, but despite Michelle's many patient explanations and reassurances, the circumstances at which she had left TIST remained moot. At fifteen, it was hard to accept why the mother she adored had foregone her studies so her husband's career could thrive. Understanding Danielle's angst and confusion, Michelle did all she could to assert that neither Joseph nor anyone else had asked her to stay at home. It had been, Michelle said innumerable times, her choice, and when Danielle would grow up, she would be free to make her own choices.

"Daydreaming?" Michelle's voice interrupted Danielle's recollections.

"Just a short trip down the memory lane." Anticipating her mother's happy reaction to the news about the PRL, Danielle poured water in the kettle and set the table for two. When everything was ready, she asked, "Will you join me?"

"I'll sit with you when I'm done. Go on. Joe and I had a coffee before he went to swim."

Danielle made a sandwich, and waited for Michelle to pour herself coffee. "I have some good news," she said proudly.

Seeing her daughter's face lit up, Michelle hugged Danielle. "My bright, clever girl. I knew your paper would be accepted."

"Did you? I was flummoxed when I saw Alec's email address. How could you guess it was about my paper, without any hint?"

"You just said it was good news," Michelle said. She sighed inwardly, but answered in her usual voice. "I knew that you were waiting for the journal's response."

"It's amazing that you thought about a paper submitted half a year ago. After so many months, it completely fell under my radar."

"I wouldn't forget a paper you submitted to *Physical Review Letters*," Michelle said. "It means a lot to me."

"I know. I expected that you'd rejoice at my news, without imagining it wouldn't be a surprise. Did you have a sort of premonition about it?"

Michelle hesitated. Danielle's question was an opening to confide the existence of another, a life-changing paper also published in PRL. Not now, Michelle decided. Her daughter might have asked in jest. Moreover, Thanksgiving was not the right time to bring up a specter from the past. When all the family gathered, Danielle deserved unconditional praise, and not revelations of a questionable legacy.

"I believe in your work, and I'm very happy," Michelle said. "You brought excellent news."

There is something Mom evades, Danielle thought. Michelle's cheerfulness sounded slightly affected, and her face looked distracted.

"Is there any particular reason you have thought about this paper?" Danielle asked.

"Maybe because you were at a crossroads just after completing your thesis. We expected you and Jonathan would decide about a wedding," Michelle said diplomatically.

"You did? Why would we consider a wedding when I was heading to King Solomon University?"

"Well, seeing you happy together, it occurred to us that you might change your mind and stay in Thorboro."

The trip to Italy. Danielle reminisced about two glorious weeks she and Jonathan had had in the summer. Back then, Sarah had fumed about them booking flights rather than buying an engagement ring.

"I don't change plans because Jon and I had a fabulous vacation. I would be nuts to sacrifice five years of hard work, especially when Green had already offered me a post-doctoral fellowship."

"No one would have taken your PhD away." Michelle sipped her coffee and quietly watched Danielle bite obstinately into her baguette. "You could have looked for a post-doc at TIST or somewhere else near Thorboro."

Danielle ate most of her sandwich before saying "Mom." Michelle looked at her inquiringly. Knowing she could not say the suggestion was ridiculously naïve, Danielle attempted to explain the stakes.

"A few weeks ago the physics department issued a call for candidates for a junior faculty position. To be considered as a candidate, one has to have three glowing letters of recommendation from well known physics professors."

"Are you considering to apply to King Solomon University? I thought you wanted to return to TIST."

"I could have also considered winning the Nobel Prize," Danielle said impetuously. "My point is that without a post-doctorate with a leading group in a high ranking university, I won't stand a chance to ever return to TIST."

Seeing her mother's expression, Danielle softened her voice. "Where and with whom one works matter almost as much as the research itself. I don't regret staying at TIST, but in hindsight, it would have been smarter to go to a graduate school at a better university."

Michelle sighed. "I didn't realize how ambitious you have become."

"Ambitious? I'm trying to be realistic, or, as Aunt Sophie likes to say, practical."

"It sounds more like opportunistic. I realize that some professors and physics departments would always promote this attitude, but my advice is to think carefully before you start conforming."

"As if universities' requirements are open for negotiation," Danielle blurted out. It was easy to advocate nonconformity when you were not obliged to bend to professors' whims and requirements. It was even easier when you were clueless about the complexity of pursuing an academic career.

"Even a full professor like my boss is expected to fit into the academic mold. Green is knee-deep in teaching, grant-writing, and various departmental obligations. I think that the only time he has for research is at nights and during weekends."

"It's not always wise to follow prevalent practices, digging in your heels and making sacrifices for a career you covet," Michelle pointed out. Perceiving that her daughter would jump at any chance to emulate her boss's career, she added, "Sometimes success takes away more than it gives in reward."

Danielle darted an accusing glance at her mother. The rewards, she wanted to say, were enormous if one had the stamina and perseverance to complete her studies alongside with raising a baby.

"I would rather do my best than be cooed and shielded," Danielle said. "Green is hardly encouraging, but he is an eminent cosmologist, and if he likes my work, I'll get my opportunity to succeed."

"Another advice is to stop deferring to your boss in everything. You will start sounding like one of those annoying women who mention their boyfriends and husbands too much."

Danielle opened her mouth, but found nothing adequate for a response - her mother was a master of striking with words without saying anything inappropriate. She silently chewed what was left of the sandwich, while Michelle drank her coffee and looked pensive. A screeching noise from above indicated that at least one of the twins woke up.

"Any more advice?" Danielle asked, to show she was not sulking.

"Wash and peel the apples." Michelle rose up. "You can also chop walnuts, and if you hurry up, I'll let you roll the dough."

Danielle told her father and sisters before the dinner that her paper was accepted to PRL.

"How many papers do you have so far?" Joseph asked after congratulating Danielle.

"Six in all. The one in the PRL is the third paper where I'm the first author."

"Excellent. We shall toast to it at the dinner."

Suspecting that her father would have said the same regardless of the journal, Danielle explained, "A paper in PRL is more than a just having my paper accepted. At TIST people used to call the journal 'Public Relations Letters.' A paper there is like entering another league."

"I treble my congratulations," Joseph said half-jokingly.

"Me too," Julia added. "One for the paper, one for your conceit, and one for sounding like a jerk."

"Me? What was wrong with what I said?"

"You assume that everyone should be familiar with physics journals," Joyce explained. "Can you name any leading medical journals?"

Danielle frowned, trying to recall the covers of journals she had seen growing up. "No," she admitted, "not offhand."

In lieu of a response, her sisters exchanged smug smiles, and the three of them went to set the table with Michelle's best silverware and china.

The Thanksgiving dinner was duly appreciated as the Mellers tucked into the tender roast beef. Joyce and Julia, who subsisted mostly on defrosted veggies, low-fat yogurts, apples, and baby carrots, praised even the green salad. The baked veggies were "scrumptious", according to Julia. After they paid tribute to the food, the twins told anecdotes from their first term at the medical school. Joseph aired his own med-school repertoire. Michelle silently picked at the food on her plate. Danielle, who was not as squeamish as their mother, savored the tastes, and blocked the goriest parts of the conversation. Halfway through the main course, Joseph raised a toast for Danielle's paper.

"Didn't you realize," Julia squeezed through her teeth into Danielle's ear, "that if you and Jonathan had set a date for a wedding, Dad would have splurged on the best Champagne available in Thorboro."

"Champagne will wait until you or Joyce sew your first patient," Danielle whispered back. "If you want top quality, make sure the patient stays alive."

When everyone was done, Michelle and Joseph beamed congenially across a vase full of chrysanthemums. Their daughters cleared the table and brought the traditional apple pie, a tray of pungent cheeses for Joseph, a tangy lemon mousse (Julia's dessert of choice), and creamy Tiramisu (Joyce's favorite).

"This year you outdid yourself," Joyce said to Michelle.

Avoiding the smelly cheese, Danielle had a serving from the other desserts. She wished Jon was with them.

Everyone slept late on Friday. In the afternoon Danielle went to visit Lucy, a high-school friend who had also studied at TIST. Despite the maternity leave, Lucy looked fazed and sleep-deprived. Two-week-old Emily had deep-blue eyes and an adorable rosy face. She made gurgling noises when Danielle gently tickled her tiny fist.

Late in the evening, Danielle spoke with Jonathan. "Nothing concrete," he summed up the meeting with a might-be investor.

On Saturday, Jonathan called from Thorboro airport. The flights were okay, he said. He and Roy had agreed about modifications he would incorporate into the software.

When they hung up, Danielle felt disappointment that Jon had not asked her to come with him to the DeWitts. Before they would be together that evening, she had to face three generations of Blooms without him.

"What's wrong?" Joyce asked Danielle in the car. Danielle quietly told her sisters about the engagement party at DeWitts'.

"Why didn't you go?" Joyce asked. "If you had told Aunt Sophie about the invitation, she would be the first one to urge you to go."

Danielle only shrugged.

"You could have been with Jonathan and mingle with interesting people," Julie said mercilessly. "But those bony preppies wouldn't be as sophisticated as Abby."

Julie rolled her eyes, Joyce giggled, and they both went on to ridicule the bony blondes and humorless blokes they met at Duke. Danielle smiled at first, but when the twins darted their comments at uncle Mark's wife, Andrea, she joined the conversation. They were poking fun at Andrea's double career as a homemaker and a mother, when Joseph parked his Volvo in front of Sophia Bloom's undistinguished and unpretentious house.

Danielle crossed a small yard with old trees and shrubs, thinking about the sprawling grounds around the DeWitt manor. She halted in front of a modest-sized house, whose furniture was outdated by the usual standards, but not old enough to be valued as antiques.

Natalie Bloom-McCormick welcomed the Mellers at the entrance, took their presents, and hugged her cousin and nieces. Joseph and Michelle went to congratulate Aunt Sophie, whereas Danielle, Joyce, and Julia stayed together, at a safe distance from a makeshift bar, where Mark handed drinks to men and voiced his concerns about the threats of global warming. On the other side of the living room, Andrea was sitting in an easy chair, with baby Max in her arms. As Joyce and Julia refused to be anywhere near Andrea, Danielle went alone to the group of women who gathered around the new mother and the baby. She waited while Andrea droned about her latest labor, and the other women sympathetically swapped their own experiences with epidural. Smiling as cheerfully as she could force her jaws, Danielle said what was appropriate and cooed to the baby. Before she managed to sidle away, Joseph gravitated to the bar, and

Michelle and her sisters left the room. Observing that she and the baby were the only ones under thirty within her sight, Danielle straightened her shoulders, lifted her nose, and headed to the sofa to give her warmest congratulations to Aunt Sophie and be coldly polite to the unbearable Moira.

Not surprisingly, the sisters-in-law sat as far as they could from each other. Sophia was upright, bearing herself like a deposed noblewoman; Moira was knitting ferociously, her yarns filling the space in between. Family lore claimed that fifty years or so of mutual dislike had began the moment the late Arthur Bloom had introduced his girl, Sophia Lichtfeld, to his sister Moira. Weddings, childbirths, and widowhood did not change what the sisters-in-law thought of each other. They belonged to the same generation, lived through similar experiences in the same little town, but could not have more different views and interests. Sophia grew soaking up her revered brother's fascination with knowledge and science. Through her life, Sophia sought the first and respected the other. Moira, who had absorbed an entirely different worldview when she had been of an impressionable age, scorned most of the things beyond her family's narrow experiences.

"Happy birthday," Danielle said, bending down to kiss Aunt Sophie. "I wish you to stay healthy and regal for many more years."

Seeing that Moira would not move her yarns, Danielle knelt before her great-aunt, cupped Sophia's hands with her own. "Hello Moira," she said dryly. "How do you do?"

"I'm well considering my age," Moira replied, without pausing her knitting. "Mark told me that your sisters attend one of the best medical schools in the country. Michelle did really well when she married Joseph."

Thanks for affirming my parents' marriage, Danielle retorted in her mind as she flashed Moira a smile. The Lichtfelds' version of family gossip insisted that few things galled Moira as much as them doing better than Blooms.

"It's a pity that you went to the same college but haven't married," Moira continued. "I cannot introduce you to someone with Joseph's means, but Abby has told me about a man whom you should want to meet."

All ancient roads led to Rome, and Moira's conversation invariably led to her most accomplished granddaughter. Before Danielle could answer, Sophia squeezed her hands, soundlessly asking her to answer politely.

"That is really nice of Abby," Danielle said sweetly. "Is she still with Eric?"

"Yes." Moira lifted her eyes from her knitting to look significantly at Danielle's bare left hand. She did not intend to be offensive, but she had to make clear that Abby's studying for a nursery school teacher's diploma counted much more than Danielle's wasting money for studying useless rubbish at TIST. "Abby won't be a doctor but she'll have a good profession. Have you heard that Eric was promoted at the bank?"

Unable to come up with a seemingly polite response, Danielle smiled nastily.

"Abby is in the basement with your sisters and other young people," Moira added. She went on knitting, leaving it to Danielle to deduce that she was too old to be welcomed by the "young people" in the basement.

How could Tali complain that Dorian was rude to Moira? Danielle thought. It was self-preservation to talk back to the hag. Before she could do so, Sophia calmly asked, "How is your research progressing?"

"My last paper was accepted by *Physical Review Letters*. It's a very selective physics journal."

"It sounds vaguely familiar." Sophia frowned, trying to recollect when she had heard the journal's name. "Have you published there before?"

"No." Danielle shook her head. Aunt Sophie's memory could compete with an Indian elephant's, but why in the world would PRL evoke any memories? Possibilities popped in her mind, and were promptly dismissed as unlikely. Then, Danielle thought about her mother's response on Thanksgiving. Something about PRL had triggered their memories. And since Sophia had only one connection to physics, Danielle's well-honed mind pointed to Aaron Lichtfeld.

Aaron was thirty or thirty-one when he died, so it was plausible that he had publications in physics journals. One of the papers might have been published in PRL. The journal's illustrious name would have figured in the stories Aunt Sophie and grandma Rachel told about their brother. Stories, which might have led Mom to study physics. Danielle warmed to the thought of being a third generation of physicists. There was something magical in closing a circle in a family legacy, she mused, envisioning herself retrieving the forgotten paper in the section of old periodicals. Aunt Sophie would be gratified to see Aaron's name in print. And it would mean a lot to Mom seeing the lost paper of her uncle.

"I see Rose and Lily," Moira said and sighed. "Danielle, can you rise up? Your kneeling must be pleasant to Sophia, but simple manners require her to welcome other guests."

"Sure," Danielle rose automatically. She stood by the sofa, a little confused.

"Can you pass by the TV room and see how Dorian is doing?" Sophia whispered. "He is babysitting Sheila and Naomi, and I'd like to know why it's so quiet there."

Danielle found the three children in Arthur Bloom's former office. Dorian, nine years old and tall compared to his younger cousins, was reading from a book titled *Norse Mythology* a blood-curdling tale about a human hero facing ferocious giants and vicious dwarfs. Four-year-old Naomi gasped, six-year-old Sheila squeaked. Seeing Danielle, Dorian closed the book.

"Hi," Danielle said. She extended both hands to embrace the girls.

"Dorian is reading Naomi a folktale," Sheila informed her oldest cousin. "In real, dwarfs and giants don't exist."

"It's mythology," Dorian corrected, "and giants and dwarfs do exist."

"They don't." Shelia pouted, looking like a smaller, cuter version of Andrea. Naomi stared wide-eyed at her sister, highly impressed by her standing up to their big cousin.

"What about red giants and white dwarfs?" Dorian asked, looking triumphantly at Danielle.

"Sheila did not mean different types of stars," Danielle said soothingly. She felt ridiculous in her role as an authoritative yet reassuring adult.

"Never mind," Dorian shrugged off the subject. "Have you heard about dark energy? It's new. Do you know that it's the largest reservoir of energy in the universe?"

Great, Danielle thought sardonically. Of all the people she had tried to speak to about dark energy, only a child brought up the topic willingly.

"Dark energy is something that makes us feel bad," Sheila intervened with ready explanation. "Mom talked a lot about different kinds of energy when we redecorated the house before Maxi was born."

"Where did you pick that up?" Danielle asked Dorian.

"I watched an interview with a professor from TIST, on channel nineteen."

"Do you remember the professor's name or how he looked?" Danielle asked.

"The professor was a lady," Dorian said. "I don't remember her name."

Slightly dazed, Danielle left the children and ambled to the kitchen, where her mother worked alongside Natalie. She offered to help, and was told to arrange more food on platters and garnish dishes. Danielle's hands did the chores automatically; her mind pondered about the first female professor at TIST's physics department. The appointment had suspicious timing, as if made in the wake of Crawford's scandal. Was TIST's first female professor in physics indebted to a careless chauvinist? Danielle wavered, darting a questioning glance at her mother. Michelle was deftly mincing dill while listening to Tali's complaints about Dorian's school. Knowing she should not interrupt, Danielle willed herself to go on, but she did not bother to stifle her bitterness.

12

THE LARGEST MACHINE

Within a week after Thanksgiving, Hopeville's shops shed their earthy brown, golden, and russet colors and adorned immaculate whites, velvety reds, and dark greens. Wintery mornings came on time; frost iced the lawns, smoky scents pervaded sleepy neighborhoods. In Fitzgerald Hall, there was little change. The secretaries' office buzzed with talk about Marjory's daughter's preparations before giving birth. The astrophysics and pizza seminars were put on hold until the spring term. Chi had bought his first laptop on Black Friday. Ben, fettered by a project in the parallel computing course, stopped coming to Danielle and Chi's office. Danielle, who had no pressing assignments from Green, spent the mornings analyzing the data streaming from the jobs she was running on the group's cluster of computers. At afternoons, she read about other groups' simulations.

On her way home in the evenings, she passed windows decorated with Christmas trees and toy trains, families carrying shopping bags and sleepy children, couples going in and out of cafés and restaurants. The Main Street was alight, stores extended their opening hours, charities appealed to holiday spirit and nudged strangers into generosity. Enjoying the atmosphere, Danielle gave donations to every earnest volunteer who stood in the cold for a cause, and smiled in response to thanks and greetings. The streets grew quieter along the familiar route through residential neighborhoods, yet the glitter of colorful bulbs made lawns, roofs, and porches look festive. Chadwick Drive houses beamed with welcoming lights, all except for a little, cold house, where she lived.

"I know I shouldn't worry," Danielle told Jonathan in one of their nightly phone conversation, "but when I do the calculations, I often have a feeling that none of the expansion rates I've picked would forge the right structures."

"Why don't you wait and see? If none of them works, you will make a better guess next time."

"I'd eventually," Danielle agreed. "But considering that each simulation should run for several weeks before it generates structures, I might find myself half a year into the post without any results."

"You can work on something else meanwhile. Did you talk with Green yet?"

"He is too busy cobbling grant proposals," Danielle grumbled. "In fact, I glimpse Cobs in the secretaries' office more often than I see Green."

"Can I tell you something off-topic?" Jonathan asked.

"Go on."

"Are you sitting down?"

"I'm lying alone on the sofa," Danielle replied.

"We got a green light." Jonathan's voice rang excited. "The beta is scheduled to become operational by early April."

"Good luck!" she said. Then, unable to resist, Danielle added, "I know you will enjoy fighting over every software component, let alone arguing on how to structure the code."

"Do you also know that I'm in charge?" Jonathan inquired offhandedly.

She bolted upright. "In charge of the beta?"

"Yes, the Californian brass required it."

"Wow," Danielle muttered. "That's great."

Jon's excitement was now perfectly understandable, but in the back of her mind, Danielle noted that he did not sound overjoyed. "Does Zeeman know about it?" she asked warily.

"Roy spoke with him after he told me. I expected a few accusing glares, but Paul acted as if nothing happened."

"That does not sound like Zeeman," Danielle commented. The Zeeman she knew would have slammed a few doors. "Is he going to work on the software?"

"Sure. I'm not supposed to design it single-handedly. Anyway, my elated position comes with a boon."

"A bonus?"

"More money isn't Roy's style. Another guess?"

"A vacation through the holidays?" Danielle's wishfully asked. Whatever Green's reaction might be, she was determined to take a few days off to be with Jonathan.

"He didn't think that far." Jonathan chuckled. "Allowing for time difference and the unavoidable jet lag, I have an official waiver to come as late as I want."

"Does it include someone kicking you out after twelve hours?"

"Nope. No strings attached."

"Then you got my congratulations. You will get much more when I'll be able to see and touch you."

There was a pause, then Jonathan asked, "Can you fly to San Francisco a day before Christmas? We can rent a car and ride along the Pacific shore, watch sunsets together."

"Like we watched the sun sinking into the Mediterranean?" Danielle teased, her voice sultry and soft. "It is an irresistible offer. I'll book the flights for a round trip."

"Wait a moment. Don't you want to celebrate the new year at Heidrun?"

They went to the Heidrun pub on every New Year's Eve since they had started dating. It was a tradition, Danielle told herself, staving off an unpleasant thought about the extra cost of another flight.

"You've got a point," she said. "When are we going to fly to Thorboro?"

"I'll take care of that." Jonathan said. "Another thing, mother has asked me to reserve January the first for something."

Happy with the prospect of vacation with Jon, Danielle did not protest about starting the year with Sarah Lerner. "Any clues about what she is planning?" Danielle asked.

"Some sort of elaborate family gathering. She is replacing toilets and faucets, and is redoing the tiles in the bathroom near the living room."

The DeWitts were also invited, Danielle deduced. Having a mental picture of Sarah stuck with a half-torn bathroom through the holidays, she wondered why Richard had not stopped the craziness in its bud.

"Dad is too busy with end-of-the-year reports and last minute haggling over the next year's budget to intervene," Jonathan answered the question Danielle did not voice. "But he cautioned against starting a project too big to be completed ahead of Christmas."

Richard was one of the wisest people she had ever met, Danielle reflected. And luckily, his capacity for clear thinking was passed to his eldest son.

Next day, Danielle went over the data she had analyzed, studied the distribution of the sizes of newly formed matter aggregates, scrutinized the typical distances between them. The plots did not point to whether the simulated universe was on the right course or not. Considering that Green was more knowledgeable and experienced, Danielle thought that he could take a look at the same data and notice something she missed. Yet, asking for his advice might backfire, if it made her seem insecure and in need of being told what to do. Deeming that more data about the toy universe would be instructive, Danielle decided to check how different light-to-ultra-heavy particles' mass ratios would affect the sizes of matter aggregates. She picked from a recent preprint five different mass ratios, fine-tuned other parameters, then made the relevant adjustments in her program. Within a few hours, she had eight different universes evolve on the group's cluster. Feeling she should stop at that, she picked a book that was almost due and went to the physics library.

As she was flipping through the most recent issue of *Physical Review Letters*, Aaron Lichtfeld's name sprang to Danielle's mind. Did her mother mention his paper on Thanksgiving? Aaron might have become a well-known physicist if he had not had the bad luck to work in an unsafe nuclear reactor. It was a shame that her mother, who had ventured into physics when women were a rarity and hardly welcome, had quit without a graduate degree.

Danielle reassured herself that she already accomplished more than Mom did. Her memories flitted to grandma Rachel's black-and-white photos, to her reminiscences about her unusually bright older brother. These stories always reminded Danielle of history textbooks, but her grandmother's old tales were probably the seeds of her mother's interest in physics. Wondering about Aaron's lasting influence, Danielle put the journal back in its place. It was about time to climb a few stairs, and look for her great-uncle's half-forgotten PRL.

Papers are destined to decay regardless of whether they merited a Nobel Prize or were completely inconsequential, Danielle observed, when the musty smell pervading the section of old periodicals hit her nostrils. She heard the thud of her own steps, and no other sound, yet she had an uncanny sensation that she was not alone. Reaching the aisle with *Physical Review Letters,* she scanned shelves lined with old volumes, found the row of those dated from the 1950s. Befuddled, she gawked right ahead. The year inscribed on the first volume was 1958, seven years after Aaron's death.

It was impossible, Danielle's mind protested. Hadn't both her mother and Aunt Sophie mentioned Aaron's paper in PRL? Transfixed to the floor, she stared at the solid evidence in front of her eyes – *Physical Review Letters* did not exist while Aaron Lichtfeld was alive. On impulse, Danielle turned to search through volumes of *Physical Review* placed on an opposite aisle, but thinking it over, she stopped. Looking for a paper which probably had never existed was pointless. She had imagined her mother's and Aunt Sophie's reactions because she had been eager to impress them with her own paper.

If Aaron had authored any research paper, Aunt Sophie would have framed and hung it, Danielle mused, as she reexamined her family lore. In terms of achievements, the Lichtfelds' physics legacy was depressing. Forcing herself to stick to the facts, Danielle could not recall any paper mentioned before Thanksgiving, when Michelle had said that a paper in *Physical Review Letters* had a special meaning. What meaning could it have, Danielle asked herself. Even if stories about Aaron's work had steered her mother towards physics, Michelle had quit it for good at the age of twenty-four. Inferring from her own ambitions, Danielle wondered whether a paper in *Physical Review Letters* had been one of Michelle's goals in graduate school. If so, then the paper Danielle and Alec had submitted to PRL could be a constant reminder to Mom that she had failed to fulfill her dream.

The realization that decades later, her mother still

remembered and cared about her crushed aspirations, shook Danielle. In her mind's eye, she saw the opportunities that the twenty-four-year-old Michelle had missed because she became a mother. Although no one blamed the baby, it was evident that she came too early into her mother's life. In a blink, the weight of what Michelle had lost was like hundreds of hefty tomes closing in. Dizzy and breathless, Danielle gasped for air.

Was it a flicker of movement or an illusion? An eerie, luring light shone between the flunking aisles. Disoriented, Danielle held the metal frames, and trudged forward. She reached the aisles' end, and unwittingly went on without support. She toppled, bumped into something solid. Muffled gongs echoed in her head.

"Don't get up yet," Jonah Cobs' voice cut through the echoes.

Danielle gingerly opened an eye, then another one. She was lying on the hardwood floor, huddled up against a leg of an enormous desk. Lifting her head upwards, she saw a glowing lamp on the table. Cobs was standing nearby, hunching forward. *Rats*, she thought, closing both eyes.

"Are you hurt?" he asked.

"My head is pounding a little and my vision is somewhat blurry." Danielle paused and squinted. "Have I really crashed into the desk?"

"Quite impressively." Cobs pulled a chair closer to Danielle. "Would you like to sit down?"

He considerately waited for Danielle to pull herself up and slump on the chair. Her pain ebbed, but the situation did not become less embarrassing. Cobs' manners were old-fashioned, his behavior was devoid of derision, yet his old eyes glinted with humor. Having little doubt that he would enjoy recounting the incident to Anne and to Marjory Klein, Danielle groaned inwardly. Why did he have to come here, when he had a roomy office where he could slack off?

Seeing color suffusing over Danielle's face, Cobs returned to his chair.

"The light startled me," she said. "I didn't expect anyone in this section of the library."

"I also was startled." Cobs waved a hand, as if dismissing the rest of what happened.

Despite the awkwardness of her situation, Danielle felt lucky it was him and not another professor.

"It's not often that someone comes here," Cobs said. "What treasures did you expect to unearth in the old tomes of *Physical Review?*"

Feeling too raw to feign an interest in some obscure physics topic, Danielle said, "An old paper that my great-uncle had supposedly published in *Physical Review Letters*. I found that it was impossible. He died in the early fifties."

"Maybe it was a letter published in *Physical Review?* You can look for his surname in *Physics Abstracts*."

Wasn't it better to let bygones be bygones? Even if she could find Aaron's paper, showing it to her mother would revive miserable memories and rekindle regrets about what might have been. Success in physics would not mend what she had inadvertently caused, but it would make her mother happier.

"I would rather leave it at that," Danielle said quietly. "I don't like to stir long-forgotten ghosts."

She expected Cobs to smile, but he looked pensive.

"Ghosts sometimes lurk in interesting places," he said. "A ghost might occasionally point to something worth knowing."

"I don't think that my great-uncle's paper, if it exists, would make any revelations. He was a nuclear physicist. He died young, a few months after a malfunction in a research reactor where he worked."

The silent empathy on Cobs' face drew Danielle to blab about her family history. She had to remind herself that despite his gentlemanly manners, Cobs was an eccentric, reclusive physics professor.

"Something I've heard at a family gathering led me to think that he had a paper in PRL." She shrugged. "I was curious to find whether he did."

"Curious to find whether he made a groundbreaking discovery, or curious in general about his work?"

Why does it matter to you? Danielle thought. Whether she cared about the work of a great-uncle whom she had never seen, or needed to know what had inspired her mother to pursue a foredoomed career, it was none of Cobs' business.

She lowered her stare and tried to stifle annoyance. Amid

volumes of *Physical Review* piled on the table, the uppermost one was from 1935. It was open on page 777. Leaning forward to see better, she read that the paper was authored by A. Einstein, B. Podolsky, and N. Rosen.

"The EPR?" Danielle whispered. She had studied about the famous paradox in a quantum mechanics course but had never seen the original paper. Wondering why was Cobs reading it, Danielle looked at the other items strewn on the table. A few pens, sheaves of dog-eared papers, old bulging notebooks. In all, she estimated, Cobs had hundreds of handwritten pages covered with equations and text. That was too much for a paper or a report. It did not look like something that Cobs did to while away a few hours a day. The sheer amount of pages suggested he was working on the manuscript for years.

"Are you writing a book?" she voiced an idea that popped in her mind.

"No, that is what my daughter is doing. Gemma is the budding author in our family."

"Does she?" Danielle echoed, unable to picture Anne's and Jonah's daughter as a writer. Reckoning that Gemma might ponder about the philosophy of science or churn out Jane Austen spin-offs, Danielle asked, "What does she write about?"

"An Arthurian space-opera," Cobs said, keeping his face straight.

The words "space-opera" brought to mind *Galactic Patrol* with its testosterone-brimming spaceships hurling through the ether. Danielle smiled, even though she was clueless whether Cobs was joking or such a sub-genre really existed.

"Is it science-fiction?" she asked.

"I guess that it's a fantasy," Cobs replied. "What Gemma writes is inhabited with seers and knights, but it also adheres to the laws of nature."

"But how can supernatural coexist with the laws of physics?"

Danielle's question took Cobs aback. He looked at her, careful not to let his disdain of her boss to filter into his observations. Danielle, he concluded, was a bit older than Gemma, pretty shy, curious and sarcastic.

"Gemma is too fascinated by nature to need time-traveling Merlin-clones," he said. "Her stories combine hard science, intuition, and rampant imagination."

As Danielle listened to Cobs speak of his daughter, his words brought back memories of times before undergraduate courses weaned her from mixing physics and fantasies. She wondered what Gemma had studied. Both literature and science seemed plausible.

As if reading her thoughts, Cobs said, "Gemma was interested in physics for a while."

"Did she study it in college?" Danielle asked impetuously.

"It would be more accurate to say that she was taught the technicalities of calculations and was indoctrinated with the inexorable physics tenets. Gemma did well for a while, but eventually she left the university." His voice trailed off, leaving bitterness to hang in the air. He sat stooped, weighted down by sad recollections.

Danielle shifted her stare and tried not to intrude into Cobs' private lamentation. She was wavering whether it was better to leave him alone, when he said "we will talk later," and gestured Danielle to go away.

Not expecting "we will talk later" to happen any time soon, Danielle went back to her office. Engrossed in thoughts, she did not notice that Chi looked askance at her. She stared at the screen, unaware that anything was amiss until Ben stormed into their office, seething with anger.

"You!" He looked balefully at Danielle. Having done nothing to provoke the rage, she ignored him.

"You choked the cluster," Ben spat.

Not understanding what he was accusing her of, Danielle looked at Chi for support. Chi shook his head and beckoned her to come closer to his monitor. Wordlessly, he showed Danielle how much CPU her jobs were using. Blushing from forehead to the tips of her ears, she muttered something about sending the runs without thinking.

Ben did not deign to reply, but his sniggering expression plainly said, "Are you that stupid?"

"I'll halt the last five jobs," Danielle said, swallowing her pride.

Ben went out without saying anything.

Making such a stupid mistake rankled, but it also convinced

Danielle that she needed Green's input. Bearing in mind his fastidiousness and lack of time, she organized the results of her analysis in several tables and plots. Next morning, she went to Green's office. He listened to her account of the toy universe's simulations, glanced at the data Danielle laid on his desk, and asked a few brisk, shrewd questions.

"Have you considered other mass ratios between the ultraheavy and light particles?" Green's equable voice suggested that such omission was a mark of ineptness.

"Yes. I planned to check five different ratios used in other groups' simulations." Danielle tersely described what the other group had done. "It turned out that the simulations are too heavy to run on our cluster simultaneously," she concluded.

"Then make your program more efficient," Green said. He gestured Danielle to leave.

"Don't let me impose on your time," she grumbled on her way to her office. Green's evident lack of interest in his own model did not bode well. Reminding herself that she would soon roam the Californian coastline with Jon, she stifled the bad feeling and immersed herself in programming.

* * *

Days slipped by while Danielle struggled with subtleties of programming. Fourteen-hour-long days, during which she had no time to dwell on physics, or, in fact, on anything that could not improve the code by making it more economical and efficient. A couple of days before the winter recess, she received an invitation to the departmental colloquium.

You are cordially invited to a physics colloquium, to be held on Thursday, December 16th, at 4pm, in the Auditorium (room 11a) at Fitzgerald Hall. Armand Brochard from CERN will talk about:

Looking for the origin of mass at LEP.

Teas and light refreshments will be served in the Lounge (room 10), at 3:30pm.

Abstract:

The Large Electron-Positron (LEP) collider at CERN was designed to study the theoretical predictions of the Standard

Model of particle physics, its three families of quarks and leptons, four vector bosons carrying the electro-weak interactions, and a zero-spin Higgs particle.

Throughout the decade that LEP has been operational, numerous precision experiments were conducted. All of them are in agreement, within experimental errors, with the particle physics standard model.

In my talk, I'll survey LEP's four detectors and the two phases of its operation, with a focus on the unique role of the Higgs particle in the standard model, and the possibility of its discovery at LEP.

A nice, lighthearted topic before the holidays, Danielle observed sarcastically. The Higgs boson was the only particle in the standard model that was neither matter nor a force carrier. Its counterpart, the omnipresent Higgs field, interacted with electrons and quarks and the particles mediating the weak force. If it wouldn't, these particles would have remained massless, and like photons, would have dispersed in space. In short, the Higgs boson was not yet another short-lived, esoteric particle. It was high-energy physicists' holy grail.

Well, if Aunt Sophie could have attended the colloquium, Danielle mused, picturing Sophia's shock at the sight of the refreshments, she might have accepted that no one is hoarding an arsenal of super-weapons underground between Switzerland and France.

On December 16th, Danielle, Chi and Ben came early to the Lounge. Other grad students and post-docs, who reasoned that the department would honor the guest from CERN with better-than-usual refreshments, trickled in and hung around a long table laid with the usual assortment of greasy and overly sweet cookies. Wanting none, Danielle stood in a quiet spot and watched those who went to scour for edibles, and the others who joined the line for hot water and coffee. She saw that Green and Lisitsin skirted the long table. After a while, everyone she could think of was in the Lounge, except the speaker. Physicists were milling about the crowded room, talking shop, bickering and schmoozing.

A bright ginger gleam caught Danielle's eyes, but a group of animated guys from the fourth floor obscured the rest of him. She shifted aside, peered between the men. The redhead held a plastic cup in one hand and clinched cookies in the other. Unable to see who he was talking to, she took a couple of steps sideways, craned her neck, and saw Jonah Cobs standing under a portrait of a Victorian physicist. Both Cobs and the redhead stood by themselves. The redhead looked scheming, Cobs seemed reluctant. Surprised and curious, Danielle edged closer, intending to remain hidden, yet within earshot.

"I should have known they won't take Brochard to King's Kitchen, but show off with a three course lunch at l'Offroy," Danielle heard the redhead saying. She could not hear whether Cobs replied.

"Has anyone thought of inviting you?" the redhead persisted.

Who would do that? Danielle wondered. The only person who paid any attention to Cobs in Fitzgerald Hall was Marjory Klein. Wanting to hear Cobs' reply, she moved a bit closer.

"I usually cannot read thoughts," Cobs said quietly.

"You were not invited, even though..."

"Why would they invite me, when I have not been collaborating with any of them for many years?"

"For the same reason you came to hear Brochard." The redhead guy's voice dripped sarcasm. "When have you met last time?"

"At Gene Harbinger's sixtieth birthday. It was soon after you returned to King Solomon."

Cobs' response must have caused the redhead discomfort, for he looked like a frisky puppy who had just been scolded. His murmur was not intelligible. Keen to hear their conversation, Danielle stepped aside. She was spotted by Cobs. Before she could retreat back, he beckoned her to come closer.

"Danielle, Isaac," Cobs introduced them. Nodding to Danielle, Isaac flashed a sardonic smile which acknowledged that Jonah had succeeded in evading him again.

"Danielle is a post-doc with George Green. Isaac is a faculty member at the university. He is a former graduate student of mine."

"Simulations of early universe?" Isaac asked, his voice intoning that the question was a greeting rather than an interest in Danielle's work. He swirled the murky brown liquid congealed in his cup, decided that it was undrinkable, then popped a cookie into his mouth.

To Danielle it was evident that Isaac did not welcome her presence, but Cobs' look compelled her to stay.

"Structure formation in toy universes with various ratios of dark to regular matter," she answered belatedly. "My simulations focus on the role that dark energy plays in the early stages of these universes' evolution."

"Do you do something besides toying with initial conditions?" Isaac asked, switching from a pointed lack of interest to a mild glee.

Jonah shook his head. "I would not have introduced you," he said, "if I doubted you can speak without glee about others' research."

Isaac's sorrowful expression was as convincing as a boxer's sad looks while it was gnawing a bone.

"That's all right," Danielle said amiably. There was something candid and lovable about Isaac, which made it difficult to be offended by him. "Toying with parameters and analyzing the outcomes is a big part of what I do."

Both professors smiled. "Admitting that whatever you do is 'toying with parameters' is asking for being passed over," Isaac instructed good-humoredly. "You should boldly imply that your work is groundbreaking or at least at the frontier of cutting edge research."

"I thought you were done with wheedling for grants," Jonah dryly commented.

"The holidays are a short hiatus. Like Sisyphus' job, that task never ends."

Danielle also smiled. Isaac was not kind or even polite, yet he was the most refreshing faculty to be around.

Jonah turned to Danielle. "What else do you do?" he asked encouragingly.

Since "cursing the darn program" was a truthful yet inadequate answer, Danielle said, "I'm looking for the origins of dark energy."

Isaac cocked his brows, popped in another cookie, then asked, "What kind of explanation are you looking for?" He did not sound mocking. In fact, Danielle discerned some interest in Isaac's voice.

"A cosmological source that can explain why dark energy acts like a cosmological constant," she said. "Why, contrary to what happened with radiation and matter, dark energy's density wasn't diluted through the universe's expansion."

Feeling ill-at-ease for voicing what baffled her, Danielle lowered her face to look at her watch. She did not notice the meaningful glance Isaac darted at Jonah, a speculative glean in his eyes. She heard Isaac whisper, "Any chance you'd mention your work?"

"You know that I don't toy with the career of any student bright enough to be worth the trouble," Jonah said firmly. "And this is not the right place to bring up my work."

"Where else can I find you?" Isaac grumbled. "I might eventually nudge Marjory into telling me, but aren't we too old to play hide-and-seek?"

The section of old periodicals, Danielle thought. Intrigued, she kept her stare cast down.

"You can take a break from calling Marjory," Cobs advised. "She will fly to Houston on Saturday."

"Laura?" Isaac asked, his smug smile completely confusing Danielle.

Clapping came from the door, and then came a call to leave the food and drink and come to the auditorium. For Danielle, it was a relief to sit at the very back. She saw Green sitting in the center of the third row between Brophy and Lisitsin. Isaac and Cobs took seats near the edge of the third row.

A professor from high-energy physics introduced Armand Brochard, reading from an index card the highlights of his illustrious career. None of what he said prepared Danielle to see Brochard in person. The French professor was about Cobs' age, not very tall, but very visible, wearing an elegantly tailored jacket over a shimmering electric-blue shirt. He should have looked ridiculous, Danielle reflected, but he did not. As if he was not conspicuous enough, Brochard raised both hands above the shoulders in a theatrical welcome.

Suave, Danielle concluded. She eyed the professor, whose behavior suggested he had too much wine with the three-course lunch. Brochard, however, walked straight, first stepping down from the platform, then ascending to the third row. He stopped before Jonah Cobs, both hands extended forward. Cobs stood up and both men hugged.

The audience responded with silence, which could express anything. No one peeped until Brochard returned to the podium.

"Before I speak about the LEP and our search for the Higgs boson," he said jubilantly, "let me disclose that Jonah and I have a long-standing disagreement about the origin of mass. About a year before the LEP became operational, we made a bet."

"The bet was on finding the Higgs boson," Cobs said. "Have you brought the bottle of Champagne?"

"Not so fast, mon ami. You'll bear with me while I describe our magnificent flagship and dash through the standard model. Then I'll tell what we have found about the Higgs boson."

If the largest machine in the world entrusted to scientists, the Large Electron-Positron collider, needed someone to introduce it, Brochard was the right person. With great élan, he described the milestones of the LEP construction. When he spoke of its cosmopolitan setting near Geneva, Brochard stepped aside, so everyone could see the aerial view, which was worth a thousand words. Although Danielle had no particular interest in high-energy physics, for ten minutes she was tempted to face its inconceivable math, if she could spend half a year between Lake Léman and the French Alps. The collider itself was underground. Its four formidable detectors brought to Danielle's mind the catacombs of Rome and Italy's ancient temples. A quick succession of more detailed slides opened a window into the detectors' complexity, and convinced Danielle that she would be better off above the ground, studying cosmology.

The following slide was a schematic illustration of electron and positron beams superimposed over a photo of an underground tunnel. "The beams," Brochard pointed at two needle-thin shining rods, "are accelerated as they pass through superconducting cavities. The powerful magnetic fields circle the electrons and the positrons over and over through the tunnel, until the particles almost reach the speed of light."

His voice brought to life the rattle of machinery, the power of invisible fields, the huge energy accumulated in the zooming particles. "The beams are squeezed before collision," Brochard explained. "When the collision occurs, the electrons and positrons disintegrate, transiently creating new particles."

"At the first phase of LEP operation," Brochard flipped a slide, "an annihilation of two beams, with an energy of forty-five GeV each, created a neutral Z particle, which decays into pairs of fermions." Other slides followed. Feynman diagrams elucidated the various ways super heavy electrons and positrons could disintegrate when they collided.

"Z decays into a quark and its anti-quark," Brochard pointed to the relevant diagram. "The quarks turn into hadrons and the hadrons generate jets of particles that hit the detector. The decay of a Z particle into neutrino and anti-neutrino does not leave tracks on the detector."

"All decays of the Z particle predicted by the standard model are accounted for. The experiments have confirmed the existence of exactly three families of quarks and leptons." He looked triumphantly at the audience. "Being able to show something definitive early on in the LEP operation gave us a great boost."

The clock on the wall indicated that a major part of the hour allocated for the lecture was over. Ignoring it, Brochard said to the audience, "In the LEP's second phase, new superconducting cavities were gradually installed. The energy of electron and positron beams was increased in stages."

Higher beam energy translated into higher collision energy, thus producing new particles that were not detected previously. Brochard's survey highlighted the tremendous work done to gear up the gigantic machine. A meaningful "ahem" from the first row caused him to skip a few slides.

"Here the electron-positron collision produces a pair of positively and negatively charged W+ and W- particles." He pointed at a Feynman diagram. "Their modes of decay agree very well with the standard model."

More diagrams trailed each other in quick succession, to demonstrate that "all of the members of all three families are accounted for."

"The top quark was discovered at Fermilab," someone called.

Brochard smiled, then asked, "Anyone not familiar with the

mechanism of spontaneous symmetry breaking?"

Murmurs followed the question, but no one raised his hand.

"Good, we can skip the Mexican hat. I surmise that the electroweak phase transition is also well known?"

Brochard looked around, then skipped to a slide that summarized what had happened around a hundred giga-electron volts. At this energy (which corresponds to a temperature of about a hundred tera-degrees Celsius), the Higgs field first came into being. It permeated the space. It gave mass to every quark and electrically charged lepton. It split the primordial electroweak force into electromagnetic and weak interactions. The carriers of the short ranged weak force, the W and Z particles, gained their masses. The carrier of the electromagnetic field – the photon – remained massless.

Duly impressed with the energy that had pervaded the Universe at the time of the electroweak phase transition, Danielle noted that the Higgs field existed since about a picosecond after the Big Bang. There was something awe-inspiring at the thought that it filled the space ever since. Without the Higgs field to render mass to particles, they would have dispersed all around at the speed of light. The simulations she was doing suddenly seemed totally insignificant.

"For the standard model to succeed, the acquisition of masses had to undergo a coupling to a Higgs boson. Bear in mind that the Higgs boson is unique in a way: it couples to any particle having a mass. The strength of the interaction is proportional to Higgs's mass and to the mass of the other particle. The heavier the Higgs's mass is, the stronger is the coupling."

He paused and looked straight at Cobs. Wondering whether Cobs would challenge Brochard's assertion, Danielle felt the build-up of anticipation.

"All four LEP experiments have recorded collisions that show potential evidence for a Higgs particle, but the evidence is far from being conclusive."

So, it might still turn out that the high-energy standard model does not solve the mystery of the origin of mass, Danielle mused. She had no idea what Jonah Cobs' objections were, but she wished them to be grounded in cosmology. High-energy physicists had enormous advantage over cosmologists – they recreated the conditions of a very early universe, under the border between Switzerland and France. On the other hand, their celebrated standard model did not account for gravity, dark matter, and dark energy.

A half an hour after the talk was scheduled to end, the professor who had introduced Brochard stepped forward and thanked him. The audience clapped, then the questions began. The first few questions were technical. While Brochard answered, people discreetly sidled to the exits.

"One last question," said the same professor after another quarter of an hour. "Yes?" he pointed to someone sitting in the middle of the auditorium.

"Popular science papers and general press often refer to Higgs boson as 'God's particle'. What do you think about it?"

"It's stupid," Brochard said promptly.

Some laughed and some sniggered.

"Hundreds of physicists from around the world have been working on the project. We ask our governments for substantial monetary contributions." Brochard raised a hand to stave off comments. "As far as we know, there might be no Higgs particle, one Higgs particle, or more than one Higgs particle. Moreover, the Higgs mechanism might be a manifestation of a more complex theory than the standard model. I share with many others at CERN a belief that finding Higgs boson is important for our understanding of the foundations of Nature. But should we attribute our ignorance to divine sources?" Brochard shrugged his shoulders. "Personally, I don't think so."

There was laughter and applause. Someone cried, "Are you taking new bets about finding Higgs?"

Brochard grinned. "I don't think so."

13

A GIRLFRIEND AND A FIANCÉE

The Highway #1 bended and curved between hills sloping down to the Pacific ocean, winded between grassy meadows and swaths of green coppices. The waters below were of an opaque shade of blue tinged with gray. They seemed to stretch indefinitely, even though the shore was close enough for the ocean's rumbling to be carried into the rental car, where Ray Charles was bidden to "Hit the road, Jack." The traffic was light. Jonathan Lerner drove as he pleased, merging the car with the sinuous road, taking its curves without slowing.

Jon was unwinding, Danielle mused, pleasantly heady from the scenery and the car's motion. It was not only the driving, she thought, looking at a three-day stubble surrounding his mouth. They both needed to hit an unfamiliar road and go whenever they wanted, without having reservations or any predetermined list of places to visit. They were together without distractions, for even Jon's cell phone was switched off. After three days and nights, not much was left bottled up after their long abstinence.

"Drowsy?" he asked after Ray Charles was done.

"No, not really. The coastal view is very pretty."

"Which means that you need a strong coffee," Jonathan suggested.

Danielle did not contradict him. They detoured to a village. Over coffees and cinnamon rolls at a local bakery, she asked Jonathan why he thought she could not quietly enjoy a pretty view.

"I did not say you can't enjoy it, but prettiness usually doesn't entrance you."

"I'm not impervious to impressions," Danielle protested, frowning at her sticky roll. "You know that I'm moved by inspiring sights and scenes."

"By awe-inspiring and powerfully consuming," Jonathan affectionately corrected.

"Is that a criticism?"

"Hardly so."

"If you say that to tease, at least let me know what your teasing is about."

"I'm just pointing out that prettiness fails to imprint a strong impression on you."

"Is that a hint that I haven't honed my sensitivity?"

"No. It's an observation. Whatever draws you in has to have potency and enigma. As far as I see, only sex and cosmology have what it takes to stir and seduce you."

"Plainly said," Danielle commented. "About which of them do you expect me to feel more uncomfortable?"

"Neither. You don't bother to feign emotions, and I like that."

"Great," Danielle replied. The tone of her voice intoned the opposite.

"It's fascinating to watch you go beyond the pleasantly comfortable, to a dark domain where lust entwines with destructiveness and seeps into the abyss."

"You make me sound like an oddity who has only two interests in her life."

"Two very broad interests," Jonathan said magnanimously. "Have you heard me complaining?"

"Not really. Have I missed a subtle hint?"

"It was a compliment. Even when you are dressed I enjoy the totality with which you get entranced. It compensates for the in-between brooding and spells of whining."

"Me?" Danielle made a grimace over her empty cup. "Maybe I don't beam with a perpetual sunshine, but I rarely whine."

"Perpetual sunshine doesn't mix well with sarcasm, and I wouldn't miss yours." Jonathan clasped Danielle's fingers and added before she could retort, "I want you to be fulfilled, and not only by me."

It was the most satisfying reply she could have imagined. Danielle patted Jonathan's cheek, then rubbed her forehead on his stubble. On leaving the bakery, Jonathan draped his hand over her waist. In the car, they sat looking at each other.

"What is it?" Danielle asked, sensing hesitation.

"You have changed since you left Thorboro. Remember how playful and lighthearted you were in Italy?"

Of course she remembered. Back then, she knew what she was doing and where she was heading to. Now, her career hung on a project she was not enthusiastic about from the beginning, a project which her boss had lost interest in. Add to the mix endless tinkering with her programs and the situation was bound to give rise to doubts and stir worries. Living with worries she could not put aside brought about change.

Back on the highway, Jonathan drove on a stretch of road that demanded his attention. Determined to preserve her good mood, Danielle shifted her thoughts from Fitzgerald Hall to the changes Jon had undergone. Unlike herself, he became more confident and clear-sighted about where he was heading to. What did the trick? Did having more responsibilities give Jon a sharper focus? Or was it the other way around - he got additional responsibilities because he could hold his ground in the face of Roy's insane schedules, reason with investors, and communicate with patent lawyers? Danielle weighed explanations, dwelt on psychological and self-explanatory arguments, but could not grasp how Jon became less distracted by trifles, more relaxed, and even more capable of enjoyment.

Her speculations evaporated when the car reached a breathtaking landscape. The road slithered on the shoulder of craggy cliffs and hovered above a rugged coastline. The view was even better after Jonathan turned from the main road to a lane, which ended with parking space and a well-trodden path to the edge of the cliff.

"Like it?" Jonathan asked. His voice was barely audible above the ocean's roar.

Below, the surf pounded jutting rocks, spreading iridescent white foam over silvery blue waters. The wind churned the shape-shifting surface, chilling the already cold air.

"It's magnificent," Danielle shouted.

She and Jonathan were the only people on the bluff, sandwiched between endless waters and the sky. They sat on the ground, nestling around each other and cuddling together. Kissing and necking, they kept warm.

They stayed at a motel in the area. After a late breakfast, they went hiking on a long circular trail that promised unspoiled nature and a chance to catch a glimpse of migrating whales.

"See anything large and swimming?" Danielle asked Jonathan hours later, when he was scanning the ocean with binoculars at an observation point.

"Nope," he replied cheerfully. "What about lunch?"

"I have a few cold sandwiches stowed in my backpack."

"We should have taken a thermos with coffee," Jonathan said.

They returned to the trail, which stretched between a thicket of plants. Stumbling on a horizontally-layered rock wide enough to accommodate two, Danielle pulled out the sandwiches. All around her were plants she could not name. The ocean lay below, its roar muffled into a rumble. From her vantage point, it had dormant, brooding airs.

"Thinking about physics?"

"No." Danielle shook her head, her eyes still directed at the distant waters. "I'm not fretting over a simulation I can't do anything about, not when I'm with you in one of the most beautiful places we've ever been at."

"You were murmuring about the ocean and dark energy in your sleep."

"Did I?" She paused to think about the previous night. "I can't recall having any dreams."

"Do you remember anything at all?"

It was the intonation rather than the words that caused Danielle to turn her head and meet Jonathan's eyes.

"Quite a lot," she said saucily, "but that had happened before I fell asleep."

"That's reassuring," Jonathan commented. He finished his sandwich, and started toying with Danielle's tousled hair.

"I thought you don't need reassurances." Her lips lightly brushed his mouth, ending with a kiss. "Does my talking about dark energy bother you?"

"No, not as long as you murmur and groan differently before falling asleep."

Danielle bobbed her head before Jonathan's infallible logic.

"Can you tell me why you were listening to my murmurs that late at night instead of sleeping?"

Jonathan shifted on the rock, suddenly interested in strata.

"Did you sneak to your laptop after I dozed off?"

The expression on his face was that of a guilty man.

"I won't make any comments," Danielle said. "Did you check whatever nagged in the back of your mind?"

"Yes. It simplifies the algorithm." Jonathan pointed at the wintery sun hanging over the ocean's edge. Its rays painted strokes of molten gold over skies and water. "If you are done, let's go to the beach."

They reached the wet sand before the sun touched the horizon. The land around glowed with fantastic colors, and the sky above was illuminated with a lurid, red-orange hue. Danielle and Jonathan breathed in the ocean's salty air and looked at ripples running over the waters, the vermillion wavelets rolling towards the shore. Embracing each other, they watched as the sun sank lower. Sand and water glistened with streaks of unearthly light, sweeping them with magic and beauty.

Next morning, they rounded off the trip. Jonathan shaved and turned on his cell phone. He listened to the messages. All but one were about Nickka.

"Jonathan, this is mother," announced Sarah Lerner's voice. "I don't know where you are and why you can't answer the phone." The message paused, as if Sarah wanted to emphasize she found her son's behavior offensive. "I am calling to remind you about the afternoon tea with Graham and Alice. Please be at our house around four, and be sure to dress appropriately. You've seen the DeWitts, so you understand what I mean."

Listening beside Jonathan, Danielle rolled her eyes, silently pointing as to how ludicrous Sarah sounded. Jonathan waved his hand dismissively.

"Will you tell me what is the appropriate dress code for high tea at a New Year?"

"Aren't you supposed to be the expert after reading all of Jane Austen?"

Danielle mulled over the question. "I can't recall afternoon teas in her novels, except those given by Lady Catherine at Rosing."

Jonathan stared at her blankly.

"You'll find out, once you read *Pride and Prejudice,"* Danielle said. "Now that I think about it, the families Austen portrayed usually weren't rich or aristocratic enough to engage with teas before dinner. And that makes me wonder - since when has your family started to entertain over afternoon teas?"

"I hope it's a once in a lifetime affair inspired by the DeWitts' reception. Their house and the entire setting conveyed the notion that their family belongs to the local nobility."

"Was it fancy?"

"In a way. Alice DeWitt has the aptitude and the upbringing to make an impression without going over the top. She has become my mother's new oracle."

Unbidden, Danielle thought about the self-congratulating, boisterous Moira. A homemaker from Edva must be very different from a housewife from Odinton. Yet, considering Sarah Lerner's three academic degrees and her professed admiration for career women, Danielle couldn't believe that a woman lacking both could have that much influence over Sarah.

"What kind of upbringing?" Danielle asked.

"Alice's family has been in banking for two or three generations."

"A well-heeled family, then. Did she go to a college?"

Jonathan named a formerly all-female, exclusive, and very expensive private university. He could not recall what Alice had studied there, but the name of the gilded alma mater sufficed to impress Danielle. Readjusting her mental picture of Alice, she cast away any comparison with Moira.

"Is she a snob?" Danielle asked.

"A tad narrow-minded. I barely know her, but if I were you, I would not mention cosmology."

Jon's advice was not surprising. Danielle did not mention what she was studying when the likely responses were astonished stares, ill-fitted jokes, and awkward silences before someone said that she must be very smart. Cosmology, experience had taught her and Jonathan, was not a profession one flaunts in a social gathering. It drew embarrassingly little interest, unless someone confused it with cosmetology.

"I'd expect better when the hosts and guests have higher

education," Danielle said.

"The DeWitts are by and large Amos' problem."

Agreeing with Jonathan, Danielle did not think about the invitation on their ride back to San Francisco. The subject did not arise until they checked into a hotel.

"Do you want to buy a dress for the party?" Jonathan asked. "You can check the designer brands."

Thinking about the expenditure, Danielle could not believe that he was serious. Yet, Jonathan did not look as if he was joking. A little unnerved, she realized that Jon had changed more than she had perceived.

"Since your mother will find fault with everything I wear," she said, "I'd rather see San Francisco and not its department stores."

Jonathan, who also preferred strolling the city streets to shopping for clothes, did not argue. They ambled across the downtown, stopped to look at unusual cars, and soaked up the atmosphere.

A shop specializing in fine chocolates caught their eyes. Jonathan went in. Ready to look at chocolates showcased as if they were gemstones, and accordingly overpriced, Danielle followed him. When Jonathan picked a dainty box with an assortment of pralines, Danielle winced seeing the unreasonable price.

"My mother will appreciate the little extravagance," he said.

"Little? It verges on obscene."

"In your eyes," Jonathan said very quietly and pulled his wallet.

Danielle made no other objections, knowing that with his income, Jon could indulge himself and others close to him. Determined not to worry about the widening gap between how she and Jon were living, she turned her attention to the city.

They bade farewell to the Golden Gate Bridge and rainy San Francisco on the morning of December the 30th. On December the 31st, an hour or so before midnight, Danielle and Jonathan were at Thorboro Research Park (TRP), in front of the doors of Heidrun Pub.

Celebrating New Year's night at the pub was a fairly new tradition, open to patrons over twenty-one. The owners did not advertize it, yet the trend gained momentum with the boom of start-ups. Word of mouth ensured that TIST graduates and TRP young professionals flocked to the pub with their dates and girl-friends. The regular clientele willingly splurged a dishearteningly high fee for the all-inclusive party, knowing that the proceeds would go to the Thorboro Medical Center Children's Wing; passersby and strangers grumbled at the owners' greediness and jibbed at paying. Danielle and Jonathan went in. As in previous years, they had a good time.

When Danielle woke up the next day, she saw first the opalescent glow shimmering behind the open blinds, and then lustrous specks floating downwards, like upturned tips of invisible wavelets. Distant thuds, or the hum of the Pacific ocean, echoed in her hazy head. She sniffed the air. The room smelled weirdly, but not with artificial scents of air-fresheners used in motels. Opening both eyes, she found herself in Jonathan's bed, with him sprawled on his back beside her. The dull rhythmic sounds came from his peaceful snores. Alcoholic fumes permeated the air. Beyond the window, fluffy snowflakes gleamed in pearly sky.

"A good omen," she mumbled and kissed Jonathan's slightly parted lips. Getting no response, Danielle nestled against him and watched snowflakes falling. In a few minutes, her eyelids became heavy and the white backdrop faded into a mist.

A phone ringed somewhere, persistently demanding response. Jerked from her slumber, Danielle looked wildly around. Jonathan jolted, but his eyes were still closed. Neither managed to get up before Sarah Lerner's voice shrilled through the answering machine.

"Jonathan, this is Mother. I wanted to make sure that you'll leave on time, taking into account that it's snowing and the traffic should be very slow. Please (the word grated in the bedroom) come before Graham and Alice. Also, make sure that Danielle will dress in a way that won't reflect badly on your relationship."

"I should have brought a strapless tangerine mini-dress," Danielle grumbled.

"Happy New Year!" Jonathan said, pulling her closer.

"Happy New Year." She planted a kiss on his lips. "A new snow is a good omen."

"If Nickka succeeds," Jonathan made his wish for the new year, "I want you and me to relocate to a remote island where phones do not ring before noon."

He lay pensive, looking the way he usually did when devising algorithms, an activity for which he did not need a computer at hand. Without leaving her cozy position, Danielle groped for her watch. She found it stowed under the pillow. For a moment, she merely stared at it.

"It's almost three," she cried. "We have to get up and make ourselves presentable."

Neither could think about dressing up before a generous mug of strong coffee.

"The noise still rings in my ears," Danielle said, as first sips of scalding coffee started to clear the mist in her head. "It was probably a mistake to mix jet lag and booze, but it was great to be around people I know. I didn't realize I was homesick before seeing so many familiar faces."

"Have you seen Paul?"

"No," came a curt answer. "Jon, we should get going. If we don't leave in half an hour, the year will begin with a row."

Soon they were ready. Jonathan took the keys, Danielle held the overpriced pralines. Although the snow kept falling, they reached their destination in time.

The Lerners' townhouse was wedged in a row of similar brownstones on a quiet street in a respected neighborhood. In a stroke of good luck, Jonathan found a place for his Mazda Miata, between a brand new Mercedes and a similarly new Volkswagen.

"Your parents and the DeWitts didn't come yet," he said, noting his parents' Lexus, and the absence of DeWitts' Land Rover and Mellers' Volvo.

At the door they were warmly welcomed by Richard. Sarah, who minutely inspected Danielle's jade-green silk dress, said nothing until Danielle handed her an exquisitely wrapped box.

"Thank you, dear," Sarah simpered to no one in particular.

The living room, Danielle observed, was stuffed with the same domineering, professionally matched furniture, but the oxblood-red leather sofa was moved closer to the fireplace. It was occupied by Amos, Amy and Amy's brother, Raymond.

Detesting Amos, and having no interest in Raymond's unremarkable, pleasant features, Danielle focused her attention on Amy, who sat between the men. Amy was not magazine-ads gorgeous, but she radiated a wholesome beauty, and her dress discreetly outlined a very good figure. In the light emanating from the fireplace, Amy's fair complexion looked luminous, and her long blonde hair was streaked with gold.

Amos rose to greet Jonathan. He addressed "hello there" towards Danielle, held her fingers as briefly as possible, then sat down again. More congenial greetings were exchanged with Amy and Raymond before Danielle and Jonathan took their place on an oxblood-red plush love-seat. The conversation returned to a practical course Amy was taking in her graduate program. Jonathan good-humoredly teased her about becoming a psychologist. Raymond told an anecdote from his fraternity days. Danielle was about to mention King Solomon University but Amos cut her off. His derisive glance made her see how nicely the sofa's color contrasted Amy's ecru-colored dress, and how tacky her green dress looked on velvety red. Conscious of the fact that Amos was gloating that his fiancée completely outshone his brother's girlfriend, Danielle detested her would-be brother-in-law even more than before.

The entrance bell rang before Danielle could think of a proper reaction. She heard Richard welcome Joseph and Michelle, and then Sarah ask about Joyce and Julia (even though she had been told beforehand that they would not come). Smiling at Sarah's feigned surprise, Danielle rose to meet her parents. Just then, Graham and Alice arrived.

Richard quietly took everyone's coats and a bottle of fine cognac from Joseph, while Sarah fussed around Graham and Alice, wondered aloud whether they had found a close parking spot, and told them how much she appreciated their driving when the roads were slippery and the traffic was slow. The DeWitts smiled politely. When Alice gave Sarah a homemade fruitcake, Sarah thanked Alice all the way to the living room.

The hosts made introductions between the Mellers and DeWitts, everyone exchanged the expected niceties, the women assessed each other's dresses and jewelry.

"When will your adorable grandchildren come?" Sarah

cooed.

Alice replied that James, Fiona, and their children (her eldest son, his wife and Alice's grandchildren) would not be coming. Although Sarah twisted her lips in a rueful smile, she looked relieved.

After the usual pleasantries were over, Sarah invited her guests to the dining table. Taking a small serving from the nearest hors d'oeuvre, Graham complimented his hostess – the aesthetic presentation of the refreshments assured him of their exceptionally good taste. Danielle and Michelle exchanged glances, for everything on the table, from the dainty sandwiches to the mini quiches, bore the lavish signature of the excellent catering service of Chives and Tarragon. The food was good indeed, and the conversation flowed without falling into awkward silences. Flushed with her success, Sarah brought up Amos and Amy's wedding. To her disappointment, Amy did not gush with information, and Alice ventured details only when Sarah asked her directly. Richard, aware that Graham and Joseph were not interested in the topic, discreetly offered to supplement the food with something from the bar. His offer was readily accepted. The three men left the dining table, pretending not to notice Sarah glowering at her husband.

"Ray and I could use your input about investment and dividends in IT start-ups," Amos told Jonathan after seeing that no retribution followed his father's departure.

"Sure, let's go," Jonathan replied. The three younger men unscrupulously loaded their plates and went to eat and discuss stock-options by the fireplace. The women were left to themselves.

"It must be exciting to hear a daughter planning her biggest party," Michelle said to Alice. "Mine are grown up and live in other towns, but I occasionally feel like they are hiding somewhere in the house, plotting mischief."

"Mom also used to say that," Amy said. "Now, instead of James, Ray and me, she has Lizzy, Will, and Harry around her. Will and Harry justly look mischievous. Lizzy looks angelical, even though she is the most cunning of the three."

"She is a very bright child." Alice's voice was warm and affectionate. "Lizzy is the eldest. She looks like Amy used to look at eight."

"At eight, girls are sharp and observant," Michelle agreed. "Then, before we realize, they become preteens."

Sarah was surprised that Alice and Michelle could bond while reminiscing about raising daughters. She could not understand women choosing to raise their children over developing themselves professionally. And, teaching in high school, in Sarah's opinion, did not amount to having a career. Having little to contribute to the conversation, Sarah darted little snubs at Michelle, showed pointed deference for Alice and her opinions, then turned to Amy.

"I'm looking forward to see your wedding gown," Sarah said. "With your complexion and beautiful hair, you can look fabulous in any dress style you'll wear."

Amy smiled, but did not give away any information. Her good manners did not betray whether the flattery pleased her or not.

"I've heard from Amos that you would like to have the reception at your house," Sarah continued. "I think that a wedding at home would be too stressful a responsibility for a busy young couple."

"A wedding reception at the bride's house has been a long held tradition in Graham's and my families." Alice looked fondly at her daughter. Her tone of voice, however, was intended to thwart Sarah's impertinent suggestions. "Naturally, Amy wishes to carry on that tradition."

"We will manage," Amy added confidently.

Sarah looked petulantly at the pricy refreshments laid on the table. She hoped and planned to make a big impression on relatives, friends, and coworkers by inviting them to an upscale reception at the DeWitts' country club. It felt unfair that the wedding would be a small, laid-back affair at the DeWitts' old manor, with or without her approval.

Seeing Sarah bite her lip, Danielle felt pity for her. She darted an inquiring glance at Michelle, to ask what her mother was thinking. Michelle's expression was of polite indifference.

Mom could not care less, Danielle concluded. In fact, her mother was more likely to be amused than impressed by Alice and Amy's rigid adherence to a course set by a family tradition.

Observing Michelle, Danielle did not notice what was happening around the table, until Alice said to Amy, "Ray has asked me about your Gwen. Why don't you speak to him while he sits by himself?"

Every head turned to the sofa, where Raymond sat alone. Alice waited for Amy to leave the table, and then said, "Gwyneth Vannoy and Briana Philips have been Amy's best friends since childhood. We all expected that if Amy marries first, they would be her bridesmaids."

Danielle and Michelle diplomatically pursed their lips, while Sarah pretended that Alice did not speak.

"Would Amy like to hire the services of a professional wedding coordinator?" Sarah asked.

"No, Fiona offered to do the coordination and Amy agreed."

"Your daughter-in-law?" Sarah shrieked, momentarily forgetting herself. "Isn't Fiona taking care of three young children?"

"She can spare a few hours," Alice asserted. "Elizabeth and William go to school and Harry takes naps." She looked at the untouched hors d'oeuvre, then at the men at the bar. When Sarah did not respond to the hint, Alice amiably suggested, "Would we have some tea?"

"Alice and I will help Sarah," Michelle said to Danielle. Understanding that it was her chance to escape and seeing that Jonathan did not return yet to the living room, Danielle went to her father.

The bottle of Cognac was more than half empty. Richard, whom Danielle rarely heard speak about his work as an R&D executive in a biotechnological firm, was relating recent advances in cloning techniques. Hearing her father ask about possible implementations of cloned tissues in an operating room, Danielle stopped a few steps away from the bar. Richard replied using terms that even she understood, but his succinct explanation did not make the gritty topic more appealing. She turned to the fireplace and looked at the tiny tongues of flames. They danced, restrained but never tamed, casting a bewitching, primeval glow. No wonder our ancient ancestors kept undying flame in their temples, Danielle reflected. The tongues of flames stirred cravings for something transcending the expected and the commonplace.

"No wonder that the brightest minds are turning to biology and computer science," she heard DeWitt saying authoritatively. "That's where the future of science lies."

Danielle kept her stare fixed at flames licking the half burnt logs in the hearth, but her thoughts leaped to physicists working at CERN, and then to the discovery of dark energy. She doubted that Graham DeWitt had ever heard about it, let alone that the discovery had impressed him. Maybe it was a compliment to Richard and Jon, a thought flickered. Danielle cast away the suggestion. A DeWitt, she mused, would not bother to flatter the Lerners.

She became aware that she was watched from behind, but could not tell by whom.

"You don't have to keep a polite distance," Joseph said. "Come and share your views about future trends in science."

DeWitt turned, aptly including Danielle in the little circle. "Are you interested in the sciences?" he asked gallantly. She mustered a coy smile, and nodded when Richard offered her Cognac.

"Would you agree that progress there is self-empowering?" DeWitt inquired. "Our best talent gravitates to fields that spearhead scientific discoveries. The high percentage of outstanding scientists make these fields even more likely to bear fruit."

"That sounds convincing," Danielle said tentatively, for DeWitt's tone was patronizing and his "logic" appallingly superficial. She wanted to point out that he ignored unpredictable factors, that for breakthroughs, timely luck might be more important than genius and diligence combined. A warning glance from Richard reminded Danielle how much he disliked arguments.

"If the objective is to bear fruit fast," she said, "I think the future should belong to the TRP start-ups."

DeWitt concurred by raising his glass.

"I agree that talent is attracted to what is innovative," she added, "but scientists often choose the better funded fields because of practical needs. In theoretical branches, in particular, one is faced with a choice between working with practically nothing or having to constantly wheedle for grants."

"You do not suggest that scientists indiscriminately follow

the flow of money?" DeWitt asked. His tone of voice implied that the answer should be negative. "I'd expect that promising research would draw talent. Similarly, when research is about to bear fruit, it attracts funding."

"That is hardly relevant to theoretical disciplines, which rarely spawn new technologies." As she spoke, Danielle recalled the call for candidates for a faculty position posted on the second floor notice board. "A very talented scientist who has no career opportunities outside of academia, and very little within it, would shy away from tackling complicated, fundamental problems. The penalty for not being successful is too high to take the risk."

"But that is also an advantage of the current system, which controls spending and requires results," DeWitt said with infallible conviction. "Formerly nothing prevented talented people from wandering aimlessly or contemplating useless questions."

"Useless?" Danielle echoed.

"You would be surprised how many minds had cogitated over the number of angels that could be placed on a head of a pin." DeWitt laid down his glass, and looked at the sofa, where his son and daughter were sitting. "When Amy was nine or ten, she aspired to become a famous artist. She is still drawing occasionally, but she knows better than to expect to make a living out of her paintings. Taxpayers do not assist artists, and they shouldn't support gifted scientists engaged in pointless research."

Amazed that DeWitt could congratulate himself for dissuading his daughter, Danielle promised herself to never envy Amy again.

"Who will decide what is a pointless research?" she asked indignantly.

"Policymakers, based on recommendations of other scientists," DeWitt replied. "We live in a progressive, scientifically oriented society that is willing to support ambitious scientific ventures. Yet, we cannot expect that science, and especially science within academia, will regulate itself. Without following market-forces, it will be clogged by stagnation and mediocrity."

Unbelievable, Danielle thought, recalling how much time Green had spent on polishing his grant proposals.

Richard silently poured more cognac in glasses.

"Danielle has always romanticized science," Joseph said. "She does not see its weaknesses."

"Romanticizing is believing that scientists stumble on breakthroughs and discoveries. That would be nice, but regrettably, modern science is too complex to emulate the needs of a start-up incubated in a basement."

DeWitt looked at Danielle as if he was seeing her for the first time. "A very opinionated statement," he said. "Do you work in science?"

Richard and Joseph both laughed, and involuntarily, Danielle smiled.

"I'm a physicist. My field of research is cosmology."

"She is a post-doctorate fellow at King Solomon University," Joseph added proudly.

DeWitt's courteous smile revealed neither approval nor disapproval, but Danielle felt that his indifference demeaned her profession and also her family's legacy.

"I study the effects of dark energy on formation of galaxies during the early universe, and I vouch that in the foreseeable future this subject won't bear any fruits, except of papers in scientific journals." She looked archly at the lawyer, whose cuff-links probably cost more than a post-doc's weekly salary. "Do you think that it is a modern version of counting angels on a head of a pin?"

To Danielle's relief, DeWitt's face did not freeze into a blank, stony expression.

"Can I get some background before attempting to answer your question?"

Not expecting such politeness, Danielle nodded.

"After you find answers to these problems, would they be relevant to anything on Earth?"

It was a clever question, Danielle thought, and a tricky one. She could say "yes," but also say "no." A relevance of a theoretical research mostly depended on one's point of view.

"Graham, Joseph, Richard," Sarah cooed, "how about some tea with the cake Alice made?"

The men followed Sarah. Amos brought tea and cake for Amy, who stayed on the sofa with Raymond. Jonathan draped his arm around Danielle's waist, embraced her. The fist of his other hand was balled. A vein throbbed on his neck.

"What happened?" Danielle whispered, seeing fury smolder in Jon's eyes.

"Nothing."

"What did Amos want?" she insisted.

"Later."

Jonathan took her hand and they went to the dining table. Along with tea and coffee, there were little tarts and decadently rich petit fours from Pierre's. Alice's cake, the only homemade dessert, was the centerpiece.

"It smells heavenly," Michelle said to Alice. "Did you use rum or sherry?"

Without waiting for Alice's reply, they sat close to Danielle's parents. While Jonathan seethed with anger, Danielle and Michelle quietly caught up on how the other spent the New Year's Eve.

"I know that Amos egged you on," Danielle said to Jonathan when they were back in his car. "Will you tell me what did he say to affect you this way?"

Jonathan cupped her face with his hands, and looked squarely in her eyes.

"Amos likes to assess businesses and enterprises. He estimated your prospects at getting a tenure at TIST as 'a slim chance'."

It hurt even though the remark was typical of Amos. "So?" Danielle asked.

"Amos thinks that Nickka is going to be worth millions." Jonathan stopped. Danielle's blank stare indicated that she did not grasp the connection between her failing and Nickka's success. "Amos suggested that I cut my losses and ditch you, and look for a more suitable relationship."

Danielle was only surprised about how well Jon controlled his anger.

"What did you say to him?"

"That he was an idiot who sounded more DeWitt than Alice."

14

THE FIRST CANDIDATE

Chadwick Drive looked picturesque – the houses were shrouded in pristine snow, the road was covered with glittering mounds, green fir trees were adorned with fluffy white cups. Ambling down the street, Danielle reveled in the surrounding beauty. Contrary to what Jon thought, she didn't always seek a sweeping grandeur. What a homey serenity lacked in majesty and fantastic colors, it compensated with being welcoming.

Closer to the Main Street, the snow was not pristine white and the serenity gave way to warm cafés bustling with patrons, to a familiar normalcy of a workday morning. Danielle's contemplations turned to the simulations she was running on the group's cluster of computers. She crossed the road while thinking about the fate of the toy universe, and went through King Solomon University's main entrance. She stopped right there. The campus, that had been draped in frozen, drabby browns in December, donned a glamorous mantle. The dazzling white extravaganza sparkled as if giddy fairies had scattered millions of icy diamonds over the snow.

A new beginning, Danielle hoped, as she walked along a narrow path through a knee-deep snow. Everything looked different: Alexander Hall had shed some of its dignified pomposity, and the old chapel seemed more Gothic with its turrets half-covered. Even Fitzgerald Hall's façade looked better, with snow lightening up its gray pediment.

On the second floor, the doors of the professors' offices were closed. Passing by the notice board, Danielle glanced at the end-of-term assignments and notifications about final exams, then skimmed announcements about conferences and summer -schools. In the place of the department's call for candidates was pinned a new notice.

Brian LaCompte will give a talk on:
Anisotropies in Cosmic Microwave Background Radiation.
The talk will take place in the Lounge (room 10) on Monday, January 12th, at 11am.

Wondering whether LaCompte was a candidate who made it to the interview stage, she entered into the secretaries' office. Only Amanda was there, leaning over a desk cluttered with newspapers.

"Happy New Year!" Danielle said.

"Happy New Year!" Amanda cocked her head to a box standing on Marjory's desk. "Try the chocolates. They are superb."

"Thanks. How is Marjory's daughter doing?"

"Laura is fine. She gave birth to a healthy baby girl."

Coming closer to Amanda's desk, Danielle noticed on it newspaper cuts congratulating Mr. and Mrs. Adam Klein on the birth of their grandchild. A particularly large one was from the employees of Seawell, Gilliken, and Klein, an intellectual property law firm. Other cuts were from local businesses and institutions Danielle had never heard of.

"I'm preparing a scrapbook with congratulations for Marjory." Amanda unearthed an album from under the newspapers. Its delicate pink cover brought a broad smile to Danielle's face.

"Marjory will appreciate it," Danielle said. "Do you know when she will be back?"

"Not before the beginning of the spring term."

Danielle's smile turned into an inquiring look, one that asked whether there were any problems that prevented Marjory from returning in a few days.

"It's going to rile half of the faculty when they find out that Marjory is in Houston while two candidates are coming," Amanda said quietly. "Not that anyone will say a word in her face."

"Why not?" Danielle asked. Green did not shy away from showing his displeasure and other professors could be even less polite.

Why not? Amanda repeated in her mind as she looked at the

photo of her boys. Why, in addition to doing her work and a large portion of Marjory's, she had to tackle stupid questions from highly educated people?

"Do you remember," Amanda asked, "a form you have signed that transfers all the rights to your work to the university?"

Unable to recall what she had signed back in September, Danielle shook her head.

"The law firm that handles these affairs for the university is named Seawell, Gilliken and Klein. Klein stands for Adam Klein, Marjory's husband."

Imagining the influence and the money involved in being a partner in such a firm, Danielle reflected that Marjory could do worse than drive a slick Saab and flaunt expensive jewelry.

"No one will demand Mrs. Adam Klein to show up when she is fussing over her grandchild," Amanda continued. "They'll cross their fingers and hope she won't be tempted to become a full-time grandma."

"But the distance between Hopeville and Houston..."

"Not a real problem for Marjory. Unlike the professors here, she can fly at a whim, in business-class."

Danielle envisioned a dressed up and bejeweled Marjory hopping on a plane. Even Green, she decided, would not dare to make any noises.

"Can I see the congratulations?" she asked Amanda. Getting the album, Danielle opened it on the first page and read:

"The Physics Department of King Solomon University congratulates Adam and Marjory Klein and Prof. and Mrs. Jonah Cobs on the birth of their granddaughter, Kim Eloise Cobs."

Cobs??? Danielle willed her jaws to remain in their place, but could not prevent thoughts from flickering in her head like fireflies in the dark. She remembered that Anne had said she and Jonah have a daughter named Gemma. Jonah, she recalled, had spoken about Gemma's literary ambitions and her having dabbled in physics. She could not recollect either Jonah or Anne mentioning a son, let alone a son married to Marjory's daughter.

Danielle recalled her speculations after seeing Jonah and Marjory dinning at Lucas Lodge. Had she known that they were related... She closed the album, took a wrapped chocolate candy, thanked Amanda and turned to leave.

"Tell Chi to come over and have one before grad students will finish them off," Amanda called after her. Danielle said that she would.

Ten minutes later, Danielle was reassured that her three jobs were still running, and began examining the files her program generated in her absence. After several weeks of crunching equations, the toy universe had finally passed its first billion years milestone. Excited that it reached a stage when it should start forming first structures, Danielle made a mental list of what she should look for.

When our universe was a billion years old, it emerged from "dark ages" (a period of a few hundred million years when it had been re-ionized and opaque), became transparent again and for the first time was dotted with stars. The first galaxies began to form during its second billion years. In a simulation of the toy universe, matter densities were too low to create stars. But that hardly mattered to Danielle. All she needed was for the simulation to track the essentials of galaxies' and clusters of galaxies' formation.

It took minutes for the graphics software to upload the most recent snapshots.

"Rats," she muttered seeing the first image. The toy universe on the screen resembled noodles swimming in soy sauce.

Her heart pounded faster and faster as she checked other snapshots and zoomed in and out in a search for discernible lumps of matter. At the sight of iridescent lobes streaked with dark tunnels, her shoulders relaxed. Without data analysis, it was only a guess, but the scattered clusters of dark and regular matter looked like progenitors of galaxies and of larger structures.

Reassured that nothing went terribly wrong with the toy universe, Danielle walked to the Hungry Boson to congratulate Anne. Happy in Anne's happiness, she returned to Fitzgerald Hall in an excellent mood, and set herself to calculate the distributions of dark and regular matter density for every snapshot.

In the following days, Danielle tackled the structures' characterization, quantified the correlations within and between matter lumps, and then attempted to compare her data with published distributions of dark and regular matter. Matching correlations calculated from her simulations, against correlations calculated for observed galaxies and clusters of galaxies, turned out to be painstakingly complicated. It was not like counting angels on a head of a pin. On the contrary, assessing the validity of the toy model promised to be a long, nasty slog.

Since the fate of her post-doctorate depended on having noteworthy results, she pressed herself to complete the analysis before Green's return. Meanwhile, her simulations ran uninterrupted. The toy universe almost reached its two billion years mark.

On the day Green came back, Danielle printed plots that summed the data analysis and a few snapshots that visualized different stages in matter accumulation. She had hoped that dark energy would begin to affect the toy universe's evolution, even though its density was a fraction of mass energy density. To her disappointment, dark energy did not have so far any measurable effects.

Waiting for Green's call stretched for hours. Too nervous to handle equations, she searched the preprint archive for recent papers about dark energy. As Green had predicted, there was a deluge. Narrowing her search to studies that combed through cosmological parameters relevant to her project, she found that a couple of groups were further ahead with simulations quite similar to what she was doing.

The situation, Danielle realized, was pretty serious. These groups had already submitted papers for publication, and barring a miracle, the work she was doing would not have the innovative edge required to be published in a good journal. She felt apprehension rise and cloud her thinking. She fought it, knowing she had to be at her best when she talked to Green. To while away the time, she skimmed other preprints.

By the time Green locked his office, Danielle had more evidence that dark energy inhibited the growth of larger structures and tore apart already formed super-clusters. She did not, however, stumble on any new, measurable phenomena caused by dark energy. She trudged home, suffering from a stress-induced headache. Not wanting to exacerbate it, she cast aside thoughts about why Green had not called her, and dwelt on what she had read. Dark energy was the universe's largest reservoir of energy, and it had been around for billions of years. Yet, trawling through tens of preprints concerning structures' evolution, she found no evidence that dark energy made any difference in the first few billion years of universe's existence.

That night, Danielle's sleep was fraught with dreams. She saw fantastic colors illuminate the sky, and the Pacific shore awash with vermillion and orange. She and Jon were alone, their legs and arms entwined, their tongues seeking and probing. Reenacting the steamy moment, Danielle rolled in her bed. In the dream, she also rolled, but somehow disentangled from Jonathan and kept rolling into the water. A current carried her away from the shore, towards the sun setting into the horizon. The land faded, the vivid sky above blurred, soon every trace of color disappeared from sight. She was drawn from the ocean's surface, pulled into the mouth of a gray, shapeless abyss. Danielle woke up before daybreak, to the sounds of Amos gloating that she would never stand a chance to get a tenured position at TIST.

The following day was similarly strained. Danielle tried to focus on the new data files, but a discordant chorus in her head kept grumbling that Green had forced the simulations on her, without having interest in the results. Many times that day, Danielle's stare wandered from the monitor to the window, where the snow, like her enthusiasm, had lost its spark and freshness. Shortly before six, Green phoned her.

"How are you?" Green asked when Danielle came into his office. He gestured her to sit down.

"Good." She handed Green eight colorful snapshots. "These were taken at different times between seven hundred million and two point one billion years."

"What is the mass ratio?" Green asked as he strewed the pages over his desk.

"Five to one," Danielle replied. She had picked this value because observations indicated that dark matter density was about five times that of regular matter density.

She described what the simulations did, answered questions, and sat quietly while Green studied the patterns in the structures and the network of voids.

"Have you compared your data with published simulations?"

"Yes." Danielle pointed at one of the plots she brought. "The distribution of clusters' sizes is similar at later times."

There was no hint of approval in Green's expression, nothing to indicate whether he contemplated dispensing with the toy model or looked for ways to improve it.

"These runs take too much time," he finally said. "You should work on speeding up your program."

Danielle, however, thought that the slowness of the code was the least of her problems. She expected that Green, who followed every notable trend in cosmology and regularly skimmed through papers in *Astrophysical Journal, Physical Review Letters, Nature*, and *Science*, would share his insights and would point as to how to improve the model. She had not anticipated that his input would consist of instructions which offered nothing except minute, albeit just, criticism. Her mind whirled with thoughts. Some concerned physics, others were worries that Green considered her work as inept.

A fluorescent light flickered over their heads, drawing Danielle's attention to the walls' luminescent, pearly glow. A shudder run through her spine as she recalled their first meeting, how she had caved when Green had discouraged her interest in the origins of dark energy. During the intervening months, she had tried to put into words what she felt in her bones. After being told off for doing so, she learned not to voice raw thoughts.

Yet, she could not let Green deduce that the toy model's mediocre results was the best she could do. Anticipating his frown at a suggestion that dark energy mattered even when its density was small compared to matter density, Danielle focused her eyes at the physics books behind Green.

"If dark energy density decreases with time," she said hesitatingly, "it might have been relatively small but not negligible when first galaxies started to form. I searched in the archive, but didn't find any preprints on the topic. I believe that a study of dark energy's effect on universe's evolution at early times could evolve into an interesting research."

"A vaguely defined research," Green dryly corrected. "You may spend months without getting anything worth publishing."

That was a disheartening possibility. Unfortunately, Danielle deemed that having her post rely solely on Green's toy model was an even worse option.

"If you want to succeed in science," Green added, "find a question which is bound to bear results."

Even if the answer doesn't make any difference? Danielle asked in her mind. She willed herself to look at Green. Then she said, "I know what there is at the stake if I don't find any new effects."

For a reason Danielle could not fathom, Green did not immediately dismiss what she said. She held her breath while he weighed her words.

"Did you take a graduate level course in general relativity?" Green asked.

She could not utter "yes," even though she had taken such a course. At least, not in a good conscience. The lecturer of the said course, professor Toby Butte from high-energy physics, was accustomed to work with eleven dimensions, and had been extremely uncomfortable with general relativity's four. Only Zeeman and a couple of other graduate students had followed Toby's crooked explanations, while the rest had learned preciously little from his lectures. She and others like her had relied on the first few chapters of Wald's *General Relativity* and on Toby's compassion when he marked the midterm and final exams. Seeing a flush of impatience cross Green's face, Danielle concluded she knew enough, and said "yes."

"Leave these." Green gestured at the snapshots and the pages with the data analysis, then lifted the phone's receiver. Understanding that it was her cue to leave, Danielle rose up.

"Can I implement a decreasing dark energy density in my program?" she asked.

"First work on streamlining your simulations," Green said, starting to dial.

The moment Danielle closed the door behind Green's office, she stopped suppressing her rising anger.

"He expects me to work days and nights on a model that interests no one," she ranted over the phone, while recounting to her mother what had happened. "But he's too busy to pay the smallest attention to what I suggest."

"You have said many times that Green is a leading researcher in the field." Michelle's voice was laced with sympathy, but it was not indulging. "He might have other reasons."

"I'm not questioning his knowledge or choices. In fact, in proposing to study a new aspect of structures' evolution, I counted on his insights."

"Can't you ask him for another meeting?"

A smile broke through Danielle's irritated expression. The question intimated that her mother believed in what she was doing.

"I can," Danielle said, "but it'll be useless. Green won't venture into a research without giving it an in-depth consideration. On the other hand, with candidates coming and his teaching obligations, he doesn't have any time to mull it over."

"I wonder," Michelle said, "whether Green would let a good idea slip."

"He doesn't consider my arguments as a good idea. Ironically, a tenured professor who can afford experimenting, prefers to pass up the opportunity rather than try a new approach which may not succeed."

"Did he say that to you explicitly?"

"Not in these words," Danielle grumbled. "He merely told me to work first on expediting the simulations."

"That isn't the same."

"I know." Danielle sighed. "Do you advise me to do as he said?"

"I suggest you use common sense and think it over. Now," Michelle's intonation implied that the discussion about Green was over, "when will you come to Thorboro?"

"Mom." Danielle's voice resonated with righteous indignation. "I can't take a weekend off so soon after returning from a vacation."

In Thorboro, Michelle stifled a sigh and rubbed her throbbing forehead. She and Joseph had expected Jonathan to propose over the holidays, but when Danielle talked about their vacation, she raved about the cliffs and sunsets or reminisced about local restaurants. Marriage was never mentioned. Nor any plans to share the same roof in the near future.

"We have to invite the Lerners for dinner," Michelle said. "What about the weekends before and after your birthday?"

In a little house on Chadwick Drive, Danielle rolled her eyes. "Do I have to?" she protested.

"I'll speak with your father and with Sarah," Michelle continued. "Don't worry about the airfare. It's part of our present."

Considering Green's abysmal interest in her work, Danielle did not bring up other objections. Having a weekend with Jon to look forward to made it easier to put very long hours into improving her code.

* * *

On the morning of January the twelfth, Danielle was yet again waging a war against a new crop of bugs. She did not react when the door swung and Ben stuck his head into the office. Chi got up immediately.

"Are you coming?" Ben asked.

"Coming where?"

"To the Lounge. The candidate is going to give a talk in ten minutes."

"Dr. Green will be there," Chi added, to remind Danielle that although no one asked grad students and post-docs for their opinion about the candidate, their attendance was mandatory.

Descending the stairs, Danielle pictured the candidate as a gladiator, who would shortly sweat blood in front of the faculty, gathered to watch him slip. The Lounge, however, did not have the ominous look of an arena. A white screen covered the old blackboard, and rows of chairs replaced the refreshments table, which was relegated to one of the walls. She saw the usual cookies and the urns with hot water, but also a large tray heaped with raisin and blueberry muffins, a tray with bite-size Cheddar cheese cubes, and plates with crackers shaped like snowflakes. The muffins were snatched very quickly, and Danielle ended up grabbing one of the last left. She edged to Chi, who stood by himself, staring at two untouched halves of his muffin.

"Don't you like raisins?" Her muffin was fresh and generously studded with blueberries. "I don't think there are any blueberries left."

"I don't want another muffin." Chi eyed the dark raisins. "My son nearly choked on a raisin cake."

"Did he?" Danielle asked, her voice inviting Chi to go on.

"I used it to explain to my wife how the universe expands."

Danielle smothered a smile. For some unfathomable reason, the sight of raisins in dough triggered in physicists a need to explain to non-physicists how the universe evolved. Usually they made an analogy between raisins and galaxies, and between the expansion of dough during baking and the growth of distances in expanding universe. Taking the entire cake to represent the universe, physicists used raisins to illustrate that faraway galaxies receded from each other during expansion, whereas galaxies' shapes and sizes did not change.

"I once tried to explain to my great-aunt that gravitationally bound objects don't expand while the space around them does," Danielle said. Aunt Sophie, she recalled, did not care about the raisin-in-dough analogy, but she was scandalized by Danielle not knowing the difference between baking powder and baking soda. "How did your wife like the explanation?"

"I don't know. Lei was with us, eating while I explained. Suddenly, he began to choke."

"Did you take him to the emergency room?"

"No, it was not that serious, but he screamed and was very frightened. We could not understand why."

Danielle finished her muffin and waited for Chi to elaborate.

"Lei thought the pieces of cake would keep growing inside his stomach. My wife was angry long after he fell asleep."

"I can imagine that," Danielle said emphatically, thinking about Dorian gagging in presence of Natalie.

She looked around, saw professors mingling in small groups, grad students and post-docs aggregated in larger clusters, and a few who lingered by the refreshments table. Green was not in the room.

"Is Green bringing the candidate?"

"Yes. I see them coming in."

The candidate was dressed in a navy blue suit and carried a laptop. He followed Green closely as Green maneuvered between the groups, stopping to make introductions to other professors. At ten past eleven, Green raised a hand and called everyone to sit down. The groups unhurriedly dissolved, faculty members taking their place at the front rows, students and post-docs sitting at the back. LaCompte, pale and palpably nervous, turned on his computer. In a moment, the Harvard University logo proudly shone above him.

"Evolution of Anisotropies in Cosmic Microwave Background Radiation (CMBR)," Danielle read from the screen. "Brian LaCompte, Harvard University."

She glanced at LaCompte's pasty baby face, eyed his hideously bright, poisonous green necktie, and the baggy pants he was too narrow to fill. LaCompte was younger than her, Danielle thought. His appearance brought to mind a gangly teenager forced to wear a suit.

Green, who stood erect like a lamppost beside the fidgeting candidate, looked as distinguished as the Victorians watching from the portraits on the walls. Ignoring the screeching chairs and whispering voices, he welcomed Brian to the King Solomon University and introduced him to the audience.

"Brian attended Penn as an undergraduate, Columbia for graduate studies." Green paused respectfully after each Ivy League university. "Currently, he's a post-doc at Harvard."

While Green went over LaCompte's awards and achievements, Danielle mused that no candidate could wish for a more favorable introduction. By the time Green reached Harvard, he lost his habitual self-possession and nearly drooled.

She watched LaCompte step forward, hesitantly thank the front rows for the invitation and Green for the introduction, then flip to a second slide. The screen was filled with the image of an ancient Greek temple surrounded by an azure sky. Before Danielle could cast her mind back to the trip to Italy, LaCompte clicked on the image, and the Mediterranean sky vanished, the temple was stripped of everything but a crepidoma and three Doric columns. A title, "Cosmological Standard Model," materialized over it.

"The three pillars are the observational evidence that holds together the standard model," LaCompte said. After a click, the word "expansion" appeared on the leftmost column, "CMBR" on the central one, and in very small letters, "abundance of light elements" was squeezed on the third column.

"General Relativity is the framework that enables us to analyze observations and put them into a context." With another click, "General Relativity" was stretched over the crepidoma.

"The Cosmic Microwave Background Radiation is the earliest direct cosmological evidence," LaCompte continued. "It dates back to an ionized, opaque universe, about 380,000 years after the Big Bang."

CMBR were photons that decoupled from baryonic (also known as regular) matter, when electrons and protons recombined into neutral hydrogen. Since the universe was about 380,000 years old, these photons drifted in space, hardly scattering from matter.

He clicked on the "CMBR" column and an oval, vividly orange shape filled the screen.

"COBE's detectors have measured the CMBR temperature to be 2.75 degrees Kelvin throughout the sky. This finding establishes that if the red-shift of the background radiation was isotropic throughout the sky, the universe had been homogeneous and isotropic when photons decoupled from matter."

Gravity clumped matter together, unless it was countered by an opposing force. Radiation decoupled from regular (baryonic) matter much later than it decoupled from dark matter. Consequentially, while photons' pressure pushed apart regular matter, dark matter could begin to accumulate.

"Before protons and electrons recombined, radiation pressure suppressed the growth of inhomogeneities in baryonic matter density." LaCompte went on. "Dark matter, on the other hand, decoupled from radiation at earlier times. So small inhomogeneities in dark matter continued to grow."

While LaCompte gave a quick survey of what happened with the relic photons, Danielle reflected that the years he spent at Ivy League physics departments rubbed off on his presentation. His initial awkwardness disappeared. He spoke with the confidence of one who had followed the evolution of CMBR countless times.

LaCompte stopped, then flickered to the next slide. All of a sudden, the screen burst with a lively collage of colors. The Victorian Lodge was awash with dapples of dark and sapphire-blue, patches of green that matched LaCompte's necktie, and bright spots of sunflower yellow.

"Each color describes a tiny deviation from CMBR average temperature," LaCompte said. Since radiation and matter had been in a near equilibrium at the time of decoupling, the colors also mirrored local inhomogeneities in the distribution of matter density. From this time forward, these inhomogeneities would grow immensely and become the progenitors of stars and galaxies.

"After correcting for the dipole term arising from our motion relative the CMBR rest frame," LaCompte pointed at a swath of bright red that belted the collage in its middle, "we are left with a mapping of the anisotropies in the microwave background radiation. These anisotropies are not accounted for by the standard model. They do not undermine it either."

These anisotropies, Danielle thought, were a hot research topic that involved many established and budding careers. Since they were also closely related to her work, she listened attentively when LaCompte turned to the mathematical apparatus that translated the colors into perturbations in matter density. Complex mathematical derivations were followed by slides showing how well theoretical calculations agreed with the high-resolution data streaming from COBE. Aside from briefly mentioning "Inflation," LaCompte did not discuss the inhomogeneities' origins. Instead, he described a sophisticated software that tracked the perturbations through major cosmological epochs, outlined the difficulties it encountered, and discoursed on the evolution of interrelated multidimensional variables. Next, he gave a detailed explanation on how an intricate modification to a commercial software package had helped in finding solutions.

He does what others do, only better, Danielle mused. Even though LaCompte did not spare himself nor the restless audience in the back-seats, she had little doubt that Green would be happy to have him at King Solomon University.

Wondering what other professors thought about LaCompte's research, she scanned the first row. Green sat in the middle, his head slightly bent forward as if he was lost in thoughts. Beside him, Brophy was scribbling something in semi-darkness. On his other side, Axelrod leaned back, as if he was catching a brief nap. Farther left, Lisitsin was slumped in his seat. Danielle shifted her stare, but she did not see Cobs. The monotonous sound of snoring caught her attention. To her surprise, it did not come from the back rows, where high-energy grad students barely muffled their yawns or disguised their whispering. A glance sideways revealed an elderly professor who fell asleep, with his head tilted backwards, and his mouth unbecomingly open.

LaCompte paused, his eyes scanned those seated in the first two or three rows, then returned to the screen. Stifling a yawn, Danielle looked at plots that neatly condensed the numerous results LaCompte was talking about. His best fits for the baryon density, the dark matter density and the cosmological constant density were impressive. The last slide was for conclusions; the last topic was a schematic survey of the Harvard group's ongoing research. He was done exactly on time. Green came ahead as the lights turned on and thanked Brian. The audience applauded. There were no questions.

"I bet George is ecstatic about Brian coming here," Ben said when they entered into Danielle and Chi's office. "A software that backtracks perturbations and calculates on the fly how each parameter affects the anisotropy spectrum. Don't you think it's superb?"

"It is," Chi agreed.

Danielle thought mournfully about her simulation. Whatever improvements she might make, it would never reach the level of LaCompte's or even Chi's programs.

"Did you get how he modified the commercial package and integrated it with his code?" Ben asked.

"It's very difficult." Chi shook his head. "I'm not sure it can run on our computers."

Chi's realism deflated some of Ben's enthusiasm. He turned to Danielle with, "You seem to disagree. What faults did you find with him?"

A dull presentation of a research which didn't reveal anything intrinsically new, Danielle thought.

"The sheer volume of his talk was impressive," she said. "He is good, but he'll bore any student senseless."

Unwilling to rave about the group's dream candidate, she took her stained mug and went to the kitchenette. Lisitsin was there, brewing coffee. She greeted the towering professor and waited for him to move from the sink.

"The candidate from Harvard showed excellent command of computational techniques," Lisitsin commented. "Interesting results. Pity that the presentation was not backed by a sound theoretical model."

Surprised that Lisitsin was talking to her, Danielle nodded in agreement.

"The anisotropies in CMBR spectrum might be applied to impose an upper bound on angular velocity," Lisitsin added as an afterthought.

Having no inkling whose angular velocity he was talking about, Danielle silently watched as he poured coffee.

"The equations of motion would be too complex to have an analytical solution," he warned, bobbing his head. "We'll adjust the field equations and feed them to a numerical program."

We? Danielle repeated in her mind. Aside from gathering that Lisitsin could mentally modify non-linear field equations, she was clueless of what he was talking about.

Oblivious of her bafflement, Lisitsin added, "I'll speak to George. We might need the software package they're using at Harvard."

Late that evening, she told Jonathan about the candidate's talk. "He wowed everyone with his software," she recounted the group response.

"Haven't I told you to focus on algorithms and code?"

The triumphant note in Jonathan's voice did not escape Danielle. "I'll never be good at programming, but that shouldn't deter you from patting yourself on the back for hammering the point home."

"Why do you always have to complain before you pull yourself together? You are more pigheaded than Paul when you cling to your prejudices."

"Something weird must be happening at Nickka," Danielle retorted. "My guess is that Zeeman let you have your way with the code."

"He does occasionally, when Katie occupies his mind."

"Is Katie a code name for some software?"

"She is a real flesh and blood woman," Jonathan said.

"I can hardly believe that Zeeman thinks about a woman when he fiddles with algorithms. Have you ever seen her?"

"No."

"How then did you find out?"

"Paul wrote a program that weights different presents Katie

might like to get on Valentine's Day. It runs on Nickka's servers."

That, Danielle admitted, definitely sounded like Zeeman.

"Did you tell him to stop it before Pilcher finds out?"

"Pilcher?" Jonathan echoed, clearly amused. "Roy noticed that the servers were running a heavy implementation and asked me about it. I found out what it was doing, then had a talk with Paul."

Pity crept unwarrantably. "It's sad that when Zeeman finally discovers human emotions, he does something that stupid."

"Didn't you tell me repeatedly that he is a jerk?"

"I didn't suspect he could feel anything except superiority. What do you think Roy will do? He won't sack him for misusing Nickka resources?"

"Of course not," Jonathan said between chuckles. "If Paul pulls it off, it could be worth another patent."

"Seriously?" Relief wiped out pity. "Zeeman is lucky it's up to Roy. I hate Roy's insane schedules, but I wish Green had a bit of his style."

"Starts-ups brim with style," Jonathan said lightly. "Boost your computing skills and you'll be welcome."

"Sure," she answered in the same tone. "Right after you tell me which start-up tackles dark energy."

"For that," Jonathan retorted, "you'll need to find something useful that dark energy does."

"Excellent advice," she said. "If I could pull that off, I'd receive a Nobel Prize on top of a faculty position."

15

ROTATING UNIVERSE

A week after LaCompte's presentation, graduate students, post-docs, and professors gathered again at the Lounge to hear the second candidate's talk on "Accretion of Matter by Rotating Black-Holes." When the candidate came in, Danielle first noticed that his red-and-gray striped necktie irreproachably matched a fitting dark suit. After a short observation, she found out that he bore himself more like a distinguished guest than a candidate for an assistant professor position. He looked at the muffins, cheddar cheese, and upgraded crackers, then passed the food without touching it. "There is no point in wrinkling your nose," she wanted to tell the guy. "If you are lucky to get an offer and see the refreshments at the regular physics seminars, you'd learn to appreciate when Amanda goes an extra mile."

The slight disdain on the candidate's face turned into a snooty expression when he surveyed the portraits on the walls. They aren't much of an art? Danielle cattily thought. Even if the drawings were inferior to the ones hung in his Medieval university, the somber Victorians deserved respect as part of Fitzgerald Hall traditions.

At eleven sharp, Susan Brophy introduced Mathias Kramer and stepped aside to let him say all the appropriate things. As soon as the lights were dimmed, the audience saw a pair of huge, flaming jets move on the screen. The jets shifted, changed course, and gradually started to swirl. Drawn to the fiery spouts, most of the eyes did not notice a small, spinning black sphere in the middle of the screen. It looked innocuous, unless one realized that the jets could not break out of the eye of the storm's irresistible grip. They spiraled inward, moving closer and closer, dancing with excruciating slowness all the way to the rim of the restless, devouring blackness.

The dramatic demonstration of accretion of matter by a rotating black-hole was followed by a slide with Einstein equations. Other slides methodically expounded a solution to these equations under simplifying assumptions. Danielle more or less understood the mathematical expressions on the first five or six slides. After the tenth, she began to lose the gist. She noted that Chi, who sat one chair to the right, stared at the slides with a glazed expression. Ben, who sat a couple of chairs to the left, did not even bother to look at the screen.

Concluding that the presentation was too technical to learn anything from it, Danielle decided that listening to the candidate would be a complete waste of time. Kramer did not need a sizable audience to boost his self-assurance. He would have spoken with the same pedantic authority to the few who had expertise in the field.

Having time on her hands, she shifted her thoughts to a phone call from Michelle about the dinner with the Lerners. Mom hadn't said why the dinner had to be put back to the end of February, Danielle recalled. As a matter of fact, Michelle gave no explanations and only asked her not to book a flight to Thorboro yet.

Richard might attend a conference or have a business meeting out of town, Danielle mused, but it's unlikely he'd be away for two weekends in succession. And Jon, he would have made up something to be in Thorboro for her birthday. Rats. She should have thought about Sarah in the first instance.

Clueless as to why Sarah piled delays, Danielle looked resentfully at her watch. The audience's apathy did not seem to dent the candidate's self-assurance. But maybe his overconfidence was an act. Some people, Danielle mused, can keep their pretensions even when they fawn those who snub them. Sarah, for example, acted however it pleased her with those she did not look up to, but Sarah would not decline Alice DeWitt's invitation, even if she'd have to call off a previous engagement.

A female voice suddenly said, "Thank you Mathias for the illuminating presentation," then it paused to let the somnolent audience realize that it finally ended. Someone clapped. Others joined.

"Any questions?" Susan Brophy added, her eyes skipping over the rows.

Please don't, Danielle silently implored. The gathered professors thought differently.

Green asked about the simulations that were used to create the movie. Lisitsin suggested something about the metric of rotating black-holes. Guys from high-energy physics fired questions related to quantum gravity.

It was past noon when the fuzzy physicists finally sauntered from the Lounge. Few could indulge themselves with shutting the door of their office, reclining on a comfortable armchair and lifting their legs on a desk. Professor Andrei Lisitsin did exactly so, then he folded his arms and closed his eyes, so nothing would distract him while he contemplated a brand new idea that sprang in his mind during Mathias' talk.

A few minutes later, he muttered "interesting", and after a short while, he jotted a couple of mathematical expressions on a piece of paper. The analogy between a spinning black hole and a closed rotating universe was something he would be glad to discuss with Mathias. Recalling that he would not see the candidate again, he shifted his thoughts to the forthcoming lunch with George. In all, it was fitting that George was his favorite colleague at the physics department. George Green was sharp, shrewd and pragmatical, and on top of that, an excellent physicist.

"Excellent physicist" meant a lot to Lisitsin. Physics was both his profession and his hobby, and even though he had changed wives and countries, his love for physics never wavered. His mind was intrigued by the riddles physics posed, and riddles drove him to look for solutions. He worked mostly by himself, but readily collaborated with colleagues who sought his mathematical wizardry and his thorough knowledge of general relativity. With George, the collaboration deepened into something resembling comradeship.

Before leaving his office, Lisitsin cast an appreciative glance at the equations sprawled on the whiteboard and smirked. He had already told George about his rotating universe model. Now, he could assert that his model was the key to dark energy.

"Brian will be an asset to the department," Green said as soon as he and Lisitsin left Fitzgerald Hall. "He works in the front line of research, he is quick at simulations and is also well-rounded."

Green's unusually insistent tone of voice brought a thin, noncommittal smile from Lisitsin. "What you mean is that Brian fits into a familiar mold and Mathias doesn't," Lisitsin wanted to say. George, despite his self-professed open-mindedness, was comfortable with a candidate schooled in the Ivy League universities, but not with the more refined European style. Since there was nothing new or intriguing in his colleague's prejudices, Lisitsin's thoughts returned to the rotating universe. He felt animation, an eagerness to speak about his vision, to announce that his colossal effort was on the verge of fruition. Keeping in mind that George had not shown lately even a perfunctory interest in his model, he decided to wait and broach the news properly. Meanwhile, he was willing to indulge his colleague and to find more about the departmental politics.

"I got the impression that the searching committee was looking for outstanding candidates from different backgrounds," Lisitsin airily commented.

"It was pressed to look for diversity, but that isn't why Kramer was invited. He wouldn't be here today if the committee hadn't complied to Susan's prodding. It issued the invitation, although it was evident that his specialization is too narrow."

"Mathias is a mathematical physicist." Lisitsin pronounced the words "mathematical physicist" as if it was a much coveted scientific prize. "I think that he also has a background in computers. His movie was good."

"Very good," Green tersely agreed. "Unfortunately, he didn't mention that the simulations and the movie were done by Amit Srinivasan."

"Who?"

"A graduate student in Emil Lang's group," Green explained. "Kramer's reply to my question indicated that he doesn't know much about simulations. I found a link to the movie when I checked Lang's group homepage. I've just viewed it again, this time with the acknowledgments."

"I see," Lisitsin said. George would not confront Susan, but he would ensure that whoever needed to know would hear about the movie.

They passed the faculty clubhouse, where the candidate, unaware that he would never get an offer, was having a lunch in the stuffy dining room. Lisitsin shrugged. Kramer, despite his knowledgeable and sophisticated appearance, was a sloppy fool.

"Does that leave us with Brian or are there other candidates?"

"Brian is excellent," Green said, "but I expect we'll have another round before the search committee concludes that he is the best."

They walked briskly, each professor immersed in his thoughts. Leaving the university campus, Lisitsin recollected that he hadn't yet handed in the receipts of his travel expenses. Preferring to address Marjory rather than Amanda (whom he disliked), he asked, "Do you know when Marjory will return?"

"She planned," Green stressed the last word, "to be back at the end of the month."

Knowing better than to bring up the department's wishy-washy leniency to the secretary's extended absence, Lisitsin dropped the subject.

King's Kitchen, a pub and restaurant, was half a block away from the university's main entrance. The food there was good, the service fast and friendly to regulars; the pleasantly dignified atmosphere drew professors in and scared students away. When Green and Lisitsin were welcomed in, the peak of the lunch hour was over. Nevertheless, King's Kitchen bustled with patrons.

"Well," Green said after a waitress left with their orders. He leaned back, indicating he was ready to hear about Andrei's research.

"As you may remember," Lisitsin stopped to clear his throat, "after the discovery of dark energy, I was suspicious of the many explanations that started to pop up. It still baffles me that otherwise competent physicists rushed to look for new interactions or posit extra dimensions. Likewise, I cannot understand the reasoning of those who hastened to reinstate Einstein's cosmological constant. It simply does not make any sense to do so."

"I remember," Green said dryly. Andrei shunned every explanation high-energy physicists came up with, and habitually referred to the resurrection of Einstein's cosmological constant as "sheer idiocy". Having no taste for empty philosophical discussions, Green made no comments. He had learned that without encouragement, Andrei would soon stop criticizing the shortcomings of other physicists and start talking about physics.

"It turned out that I have been right all along," Lisitsin went on. "A rotating universe is a physically plausible explanation. Equally important is that it doesn't require extrapolations or experimentally unattainable physics. In that, rotating universe stands out amid perennial models like Inflation."

Green weighed the argument while the waitress served his entree and a bowl of soup with a basket of bread for Andrei.

"Inflation is unlikely to remain unchecked for long," Green said after the waitress had left. "The resolution in the background radiation data will improve in the next generation of probes. Once the perturbations inferred from the radiation spectrum can be compared to Inflation's predictions, it would be resolved whether Inflation should become a part of a more comprehensive standard model."

Several options of what should be done with Inflation, phrased in the versatile Russian language, crossed Lisitsin's mind. He sniffed the steaming bowl, then he said:

"I can't change what mathematics teaches us. Universal rotation doesn't predict inhomogeneities in the background radiation, and neither does the standard model. But..." Lisitsin stopped, letting his meaningful "but" hover in the air, until it would sink in that what he was going to say was pivotal. "Universal rotation is instrumental in shedding light on the process that set off galactic rotation."

Green nodded that he got the message. So far, Andrei did not say anything new.

"Relating between universal rotation and dark energy took more time than I expected," Lisitsin continued. "The big leap happened during the holidays."

The big leap, Green noted, could mean various things when Andrei used it. It had been a while since Andrei had started to drop hints about working on an inclusion of a cosmological source for dark energy in his pet project. Having heard nothing about it for several weeks, Green concluded that these attempts turned into nothing.

Seeing that George was not impressed, Lisitsin drew a pen

and a sheet of paper from an inner pocket of his coat. In his mind's eye, Lisitsin zoomed over months of intense work, through countless promising thoughts and fragments of ingenious ideas, through setbacks he had overcome, false starts and aborted attempts. Excitement suffused his cheeks when he foresaw the triumphant culmination of his work. With a magician's flourish, he wrote the equation that was written on his whiteboard.

It was short and elegantly simple. It depicted the space-time of a rotating universe permeated with dark energy.

Green studied the equation without falling for its deceptive appearance. Universal rotation made the space-time more complex than that of an uniformly expanding universe with a cosmological constant. An intricate combination of rotation and expansion mimicked a time-dependent dark energy.

Yes, it was a big leap, Green thought. His eyes were fixed on the equation, his deadpan expression veiled what he felt. As a boy, he was curious. As a young man, he was enticed by the logic and the beauty of physics. That raw, youthful sense of wonderment had long been eroded, but vestiges of innate curiosity still hibernated in the recesses of his mind. He could not stop looking at the equation.

Lisitsin's face glowed with self-satisfaction. "What do you think?" he asked.

"You are the expert on general relativity," Green said. Without doing calculations, he could not assess the equation's correctness. Having learned to trust Andrei's mathematical superiority, he had no intentions to check it.

Lisitsin was not deterred by George's reticent response. Trusting that George grasped the extent of his breakthrough and started to cogitate about its far reaching consequences, he stuck a tablespoon into the creamy mushroom soup and tasted it. Green forked salad greens from his plate, cut a piece of a grilled chicken breast. He thought fast and ate slowly, all the while cautious not to show premature enthusiasm.

"It's a first step." Lisitsin said in a matter of reopening the conversation. "Now, it's time to work out Einstein equations."

Green's expression became palpably graver. Einstein equations related changes in space-time with the dynamics of objects within that space-time; they were the cornerstone for any self-consistent cosmological model. Andrei's equation described a space-time with both galactic rotation and dark energy, but it did not offer insights as to how to formulate Einstein equations for such a universe. Finding a way would take time, and having the equations did not guarantee finding a solution.

Moreover, Green reflected, Andrei could fiddle with these equations for years, and it might be too late when the model is ready. To get a burgeoning and increasingly competitive community to notice anything new, it was essential to obtain results fast.

Noticing that George's face clouded, Lisitsin's watery-blue eyes hardened, challenging Green.

"We don't need to postulate any new forces, particles or dimensions in field equations," Lisitsin stressed the advantages of his suggestion. "Do you know of any other model that can do that much?"

Green put the knife and the fork on his plate and finished chewing the chicken. He said "no," then turned to his beer. Past experience showed Green that Andrei would beat about the bush for a while, then ask to enlist the help of one of Green's students or post-docs. Assessing that it would take Andrei five to ten minutes to get to that point, Green used the time to contemplate his answer.

If after several months it became evident that Einstein equations were unsolvable, whoever he'd have assigned to help Andrei would face a serious problem. Ben was already working on an approved, solid topic, and he wouldn't want to do anything with Andrei's suggestion. Chi was overworked and he'd be even busier once the spring term commenced. Danielle was available. She would want to explore a new explanation for dark energy, Green reasoned. He took another gulp of beer, then looked at the equation. It offered clues to two enigmas: what had initiated galactic rotations and what was dark energy. What he felt was more than an occasional bout of curiosity. He wanted a stake in the model. It was not his responsibility to dissuade Danielle from taking the risk, he decided.

"I can do it alone, but that will take too much time," Lisitsin said. "I'll provide the necessary mathematical foundation."

Lisitsin's voice stressed that the lion's share of the research would be his. "But it'll be faster if your grad student or post-doc helped with the technicalities."

He paused in the middle of the pitch, even though Green made no objections. The last hurdle was to find out tactfully who, Chi or Ben, was better with intricate mathematics. "It will be helpful," Lisitsin said, "if he'd have a quick understanding of the model."

"Danielle," Green said, never thinking to ask her acquiescence.

"Danielle?" Lisitsin repeated.

"She has the knowledge you are looking for, and she'll jump on the opportunity to explore the origins of dark energy."

Lisitsin wasn't surprised that Danielle would be enthusiastic about assisting him to develop the model, yet he wondered why George preferred a female newcomer over the other members of his group. He cast his mind back to seminars she had been at, but recalled only one instance when Danielle stood out by refuting a theoretical paper. That, Lisitsin reflected, did not suffice to recommend her. Warily, he weighed his options. The rotating universe model was his own, and he didn't have to entrust it to an ambitious bluestocking. He was entitled to be choosy, or at least receive George's assurance that she was as good as the others.

"Is she tenure-track material?" Lisitsin asked conversely, his fingers toying with a soft roll.

"Everyone in my group has the potential," Green replied.

Lisitsin responded with a wily, almost derisive, smile.

"Danielle is bright and motivated but she isn't Brian La-Compte. Her skills could be more solid, but that is understandable considering that she came from TIST."

"Is she doing good work?"

"It has been steadily improving. Right now it is satisfactory."

Lisitsin hesitated. Coming from George, satisfactory wasn't a trifle. He thought of inquiring about Danielle's personal life, then decided to humor George's politically-correct sensibilities and skirted the subject.

"Time alone will tell if she is up to the challenge," Lisitsin said. His watery blue eyes locked stare with Green's stale-gray ones, sealing a silent agreement.

On their way to Fitzgerald Hall, the professors agreed on the essentials of their new collaboration. In his office, Green called to summon Danielle.

"Yes, of course," Danielle said when Green asked whether she could come. The snapshots strewn on her desk looked pathetic after Kramer's spectacular movie. Having no time to prepare anything better, she picked two recent plots and rushed to Green's office.

Lisitsin's presence was both a surprise and a distraction. Stifling her discomfort, Danielle sat in the vacant armchair, and listened to Green's equable voice explain the idea of omnipresent rotation. Rotation was prevalent in space - planets orbited around stars, stars and dust rotated around a galactic center, galaxies rotated within clusters. But rotation of the entire spacetime? Green went on, but most of his words passed over Danielle's head. She tried to picture universal rotation. The room's walls started to swim before her eyes.

"Is something bothering you?" Green's stern voice restored the walls to their place.

"Um," Danielle muttered. She wanted to say something more intelligent, but without grasping the specifics of a rotating universe, she could not decide whether the idea was crazy or brilliant. Knowing she should not look hesitant, she focused on practicalities. Green was too cautious to be engaged with speculations. He wouldn't, Danielle reasoned, speak about universal rotation if it could be ruled out. Deeming that he was too scrupulous to offer anyone in his group to work on a risky topic, she felt reassured. Green's involvement practically sanctioned the idea.

"I thought that dark energy density should decrease while universe expanded," she said aloud. "But it has never occurred to me that an accelerated expansion could arise from rotation. Such possibility is astounding."

The professors exchanged glances. Neither of them seemed to be pleased.

"Gödel introduced universal rotation half a century ago," Green said. "He solved Einstein equations with a positive cosmological constant."

Danielle stared stupidly at the plots she was holding. "Shouldn't the cosmological constant be negative to act like a repulsive dark energy?" she asked.

"Gödel's solution described a static universe," Lisitsin chimed in. "His model posited the existence of a positive cosmological constant to balance the repulsive effect of rotation."

Danielle's confusion deepened. The hypothesis of a static universe relied on an early twentieth century belief that universe, as a whole, did not change with time. But why had Gödel considered a static universe when it had been known that universe was expanding?

"Haven't you heard of Kurt Gödel?" Lisitsin's tone implied that she should have.

Danielle shook her head. She saw the patronizing look the professors exchanged, and said "no" curtly.

"Gödel was a mathematician," Green said. "He was at the Institute of Advanced Studies in Princeton when Einstein was there."

So what? Danielle thought. She wanted an explanation about the project, not more details about a dead mathematician.

"Come to my office tomorrow at ten," Lisitsin instructed. "We'll go over what you will do."

Ha? with a big question mark echoed in Danielle's mind. Maybe Lisitsin didn't notice, but neither professor invited her to work on the project, nor asked if she was willing to do so. She looked inquiringly at Green.

"You can leave those on my desk," he said about the plots she was still clutching.

Danielle rose up and smiled unconvincingly. For once, it was a relief to be gotten rid of.

Chi was not in the office when she got in. She slumped on a swirling-chair, cupped her chin, and tried to convince herself that a solution to the dark energy problem was emerging not in Harvard or Princeton, but at an office next door.

It could not be a daydream, Danielle mused. She was too excited to ponder on what Green might have told Lisitsin, but she felt gratitude. Green was rarely supportive. He has not conceded that she had argued for the dark energy to be of a cosmological origin, and time dependent, yet he bore in mind her interests and recommended her to Lisitsin. Her eyes fell on the plots and snapshots cluttering the desk. She felt pity that Green's oversimplified model did not postulate a source for galactic rotation.

The mechanism of universal rotation must be inherently different from regular rotation, she thought. Green had mentioned that, by itself, universal rotation could not predict observations, nor point to possible discrepancies with general relativity. It seemed strange to Danielle that he had not mentioned whether the notion of universal rotation contradicted any of the cosmological tenets.

Scents of ginger and other spices wafted into the office, heralding Chi and his warmed lunch.

"Have you heard of Gödel?"she asked after Chi sat down.

"No." Chi began to eat, showing interest only in his food.

Resigned to silence, Danielle pulled from the shelf her copies of *The Early Universe* and *General Relativity*. She looked at the indexes, leafed through pages, and read some bits from sections that drew her attention. Nowhere did she come across Gödel's name or any mention of a "rotating universe." Satisfied with the obscurity of the model, she turned to check Lisitsin's departmental homepage.

Andrei V. Lisitsin, Danielle read, received an MSc and a PhD in Physics from Moscow State University. He stayed at the department of theoretical physics there for over twenty years. He was a visiting professor in Sweden for two years, then moved to King Solomon University. For the last six years, Lisitsin was a Douglas and Harper Morgan professor of theoretical physics.

The list of Lisitsin's publications was considerably shorter than Green's. Danielle scanned the titles of his papers, saw no mention of large-scale rotation. Thrilled that she would work on the project from its early stages, she challenged herself to read Lisitsin's most recent paper. After an introductory paragraph, she stumbled on monstrous equations and indecipherable text. She skipped a few lines looking for explanations. The paper had barely any, except of "it is easy to see that," or even more succinctly, "therefore." Staring at the equations, she could not perceive what was so easy.

No wonder he is bored at seminars, she thought after skimming the rest of the paper. Lisitsin had plenty of mathematical tools to transform his idea into a sound, and possibly groundbreaking, model. Awestruck by his abilities, Danielle girded herself for "reading" another of his recent papers. It turned out to be even less comprehensible.

"Lisitsin might think that I understand practically nothing, and tell Green," a panicky thought rose in her mind. It was followed by, "Green will never treat me seriously again," and by a lamentation that, "It was a mistake to imply I knew general relativity in depth."

The sounds of Chi clicking on the keyboard filtered into Danielle's growing dread. She hesitated, then said softly, "Can I ask you something?"

Chi pressed on save. "Yes?"

"Have you heard about Lisitsin's model of a rotating universe?"

Chi looked at a loss as to what was she talking about. She repeated the question. His expression changed, reminding Danielle of ice thawing on a warm day.

"No," Chi said.

"Have you ever worked with Lisitsin?" Danielle asked before Chi could return to his program.

"I told Dr. Green that I can't do that kind of math."

"Neither can I," Danielle said. It was an opening for Chi to ask why she was asking or at least show a glimmer of curiosity, so she might say that she would take part in Lisitsin's new research. Chi, however, returned to his simulations, leaving Danielle to worry about her involvement in Lisitsin's ambitious project. What if it was more than she could bite, and would jeopardize her chances to carve an academic career? On the other hand, what better choice did she have? Unlike Chi, she could not count on her simulations.

She was about to go to the library to look for Gödel's papers, when a phone call from Green summoned Danielle to his office. Green asked about the plots as soon as she entered. After Danielle explained what needed to be clarified, he asked about the state of the data analysis.

"I do it whenever I have new data from the runs. When there is a visible change in matter distribution, I redraw the plots."

"Keep on doing that," Green said, "and email me the ones

you already did. Can you attach to each plot a description of what was calculated?"

"Sure, no problem. About the rotating universe..."

"That should not interfere with your work," Green interrupted. He picked up the receiver and started dialing, leaving no doubt that Danielle was to leave.

"Rats," she grumbled in the hallway.

The rest of the evening was spent on making new plots and composing explanations.

16

GODS DO NOT BAKE CLAY JARS

An hour before she was to meet Lisitsin, Danielle was a bundle of nerves. So much depended on her performance, yet she could not gather her thoughts, or stop her mind from conjuring scenarios that swung her expectations from euphoria to dread. Unable to stop the maelstrom, let alone to focus on anything productive, she prescribed herself a walk in crisp air.

She was not going to pretend she understands everything he says, Danielle decided, leaving the office. She wouldn't be cowered by him, she resolved, striding along the hallway.

Descending to the first floor, she met Lisitsin, draped in a long woolly coat and holding a briefcase, on his way up.

"Good morning," Danielle said, even though he habitually ignored her greetings.

"Good morning," Lisitsin answered.

"I'll come to your office at ten," she said, feeling obliged to say something.

"Come in ten minutes. There is no point in wasting time."

Lisitsin's office looked similar to Green's, but in place of armchairs there were upholstered swirling chairs, and the monitor was of an older model. The most notable difference, Danielle observed, were the mathematical expressions crowding the whiteboard. Reckoning that she should look elsewhere before she was completely discouraged, she half-turned towards the bookshelves. Her eyes flitted over the books' spines, looking for familiar, welcoming volumes. Most of the titles were unreadable, yet Danielle gawked at the Cyrillic letters until Lisitsin told her to sit down.

The articles, preprints, and sheets of paper scattered on Lisitsin's desk were too intimidating to look at. Averting her eyes from the formidable equations, Danielle's stare lingered on a framed photo of a girl with long, straw-colored hair. She looked around fifteen, slim and athletic; a vulpine smile lingered on her face.

"As you should have gathered yesterday," Lisitsin opened, "constructing a model for a rotating universe poses a big challenge. Our strategy is to break it up into interconnected riddles."

Danielle's eyes shifted to Lisitsin. There was a strong family resemblance between him and the girl.

"How does the angular velocity of rotating space-time depend on the scale factor?" Lisitsin asked.

Was it some sort of test? She hardly expected small-talk, but neither being unceremoniously examined.

"The angular velocity?" she asked.

"Yes," Lisitsin snapped.

Was she supposed to repeat Green's explanations? Peeping warily at the professor, Danielle saw he was ready to throw her out of the office if she dithered and wasted his time. Lowing her gaze to her knees, she made quick estimations. The scale factor (a measure of how distances grew when universe expanded) grew along with wavelength stretching. The angular velocity was proportional to the inverse of wavelength. She put aside the factors of two and Pi which she had no time to figure out, and said the approximate answer aloud.

"How does the angular velocity depend on the dark energy density?" Lisitsin immediately fired another question.

"The square of the angular velocity should be proportional to the energy density."

"Write down how the dark energy density decreases over time," Lisitsin demanded, pushing towards Danielle a sheet of paper.

She took a pen from the desk and wrote a two-lines-long derivation. When she was done, Danielle put the pen down, hoping it would cue Lisitsin it was time to end the test.

"Explain why the decrease in dark energy density is slower than the decrease in matter energy density," Lisitsin instructed.

She answered.

Other questions followed. Danielle expressed interest in Lisitsin's idea at every opportunity, but he paid no attention to her broad hints. He questioned her to his satisfaction, and ended the meeting by giving Danielle an old photocopy of Gödel's paper to read and redo the derivations.

"Lisitsin grilled me for over an hour without telling me anything about his model," Danielle summarized the experience to her mother later that evening. "In fact, I have no clue of what he wants me to do."

"Did you answer his questions?" Michelle asked.

"Sort of, I guess. His only input was to give me an old paper to go over. He said it'd be a good exercise."

"What kind of person he is?"

"Arrogant and impatient. But he is also developing a new cosmological model, which sets him apart from Green and most other professors, who basically do what others do. Thinking that his model might account for dark energy, I tend to agree with Charlotte Lucas. Lisitsin has 'a right to be proud'."

"I don't recall that Elizabeth Bennett accepted such a right," Michelle said. "By placing him on a pedestal, you are belittling yourself."

"Don't you think that Lisitsin's lousy manners are excusable if he is some sort of creative genius?"

An uneasy feeling that eluded translation to words settled in Michelle's gut. She said, "One may admire a genius and even allow a creative person some leeway about social niceties, but I wouldn't put up with a lack of respect from someone you work for."

"Lisitsin isn't that bad," Danielle countered. "His manners probably reflect his foreign upbringing. Who knows what degree of loftiness is acceptable at Moscow University's physics department?"

"You are old enough to draw the line." There was a pause, then Michelle added, "My advice is to give it very serious thought before you commit yourself."

In Hopeville, Danielle shook her head. Her mother had left academia too early to grasp how much she needed the collaboration with Lisitsin to spur on her lagging post-doctorate.

"Mom, if Lisitsin offers me to work on his model, I'll take the chance. There is little point in mulling over the pros and cons when I have nothing better to be choosy about."

A shiver ran through Michelle's spine – Danielle's earnest words stirred up unwelcome memories. "What did Jonathan say?" Michelle asked.

"He said that he can't be in Thorboro on the weekends before and after my birthday. I didn't feel like telling him about the meeting after that."

"But you will," Michelle said, showing uncharacteristic lack of concern.

Despite the prediction, Danielle did not bring up working with Lisitsin when she spoke later that night to Jonathan. She mentioned reading Gödel's paper. To her surprise, Jonathan was familiar with some of the mathematician's work.

"I didn't know he was famous," Danielle said. "His cosmological solution has closed time-loops."

"And why does that ruffle your feathers?"

"It takes a mathematician to ignore the fact that closed time-loops are unphysical."

"And the fans of science-fiction," Jonathan teased. "We need time-loops for time-traveling."

* * *

Swamped with new data streaming from simulations, Danielle did the derivations for Lisitsin's assignment in between the data analysis she did for Green. After a week had passed without any message from Lisitsin, she decided that she could have spared herself reproducing the derivations. She mulled over going to Lisitsin's office on the pretext of returning Gödel's paper, but dismissed the idea. Maybe Lisitsin did not call her because he deemed that she was not good enough. Anyway, she was not going to plead about getting a try. Danielle took her mind off the rotating universe and channeled her disappointment into code-writing. Even though programming was not her forte, her progress was much faster than in the fall.

It was Friday, the last workday before the beginning of the spring term, when she passed Lisitsin in the hallway. Unsure of what to say, she affected a smile and muttered, "Hello."

Lisitsin stopped, said "Come to my office at five," and

walked away.

Reassuring herself that Lisitsin had not yet made up his mind about her, Danielle reread Gödel's paper, tracked her own derivations, studied the various steps as if she was preparing for an important exam. She did not notice how late it was until her stomach rumbled in protest.

"Jonathan called," Chi said when she returned with a sandwich.

"Did he leave a message?"

"No."

Unable to recall where Jon was scheduled to be on Friday afternoon, Danielle unwrapped the sandwich, looked at the greasy blots on the waxed paper, and noted a suspicious smell. Reasoning that the food-venue on the campus wouldn't sell it if it was inedible, she took a bite and turned her mind back to the conditions for universal rotation.

It was dusk when she left for Lisitsin's office. The secretaries' office, Green's and most of the others were already locked.

"Have you read Gödel's paper?" were Lisitsin's first words.

"Yes."

"Write," Lisitsin waved to a corner on the whiteboard where nothing was written on, "the condition for rotation without closed time-loops."

Congratulating herself on working out the answer beforehand, Danielle did as she had been told.

"Do you understand what is our main difficulty?"

Danielle itched to retort that her main difficulty was not knowing what Lisitsin had done so far. She sat silently, and looked for a more acceptable answer. If Lisitsin was wavering about accepting her, it was unwise to ask for explanations.

"How does universal rotation impart angular velocities to galaxies?" she voiced what puzzled her most.

"You should be more precise. The question is how the vorticity of matter-sources enters into Einstein equations," Lisitsin corrected, pointing at a tangle of equations in the middle of the whiteboard.

Unsure what exactly vorticity was, Danielle assumed that the mathematical expression described matter's rotation.

"We'll start with a rotating cold matter and write a self-consistent solution that mimics the effects of dark-energy," Lisitsin continued. "Why contributions arising from the background radiation should not be considered?"

"The corrections are small," Danielle said with more confidence. "By the time galaxies formed, background radiation contributed very little to the universe's energy balance."

"Now, to calculate galactic vorticity..." Lisitsin stopped, seeing Danielle's incredulous expression. "Any problems?" he asked airily.

"I thought that rotation was a part of universe's evolution from earliest times. If it wasn't, what set it in motion later on?"

"Your objection is irrelevant." Lisitsin's hand rose in a gesture intended to forestall further nonsense. "Initial conditions would take these into account."

Clueless of how he was going to formulate such initial conditions, Danielle nodded diffidently.

"We need a computer program that calculates the rotation of various matter sources," Lisitsin instructed. Having sparse knowledge about software, he did not delve into details. "Bear in mind that we cannot waste time."

He eyed Danielle to make sure that she understood her assignment; she merely looked overwhelmed. It's too early to conclude she was inept, Lisitsin reasoned, shifting his stare to his pretty daughter. Svetlana's smile reminded him that young women were more responsive to encouragement than disparagement.

"There is a saying in Russian which I often repeat to my girl. Loosely translated, it says that gods do not bake clay jars."

Gods? Danielle wondered. Had they anything to do with physics?

"It sounds better in Russian, although the meaning is universal. If gods do not bake pottery, then someone else does."

Does "gods" refer to professors of theoretical physics? Danielle asked herself.

"People?" she said tentatively.

"Exactly." Lisitsin flashed a foxy smile. "Do you see what it means?"

"Not really."

"People shouldn't wait for a divine assistance, but make their own clay jars," Lisitsin explained. He rose up to escort Danielle out.

"First and foremost find a computer program," he bode at the door. "Ask for help if you need to, but don't sit and wait for the program to materialize out of the blue."

As Danielle walked away from Lisitsin, the pressure in her head ebbed, her shoulders relaxed, she looked straight ahead. A man was sitting on the floor by her closed office, a stranger whose face she could not see. She stopped, her heart pounding fast and loud. The man, awash in fluorescent glow, was hunched over something. She squinted, tried to see what he was doing. Something about him was very familiar.

A few heartbeats later, she was joyously running forward.

Hearing footsteps, Jonathan Lerner turned his head, smiled, saved the changes on his code. By the time Danielle reached him, he had put the laptop aside and was standing, ready to catch her with a big hug.

"You spooked me," she gasped in Jonathan's arms. "What are you doing here?"

"Surprising you. You didn't think I'd miss your birthday?"

"Coming from Lisitsin's office, I can barely think at all." She rubbed Jon's chin with her brow, rose on the tips of her toes and lifted her lips to his.

"Is Lisitsin the guy who is watching us?"

"What?" Danielle turned fast, glimpsed Lisitsin go into his office, and pulled away from Jonathan. "Let me pick up my backpack and coat." Her hand fumbled for a key in her pocket. "I want to get out of here as soon as possible."

They smooched in the rental car and on the steps of the little house at Chadwick Drive. When Jonathan finally could speak in entire sentences, he said, "I made reservations at Lucas Lodge."

"For tonight?" Danielle asked hopefully.

"For the weekend, including a dinner tomorrow and rented ski equipment."

Too happy to say she was happy, Danielle kissed him and rushed to pack.

It started to snow a short while after they left Hopeville. Big flurries accompanied the car, adding evanescent glimmer to shadows blurred in the dark. Suddenly apprehensive, Danielle wondered if it was too good to last.

"Can you drive slower," she asked, "without testing the car on the slippery road?"

"Sure," Jonathan grinned and slowed down. "Will you tell me who is Lisitsin?"

"It's a long story." Danielle recounted what had happened in Green's office, what she understood about Lisitsin's idea, her expectations, worries, and dreams. Jonathan listened, paying varying degrees of attention; he let physics pass over his head.

"What if it doesn't work?" he asked when Danielle was done.

"I still do simulations for Green's toy model. The rotating universe is a bonus, a rare opportunity to do something different, the kind of research physicists did long ago, when they turned the classical world upside down."

"The turn of the century? I thought you were pining for Jane Austen's times."

"She is great, but I wasn't brought up for a manor. Nevertheless, I'm a third generation of physicists."

"And a good one," Jonathan said affectionately.

"Do you think so? Am I good enough to work on a new, fundamental problem?"

"Since both Green and Lisitsin think so, who am I to raise doubts?"

Missing the irony in Jonathan's voice, Danielle's eyes lit, gleaming with visions.

"Rushing headlong into the land of discoveries?" he teased.

"I wouldn't call patiently waiting for Lisitsin to make up his mind 'rushing headlong'," Danielle retorted.

"You wouldn't," Jonathan agreed. After a short while, he asked, "Do you really want all of the juggling involved in accommodating two demanding professors?"

"Aren't you the last person who may question others' unreasonable workload?" Danielle countered. "I, at least, won't be flying back and forth across the country, nor ram heads like you do with Pilcher."

"I hope, for your sake, that Lisitsin is not an idiot like Pilcher. Life is easier when professors put their names on research papers without messing up your work."

"The gods do not bake clay jars," Danielle cited. Seeing Jon's expression, she repeated Lisitsin's explanation.

They talked about Nickka's patent application and the beta, until Jonathan turned to a country road leading to Lucas Lodge. Stepping out of the car, they felt the soft, fluffy snowflakes landing on their faces, smelled the smoke rising from chimneys, and grinned at the soft lights filtering from rustic cabins and the main house. The Lucas Lodge's entrance was as elegant as Danielle remembered, with an added benefit of warmth. Jonathan got a key from a courteous receptionist, who also told them about breakfast and wished them a good night. A magical night, Danielle thought, quietly ambling with Jon through the enchanted woodland. Despite the snow, they both radiated heat.

"My lady," Jonathan said when he opened the door.

He bent over the hearth to light the logs, leaving Danielle to discover a fondue dish ready to be warmed and eaten, a bottle of white wine, a tea set for two with bread, buttery shortbread, and an assortment of chocolates. When he rose, he did not need to ask whether she liked this or not. Danielle glowed.

"You look good," Jonathan said.

"Better than in a full light?"

"Different."

Danielle's ruddy cheeks turned redder; her eyes turned to the massive wooden bed. The lily-white, crisp bed linen had an exquisite pattern of wild flowers. A musky smell permeated the cabin.

It was almost midnight when they reached the food. Burning logs crackled, red flames glowed in the fireplace; they drank wine and munched pieces of bread coated with cheese.

"This is exactly what I'd have asked for my birthday, if I would have thought that it's possible." Danielle toasted Jonathan with what was left in her glass. "You've accomplished mind reading."

"I expected you would rather undress than dress up tonight."

"Very far-seeing." She smiled at Jonathan's clothes, which were tossed near the bed. "When did you plan that?"

"At the New Year tea at my parents." Jonathan popped a chocolate in Danielle's mouth. "I wanted to be with you alone in front of a lit fireplace."

"How could you think about that in their living-room?" she

managed to ask.

Jonathan showed her.

* * *

They fell asleep sated and spent, and slept blithely while the snowfall intensified and gusts of wind circled the cabin. The first sound Danielle registered was a distant pounding or a muffled hammering. She stretched luxuriantly, and without opening her eyes, moved towards Jonathan. Her skin felt the silky touch of creased linen, a soft pillow; her hand almost reached the edge of the bed, but it did not find Jonathan.

"Jon?" Danielle murmured.

"Up here." The voice came distant and concerned. Opening both eyes, she saw Jonathan half-dressed, ransacking a suitcase.

"You better get up," he said, "and dress for outdoors."

"Has anything happened?"

"There was a heavy snow. Blizzard conditions are expected to develop later in the day."

"How do you know?" she asked, baffled.

"Take a look at the window, or better yet, try to open the door. The snow is already two feet high."

Completely awake, Danielle started to dress.

"Didn't you hear a pounding on the door a few minutes ago?" Jonathan asked.

"I thought it was a dream."

"Nope. The guy who runs the place is rounding everyone up. He said to pack a change of clothes and move to the main building while the visibility is still pretty good."

"Do they have guest rooms there?"

"They have a supply of firewood, food and other necessities. We might be cut out from civilization for a couple of days."

A few minutes later, two bulky figures dashed into the mounting snow, holding each other and a backpack. It was almost dark and brutally cold. The wind whined hoarsely, swirled the descending snow, and shook trees in a mad frenzy. Hands clasped, Danielle and Jonathan waded through drifting mounds, slowly progressing while struggling to stay on their feet. Whistling like a maniac, the wind lashed at every piece of unprotected skin, thrust them in every direction, and toppled them onto the snow.

Despondency engulfed Danielle; sadness seeped into her mind. The magical wood from the previous night transformed into a bleak, outlandish world. Snow moved in surreal white currents; snowflakes circled all around in incessant, random motion. Something was very wrong in this mindless, raging chaos.

"Come on." Jonathan's voice was barely audible. He tugged Danielle's shoulder and pointed. She squinted in the same direction, then nodded. Through the darting and swirling snow, Lucas Lodge looked like a phantom house, an illusion conjured to mislead and to lure. Fear froze her motions; she did not budge. An impatient pull from Jonathan broke the spell. She squeezed his hand, and they went on plowing through the tempestuous snow. Buffeted by the wind, panting and shivering, they reached the house. The door was unlocked.

A casually dressed woman stood by the entrance. She brightened seeing Danielle and Jonathan.

"Never mind the boots, just come inside," the woman said. "My name is Rebecca. Please, leave everything here and warm yourselves in the breakfast room. I'll bring some hot coffee."

"Thank you," Danielle said. She was gasping and shaking.

"If you need anything don't hesitate to tell me," Rebecca added. Despite her composed voice, she was looking impatiently at the door.

"We are fine," Jonathan said. "Are you waiting for someone else?"

"My husband, Peter, and another couple."

The lodge was warm. Following a waft of burning wood, Danielle and Jonathan came into a large room whose ceiling and walls were paneled with dark rustic wood. The decor recreated the ambiance of a morning room in a country manor, but its splendor was lost on Danielle and Jonathan, who headed to the fireplace. A man and a woman in their sixties were warming themselves before it; the man moved aside to give them a place.

"Filthy weather, isn't it?" he commented. "My wife's name is Mary. I'm Edgar." Edgar proffered his hand.

Jonathan introduced Danielle and himself. By the time a grumpy looking pair in their mid-forties joined them, Danielle stopped shivering. Everyone moved to let the newcomers have a place by the hearth.

"Oh my gosh," the woman groaned. "It's freezing outdoors."

"Let's cross our fingers and hope there won't be a power outage," the man said. "Has anyone seen any other staff except Becky and Pete?"

"We've met only with Peter and Rebecca," Edgar said calmly. Smiling to his wife, he added, "We are Mary and Edgar."

"Jonathan and Danielle," Danielle said.

"Ken and Pamela," Ken said. "Pete and Becky live here. If no one has come through in the morning, I expect that all the roads are already closed."

"Oh my goodness, we're stuck in a forest," Pamela moaned.

"Not in the woods exactly." Edgar waved a hand at the elegant room. Pamela looked around and giggled embarrassingly. "Oh, dear. We were in such a hurry, we put on the first thing that came in hand."

"None of us thought of dressing up." Mary smiled reassuringly. "I'm convinced that the Webers won't hold that against any of us."

"Not at all," Rebecca said, coming in with a steaming pot of strongly smelling coffee. "I understand that everyone's plans have changed, but I hope that all of you will have the best possible stay at the lodge."

She left to bring cups and saucers, sugar and milk.

"When was the last time we were stranded in the woods during a blizzard?" Edgar reminisced. "About thirty years ago?"

"Closer to forty, but I still shudder whenever I think about it," Mary corrected, patting Edgar's shoulder. "That was a humbling and exalting experience, even a miracle, considering that we came out of it unscathed. Today's blizzard is barely an inconvenience. We can watch the elements rage while we are safe and cozy inside."

Glancing at Pamela and Ken, Danielle observed no inclination to be thrilled or awed. They looked quite annoyed that the capriciousness of nature played havoc with their plans.

"We were about to leave after breakfast," Pamela complained. "We had to go, but the roads are closed."

"I should have brought my laptop," Jonathan whispered to Danielle. Unable to think of a retort, she rolled her eyes.

"Good morning and welcome again to the Lucas Lodge," Peter said as he and Rebecca walked into the room. His face was red, his hair tousled. "We are all stranded here for several days, but I don't expect it'll be a harsh experience. We can brave both the weather and Becky's cooking."

"You may ask Peter to cook," Rebecca suggested.

Pamela and Ken looked at each other irritably; Edgar and Mary exchanged amused glances. Peter stepped closer to the fireplace.

"We had blizzards here many times, and no one ever was in any danger," Peter said. "We'll take care of sleeping arrangements later."

"The Lodge has very comfortable folding beds we often use for wedding parties, and an ample stock of linen and spare blankets." Rebecca came closer to Danielle and Pamela. "Ask me if there is anything personal you may need," she added quietly.

Peter and Rebecca left their guests to serve themselves coffee. After a while Peter returned. "Our living room, the T.V. room and the library with its contents are at your disposal," he said to the guests. "Let me show you around, while Becky tries her hand at rolling croissants."

Mary and Edgar, keen to make the most of the situation, went along and readily talked with Peter. Their enthusiasm had little effect on Pamela and Ken, who tagged along as if doing others a favor. After Peter left, Edgar and Mary wandered around. Pamela and Ken turned to their cell-phones.

"Mary and Edgar behave like wide-eyed children," Danielle whispered to Jonathan. "I wish we could be that adventurous at their age."

"Let's hope we won't go through Pamela and Ken's period first," Jonathan quipped. "They give a bad name to the middle age."

For breakfast, the Webers set the tables with porcelain dishes. They laid out soft-boiled eggs, toasted slices of bread, butter, honey, marmalade, and plum jam. Both Peter and Rebecca looked more like vacationing millionaires than waiters, yet they circled around good-humoredly, serving tea, coffee, and quirky looking croissants.

"A penny for your thought?" Danielle offered Jonathan over

their second cup of coffee. They were sitting at a table for two.

"Those who think in Java are not paid with pennies, but you can get mine for free."

"You were thinking in Java?"

Jonathan grinned and put the rest of a croissant in his mouth.

"How can you in the middle of a snowstorm?"

"I was running an algorithm in my head, but I can stop any moment. What do you want to talk about?"

"Something heartwarming and jolly. After braving wind and snow, I don't want to speak about code or think about Green and Lisitsin."

"We can," Jonathan paused to look at Danielle suggestively, "reminisce about last night."

"At this place?" Danielle smiled. "Oh my gosh," she imitated Pamela's intonation.

"I see your point. No sex, code or work."

"Your challenge is to think of something silly, pointless, and funny."

"Okay." Jonathan took another croissant. "Yesterday, while I was waiting for the flight, my mother called."

"Is that supposed to be funny?" Danielle muttered.

"She wanted me to arbitrate between having the wedding invitations engraved and letter-pressed."

Danielle burst with laughter. "Do you know the difference?"

"That was easy to find out. Engraving is what mother wanted. Amy has chosen letterpress."

"I like a tempest in a teapot. What about Amos?"

"He supports Amy. Before calling me, mother asked my father to intervene."

"Did he?" Danielle asked. Richard usually avoided taking sides in the Lerner household.

"Of course not. He is as neutral as Switzerland."

After the breakfast, she read and socialized, leaving Jonathan to do whatever work he could do without a laptop.

The four couples sat together for a dinner. Rebecca's culinary efforts brought more jests than compliments, but her cooking went down very well with the wines from the Lucas Lodge cellar. At about nine, Peter and Jonathan brought the folding beds. These were barely used, for Edgar, Mary, Ken, Pamela, Jonathan, and Danielle played Monopoly until the wee hours. By Sunday morning, the wind abated and the cold wintery sun glimmered between clouds. Determined not to abuse the Webers' hospitality for more than necessary, everyone went out and started shoveling. Their reward was two nights to be used at each couple's discretion before the road was opened on Tuesday afternoon.

17

NONSENSE AND RUBBISH

The spring term has commenced on Monday, amid an uncommonly harsh spell of seasonal flu. While feverish students stagger to meet King Solomon University's unflagging expectations of excellence, many are questioning the...

Reckoning that working for Lisitsin and Green, she would get all the "unflagging expectations of excellence" she could muster, Danielle folded the *Hopeville Herald,* stowed it in her backpack and headed towards Fitzgerald Hall. After five days at the Lucas Lodge, even an outbreak of flu could not dampen her optimism. Thinking of it, a bout of flu actually made her absence self-explanatory, and gave it a reason no one could frown at. Shifting her thoughts back to the rotating universe, Danielle unlocked the office. On her desk waited a note dated from Monday, telling her to come to Lisitsin's office. An email from Green asked her to read an attached preprint and track a brand new analysis it presented. She downloaded the preprint, groaned, and began reading it. Why, she wondered, did Green insist on treating matter aggregates as galaxies, even though they did not rotate? Why the dark energy was to be represented as a number added ad hoc into the code? She toyed with the idea of introducing rotation into the toy universe simulation, but decided that Green would not allow it. Without formulating Einstein equations, her suggestion was indeed pretty meaningless.

At quarter after ten, the phone rang. "Come right away," Lisitsin demanded.

She rushed to Lisitsin's office, her hopes high that he made some progress. Lisitsin was pacing back and forth, deep furrows creasing his brow. Without stopping, he waved Danielle to sit down. Ready to witness physics in the making, she raptly waited for explanations.

"Representation of rotating galaxies is the bottleneck," Lisitsin said abruptly. "We cannot go further before we examine the various possibilities of how matter spins in the universe."

Danielle nodded. At Lucas Lodge she had fiddled with imaginary scenarios, filled pages with doodles of swirling and accelerating snowflakes. Eager to find out how Lisitsin tackled the problem, she watched as he paced and muttered, jotted mathematical expressions on the whiteboard. She willed herself to follow Lisitsin's disjointed sentences, to soak up the underlying physics. After some hesitation, she asked about one of the terms. Lisitsin impatiently waved the question aside, scowled to nip in the bud any further attempt to interrupt the flow of his thoughts, and went on scrawling equations on the whiteboard. Humbled by his brilliance and her inability to grasp most of it, Danielle bashfully gazed at mathematical expressions and waited for Lisitsin to take further notice of her presence.

At last he stopped and turned to Danielle. "If we combine this," Lisitsin pointed at an expression, "with that," he pointed at another expression, "we get an interesting possibility."

And? Danielle thought, waiting for an elaboration, which did not come. In the ensuing silence, it dawned on her that there would not be any discussion or clarification, that she was expected to understand the "interesting possibility" on her own.

"When you work on the riddle, take these into account," Lisitsin pointed at a couple of complicated expressions.

Wincing inwardly, Danielle stifled her disappointment and started to copy the "riddle" from the whiteboard.

"What about the computer program?" Lisitsin inquired.

Danielle said that she would ask around, after which she was dismissed.

Passing by the secretaries' office, she went in. Marjory was alone, sporting a new haircut and highlights, which made her look strikingly non-grandmotherly. Paperwork was lain again on her desk. On a wall nearby hung a collage with a dozen photos of a baby.

"Congratulations," Danielle said, cocking her head to the photos. "How is your granddaughter?"

"Kim is growing and becoming prettier every day. Doesn't she look sweet?"

Deeming the question was an invitation to take a better look at the photos, Danielle glanced at the newborn, then at the slightly bigger and rosier baby. Finding nothing of interest in the same little face and wispy hair repeated a dozen times, she studied the baby's garments. Kim wore pearly whites, soft pinks and lavenders, dreamy mauve and delicate peach. In one of the photos, the baby was draped in a large piece of what looked like a heirloom lace.

"Beautiful," Danielle said earnestly. "Kim looks like a little princess."

Noticing what Danielle was staring at, Marjory smiled.

"Laura has always been a tad extravagant with clothes, but the Victorian lace is a gift from Kim's aunt. It hasn't been long since I fussed over Laura's dresses." Marjory sighed. "And now, Laura is a mother, and a boy she used to play with is coming to give a talk."

"Is he a faculty member?"

"A candidate." Humoring the curiosity written all over Danielle's face, Marjory added, "Rory and Laura went to the same elementary school when his father was on a Sabbatical at the university. Back then, the McDowells lived nearby."

"Is his father also a physicist?" a question slipped out.

"Yes, he is."

Seeing that Marjory was not inclined to talk, Danielle made some admiring noises about the baby and backed from the room.

"Have you heard that another candidate is coming?" Danielle asked Chi later that day.

"No," Chi said, without raising his head from the weekly assignment he was preparing for Green's course. This semester, he was Green's unofficial teaching assistant. Ben, being Green's graduate student, should have prepared the assignments, checked students' work and written down the solutions, but he had weaseled out of the job. Sympathizing with Chi, Danielle switched the conversation to another topic.

"Have you encountered Einstein equations with vorticity?"

"No."

She outlined Lisitsin's model; Chi listened with an undisguised respect.

"I don't have a program that solves them numerically. You better ask Ben. He will know if someone in Dr. Brophy's group uses them to study accretion disks."

Like hell, Danielle said in her mind. She'd ask for Green's help before groveling for anything from Ben.

She analyzed data from the toy universe's simulations, then went over the preprint, which garnered as much enthusiasm as the gloomy February evening outdoors. That very night, she started to work on Lisitsin's "riddle." His self-confidence was infectious, his ideas fascinated her. Having never encountered someone like Lisitsin, she believed that his genius would quickly overcome the obstacles the rotating universe model was facing.

Thursday brought the first colloquium of the spring term, a talk about "A Glassy Phase Transition in Proteins," to be given by professor Karen Gould. Although Danielle had only a vague notion what "a glassy phase transition" meant, she was in the Lounge on time to observe that Lisitsin and most of the guys from high-energy did not deign to come. Gould, she learned, was the head of a large group and a recipient of several prestigious awards. Finding the woman more interesting than the biophysical subject, Danielle gleaned preciously little of what Gould was talking about. She surveyed the audience and noted Isaac among many unfamiliar faces.

It soon became clear that Gould was an assiduous careerist who wouldn't go to a getaway weekend without stuffing her suitcase with papers and grant proposals. Danielle pictured her working while others whiled away the time roasting marshmallows and playing Monopoly. Although that did not make Gould any worse than Green, Danielle did not find the woman and her notable achievements inspiring.

"Would you come to my office?" Green asked, overtaking Danielle on her way to the second floor. Anticipating that he would ask about her simulation, Danielle was surprised when he said, "Can you summarize the method reported in Taylor's preprint?" as soon as they sat across his desk. She recounted what she had gleaned from the preprint.

"You should start implementing the method."

"I don't think that the extra calculations will improve the analysis I'm already doing," Danielle replied.

"You guess that they won't," Green corrected.

She itched to retort that having devoted so much time to analyzing the data, she got a sense of what would work and what would not. Reminding herself that she needed Green's systematic thinking and superb knowledge, Danielle restrained her tongue. She listened silently to his instructions and nodded in all the expected places.

When he was done, she opened with, "About the rotating universe model..."

"That's an extra you should work out yourself," Green said. Without losing an iota of his equable politeness, he brushed Danielle off.

She left his office infuriated; Green could carelessly add to her workload, but not spare any time on a problem she was struggling to solve. His narrow-mindedness made her more appreciative of Lisitsin's unconventional thinking. His riddle was time-consuming, but at least it served a purpose and was not needless work.

Danielle was less inclined to glorify Lisitsin's freethinking after another brainstorming session in his office. Going there, she had expected to hear revelations about his model; when she left with another "riddle" to grapple with, she was fuming. Lisitsin, completely unencumbered by manners, dismissed whatever she asked as "nonsense" and referred to her timid suggestion as "rubbish." It also rankled that he had no regard for her time; she was required to listen to his ruminations as if she was an animated soundboard.

After she cooled down, Danielle gave some thought to what would cause Lisitsin to treat her more seriously. Zeroing in on the software he wanted, she went to ask one of Brophy's students where one might acquire software that solves Einstein equations with vorticity. Only Ben was in the graduate students' office, skimming through conferences and summer-schools.

"Hi," she said. "Any conference you recommend?"

"The one George is going to in May, and there is also," Ben

scrolled back until he found the announcement, "a two-week-long summer school in Cargèse in April."

"But the registration ended yesterday."

"Yeah," Ben drawled. "Have you signed up?"

Itching to needle Ben, Danielle told him about having started to work with Lisitsin.

"Do you think that this will give you a head-start?" Ben stressed the word "this" derisively.

"Lisitsin's model aims to explain both galactic rotation and dark energy," she said, letting the enormity of the impact hang in the air.

"It's up to you if you want to waste your time, but trust me," (*trust you?* Danielle sneered in her mind), "working for George is the best option. If you need another recommendation," Ben added, "try to fawn Cobs."

The ugly implication that she could not succeed on her own hit the mark. Feeling disgust and loathing for the schmuck, Danielle willed herself not to give away how she felt.

"Why Cobs of all people?" she asked when she was able to speak carelessly.

"A recommendation from him opens the doors to many places."

"Really?" Danielle asked sarcastically. "How can Cobs exert such an extraordinary influence after he hasn't published or collaborated for years?"

"Don't you know that ALL of his students and post-docs became faculty members?" Ben gave her a scornful glance. "Quite a few distinguished professors owe him their elevated positions."

Refusing to believe anything Ben said, Danielle wordlessly turned on her heels.

Through desperation and grit, Danielle managed to solve both riddles before she got another call from Lisitsin. She entered his office, feeling quite complacent for having done her part. Noticing the deep furrows lining his brow, her self-confidence evaporated. She sidled to one of the chairs, sat down, and silently watched as he walked back and forth. His strides were forced and agitated; he flailed his hands. After a while, Lisitsin's steps slowed, the creases straightened on his forehead. He looked with a chilling tenderness at the squiggles sprawled on the whiteboard and wordlessly examined his brainchild. Danielle heard her heart pounding as she waited to hear his verdict. A predatory look on Lisitsin's face foretold her what would be his conclusion, before he systematically erased the whiteboard.

"Now, what about the software?" he asked turning to Danielle.

"I haven't found anything yet." Danielle's voice faltered when watery-blue eyes disdainfully bored into her. She cringed, her stare fell at the solutions to his riddles she was holding. Too embarrassed to speak, she put the papers on his desk.

"Is there anything you can do?" he meanly inquired and gestured Danielle to leave.

Tears were held in check while Danielle walked to her office, took her coat, and without a glance at the monitor, got out and ran down the stairs, away from Fitzgerald Hall. The freezing-cold air did not wipe out the humiliation. Her face was burning, her eyes stung. Even worse, she could not lay all the blame on Lisitsin's rudeness and insufferable arrogance. If she hadn't dumbly followed his movements when the situation called for speaking out, most likely she wouldn't have been shown the door.

The knot in Danielle's throat started loosening when she thought about solving Lisitsin's riddles while keeping the simulations' data analysis in good shape. She sauntered between the Greek Revival edifices, reflecting that even though she did not have Antigone's fortitude, she was not entirely inept.

If only Green could give more input and Lisitsin much less, she thought. Yet, by some bad lot, Green scarcely came up with ideas. Lisitsin, on the other hand, was a fount of ideas.

Cogitating about her woes, Danielle did not notice a group of young women standing in front of Austen Hall until she heard their animated voices. A swift glance noted their pampered hair, long ebony coats, and knee-long boots snugged prettily to the calves. She stopped, suddenly aware that the coat she had bought two years ago was too short and of the wrong color; her drab footwear could not bear any comparison.

Rats, Danielle thought, envying their lightheartedness, the easy way they fit into a group. Curious who they were, she started to pay attention to fragments of conversation that reached her ears. She heard of "true symbolism" and someone named Harry Potter. A "Philosopher's Stone" was mentioned as both a physical and metaphorical elixir of life. Concluding that they raved about a fantasy story, Danielle resumed her stroll. Even though she was ordered out of Lisitsin's office, she was too much of a physicist to swoon over mythical heroes or to envy women who studied entertaining fluff.

You wouldn't be so feisty and chatty if you were coming from Green's lecture, she told the women in her mind. Or if you had to listen to Green disparage anything imaginative that wasn't formulated and at least numerically solved. Maybe you'd giggle when Lisitsin tells you that gods do not bake clay jars, but soon enough you'll find out that he is a conceited bully.

She ambled between Austen and Campbell Halls, drawing pleasure from mentally abusing the professors. Knowing that Green and Lisitsin were adverse to anything uplifting, she conjured galloping warriors, gallant knights and treacherous gnomes. In her mind's eye, she saw forsaken civilizations, the bygone times when gods mixed with heroes and monsters interbred with beasts. Her childhood heroes were all brave, noble and just. And none of them, Danielle realized, would have made a successful professor of physics, nor even a candidate for a tenured position.

She smiled at the thought. Leaving fairy tales and mythical heroes behind was a natural process of growing. Like many others, she had turned to science fiction, where she had discovered alien worlds, hyperspace and time-traveling. Her fascination with space was a prelude for studying physics, a profession that transcended societies and explored the uncharted waters of nature. After all these years, she readily burned the midnight oil until a simulation would run or equations would be solved, but she was tired of working hard to fulfill every professorial whim, only to be silenced or treated as if her work was nonsense or rubbish. Rebellious and longing for human empathy, she left the campus and turned towards the Hungry Boson.

In the teashop, she saw unhurried patrons; red and pink roses decorated every table. After greeting Anne, Danielle looked inquiringly at the crimson flowers that burst from a big vase on the counter.

"It's Valentine's Day," Anne said.

How could I forget? Danielle thought. "I was engrossed by work," she said miserably. "Somehow it slipped my mind."

"The day isn't over yet," Anne said encouragingly. "Do you want cappuccino as usual?"

"Yes, and a chocolate éclair please."

"Now, why don't you tell me what you were working on?"

"It's a new model that aims to explain why galaxies rotate, and why universe undergoes accelerated expansion," Danielle opened. She sat on a stool, gratified that Anne wanted to know about her work, and that she would be able to use unscientific and intuitive terms.

The cappuccino was ready, while Danielle described galaxies as swirling eddies in celestial ocean, and dark energy as an invisible force that spun these eddies while pushing them apart.

Seeing Danielle's entrancement with space's sweeping grandeur, Anne silently put her order on the counter.

"Thank you." Danielle raised the mug and sniffed it appreciatively. "The last time I had coffee not on my desk was at the departmental colloquium over a week ago. Honestly, I shouldn't call that turbid concoction a coffee."

"That tradition of the physics department also appalled the speaker of that colloquium. Isaac brought her here to show that she could have a decent cup of coffee within a stone's throw from the campus."

Isaac? Danielle registered the link, then said, "I'm sure she liked it here very much."

"She was very nice about the Hungry Boson. Did you find her lecture inspiring?"

"Not really. I know very little about the topic."

"I thought that having so few successful female physicists to look up to..." Anne did not finish the sentence.

Frankly, Danielle thought, she was way more impressed by Olivia Birkhead becoming the first female faculty at the TIST's physics department than by a successful professor who spoke about something she was not interested in. Since she could not tell that to Anne, Danielle cast her mind back to Karen Gould's talk.

"Her career is outstanding," Danielle said. "It was clear that she is a motivated, no-nonsense scientist, but personally I thought she was a tad too diligent to be really inspiring."

"You're too young not to be judgmental." Anne's voice was tinged with a reproach. "It must take a lot of determination and hard work for a woman to reach a high academic position."

"It certainly does. I should have appreciated more her academic position regardless of her research topic, but I have that flaw of focusing on what one researches. Well, I suppose that such outlook reflects my lack of ambition."

Anne did not respond immediately, thus causing Danielle to wonder whether she had made another faux pas. When she spoke, Anne's voice was very low. "Your ambition goes beyond getting and holding a position. Since I know only few physicists who aspire to that much, I'd say that you are among the most ambitious physicists I've met."

Danielle did not reply, but after returning to her office, she searched for Isaac on the homepage of the department of biophysics and bio-informatics. A single name emerged - Isaac Gurevich, an associate professor. She read his research interests (protein folding, nucleic acids and some other, unfamiliar, biological terms), skipped his recent publications, then clicked on the résumé.

"BSc in physics from MIT. A PhD in physics from the King Solomon University. Thesis adviser: prof. Jonah Cobs."

So, one of Jonah's last students got a tenure in biophysics, Danielle reflected. She looked at Isaac's photo, and wondered if he was enticed by the more rewarding pasture than theoretical physics. At twenty-eight, she had seen enough to accept that bright and properly ambitious physicists preferred to get a tenure at a good university rather than to nourish hardly achievable dreams. Isaac's face, framed by ginger hair, brought to mind a lovable puppy, one that was too smart to be trained to do what it did not want to.

"You may look guileless, but you wouldn't let your work be overlooked or belittled," she told the photo. A latent humor in Issac's expression implied that the mere suggestion was a lame joke.

Closing Isaac's homepage, Danielle returned to Taylor's preprint and her simulations' data. It was late in the evening when she completed a new set of calculations and could summarize her findings.

"Hi, George," she typed. "The universe in the simulations is just over six billion years old. It's on the verge of an epoch when dark energy density equals matter energy density. Attached is the data analysis of the matter aggregates that were forged in the various runs. As you can see, after months of tinkering with correlations, I have a fair idea what the data would yield without the new analysis. What the simulation needs is a more relevant physics, and not a new method of toying with data. Danielle."

Feeling more tired than triumphant, she reread the email, then deleted everything from "As you can see" up to "toying with data," and sent it to Green.

On her way home, she contemplated a new algorithm that would assign every galaxy a random axis of rotation and a random angular momentum, while still imposing conservation of the total angular momentum. Cogitating on how to introduce universal rotation that would force faraway galaxies to recede from each other faster and faster, she hit a roadblock.

Late in the evening, Jonathan phoned. For Valentine's Day he had excellent news: the technical part of the patent application was completed, and he would stay in Thorboro for the foreseeable future.

"Any plans?" Danielle asked suggestively.

"We should be ready for the beta in early April," Jonathan answered, implying that his plans amounted to work, work, and work.

When Michelle heard from Danielle that Jonathan would be in Thorboro during February, she lost no time in arranging the family dinner with the Lerners. Jonathan readily cooperated. Sarah's response was less definite and less pleasant, but Michelle managed to secure a date within a handful of phone calls and without too much hassle. Telling no one but her husband, Michelle also invited Aunt Sophie, Natalie, and Dorian.

* * *

A few days later, Lisitsin summoned Danielle to his office.

Please, not another riddle, she wished while walking along the hallway. And if he hadn't made any progress, let the brainstorm be short, she added to the wish list before knocking on his door.

"I went over the solutions you left me," Lisitsin said. "What I've noticed is that you have difficulties handling the more intricate calculations."

Danielle opened her mouth to say that the main problem was the sheer amount of calculations, but Lisitsin raised a hand, indicating he was not to be interrupted.

"I understand that you want to continue in science after your present post-doc," he said.

Considering their last meeting, Lisitsin's friendly interest was unexpected.

"Yes," Danielle said.

"Then you need to hone your skills and expand your horizons."

Alarmed that the next riddle was going to be excruciatingly hard, Danielle darted sideways glances at equations filling the whiteboard.

"For example," Lisitsin went on, "can you read and understand current theoretical papers?"

"I read papers related to my work, but I hardly have time to keep track of papers in other fields."

"Yet you must do so if you aspire to stay in academia." Although Lisitsin spoke firmly, a foxy smile lingered on his face. "As it's easier to stay updated in a stimulating environment, I recommend that you join our journal club."

"What?" the cry burst from Danielle's mouth. How could Lisitsin present such a demand as if it was a benevolent suggestion?

"It's very informal, a few graduate students from high-energy, a graduate student from applied mathematics and an undergraduate majoring in physics. We meet twice a month to discuss a recent paper that everyone reads in advance."

"I really don't see," Danielle said as she racked her brains for an excuse to decline the invitation without flatly refusing it.

"Our next meeting is on last Friday of the month, at two, at the seminar room." Lisitsin handed her a paper. "Make a photocopy of this and read as much as you can."

Silently cursing, Danielle took the paper and left. Any time she could spare from data analysis, she intended to use on incorporating galactic rotation in the code. She planned to launch new runs before leaving for the weekend. Instead, she was obliged to go to a journal club several hours before her flight.

She skimmed the abstract on the night before the journal club meeting, and dozed off at the beginning of the introduction. Soon after that, Danielle found herself alone in a bleak, lifeless landscape, surrounded by milky-white currents of snowflakes. Sundered from Jon, buffeted by a ferocious wind, she staggered on her feet, tried to keep moving despite the turbulent snow that thrust and pounded her at random. Walk where to? There were no cabins in sight, nothing but a rapidly moving snow. She could go anywhere or stay in place, for all directions looked alike. She stood transfixed, shaking with fear. Something lurked in the raging chaos of swarming snowflakes. Besides the mayhem of white flow, a menacing presence stalked the forest. She strained her eyes and looked around. A bronze shape flashed in the distance, a blur of red-brown color. About to scream, Danielle woke up.

Mulling over the dream in the morning, Danielle decided that the scary figure was a fox or a little fawn. Reaching the office, she had no time to wonder about the dream's meaning. Her program finally ran with rotating galaxies, which were pushed apart by a constant dark energy. Too excited to delve into calculations, she turned to the graphics software. On the monitor, hundreds of specks blinked over an inky-black background, filling the universe with tiny spin-tops. Delighted, she rotated the image and zoomed in and out, changed the background to white, blue, and then to gray. At least in the very beginning, the addition of galactic rotation did not cause any visible changes. Yet, it was a relief that the new addition did not stall the program, which went on churning even more equations.

At two o'clock, Danielle took the paper and went to the seminar room. Lisitsin arrived before she could make any progress with the introduction. Five minutes after everyone sat around the ebony table, Danielle gathered that the paper studied a twisted space-time. After another five minutes, she concluded that the study concerned a universe governed by physics that made

Einstein's general relativity look comprehensible by comparison. A quarter of an hour after they began, Danielle dumbly stared at other participants, without making any attempt to follow them or even find out how many dimensions that universe had. She tried, yet she could not discern the math student from the high-energy physics graduate students. Their cockiness, the frightening brainpower and the innate loftiness were all too familiar. A huge mistake, Danielle decided, finding out that she was enclosed for at least an hour with three Paul Zeemans keen to show off their enormous intellect. She felt out of place, and embarrassingly conscious of being the only female in the room. Hoping to remain unnoticed until it was over, she drew a small consolation from the quietness of the undergraduate student, who looked like a teenager. His lack of understanding is excusable, she reflected, painfully aware that hers was not quite so.

For a while the graduate students sparred with equations and with each other, Lisitsin fired equations and cried "nonsense." During a momentarily silence, the teen made a lazy remark. Impressed that he ventured to speak, Danielle darted a furtive glance at Lisitsin. From his and others' responses, she gathered that the remark was aimed precisely to the point. Awestruck, she realized that the kid had already mastered the content of the paper and was simply bored.

The moment passed, and others joined the fray, tossing mathematical expressions with unwavering confidence. Keenly aware of her inferiority, Danielle thought that Susan Brophy, Olivia Birckhead, or any other competent female theoretical physicist, should be sitting in her place, for she would never be able to hold her own against the guys. A mist of misery fogged her vision; her head felt heavier. Others went on and on; their voices ricocheted, turning into a meaningless buzz. In her mind's eyes, galaxies shrank and became snowflakes, which darted in all directions. She sat motionless, doing her best not to draw attention, while her mind attuned to uncoordinated motion of objects spinning and drifting in front of her eyes. In a flash of insight she grasped why the horizontal currents of snowflakes felt incongruous. There had to be a tiny preferential orientation – the Earth's pull made the motion not entirely random.

In a leap that took very little time, Danielle formed a picture of a seemingly random galactic rotation superimposed on a barely detectable universal rotation. She was contemplating the idea when a squeak of moving chairs indicated that the others were rising.

"You didn't say anything," Lisitsin's voice rumbled disapprovingly. "Did you follow any part of the discussion?"

"No." Danielle turned her face to Lisitsin, but in her mind's eye dust-like galaxies were spinning and receding. "But I did some useful thinking, so it wasn't a complete waste of time."

"Will you tell me about it?" Lisitsin asked all-too-kindly.

"The orientation of clusters of galaxies is usually assumed to be random."

"And what do you think?" Lisitsin interrupted, his voice oozing sarcasm.

Elated by her vision, Danielle was oblivious to the mocking of someone too big to count as a snowflake and too small to overshadow a galaxy.

"There might be a spatially oriented component," she said. "If one envisions galaxies as snowflakes during a blizzard and one looks for a short period of time, then the snowflakes dart in every direction and their movement looks random, even though they are always pulled by gravity. Eventually, each snowflake falls down."

"Are you suggesting a blizzard of galaxies? That's rubbish."

"It's not about a blizzard," Danielle said impatiently. The image was still clear in her head. "What if galactic rotation had originated from local phenomena, but it is superimposed with universal rotation? The axes of rotation of clusters of galaxies would have a tiny preferential orientation, which is masked by a large random component."

Liking the idea more and more, she did not wait for Lisitsin's response.

"I'm going to add universal rotation to my program. If it works in the simulation, we might be able to see whether it accounts for the dark energy."

"Nonsense," Lisitsin barked before he strode out of the seminar room.

18

DINNER AT MELLERS

"Can you put the tulips in the center?" Michelle asked.

Danielle laid the vase on an alabaster-colored linen tablecloth. The contrast of tulips' yellow, red, pink and dark-purple colors enlivened the otherwise homey, placid surrounding; the effect was bold and beautiful. Opposites don't always blend that well, she noted, finding yet another reason as to why Aunt Sophie and Sarah Lerner should not have been invited to the same dinner.

"Have you told Sarah who your other guests are?" Danielle asked Michelle, when Michelle brought a stack of very fine porcelain plates from the cupboard.

"No, I didn't."

"I'm always glad to see Aunt Sophie," Danielle added, "but she and Sarah belong to two different, incompatible spheres."

Seeing that her mother was not concerned, Danielle went on. "Sarah is too used to worship status and money. She won't deign to show the least respect for Aunt Sophie's archaic views and her ingrained dignity. Since Aunt Sophie abhors vulgarity in opinion even more than in conduct, we can imagine how she'll respond when Sarah extols the DeWitts and drones on how amazing the wedding is going to be."

"Sophia can be forthright on occasion, but she'd never say or imply anything improper at a family dinner."

"No, she will just let her eyebrows go expressively up and down. After a while even Sarah may notice the meaning of Aunt Sophie's hawk-eyed stares."

"So?" Michelle asked. "We might have an entertaining dinner."

"Or a bumpy one," Danielle countered. "I won't be surprised if there will be a war of titans or a tight-lipped silence."

Determined not to worry beforehand, Michelle took a plate and fondly brushed her fingertips over the delicate pink rosebuds painted on the ivory-white background. She and Joe had acquired the matching dinner and tea set during a vacation in London, in a shop that specialized in selling fine china for two or three centuries. The price still made Michelle squirm.

"The pattern is old-fashioned, but the craftsmanship is exquisite," Michelle said. She traced a gold circle along the plate's rim. Several years after she had entered that shop to indulge a tourist's curiosity, the sets were becoming a family heirloom.

Knowing her mother's fascination with English aristocracy and the highbrow British culture, Danielle said, "Aunt Sophie will appreciate your using the set while Dorian is here."

"I thought that everyone would enjoy sitting down to a nicely set dinner."

"Did you?" Danielle asked incredulously. "Tali will fret herself that Dorian might knock something, Richard won't care and Sarah can't distinguish between fine porcelain and a cheap imitation. If you really want that snob to appreciate the craftsmanship and beauty, clip a price tag to her plate and drop the name and the location of the shop where you bought it."

Although Michelle privately agreed with the portrayal, she shook her head. Sarah's want of sophistication did not take her mind off Danielle's grouchy mood.

"What about you and Jonathan?" Michelle asked.

"Jon? He barely notices what he eats, let alone such trifles as plates and utensils. His mind is set on whatever is going on at Nickka."

There was a rift, Michelle concluded, looking at her daughter's defiant expression. When Jonathan had asked her to postpone the dinner, Michelle had no doubt what would be his surprise for Danielle. Her expectations to hear about the long-awaited engagement ebbed after Danielle returned from Lucas Lodge. Her daughter had had "a fabulous time, and best birthday present I could wish for," but no proposal from Jonathan. Remembering several alarming premonitions she had had in the intervening weeks, Michelle felt she should get to the bottom of her daughter's discontent with Jonathan. She wanted Joe to add his weight to her warnings, but he was upstairs, catching up with sleep after operating in the wee hours.

"It's a stressing period for Jonathan," Michelle gently observed. "Maybe you could spend more time in Thorboro, be here when he needs you."

"If I slack off another weekend I might as well leave Green's group," Danielle retorted. "Besides, Jon doesn't need me to hover around. While you and I set the table, he attends meetings at Nickka. He will go back to work after the dinner."

Remembering her husband's typical schedule when she was at home with a child and two babies, Michelle did not bestow much sympathy on her daughter. "If you are fine with that, why do you grumble as if you aren't?"

"Jon doesn't let anything distract him, and we all respect him for that. But when I show a similar tenacity, why is that a strain on our relationship?"

"A woman cannot immure herself without consideration of others." Michelle stopped, seeing her daughter bristling with irritation.

"And yet," Danielle commented, "she is expected to hold out against hordes of brilliant guys vying for every available tenure-track position."

Michelle looked ruefully at her daughter's stubborn expression. "I've never dismissed your aspirations to return to TIST as a faculty member, and I'm not discouraging you from competing with men. All I ask is that you bear in mind that there is a fine line between ambition and obsession."

Ambition and obsession. Danielle repeated the words in her mind, and wondered if her mother really knew what they meant. Could Mom understand how it feels lying awake for hours because the mind cannot stop looking for answers about aligned rotation? Or having these recurring dreams, where whirlwind currents spin gray, misty substance? No, Danielle concluded. If her mother was aware of the travails of cracking something unknown, she wouldn't caution so easily about fine lines.

"My research isn't an obsession," Danielle said. "It's an opportunity to do my best. Regardless of Nickka's success and

Jon's and my need for a steady income, I'll never be at peace if I add nothing to the understanding of dark energy."

Michelle's head threatened to implode as it sank in that given a chance to pursue her career, Danielle might not go back to Jonathan. She rubbed her throbbing temples and trudged to the cupboard for the silverware. Upon returning, Michelle silently started to place forks, knives and spoons with immaculate precision.

Seeing her mother's subdued face, Danielle reached Michelle and embraced her.

"My interest in physics came from you," Danielle whispered, then moved a bit and held her mother's hands. "I don't know if the discovery of dark energy heralds another golden age in physics, but it's one of the few discoveries that weren't predicted theoretically. It'd be a huge mistake not to take a part in the ongoing effort to understand the origins of dark energy."

Michelle's face paled as recollections she had quelled long ago threatened to open the floodgates. Fighting to compose herself, she pulled her hands away and went to bring wineglasses. She suppressed her memories, stifled unwarranted emotions until she felt only a dull ache. She returned with sparkling crystals and sent Danielle to bring linen napkins. She waited for Danielle to fold some, then said, "I wish your research to succeed, but not at the expense of your relations with Jonathan. When all is said and done, your self-fulfillment shouldn't depend entirely on making a mark in cosmology."

Danielle finished with the folding, then arranged the napkins by the plate. "It doesn't work like that with Jon and me," she said. "We thrive on forging something new and unconventional. Take that away and we won't be able to adore each other so much."

Remembering similar arguments she herself had said almost thirty years ago, Michelle let the subject go. After the table was set, they went into the kitchen, where Michelle cooked and Danielle washed vegetables. Their conversation flitted between general gossip and family matters unrelated to Danielle's affairs.

To no one's surprise, Sophia, Natalie and Dorian arrived almost an hour too early. After the usual exchange of hugs, kisses and comments, Michelle took her aunt, with Dorian in tow, to inspect the table. Natalie reposed in the kitchen while Danielle unpacked two large bags from the Hungarian Café.

"Guess what I chose," Dorian asked when a nuts-and-raisins strudel, a cherry strudel, a Viennese Sacher cake, and a tray with brownies were lain on the counter. Danielle pointed at the brownies and thanked Natalie.

"Mrs. Lowery phoned last evening," Natalie said after Sophia and Michelle came into the kitchen. Without waiting for Natalie to relate Dorian's latest escapade at school, Michelle wordlessly gestured to Danielle to whisk him upstairs. In Danielle's former room, Dorian recounted the incident from a very different perspective.

"I sat in the class quietly minding my own business. All of a sudden, I heard Mrs. Lowery yelling 'Dorian McCormick, stop gazing at black-holes and answer my question.' Just like that, out of the blue."

"What did you do?" Danielle asked solemnly. For Dorian, a teacher asking a question during a lesson was indeed an unprovoked intrusion.

"I explained that one cannot gaze at black-holes because light is absorbed by their huge gravitational field, but that it's possible to gaze at jets a black hole thrusts outwards."

"Did you have to?" Danielle moaned, not expecting an answer. Dorian was usually clueless about what he had done wrong. She weighed the advisability of bringing up some rudiments of social behavior, but decided that it was more important to prevent mishaps during the evening.

"Do you know that Jonathan's parents are coming to dinner?"

"Yeah, I got a long lecture about manners on our way here." Dorian grimaced to convey what he thought about it. He circled the room, looking for something interesting to do.

"And?" Danielle prompted.

"I forgot most of it, but I made a list of subjects I'm not allowed to talk about."

"Good. Tell me what they are."

"Mrs. Lowery, school, the board of education, the stupidity of the educational system in whole."

"Very wise," Danielle agreed, thinking of Sarah Lerner.

Dorian meanwhile stopped in front of a set of Asimov's

books. "Do you like *Foundation?*" he asked.

"Of course."

Encouraged, he launched into a comparison between *Foundation* and *Star Wars*, mind tricks and sortilege. After airing his views and not succeeding in changing Danielle's, he asked to play on the computer.

"Chess or Mahjong?" Danielle offered, turning it on.

Dorian looked at her pityingly. "I brought a game," he said, dashing downstairs. A minute later, he brandished a computer game in front of Danielle's eyes."Do you want to play?"

"No, but I will stay to watch you."

Enemy spaceships popped in the space between stars. Trying to outmaneuver them, Dorian moved his spaceships, transported stealthy fighters, and deployed troops. He moved fast, exchanged intense fire with the enemy fleets, then he grinned happily, satisfied with blasting the enemy strongholds.

To Danielle's relief, Jonathan arrived on time. His parents came, as expected, pointedly late.

Joseph welcomed the latecomers, took their coats, and invited them to the living room. Sarah went in first. She registered everything from the furniture to the two unfamiliar women, affected a polite smile, and handed Michelle a box from Pierre's.

"Sarah and Richard," Michelle introduced. "My aunt, Sophia, and my cousin, Natalie."

A two-faced shrew, Danielle silently summed up Sarah's behavior some ten minutes later. Although Sarah sat on the sofa with Aunt Sophie, she completely ignored the older woman while skillfully fishing for professional and personal details from Natalie. Digging up that Natalie held a relatively low position at a pharmaceutical firm, and that she was a single mother, Sarah pigeonholed her as a failure. The mouth of the loud proponent of career women twisted into a forced smile; she excused herself, and went to the fireplace where Richard and Joseph talked.

"No one talks about the glass ceiling," Sarah commented, butting into the men's conversation. "Even open-minded, liberal men forget the hardships mounting in front of the less-privileged working mothers."

"Dinner is ready," Michelle announced. "Call Dorian," she quietly told Danielle. "And on your way, turn on the lights above the dining table."

"Isn't it magical?" Danielle whispered to Dorian when they neared the table. A soft glow illuminated the old-fashioned, dainty china. Silver utensils gleamed. Countless crystal facets reflected the flame-like colors of the blooming tulips, and dappled the tablecloth with gem-like glitter.

"It's boring," Dorian whispered back. "I wish we could enact an attack of trolls or an explosion."

We might have both, Danielle thought, darting a glance at Sarah.

Michelle asked Sophia to sit first, then, leaving an empty chair, she invited Sarah and Richard to sit down. Joseph sat next to Sarah, and before Natalie could protest, she was directed to a seat between Joseph and Jonathan. Danielle sat by Jonathan's other side. Subtly but firmly, Dorian was flanked to a chair between Danielle and his grandmother. Finally, Michelle sat between Sophia and Richard.

Mom could have a career in diplomacy, Danielle reflected. Looking sideways, she saw her father smiling as he poured French and Californian wines; Sophia approvingly examined the smoked eel that was placed in front of her. Dorian seemed to be mesmerized by paper-thin slices of Italian salami. Richard did not examine the food, yet he looked pleased. Even Sarah, Danielle observed, lost some of her petulance while scrutinizing sophisticated appetizers from Chives and Tarragon. Danielle smiled at Jonathan. The quaint atmosphere, a synergy of refined food, pretty china, flowers and lights, all melded into a spellbinding moment, to enjoy and to treasure as a memory.

The first course proceeded pleasantly, until Sarah affected a benevolent smile and addressed Dorian.

"Your mother told me you are a good student. Do you like school?"

Dorian raised his eyes; his stare tried to vaporize Mrs. Lerner. Danielle kicked him under the table.

"It's fine," Dorian muttered, recalling the correct answer.

"That's good," Sarah said approvingly. Addressing no one in particular, she added, "With so many resources invested into improving education, it is reassuring to know that our efforts bear fruit."

Sophia's veined hand clasped Dorian's hand before he could utter a single word, and it stayed there until Dorian lowered his stare to his plate. Sarah noticed the gesture, which spared her from finding out what Dorian thought about School or Education. She deemed that the child was shy.

"What is your favorite subject?" Sarah asked encouragingly.

The conceit, patronizing voice reminded Dorian of Mrs. Lowery's tacky bouts of false friendliness. Categorizing Mrs. Lerner as a phony, Dorian squeezed though his teeth, "Psychohistory."

Sarah looked surprised. She did not expect from a boy in an elementary school to hear about the peripheral discipline. She studied Dorian's childish mouth, his round chin and undeniably intelligent bright eyes. A likable boy, Sarah reflected.

"Did you hear about psychohistory in a gifted-and-talented program?" Sarah asked.

"I read about it in a trilogy called *Foundation*. I usually read books during the lessons, unless we have a quiz or an exam."

"Schools in the district offer an accelerated curriculum for the most advanced students," Sarah said to Natalie. Her voice left no doubt that it was a mother's fault when a child failed to follow the approved syllabus. "His teacher should be able to advise you about the existing options and recommend tests that Dorian may take. I'd cooperate with the system instead of letting him read who-knows-what in class."

"Who-knows-what," Dorian scornfully hissed, darting Sarah a scorching glare.

"Don't even dream of replying," Danielle hastily whispered into Dorian's ear. She looked at her mother, wordlessly asking her to draw Sarah's attention from Dorian. Michelle gave a tiny nod and turned to Sarah.

"Are Amos and Amy using a bridal registry?" Michelle asked amiably.

"No, Amy prefers old heirlooms over anything new and modern." Condescending to be gracious to Michelle, Sarah added, "Amy might like your set. It's in a very good condition."

"Thank you," Michelle said, her eyes glinting with laughter. "If you are interested, I'll find you the address of the store."

A minute ago Sarah pondered on how to flip her plate discreetly to check the manufacturer's details. After Michelle had spoken, Sarah quickly removed her fingers from what she now believed to be a cheap imitation.

Pretending not to notice, Michelle said in the same pleasant voice, "Joe and I bought it in London." She named the store. "I'm pretty sure they offer international shipping."

Sarah's narrowed eyes quickly returned to their usual size. She thought that Amy would appreciate a royal coat-of-arms on a saucer, and even Alice might be impressed if she dropped a word about shipping from London. On the other hand, Sarah reasoned, Alice would expect them to buy soup tureens and a variety of covered dishes along with complete sets for two dozen guests. There would be a lot of expenses, all of which might be needless.

"Amy will prefer to choose her china with Alice and Fiona," Sarah said. "Amy has an excellent taste, but she defers to her family. Alice and Fiona are orchestrating the reception..."

"Which will turn out beautifully," Richard added, before his wife could start mewling about DeWitts monopolizing the wedding and deciding how much everything would cost. "It'll be subtly elegant and reasonably traditional."

"That must be a relief for you," Sophia said. "It's a good sign when a young woman doesn't insist on making an embarrassing display of shallowness and extravagance out of her wedding."

Sarah managed a lopsided smile, then turned to discourse on Amy's accomplishments, which ranged from having chosen a perfect profession to being brought up in lovely house in Edva. Dorian twiddled his napkin and twisted his legs around the chair. Michelle waited for the men to be done with the appetizers, then cued Danielle to help her clear the table and bring the next course.

Danielle brought salad bowls made of the same exquisite china, then carried a matching covered dish with tiny potatoes baked with olive oil, thyme and rosemary. At last, Michelle came in with her signature roast beef. Joseph poured more wine. Danielle and Jonathan grinned to each other. Sophia complimented Michelle on the tender and juicy roast beef. For a while the only sounds were of cutting, sipping and chewing.

Seeing that Jonathan emptied his plate, Michelle offered him a second helping. Joseph asked about his work.

"We are pretty much on schedule. Roy hired a team to work on quality assurance before the beta. They are starting next week." Half-turning to Michelle, Jonathan thanked her and tucked into the potatoes and roast beef.

"We are also having a round of hiring," Richard said. "I heard that other firms at TRP are also doing so."

Danielle, not being interested in the concurrent hiring at Thorboro's Research Park, half-listened to Aunt Sophie persuading Dorian to taste the veggies on his plate. *I was wrong,* Danielle complacently thought. A mutual dislike between Sophia and Sarah did not escalate into an open enmity.

"If you seriously intend to return to Thorboro," Sarah's forceful voice was, strangely enough, directed at Danielle, "you should take advantage of the boom in the Triangle."

Considering that she was working very hard to be able to return to Thorboro, Danielle found Sarah's "if" quite insulting. She thought that Jonathan would step in on her behalf, yet he continued to fork tiny potatoes, apparently unaware of his mother's suggestion.

"I don't know much about software or bio-technology," Danielle said lightly, "nor anyone at TRP who might hire cosmologists."

"Doesn't that make you rethink your profession?" Sarah tilted her head towards Natalie, hinting at a cautionary example of a woman who failed in everything.

"I don't see any reason to make changes in the midst of a post-doctorate at a leading group in the field," Danielle countered. She kept her voice reserved and slightly condescending, both to avenge Tali and in the hope that it would deter Sarah from making other snide suggestions.

Tension solidified around the table.

"I'd have expected someone at your age to be reasonable about her prospects of getting a tenured faculty position," Sarah said. Her voice was impersonal, as if she was addressing an audience of strangers. She registered Danielle's hurt expression and the old woman's tightly pressed lips. Michelle was staring expressionlessly at her flowers. Richard and Jonathan looked embarrassed; the doctor remained unruffled.

"What else would you expect?" Danielle asked, forcing

herself to remain civil.

"That you would make a good use of your PhD and of being a postdoctoral fellow at King Solomon University. Take some courses in business administration and start applying for an entry level management job."

Danielle stifled a snigger. The idea of her in a managerial position sounded more absurd than applying for a job in software development or in bio-technology.

"Do you also want me to work my way up?" she whispered to Jonathan.

Before Jonathan could answer or Danielle and Sophia could stop him, Dorian sprung to his feet, his face contorted with detest. He looked at Sarah, as if she was one of the laser monsters, more grotesque than vile.

"Does Danielle have to leave cosmology to marry Jonathan?" Dorian cried. "She doesn't like to boss others around. She wants to make discoveries and become a famous physicist."

Every adult around the table smiled, except Sarah, whose face reddened.

Sarah weighed her options, wavering whether to ignore Dorian's impudence. Seeing Sophia patting his arm, Danielle smiling gleefully and others looking amused, Sarah's face puckered. Affronted that no one checked the boy, she felt it was too much being put down by a child and then laughed at and humiliated by his pathetic relatives. Seething with righteous mortification, she decided to leave immediately, even if she would have to drag Richard from the table.

Sophia Bloom's hawkish eyes saw a selfish woman flying into a temper. She addressed Richard:

"Dorian's childish outburst must sound strange to those who are not familiar with our family's history."

"Which part?" Sarah mocked, gesturing Richard to get up. "Making discoveries or becoming a famous physicist?"

Having fifty years' worth of experience with Moira, Sophia knew better than to take any notice of Sarah. She sat upright like an old gentlewoman, a cloak of dignity draping her old-fashioned clothes and wrinkled skin.

"Danielle is a third generation to go into physics. My brother, Aaron Lichtfeld, studied physics. He was in a pioneering field in his time. He was cut down by an explosion in a nuclear reactor he worked at."

"I'm sorry." Under the table, Richard put a firm hand on Sarah's thigh, restraining her to sit down.

"Aaron died young, before having a family," Sophia continued, "but my sister Rachel and I have tried to keep his legacy, telling about him to our children. Michelle picked up the torch when she chose to study physics."

"Auntie," Michelle said very softly, as if reminding something to her aunt. Shaking her head to stop interruptions, Sophia went on.

"In the early seventies very few women ventured into physics. Michelle did. She graduated with honors and was accepted into TIST's graduate school."

"Grandma," Dorian whispered. He seemed to dread what was about to come.

Sophia again shook her head. "My niece and grandson are uncomfortable when I ramble about our family," she told Richard. "To some people the story is bound to sound pointless. Our legacy has nothing to do with estates and heirlooms."

"What you say is very interesting," Richard said gallantly.

"I see where Jonathan comes from." Sophia's voice emanated respect. "Michelle and Joseph were married in the summer before Michelle began her graduate studies. She did well there, working throughout her pregnancy. Michelle left TIST's graduate school after giving birth to Danielle."

Please stop, Danielle silently implored Aunt Sophie. She heard Michelle taking a deep breath.

"When Danielle was growing up, she found it difficult to accept that Michelle had dropped graduate studies for her." Sophia's voice became gentler. She looked old and vulnerable. "Being a clever girl and occasionally rebellious, Danielle often questioned Michelle's decisions. But inheriting her mother's love for physics, she followed in her footsteps."

Thank you very much for sharing all that with Sarah, Danielle said in her mind.

Jonathan draped his hand around Danielle's shoulder. Sarah snickered.

"It is not an easy legacy," Sophia concluded, looking at

Jonathan. "Danielle is stubborn, and being a Lichtfeld, she is not very practical. Are you uncomfortable with what she does and does not do?"

"I'm very comfortable," Jonathan solemnly assured Sophia, yet his eyes glinted with mischief as he turned to face Danielle. "On the other hand, if you would rather model lingerie, I will accept your decision."

Sophia's thin lips curved into a heartwarming smile; there was a telltale mist in her eyes. Michelle beamed happily, while striving not to look triumphant. Joseph smiled broadly, and even Richard, although he did not dare to smile, looked pleased. Natalie, acutely aware that she had no loving man to share her and Dorian's life with, covered her quivering lips with a hand. Sarah wore a stony expression. Dorian made retching grimaces.

Knowing she had made her point, and cautious not to overdo it, Sophia said, "Danielle, if you are done, would you take Dorian upstairs until we are ready for desserts?"

Danielle rose up, feeling that she also needed some time away from the table. She hoped that Jonathan would join them soon.

"Your modeling underwear, that was disgusting," Dorian said as soon as they were out of earshot.

"He was kidding," Danielle explained, smothering a smile.

She expected Dorian to go straight to the computer, but he slumped on her former bed.

"It's lucky you're not superstitious," he said pensively.

"Aha," Danielle replied, thinking of something else.

"Do you believe in fate?"

"Fate?" Danielle echoed. "Are you talking about a godly power encountered in mythology or a predestination of future?"

"Not the three Moirae," Dorian groaned. "A Fate, like having a destiny."

Rats, Danielle said to herself. Discussing "A Fate, like having a destiny" would force her to thread onto a topic where the subtle differences between mythology, *Star Wars,* and reality were completely blurred. Aunt Sophie always discouraged such conversations and Danielle usually saw her point. Yet, she deemed that Dorian deserved to be heard after his tussle with Sarah.

"Mythological heroes or Jedi knights might have destinies," Danielle said, "but supernatural powers do not currently dwell on Earth. Nothing governs or predetermines our choices and actions."

"That's," Dorian stopped, stumbling on adjectives belonging to the forbidden-words list.

"You can say nonsense. That might be lame but it's not bad language."

"You can't say nonsense about fate and destiny," Dorian protested.

"I didn't say that they are nonsense, only that they are figments of human imagination."

"Then how do you explain that you are the only one in the family who went to study physics? That you left Thorboro instead of marrying Jonathan?"

"Probably because I'm the only impractical Lichtfeld."

"It's all a part of your destiny. It was determined at your birth."

Pity welled when it dawned on Danielle that her overly imaginative cousin believed in what he was saying. Reflecting how hard it must be to grow without a father, she dearly wanted to soothe Dorian's confounded mind.

"I think that you confuse destiny with legacy," she gently suggested.

"I'm not a five year old or as stupid as Mrs. Lowery thinks."

"Okay," Danielle conceded, "you know the meaning."

She racked her mind, wondering what the heck she was supposed to say next.

"Do you want me to tell you about your destiny?" Dorian asked, clearly eager to share the information.

She wanted him to just read a book or play quietly on the computer. Unwilling to offend him, she said:

"If you are privy to Fate or Destiny or have eavesdropped on someone and want to spill it, I'm listening."

A blush spread over Dorian's ears, indicating that the source of his information was human.

"I don't know why, but you almost died at birth," he whispered conspiratorially. "Aunt Shelly saved you by making a vow that she'd leave physics if you survived."

If Dorian used telekinesis or ate a grapefruit, he could not have shocked Danielle any more.

"Where did you hear that?" she rasped.

"Grandma and mom argued what would you do if Jonathan proposed. Mom thinks you will return to Thorboro and get married. Grandma thinks you will stay at Hopeville."

Common sense required that she would not listen to a concoction made out of family history, fantasy and whatever Dorian had gleaned from eavesdropping on his mother and grandmother. But too many thoughts vied in Danielle's mind, muddling her reasoning. A sense of foreboding slithered in between. She felt that Dorian had glimpsed into something.

"Dorian, listen carefully. You know that my mother is not superstitious. Why would she try to avert a medical emergency with vows?"

"Maybe she was desperate?" Dorian whispered. "Or maybe she had a vision?"

"It must have been pain and dread rather than a vision," Danielle pondered aloud. She did not know what exactly had happened at her birth, only that she was born a couple of weeks prematurely. "Even in case of emergency, vowing to leave physics for good doesn't make any sense. Mom couldn't believe that it might actually help."

"I think it is somehow related to a paper Aunt Shelly was writing," Dorian added his insight.

"What paper?"

"I've heard grandma speaking of it, after you told her about yours."

"Impossible."

As soon as the denial slipped from Danielle's mouth, memories started surfacing: Thanksgiving day, Aunt Sophie's birthday, the search for Aaron Lichtfeld's nonexistent PRL, and earlier incidents. Was that why? Danielle asked the memories in her head. Dorian's farfetched tale explained why Michelle evaded questions as to why she had quit, yet always insisted that she had not been pushed to drop. But why did Mom keep her sacrifice in secret? Danielle wondered. Was it to shield her from a burden?

When Danielle went downstairs, her knees were weak; the dining table and people around it seemed to be shrouded in mist. She saw Sarah looking skeptically at the strudels, heard

Jonathan and Richard discussing Italian cars. She got a coffee and a plate with a slice of each cake. Without attempting to speak, she put some chocolaty cream into her mouth. Even sweetness did not lift the veil – everything, except her mother's votive offering, felt unreal.

19

IRONY OF FATE

By Monday morning, Danielle was ready to shrug off the tale Dorian had concocted. Her mother might have decided to leave TIST while in labor, but fate and destiny were wishful embellishments, and the rest of the story seemed fabricated. Michelle wouldn't have made an arcane vow nor considered it as binding. She would have resumed her studies after a while, if someone had not put his foot down.

Walking along Chadwick Drive, Danielle laid the blame on Michelle's adviser. She dismissed the allegation before she reached Main Street. Most physics professors would have appreciated a grad student with a paper accepted by *Physical Review Letters*, so even if the chauvinist adviser had turned his back on a young mother, Michelle could have gone to someone else. Wondering why her mother had never returned to physics, Danielle entered the campus. Lost in thoughts, she hardly noticed anything until she reached Fitzgerald Hall.

She halted before the imposing Victorian façade, wavering whether to go to the office to check on galactic rotation or head straight to the section of old periodicals. In half an hour, she could refute once and for all the existence of the PRL. But what if Michelle had conducted a brilliant research during pregnancy, published a paper, and then inexplicably severed all her ties with physics? Danielle tossed her head and saw an ugly gargoyle jutting out from the pediment, a beastly creature she had not noticed before.

"There is nothing I can do to atone for what mom suffered giving birth to me," she told it. "After twenty-eight years, her decision is irreparable."

The gargoyle, naturally, did not respond. Danielle eyed it more carefully. Dorian's tale was probably looming in her mind, for it looked like something copied from an ancient Greek temple, a mythical creature from the same pantheon as the Fates.

"If Fate entwined my future with physics it should have endowed me with much more brainpower," Danielle told the gargoyle. She took the stony stairs, opened the entrance door, and ascended to the second floor.

The fluorescent-lit, stark hallway had nothing mythical in it. Walking on dirty carpets, Danielle's thoughts turned to Zeeman and Isaac. Each of them had a better chance than she could ever have, and yet both had opted to carve out a career outside of theoretical physics. Was it perseverance or impracticality that kept her so long in the field?

"Aren't you too old to fantasize about a talisman passed to you at birth?" a voice snickered in Danielle's mind, uncannily combining Green's cold disdain with Lisitsin's arrogant sneer. Automatically, she turned her head and glanced at their offices. Both doors appeared to be locked.

The secretaries' office was also closed. In a central place on the notice board an announcement was pinned:

Rory McDowell will give a talk on:

Inflation: a bridge between
quantum fluctuations and cosmology.

The talk will take place in the Lounge (room 10) on Monday, February 28th, at 11am.

"A very long bridge," Danielle muttered. Inflation's scenarios were based on a premise that at its very beginning, the universe was filled with negative pressure over a hundred orders of magnitude larger than the observed dark energy. That pressure was hypothesized to drive a mind-boggling expansion of distances in an imperceptibly small fraction of a second. Quantum fluctuations embedded within a miniscule volume had stretched during the expansion to occupy cosmological lengths.

If one could make a career by studying a hypothetical process which ended way before the universe was one second old, Danielle reflected that she shouldn't dismiss a remote possibility that a paper had changed her mother's life. She sidled past her locked office, towards the library.

Dim and cavernous, the section of old periodicals was as welcoming as a forsaken graveyard. Danielle walked slowly, her nostrils twitching in protest against the dust and the musty smell of decay. Shadows flitted; phantoms stalked this tenebrous burial ground. Fate and Destiny lurked, as real as the knowledge that Michelle's PRL was buried in a dust-ridden tome.

"Let it go," ghosts seemed to be whispering. "It's Michelle's secret. Let her decide what to tell."

Danielle stopped, fighting an urge to turn back.

"Seeing the paper can't affect what Mom might tell," Logic brushed aside imaginary warnings. "And it certainly can't change what has already happened."

Danielle walked to the aisle stacked with volumes of *Physical Review Letters*. She reached with a shaking hand to pull a tome dated from the year she was born. She held the bounded volume. It felt as if she was holding Pandora's box.

"If Fate exists..." an errant thought flickered.

"Superstitions," Danielle dismissed the uncanny sensation and flipped the cover. She inhaled the rising dust as her fingers, tingling with expectation, leafed through the yellowing pages. Nothing happened. Fate, if it was privy to Danielle's expectations, chose not to make spectacles.

Hundreds of pages later, the fingers holding the tome froze. Petrified, Danielle registered only three lines: "Michelle Wiseman-Meller and Alexander Dobrovsky," "Thorboro Institute of Science and Technology," and "Manuscript was received on February 27th." The rest of the page was blurred by raw pain encapsulated in tears.

Fate might have watched Danielle when the connection between her birth and the paper sank in, but it offered neither revelations, nor magical aid. Left to her own means, Danielle pictured Michelle as a young woman, filled to the brim with possibilities. In her mind's eye, she saw Michelle taking part in discoveries, building a flourishing career, getting every perk and reward that comes with being a respected professor. A stubbing pain shattered the vision - a phantom of the untimely labor which had reduced the gifted physicist into an ordinary stay-at-home mother. Unable to withstand the colossal waste, Danielle crouched in the gap between two aisles. The PRL tome tumbled. Her tears became bitter and hot, her sobs lost any restraint, then she slipped into oblivion.

Eerie quietness seeped through Stygian blackness, cleared some mist and brought home to Danielle where she was. She rubbed stinging eyes and cast a wary glance at the closed tome laying at her feet. It was too solid to be a specter from the past. Yet, she had a ghostly sensation that she was not as secluded as she ought to be.

"Rats!" Danielle squeezed through her teeth, glimpsing a faint light slanting between the aisles. Someone had been there while she had cried uncontrollably, and, even worse, someone was still loitering in front of the aisles, cutting off her retreat. Since no one in his right mind would have the slightest interest in old papers on Monday morning, Danielle deduced that "someone" was Jonah Cobs. That fitted. Who else could she stumble upon when she looked for the legendary PRL?

Shuddering at the thought of having to give explanations, Danielle picked up the dropped volume and stacked it in its place. She shifted from leg to leg, stretched her arms, and smeared the tears that did not dry yet. Tiptoeing along the aisles, she planned her escape. The passage was pretty dim; she might be able to pass a couple of feet from Jonah without him taking notice of her blotchy complexion.

Thump. The sounds of leather soles stepping on hardwood floor heralded another intrusion - someone walked into the passage, blocking her retreat. Danielle pressed her back to the aisle and peered forward. The footsteps came closer - a silhouette of a man wearing a jacket passed, casting a shadow. She quickly backed. The footsteps dithered, then halted.

"Jonah?" the stranger asked. "Dr. Cobs?"

"One and the same. How can I help you?"

"My name is Rory McDowell." The voice hesitated. "Mrs. Klein told me I could find you here."

There was a pause. Danielle envisioned Jonah slowly turn his head and study the candidate. Her watch showed it was a quarter past ten. So, McDowell could not stay in the passage for long.

"Come and sit down," Jonah's voice greeted. "Such a pleasant surprise to see Walter's son."

"I have been looking forward to meeting you," Rory said. A pause ensued, as if Cobs and McDowell shook hands. "I was amazed to find that we are not scheduled to meet today."

"I see you've bypassed that little omission," Jonah said pleasantly. "It's not easy to cajole Marjory into disclosing my whereabouts, and the section of old periodicals is usually left out of the departmental rounds."

"Mrs. Klein remembered me and my father." A pause. "She also mentioned that you won't come to my talk."

"Marjory must have explained to you that I have nothing to do with the candidates for the position. I don't take part in the interviews, and don't attend the lunches. I do not form or express any opinions."

Although there was warmth in Jonah's voice, he uttered the words with a finality, which surprised and intrigued Danielle.

"But why?" The disbelief in Rory's voice was carried to the aisles. "You of all people, the seer of the physics department?"

The seer of the physics department? Danielle echoed in her mind. She pinched her arm slightly.

"Nowadays, I refrain from dubbing in prophecies and from meddling in the departmental affairs. Speaking plainly, I leave the choice of my successor in the hands of those who will be his colleagues, and dedicate my time to research."

Danielle heard Rory's voice, but could not discern what he said.

"Thirty years is a long time to change one's outlook," Jonah replied. "How is Walter doing?"

"He is at CERN, a member of one of the LHC's planning committees. Father is steadfast in his interests. He is intent on finding the Higgs boson and further evidence for CP violation."

It was clear that Jonah chuckled, but what he said about "fascinating discovery" and "dark energy" were indistinguishable.

"No, that has not drawn his attention to cosmology," Rory replied.

"Walter has always regarded cosmology a soft-science,"

Jonah reminisced, "but so did most high-energy physicists. Have you heard about Gene Harbinger from Harvard?"

"We met when he visited Edinburgh. By the way, he moved to Arizona three years ago."

"Did he?" Jonah's voice sounded ponderous. "I haven't heard from Gene for a while."

A hiatus was followed by Rory saying, "I have to go shortly."

"Yes, of course." Danielle could almost see Jonah smiling. "I wish you good luck."

"Thank you. I'm sorry we didn't have time to speak. I have been looking forward to hearing your opinion about Inflation."

In her hiding place Danielle reckoned that if the outstanding candidate wanted to hear the most eccentric opinion in the physics department, he was likely to get what he asked for.

"Notwithstanding its correctness," Jonah said, "it is a very elegant paradigm."

Told you so, Danielle jeered in her mind.

"No, don't look affronted," she heard Jonah's voice. "You shouldn't mind my subversive comments."

"I'd appreciate hearing your reservations."

"No reservations, only questions," Jonah's voice reassured.

Rory's response might have been a gesture, for Danielle did not hear him.

"Look at any two objects," Jonah continued. "How do you picture the physics of a distance between them?"

Wasn't that obvious? Danielle wondered. It could be painstakingly difficult to determine the distance to a remote object in space, but the problem was not a conceptual one. Everyone knew what a distance was.

Rory probably looked as puzzled as she felt, for again she heard Jonah's voice. "Will you talk about an exponential stretching of distances?"

A pause ensued, which Danielle interpreted as Rory's nod.

"Can you tell me then," Jonah asked, "what is the physical interpretation of an interval of length either before or after it was stretched?"

In her mind's eye, Danielle saw a grayish, opaque mist. The metallic shelves filled with heavy volumes dissolved into a tangibly fluid entity, landscaped with sinkholes and whirlpools.

Stop it, she ordered herself.

"I think that the stretching of distances is completely accounted for by special and general relativity," Rory said. "Universal expansion has been verified by countless observations. Moreover, the discovery of dark energy scarcely leaves any doubt that the expansion accelerates."

"Are you satisfied with the overall picture?" Jonah prompted.

Danielle waited for Rory to say "How could anyone be?" or point out that dark energy could hardly be vacuum energy when its theoretical value is a hundred and twenty orders of magnitude off mark.

"Inflation requires some ironing out," she heard Rory saying. "I've been working on a scenario in which dark energy sits on Inflation's tail."

"That sounds very interesting," she heard Jonah saying.

"I'll present the essentials of the derivation in my talk." Rory's voice intimated that Jonah was welcome to change his mind.

"No doubt, but I must pass your invitation. My presence at Walter McDowell's son's talk will set tongues wagging. It's better not to give certain members of the faculty the impression I'm putting my oars in."

Very considerate, Danielle thought, observing that Jonah's response, albeit thoughtful, was also an excuse not to budge from his chair.

"I'm used to people dragging in Father's influence. It's a sort of a birthright, like an aptitude for mathematics and physics."

"A birthright?" an incredulous voice sniggered in Danielle's mind. Physics occasionally felt like a vocation, but a birthright? A birthright was a privilege, not a burden kept in secret. "Oh, Mom," she mouthed, yearning to be in Thorboro and get the entire story. Her thoughts revolving about Michelle's legacy, Danielle paid little attention to the voices carried from the passage, until Rory's amazed voice asked, "How did you know?"

"You do not strike me as an overconfident fellow, yet for a candidate at the beginning of the day, you are uncommonly relaxed. Seeing that you are not anxious about an offer from King Solomon University, I deduced that you already have another one."

"I'm negotiating with Edinburgh," Rory's cheerful voice echoed between the aisles. "I married last June and my wife wants to stay closer to home."

It added insult to injury that Rory was married and had an offer for a faculty position at his hometown. In fact, Danielle mused, he had everything she pined for, including a parent who assisted his career rather than burdened him with guilt. Fate, if it existed, gloried in being unfair. It awarded a few chosen ones all of the advantages and laughed at the rest.

"A very reasonable wish," Jonah agreed. "Hopeville is a nice but pretty provincial town. It has several overpriced restaurants, but not a single decent pub."

"Really? I can hardly reconcile that with father's fond recollections."

"Hopeville has changed, and the recollections of youth tend to be as misleading as an old man's grumpiness. Whatever decision you make, bear in mind that King Solomon is a good university and that its physics department got its solid reputation rightfully. My colleagues successfully follow the concurrent trends and are at the forefront in their field."

"I really must go."

"Good luck. Don't forget to give my regards to Walter."

An unintelligible murmuring was followed by a shuffling sound, probably a heavy chair being moved. Hearing the thud of receding footsteps, Danielle inched away from the metallic shelves.

"You can get out if you are done," Jonah's voice said.

Blushing crimson, she walked to the edge of the gap between the aisles. Jonah sat hunched over a desk cluttered with old volumes, bulging notebooks and dog-eared papers. Engulfed in a softly glowing circle of light, he looked like a scholar in an old Dutch painting, albeit donning modern clothes.

Stepping out of shadows, Danielle said, "Good morning."

"An interesting morning. You are welcome to stay here if you are not going to Rory's talk."

Danielle pulled a chair and sat down, her eyes scanned the papers on the desk. A cursory look did not reveal what Jonah was working on, but the sheer amount of the amassed material incited Danielle's curiosity. Gauging it would be bad manners to be too forthright, she started with, "I am sorry about overhearing your conversation."

"No need to. I knew you were there, and no harm is done as long as you don't ask me to foretell how your career will turn out."

Unsure whether Jonah spoke in jest or seriously believed he could foresee one's future, Danielle chose to skirt round his eccentricities. "Can you tell what dark energy is?" she asked.

"I have some ideas, none of which I've checked. I have too little time even without considering cosmological aspects."

Too little time? Danielle repeated in her mind. Jonah seemed to have all the time in the world. So what was he doing? Casting her mind back to the exchange between Brochard and Jonah, she doubted that he had filled all these pages with cogitations on what empty space is.

"Since I've started a quarter of a century ago, I considered various possibilities," Jonah continued. "But in the intervening years, I came to realize that I cannot delve into every promising course. In the past decade, I have focused on elementary particles."

Even a decade sounded like a formidable stretch of time; twenty five years felt like an incomprehensible obsession. What kind of idea could drive an accomplished physicist to work that long without seeking others' approbation? Was it some sort of delusion?

"Why do you work by yourself?" the question slipped before Danielle could stop herself.

"Isn't it evident?" Jonah's quiet voice vibrated with fury. "I cannot take the responsibility of steering a promising student or a post-doc into research that has a slim chance of speedy progress. I want to complete this," he waved over the desk, "in my lifetime, but not at the expense of ruining someone's career."

The ferocity of Jonah's conviction brought to mind the wrathful seers of olden times. His integrity, Danielle thought, was endearingly human.

"Can you tell me about your work?" she asked.

An indignant silence insinuated that it was a wrong question to voice.

"I didn't mean to offend," she muttered.

"No, you didn't, but nevertheless your request is presumptuous. Do you expect to grasp in a few hours or even in days how the material world and the space are constructed?"

No one can relate the principles that govern everything from single particles to the observable universe, Danielle retorted in her mind. The foundations of physics she had studied did not connect the material world on atomic level with the nature of space.

"I wish I could learn that in a lifetime," Danielle said. She looked at the sea of aisles. The hundreds of volumes she saw comprised thousands of papers. One of them was her mother's. "What I asked," Danielle added, "is a distilled overview of the rudiments."

"That we can accomplish in a minute. Everything, the material world, the space itself consists of a single substance. For historical reasons, I like to refer to it as aether. Time has a meaning because aether flows."

Gray substance started spreading in Danielle's mind eye. She discarded the image before currents and eddies pervaded her vision.

"I'm afraid that this is too abstract," she said. "How can the same aether be an empty space and an actual matter?"

"To understand how interacting aether currents form elementary particles, how these interactions give rise to the familiar forces, curve space..." Jonah paused when he noticed that Danielle was holding her breath. He shouldn't have mentioned aether currents, he reflected, nor imply that he understood what are the fundamental forces. "In short, to reconstruct the physical world and its laws, you'd have to follow these derivations," Jonah pounded his hand on the closest notebook, "and many others."

She listened awestruck - even Einstein did not have all of these answers. A single physicist couldn't develop a theory with such far-reaching consequences. Moreover, if Jonah deemed that his work had a potential to upturn physics, why didn't he subject his results to the scrutiny of the theoretical community?

"Will you ever publish it?" Danielle blurted out.

The words hovered unanswered, until it dawned on Danielle that her question was crass. Duly embarrassed, she stared at the papers strewn over the desk.

"Everything has its own time," Jonah said after a while. Deducing that Danielle did not recognize the citation, he added, "A proverb from Ecclesiastes. It is engraved on the gray arch behind Fitzgerald Hall."

Danielle rose to leave. Jonah's courteous words implied that he would rather have his desk to himself than speak about his work.

"Keep this proverb in mind," Jonah advised, "but for the time being put aside what I told you about aether." He lowered his stare to a derivation he was working on, but he could not in good conscience ignore the disappointment he saw in Danielle's swollen eyes. "Life puts forks on one's road," he said. "Someday, you may take part in the endeavor."

Danielle nodded, added the advice to the same compartment where she stowed Fate and Destiny, and silently walked away.

Jonah gazed into the passage until the sound of Danielle's footsteps petered out; then, he heaved a sigh. He fully endorsed the maxim that "everything had its own time." Unfortunately, one found whether the time was right only in hindsight. Determined not to dwell on memories, he rose up and sauntered to the aisle with *Physical Review Letters*. He scanned the bounded volumes, found and pulled out the one placed upside-down. Thumbing through yellowing pages, he stopped at a page blotted with dried tears. Jonah leafed forward to check that it was the only page smeared with tear stains, then started to read a paper about CP violation authored by Michelle Wiseman-Meller and Alexander Dobrovsky.

* * *

Although Danielle could not put out of her mind what had happened in the section of old periodicals, she set herself to analyze the data generated during the weekend. Absorbed in calculations, she noticed that dusk was falling only when Green called.

"Can you come to my office right now?" he asked.

Having nothing ready to show and very little to say if Green brought up the candidate's talk or her truanting the entire weekend, Danielle itched to say that she would actually rather not.

"Sure," she muttered.

Green would not waste his time on petty rebukes, Danielle reassured herself on her way to his office. A premonition that he was about to broach something important made her stop before his door. Apprehensive of what he might say, a gut feeling urged her not face him. Danielle gave herself a brief mental shake and stepped into the office. Green sat imperiously behind his desk; Lisitsin slouched on another armchair, a smirking expression on his face. They looked like a wise king and his wily jester.

Sitting down, Danielle adjusted her impressions: Lisitsin oozed smugness, Green exuded contentment. Had Lisitsin had the temerity to use Green as a soundboard during one of his brainstorms? Considering Green's knack for finding faults and mistakes, Danielle thought that Green wouldn't be looking impressed if Lisitsin hadn't made notable progress.

Regretting that she missed that critical leap when an idea transmutes into a tangible scenario, she half-turned to look at the whiteboard. In its center was a rough sketch of darts piercing tilted disks and of arrows aligned upwards. The sketch was surrounded by mathematical expressions jotted with red, blue and black markers.

"Andrei made a very interesting suggestion about the detectability of universal rotation." Green nodded to Lisitsin in a gesture of appreciative acknowledgment. "Observations indicate that galaxies rotate around axes pointed in random directions. Having data about the random component of galactic clusters' rotation, we can subtract it from the total signal and get an estimate of the residual aligned rotation."

Getting some inkling of what was depicted on the whiteboard, Danielle tried to relate between the mathematical expressions and the sketch. The circular shapes, she assumed, referred to galaxies. The darts were the axes they rotated around. The parallel arrows represented the direction of the aligned rotation – a rotation that revolved each galaxy in the same direction along a much longer radius. The superimposed rotation brought to mind Earth-like planets, each spinning around its axis while orbiting around the Sun.

Danielle cast the image away, for one could not attribute a

single center to the aligned rotation. Involuntarily, another image sprang. Snowflakes whirled in tiny funnels, their descent almost imperceptible.

Green's voice, methodically explaining their groundbreaking idea, cut through the vision.

"Andrei and I have followed Gödel's model. As you can see on the whiteboard, we picked up a universal alignment without attributing to it any specific axis in space."

It was evident that Green was intrigued with their clever idea and that he expected it to branch into new collaborations and grants. After a while, Danielle noticed that he often paused, and that he elaborated everything as if it all was brand new for her. But why? All they did was to give a mathematical formulation of her snowflakes vision, the very idea Lisitsin had dismissed as "nonsense" on Friday.

How come Green had heard about it? And why was he expounding it to her? Danielle's suspicious eyes turned to Lisitsin, but reverted to Green the instant she glimpsed Lisitsin's triumphant smile. Only one explanation suggested itself: Lisitsin had appropriated her idea and presented it to Green as his own. The airless, cloyingly gray office was stifling. Nauseous, Danielle exerted all her willpower to stop gastric juices from welling up.

"It will take you some time to get used to our approach," Green said. His intonation implied that he was not surprised by Danielle's inability to grasp it on the fly.

The understanding that Green was absolutely clueless of what had happened brought Danielle back to her senses faster than any conscious effort.

"I don't see Einstein equations for the model," she said.

"It's a toy model George and I have constructed to mimic an azimuthal, universal rotation," Lisitsin butted in, as if this was the only explanation Danielle needed.

His nerve astounded her. Anger rose like a bonfire. Her face radiated heat.

Rage, however, ebbed as fast as it surged, leaving a disheartening realization that a person who could brazen it out was capable of denying everything if he was confronted. Dumbfounded, Danielle's thoughts wandered to her mother's paper, to Michelle's shattered dreams, then to Green. He knew her way of thinking, and he was too shrewd not to discern it in "their" model. Bracing herself, she looked directly at Green, her eyes mutely implored him to use his power to right the situation. Green's slate-gray eyes met hers, and without flinching, they smothered her naïve request.

"Formulating Einstein equations is a related but different problem," Green said. "Judging by a lack of advancement in your analytical efforts, Andrei and I prefer that you return to numerical simulations. It's a simpler problem, and it's bound to generate results."

"What?" Danielle croaked. Green was not a sadist, but a politically correct, successful professor. He was not supposed to wield power arbitrarily.

Green heard the outburst, saw Danielle's overwhelmed, muddled expression, and deduced that she did not grasp what she was assigned to do. He considered Danielle's overall disappointing performance, the inexcusably slow code-developing, her lack of initiative while professing interest in theory. He recalled that she had not attended McDowell's talk in the morning. His face hardened.

"You'll use a fictitious radius," Green continued. "For a qualitative estimation, we've taken it to be proportional to Hubble distance. In the simulation, you'll have to fine-tune the constant."

Danielle winced at the thought of fine-tuning, which neatly summarized who-knows-how-many short runs interposed between code adjustments. Even worse, she abhorred the fashion in which Green thrust the assignment on her. Yet, self-interest demanded that she'd show no discontent. Half a year into a post-doctorate, it was high time to zero in on a well-defined, concrete research topic. It was her opportunity to explore a fascinating new ground and work on her own, without depending on Lisitsin.

Reckoning that she should show that she had also considered the interrelation between dark energy and universal rotation, Danielle cleared her throat and said, "The model doesn't specify how universal angular velocity decreases as the universe expands."

"Don't worry about Einstein equations," Lisitsin ordered.

"I'm going to continue my work on the dynamic solution," he told George. "What Danielle should do is simple, straightforward programming."

"For simplicity's sake, assume that the universal rotation is aligned along the Z-coordinate," Green went on, as if no one had interrupted. "In the azimuthal direction, galaxies are pushed away from each other. To get a rough picture, think of marbles scattered all around from a rotating platform."

"Wouldn't that leave the Z direction distorted?" Danielle asked. Fine-tuned rotation might mimic the effect of cosmological constant in the X-Y plane, but there was no force to accelerate the galaxies as they receded in the Z direction.

"You'll insert a value equal to the cosmological constant," Green instructed. "Later on, through calculation of the correlation functions, you'll measure the extent of the arising anisotropy."

"Ah," Danielle mumbled.

It was a weird day, and she was too tired and disgruntled to try to convince professors who deemed themselves infallible. Wanting to get it over with as soon as possible, she did not voice any other reservations, but listened to Green's specifications of how to conduct the numerical fine-tuning, nodded to show that she followed his instructions and said "yes" when it was expected.

20

INVOLUTE CONUNDRUMS

"Are you done with whining?" Jonathan asked, while he scanned the output streaming on his monitor. He had fixed the latest glitch, but the software required another round of quality assurance.

"It's not only that Lisitsin stole my idea." Danielle resentful voice carried through the receiver. "He and Green..."

"We already agreed that they are schmucks," Jonathan cut short the tirade. It was after midnight, and Danielle added nothing to what she had already said about the professors throughout the last week. "What else do you want me to say?"

"Something about decency and fairness. Green didn't bring me in when they fleshed out the physics, but he has no qualms to demand that I translate 'their' research into a flawless simulation ASAP."

"You have said it all, and it sucks. But when it comes to the point, you can either slam the door like Paul did, or pull off that program."

"When it comes to the point," Danielle retorted, "it doesn't bode well that my supposed mentor treats me as his technician and not as a junior researcher." She had tried, in vain, to explain to Jon how that harmed her prospects, but seven weeks before the beta-version release deadline, last-minute modifications and glitches eclipsed everything else in his mind. She swallowed a rising bitterness and asked, "How is the quality assurance progressing?"

Jonathan cursed. "On the brighter side," he added, "Paul and I have started incorporating a new visualization."

"Do you sleep and eat at all?"

"I caught some sleep in the morning, and Susanna stores healthy snacks and restocks the fridge with salads. She vouches for whole grains and fresh veggies to neutralize the late-night pizza."

"You are lucky that the only sane person in the bedlam takes cares of you all," Danielle said about Nickka's secretary.

"Oh, Pilcher is sane, although I won't insult Susanna by making any comparisons."

"Why?" Danielle asked. Jon had not mentioned Pilcher for a while. "What did he do?"

"Who knows?" Jonathan's voice intoned *who cares?* "We see him occasionally, parading in and out in a suit, looking important."

Picturing Pilcher swagger into a room where half a dozen disheveled programmers feverishly worked, Danielle laughed for the first time since the conversation at Green's office. Jon's rational wit was what she needed. That and his unswerving determination.

Resolute to take a leaf out of Jonathan's book, Danielle engrossed herself in constructing a new universe. In her mind's eye, space was dotted with swirling spin-tops. In the code, the largest matter aggregates were programmed to spin around randomly directed axes; the aggregates' initial angular velocity was to increase incrementally until it reached predetermined values.

The effect of the omnipresent, universal rotation was harder to fathom. Danielle cogitated over the mathematical expression she had copied from Green's whiteboard. She scrutinized Green's sketchy instructions, yet she did not get hold of the trajectories involved. Universal rotation differed from other modes of rotation: it was not concentric, and the revolving matter did not move along enormous rings or any other closed orbit. Looking for analogies, she could not come up with anything useful.

Pressed for time, she deconstructed each mathematical term. The different representation reminded Danielle of something similar she had encountered in one of Lisitsin's riddles. Her hand pulled open a drawer, her head turned to where her solutions were stowed. The reams of derivations lay undisturbed, as forsaken evidence of her hard and thankless work. In a flush of anger, her hand jerked to slam the drawer.

A thought about her mother stopped the hand, drowned the bubbling anger. The past was beyond redressing, but the future depended on her. She could make a drama out of what Green and Lisitsin had done, or she could show that she had what it takes to succeed.

Forcing herself to focus on physics, Danielle turned to Lisitsin's riddles. She trawled through the handwritten pages, her pigheaded and increasingly agitated search continuing after Chi left the office. When nothing turned up, she started to pull books from the shelves over her head. She thumbed through each book, looked at every loose piece of paper, in case it was a forgotten or an unfinished calculation. The number of crumpled notes on the floor grew steadily. A volume of *Numerical Recipes* got a shake, even though it was unlikely to hold anything useful. When a paper fell from between its pages, Danielle picked it up and unfolded it. The covariant derivatives were what she was looking for.

The expression was too complex to picture, but she deemed that it described some kind of a tilted spiral whose circumference grew proportionally to the Hubble radius (a distance comparable to the observable universe). She imagined a very young universe dotted with hurricane eyes; the primordial matter swirled ferociously around those centers. Distances stretched as universe grew older, the swirling matter slowed down; initial trajectories evolved into giant spirals, with arms as large as the Hubble radius.

Danielle doodled a spiral, added a tilted spin-top to illustrate a chunk of matter moving along the trajectory, then put the sketch aside and resorted to mathematics. It took a couple of days to construct a blueprint for universal rotation. Once she had a satisfactory algorithm, she began to translate it into a computer program. It was pretty straightforward to encode the covariant derivatives. It came as no surprise that setting initial values was a big headache.

"Everything depends on the values the simulation starts with," she told Jonathan one night. "I estimated the range of initial values for galactic rotation by extrapolating from observations. But if the initial values for universal rotation are wide of the mark, the entire simulation is meaningless."

"Don't you have any data to rule out unrealistic values?" Jonathan asked.

"Undistorted galactic rotation sets an upper limit on universal rotation at the time galaxies were formed. If we posit that universal rotation is the source of dark energy, it'd give a lower limit."

"Can you sum up what that means without a lecture in physics?"

"That I need a miracle, or at least a lucky guess, to save months of fine-tuning through trial-and-error."

* * *

Miracles did not happen while Danielle modified the computer program. Days slipped by, very long days that started with a strong coffee at about seven in the morning and ended with bleary eyes and a headache after midnight. She said nothing when Ben informed her and Chi that he was accepted to the summer school in Cargèse, and only cursed again the Sisyphean task the professors had thrust on her. Tired and frustrated, she constantly bore in mind the consequences of her mother's lack of stamina. Resolute to succeed where Michelle had failed, Danielle willed herself to persevere. When her head reeled and the monitor seemed to spin, she steadied herself with more coffee and an occasional nondescript sandwich from Lawrence Hall's vending machine.

One afternoon, she met Green in the hallway. He stopped unexpectedly and inquired about her progress.

"I wrote the computer program, but it doesn't run yet."

"Can you make it run by the end of the week?" Green asked, his voice polite and completely neutral.

Perfectly understanding that it was not a question, Danielle said, "I intend to," to which Green responded with a tiny nod before he went to his office.

Alight with new urgency, Danielle made a strenuous, almost desperate effort to purge the code of errors.

Debugging was over by Friday. Content that the program was running through its first test, she went to the seminar room, where Green was to rehearse a talk for a conference in Boston.

The second slide listed Chi Wang and Ben Cox among his collaborators; other slides showed graphs and plots from Ben's and Chi's simulations. Danielle followed the thirty-five minute long presentation, acutely aware that it did not allude to her work even once. While she had no grudge against Chi, who more than deserved being noticed, she left the seminar room envious of Ben and resentful of Green.

Saturday brought new reasons to feel disgruntled. Danielle came to the office expecting to go over the first files the program generated, but there was no output. By the time she discovered that the damned program only appeared to be running, Danielle barely restrained herself from yelling at the idiotic computer. Before she could track the source of the problem, Green summoned her to his office.

"Do you have any images of the rotating universe?" he asked.

"I have several snapshots that qualitatively show galactic but not universal rotation." Danielle paused seeing Green's face twitch. She took a deep breath. "I was curious to see what galactic rotation might look like, so I added it to the simulation of the toy universe a couple of weeks ago."

"But you didn't include universal rotation?" Green asserted his dissatisfaction without waiting for a reply.

"A run I sent yesterday stalled. I'm going to restart it with a different set of initial values."

The slate-gray eyes emanated chilling coldness. "Email me the snapshots first," Green instructed, gesturing Danielle to leave. She sent him the best snapshots, then went back to the code.

The conversation with Green was not mentioned when Danielle talked to Jonathan that night. Her head throbbed. She silently listened while Jon recounted how they integrated the new visualization into Nickka's software. For Jonathan Lerner, she thought, sixteen-hour-long workdays were nothing to complain about.

Danielle did bring up "a few problems with the program" when she spoke with her mother on Saturday. Michelle, who fretted about Joyce and Julie overworking themselves at the med-school, did not ask Danielle to specify.

After Green flew to the conference, Danielle went again over the entire program. She rewrote a few functions, but did not find errors that could explain the stalling. Having no lead as to what was wrong with her code, she leaned towards blaming the universal rotation. She was staring balefully at the subroutine that handled it when Ben poked his head into the office.

"Hi," he said. "What's up?"

"Nothing much," Danielle grumbled.

"The universe doesn't rotate yet?" Ben asked with unwarranted cheerfulness. Without waiting for her answer, he approached Chi's desk. "Will you look at a short movie I'm making for the summer-school?"

Chi, who was polishing yet another draft of his paper, kept a stoic expression. Danielle did not believe that the expression was genuine. Even Chi, she mused, must be miffed by the fact that Ben is going to bask under the Mediterranean sun, while he is left to follow Green's whims in the cold, gloomy Hopeville.

"Yes," Chi said without turning. "Are you going to have a poster?"

"A ten minute talk." Ben's self-congratulation oozed from every syllable. "After George heard it will be a paper in the summer school's proceedings, he agreed to shell out for the airfare."

Feeling spiteful and mean, Danielle bit her tongue, stuck her nose closer to the code spread over the monitor and pretended to be very busy. She should be very busy, she corrected in her mind. The program had to run by the time Green returned. She contemplated the initial values that stalled the program, assigned three different, yet plausible values for the angular momenta, and sent the program to run on the group's cluster.

Hours passed as she monitored the messages that appeared on the screen. Her hopes rose when it seemed that she struck it lucky this time; but one of the runs stalled before she left for home. She aborted the other two runs on the following day. Disheartened, Danielle repeated the process with new values. The waiting for messages, she found, was as draining as a full day of work.

On Thursday night, she slipped over ice and tumbled on Chadwick Drive's sidewalk. Scared and in pain, she limped along the deserted street to her house. "It'll be okay," she reassured herself after finding no signs of injury. A cup of herbal tea and a good sleep could heal everything.

After she wrapped herself in a blanket, Danielle waited for sleep to take her under its wings. The wind kept whining and groaning. Its muffled howls brought back the blizzard, the frisson of the fear she had felt. The fear was still there, Danielle discovered. And also a sense of foreboding. Jon? she thought, rising up in alarm. No. He sounded impatient; he might be exhausted but otherwise he was fine. The wind whimpered mournfully while Danielle prayed for everyone in her family. Then she lay down, listened to the wind's lulling sough until she slipped into dreamland.

The runs' output Danielle saw on Friday indicated that the initial angular momenta she used were an unlikely source for the program's stalling. As far as she could check, neither the initial values nor the code were the culprits. Uneasy about the aligned universal rotation, she perused the algorithm and compared it to the code. The program reflected the algorithm faithfully. The algorithm did its job, unless it misinterpreted the model.

She was not an idiot to misunderstand a model based on her own idea, Danielle thought. Yet, the fact remained that the simulation did not run. Moreover, she had no time left to tinker with initial values, and she could not check the code indefinitely. A gut feeling wasn't a substitute for an unbiased, knowledgeable feedback, Danielle reasoned, then grimaced. The most reasonable course was to consult Lisitsin. Yet, the mere thought of asking him anything was abhorrent.

"When the push comes to shove," Reason chided, "it's better to take desperate measures than to fail."

On her way to Lisitsin's office, Danielle girded herself for talking to him.

Lisitsin was cogitating over a different problem when he noticed Danielle standing at the door. Recalling that they had not spoken since the meeting at George's office, he beckoned her to come in. "Well?" he asked, anticipating to find out how his idea had turned out.

"I have problems with the program," Danielle said. "It doesn't run properly."

Lisitsin's forehead furrowed."Why not?" he asked.

"I think that something related to universal rotation stalls it, but I cannot determine what."

"All you had to do is to write a short program," he said petulantly. "It's a job for an undergraduate student."

Danielle reminded herself that Lisitsin's knowledge of programming was somewhere in between scant to nonexistent, straightened her shoulders, and pointedly looked at the professor.

"Did you check for bugs?" Lisitsin asked.

"Yes."

"Then you should pay a closer attention." Without waiting for Danielle's excuses, Lisitsin added, "Did I give you a paper to go over for our next journal club?"

Astounded that he brazenly referred to the journal club, and in all acted as if he had not appropriated her idea, Danielle moved to leave the office. "Beggars can't be choosers," Reason hissed. "If you want a career, you can't quit."

"I can't spare the time for the journal club before I fix the program," Danielle said.

Lisitsin crossed his arms. His airs demonstrated that she was not worth the effort of rising objections. A sickening sensation squeezed Danielle's throat. She averted her eyes.

"I've checked the code several times." She directed the words to the whiteboard covered with mathematical expressions. "It follows the algorithm, which I based on what you and George told me."

"Really?" Lisitsin's voice resonated with insolence. "Do you have any suggestions as to what might be wrong?"

"I have," Danielle said. Lisitsin's mocking provoked her to voice her suspicions. "Unless I'm missing something obvious, the problem is in the model."

"That's interesting." Lisitsin rolled the words contemptuously. "Am I correct that you claim your code fails because of a fault in our model?"

"The problem lies deeper than programming. I think that it stems from the assumptions made about universal rotation."

"Nonsense," Lisitsin barked, "utter rubbish."

How dare you? She couldn't believe that once again Lisitsin waved aside her suggestion, using the same words he had used to dismiss her idea at the journal club.

"Haven't you learned anything while you worked with me?" he snarled. "You don't do physics with feelings, you solve equations, make calculations."

Danielle's mouth opened, but she could not utter a word. So many times she agonized about what Lisitsin had done, yet it never occurred to her that he heard her speak about swirling snowflakes, gleaned the underlying physics but did not register that she, Danielle, came up with the idea.

Awash with shame, she realized that Lisitsin never noticed what he had done, for he did not see her as a physicist. For him, she wasn't even an assistant. She was a cog used to facilitate his work. Without uttering a word, she turned and left the office.

She wanted to run away, to be free of the professors and never return to Fitzgerald Hall. But giving up was the easiest route. If her mother had the backbone, giving birth would not have cost her a good career. Afraid of the writing on the wall, Danielle returned to her desk. She quelled self-indulging urges and started to document every detail of the diagnostics she had run so far.

* * *

Green was back on Monday. By the time he stepped into his office, Danielle had a summary, complete with tables, ready to support her claim. The numbers pointed to a pattern: the slower the angular velocity of the universal rotation was, the longer the program ran before it stalled. The only case the program succeeded to simulate was the most undesirable one – a non-rotating universe devoid of dark energy.

Green called Chi after lunch. Danielle waited for her turn, but the day ended without any notice from Green. Her frustration and anxiety grew when the same repeated on Tuesday. When Ben bragged about Green's response to his movie for the summer school, she was tempted to wish Ben a severe diarrhea before, during, and after his talk.

On Wednesday, Danielle's nerves were frayed. To occupy herself until Green would summon her, she toyed with the universe's expansion rate. The subroutine did not cause any problems. Reckoning that it would take her mind off Green, she began a new set of simulations, in which the value of the expansion rate changed along with the parameters responsible for universal rotation.

When the phone rang on Friday, Chi answered, then hurriedly left the office. Twenty minutes later, he returned with his son.

"Sorry that I had to bring Lei. I have an appointment with Dr. Green in half an hour. I'll take Lei home after it's over."

"No problem." Danielle smiled to the boy, who inched closer to his father's hip. "Hi," she said to Lei.

Resigning herself to boisterous childish noises, she watched Lei sit next to Chi without making a pip. Chi silently resumed his work. Lei pulled crayons and a worksheet from his backpack and started to color industriously. A few minutes later Danielle rose up and headed to Green's office.

"Come in," Green said when she knocked.

He was reading from the monitor, but seeing Danielle, Green took off his glasses. He motioned her to sit down, then asked about the computer program.

"It stalls after I launch it." Danielle described the tests she had run. She ended with, "I checked for bugs, but found none."

"Do you keep track of the parameters you are using?"

"I wrote down everything, but, in a nutshell, the program runs longer for slower rotation. The time interval before it stalls also depends on the rate of the universe's expansion."

"There might be a way to reanalyze the last survey of galactic rotation," Green said after a short reflection. "I spoke with a few people at the conference, and they expressed an interest to see your simulations."

With whom? was Danielle's first thought. On second thought, she preferred to find out whether the survey had any relevance to universal rotation and dark energy. Wary that Green would end the impromptu meeting, she swallowed her questions, and brought up the algorithm. His expression turned more somber, but he did not stop her from outlining what the algorithm aimed to do and how it was incorporated into the program.

"You haven't figured out how to perform both expansion and rotation?" Green asked.

"No," Danielle admitted, impressed by how quickly he saw the crux of the problem.

"You have been working on the rotating universe for four

months. Wasn't the last month dedicated to rewriting your old program?"

"Yes," Danielle murmured. Green made the situation sound entirely unjustifiable.

"You've told me that you were looking for an academic career in physics."

Danielle nodded.

"Andrei can afford spending a few months without making progress. Do you understand that in your position timely results are essential?"

"Yes, I know," Danielle said, feeling nauseous. There was a knock on the door.

"Wait a few minutes," Green called. He saw on Danielle's face both apprehension and defiance. Reluctant to make a harsh decision, he asked, "Do you think that given a few more days you can find and fix the problem?"

"No." Danielle shook her head. "I've already checked everything I could think of."

Green leaned forward, his shrewd, slate-gray eyes looked sternly at her. "Do you understand how important it is to get the simulations ASAP when there is an interest in the model?"

"Yes," Danielle muttered. Trapped between Green's high expectations and his unwillingness to delve into the root of the problem, she looked helplessly at her knees.

"I don't have the time to lead you by hand when you can't work out the problems by yourself," Green said. Convinced that he did all he could to help Danielle, he added, "Go over everything you did and prepare a concise report on your algorithm and the state of the program. And ask Ben to schedule a pizza seminar for next Friday."

A pizza seminar? The words reverberated in Danielle's head, starting a panic. It was pretty obvious why Green wanted Ben and Chi to participate. Chi programmed better and faster, and Ben, although not as good as Chi, was Green's favorite. All of a sudden, a sword of Damocles hovered over her head.

It's paranoia, Danielle soothed herself. She worked on the model from the beginning. Even if Green did not recognize her idea, he would not hand her research over, just because there was a chance the project might take off. "Nonsense," an ugly voice snickered in Danielle's head. "Green will push it further, with or without you."

Dreading another week of suspense, she asked, "Are you taking the project out of my hands?"

"We shall see after the seminar," Green calmly replied. "Can you tell Chi to come in?"

Danielle wobbled to the door, held it open for Chi. In the hallway, her legs almost buckled.

Lisitsin, who was waiting in the kitchenette for the water in the kettle to boil, saw Danielle prop herself against the wall. Intrigued, he went to inquire after his model. "Any results?" he asked.

"No."

"Did you find the error at least?" Lisitsin insisted.

"No, I didn't."

They saw Amanda leaving the secretaries' office, with Lei trailing after her. Amanda smiled when she came closer and rolled her eyes towards the restrooms. Danielle mustered a wan smile. Lisitsin eyed the secretary's creamy neck on the background of a cascade of bright brown hair.

"She should not bring a sick child to work," he said after Amanda was out of earshot.

How can he find fault in Amanda's good deed? Danielle wondered. Then it sank in that Lisitsin assumed Lei was Amanda's son. She stifled a hysteric laugh. Lei resembled Chi. His Chinese ancestry was written all over his face. There was no way Amanda Hogan could be his biological mother.

"Are you working on the program at all?" Lisitsin inquired irritably.

Not trusting her voice, Danielle gave Lisitsin a look that caused him to mumble about "unbalanced female hormones" all the way to the kitchenette.

She went down the stairs and out of Fitzgerald Hall's backdoor. The alley stretched forward, flanked by gnarled trees that towered defiantly against the cloudy sky. The air was damp and refreshing. Breathing deeply, she skirted the thawing snow and muddy puddles, and walked under the canopy of barren trees.

"Your branches will bud in a couple of weeks," she told a majestic oak. "But if Green won't extend my fellowship, I'll be laid off at the end of August."

Tears gleamed in her eyes. Green, if he wasn't such a self-serving bigot, could have invested some time in reexamining the model. But he cared only about getting the results ASAP. It was her misfortune that Lisitsin was even worse.

Damn Lisitsin, Danielle bitterly thought as she trudged under the canopy. How gullible she had been to admire his brilliant, unconventional thinking. The crackpot claimed to have insight into the Universe, but he could not see that Lei wasn't Amanda's son.

"The idea of matter subjected to a weak rotating force was mine," she told the trees. Through tears, her vision was dotted with lustrous snowflakes that spun and swirled, in a seemingly random fashion. In her mind's eye, Danielle dragged the snowflakes outwards. Still swirling, they moved apart.

Slowly shuffling, she reached the arch. The enormous marble form confounded her for a moment, then a flash of inspiration culminated weeks of relentless work.

"Rats," she said, grasping why she had never succeeded in visualizing the professors' model.

"Rats," she said again, understanding why the simulations always stalled. The reason she could not incorporate universal rotation into the code was so simple – such rotation was incompatible with expansion.

The spinning snowflakes in her vision were pulled by Earth's gravity. This pull was constant during the short time the snowflakes existed. Galaxies, on the other hand, rotated in a universe subjected to accelerated expansion. Circumventing the fact that universal rotation ebbed over time, the professors' model inadvertently introduced an inconsistency.

Luckily, she knew the code inside out. Back in her office, Danielle split the simulation into two separate programs: one that generated universal expansion without rotation, and another that facilitated universal rotation without expansion. Completing the debugging early in the evening, she launched both runs, and left Fitzgerald Hall without waiting for printed messages. Her stride was brisk and self-assured, for she felt in her bones that universal rotation and expansion could not co-exist.

21

PIZZA SEMINAR

Licking the last vestiges of dulce de leche ice cream, Danielle looked with some surprise at the empty carton. Usually she did not pig out at the kitchen, but this Sunday was different. Powerless to do anything about her simulations, she stayed at home, and without noticing, her ice cream servings spiraled out of control.

On Saturday, she had busied herself with plotting charts and filling tables, and more importantly, checking every half-hour that the two runs, on which her post-doctorate depended, did not stall. By the end of the day she estimated that if the programs continued to run, they would generate data by Monday morning.

"Patience," Danielle told herself. Her hunch was a timely shortcut, but insights did not suffice to convince Green that her simulation worked correctly and that she was not inexcusably incompetent. Maybe in the future her words would carry some weight with Green. Yet, even the best-case scenario had a downside: after demonstrating that universal rotation was incompatible with an expanding universe and dark energy, her research would be back to the starting point.

Dark energy. Danielle's mind, sated with sugar, dwelt on the words. Dark energy could be something entirely different from everything else known to physicists.

This tantalizing possibility drew Danielle's thoughts. Her mind stopped worrying about Green not extending her postdoctoral fellowship; her body loosened as questions about dark energy's origin resurfaced in her mind. A fog-like substance percolated through her field of vision, filled it with eddies and whirlpools teaming in a mist. Languorous and hypnotized by the cyclic motion, Danielle was unaware of another sensation feeling its way. That sensation had flashed before, disguised as Affection or Attraction. It had come and gone during the years she was with Jonathan. This time, it emerged fully-shaped, mesmerizing and powerful. When Danielle saw daylight filter again into the kitchen, her mind was crystal-clear and every sense sharpened and attuned. A new force eclipsed the lure of dark energy, dwarfed her ambitions. Unable to direct or control it, Danielle fell under the spell of Love.

When the spell became a "revelation," she called Jonathan.

"What now?" he snapped after the first ring and before she could utter a word.

"It's me, Danielle." Still thrilled, she tried to speak coherently. "What happened?"

"Nothing much. My mother called five times last hour. Five minutes ago she wanted to know whether we had been invited to the wedding of a niece of Richard's second cousin."

Reality pushed its way uninvited, its gritty fingers clawed the joy and sapped the magic. A dull ache rolled to the back of Danielle's head, where Reality's cohort, Disappointment, settled.

"Why should Sarah care, all of a sudden?" Danielle asked.

"She is finalizing the invitations to the wedding over the weekend, and dad is out of town."

"It's your brother's wedding. Can't you put Nickka out of your mind for a while?"

"You forget that the beta is due on April 13th. We are scheduled to present it before the investors on the 20th and then at a software exhibition at the end of April. Now, try to impress that on my mother when she dreads that the Lerners' invitations won't arrive on time."

"Tight schedule," Danielle remarked sardonically. "Should I stop calling you for a month?"

"Of course not, just don't call that early."

"I will not."

Danielle's tone of voice caused Jonathan to reconsider her unusual timing. "What's wrong?" he asked.

Could "wrong" apply to an unanticipated and unplanned

magic that overturned her interests and priorities? Danielle craved to say that Love dispelled other concerns, but these words would be lost among deadlines. She would tell Jon after the beta is over, she promised herself.

"Nothing," Danielle said.

"Any news about your runs?" Jonathan asked, recalling Danielle's new simulations.

"I'm not expecting to get any data until tomorrow," Danielle replied. Her blithe tone of voice indicated that she was not worried about the outcome.

"I told you that you can solve it," Jonathan said triumphantly, then in a more serious voice, "but don't show Green anything before you double-check it."

"You shouldn't caution me against overconfidence. Green doesn't pay attention to what I say if it isn't backed by hard data."

"Just make sure."

"I always do that," Danielle pointed out. Feeling too happy to hold on to resentment, she added: "Green is demanding and prejudiced against hunches, but solid analysis of reliable data goes a long way with him."

"I have no doubt, but no one likes to be proven wrong. Especially," Jonathan stressed the word, "after he blabbed prematurely about the model."

"Rats," Danielle squeezed through her teeth. Imagining her work finally appreciated, she forgot that Green had a vested interest in the success of "his" model.

Love outshone the new worry until Danielle fell asleep. In a dream, she and Jonathan were snuggling in a bed, her hand patting his chest, her legs entwined with his. She was just starting to tell Jon about the revelation when he vanished, and she reappeared, fully dressed, in Fitzgerald Hall's seminar room. The pizza seminar, Danielle realized. She was about to speak, but the walls dissolved before she presented the first slide, the floor sprouted thick grass, the ebony table shrank. She was sitting disoriented and alone at a prettily set table, with Michelle's PRL laying on her lap. Seeing a lavish and unfamiliar manor, Danielle concluded that she arrived early to Amos and Amy's wedding. Someone laughed huffily. She turned around, and found herself in the full view of Lisitsin and Sarah Lerner. The shock woke Danielle up.

When dawn broke, she rushed to the university. The programs were still running, each run had generated an output file. Panting, she scanned the snapshots of the two universes. They looked similar. She zoomed in, varied the angle of the display, minutely examined the positions and the rotation of the aggregates, until she spotted several tiny differences.

"The data supports my hunch," Danielle emailed Jonathan.

Noticeable differences in a single set of initial values was a promising finding, but more was required to convince Green and Lisitsin. She spent Monday adjusting the code and fine-tuning parameters in both simulations. By the time Danielle left Fitzgerald Hall, she was in a state of exhaustion, but four different versions of the program were running on the group's cluster.

"It was an intense day," she told Jonathan that night. "The runs should generate data by Thursday, which will leave me enough time to make four or five pithy slides. I don't harbor any delusions that the problem of rotating universe can be solved within a few days. All I intend to show is that the model leads to inconsistent scenarios."

Later on she and Green might agree on expanding the scope of the simulations to make a systematic study, Danielle mused when she lay in bed. It wouldn't be published in PRL, but it could be a solid, comprehensive paper. Daydreaming about authoring a paper with King Solomon University's affiliation, she forgot to email Ben about the pizza seminar until the next morning.

"Hi, Ben," Danielle typed. She took a sip of scalding coffee, winced and went on, "George asked me to talk about my simulations at our next pizza seminar. Can you email the cosmology group that we'll meet this Friday, March 31st? The title of my talk is 'On Universal Rotation, Expansion and Dark Energy'." She halted, reread the title, then sipped more coffee while looking for a less pretentious wording. Unable to think of anything better, she shrugged it off as the least of her problems, and concluded the email with, "Thanks, Danielle."

A couple of hours later, Ben smirked at the pretentious title, then pasted it in a notification to the cosmology group's mailing list. When George Green read the pompous title, he shook his head disapprovingly. The equivocal wording belonged to popular science aimed to lure a lay audience. It had no place in his group.

"Stupid cow," Lisitsin grumbled when he read the same notification. "Instead of letting us know what you have, you waste time on redundant, frivolous titles."

"Did you find what stalls your program?" Chi asked Danielle, after reading the email.

"Yeah," she replied, too focused on calculations to elaborate.

Jonah Cobs checked his emails once a day, before he picked up his notebooks and reams of papers and headed to the section of old periodicals. He saw the notification about a forthcoming pizza seminar and glanced at the title. He intended to forget it immediately, but the high-flown mishmash drew his attention. It was the sort of title that Gemma would have favored. "On Universal Rotation, Expansion and Dark Energy," Cobs reread, feeling an incongruous puzzlement. Admittedly, he did not follow the current trends in research, but it was inconceivable that George would have engaged a post-doc to study the effects of universal rotation and expansion.

Bloody stupid, Cobs thought, and very unlucky for Danielle's career. Irritation nudged him to go to George's office. But Jonah's eyes turned to a framed caricature cut out of an old issue of *King's Monkey*. In one of her most poignant sketches, Gemma depicted an elderly man sitting in a whale's belly, refusing to go ashore before completing his "Great Theory of Everything." Cobs sighed, feeling too old to squabble with his colleagues or meddle in their research. Danielle wasn't his student, he quieted the feeble protest of his conscience. At the section of old periodicals, Cobs went to his usual place in the passage between aisles, piled the notebooks, and immersed himself in equations. An intersection of two swirling aether currents eradicated every concern from his mind, except of how these currents interacted.

At the same time, Danielle collated data from the simulation she had launched on Friday. She paid little attention when Chi left the office, but when he came back, it was impossible not to notice that Chi beamed as if he had just been invited to Harvard University. In his hand were clutched stapled papers.

"Good news?"

"Dr. Green agreed our paper is ready for submission."

"Good luck," Danielle said, marveling that Chi could rejoice over Green's approval after all the protracted revisions he had gone through. Her thoughts wandered from Chi to herself, and to how Green would respond to a suggestion to expand her study. That brought back Jonathan's cautionary words. Bearing in mind that her fastidious boss might ask for more evidence, she went back to scrutinize the data.

The day was drawing to a close when an influx of new files flashed on the monitor. Four of these were the first snapshots generated by the runs she had launched on Monday. Willing to trade off food and rest against saving her post-doctorate, Danielle picked the most food-like item left in the Lawrence Hall vending machine. Back at her office, she washed down the overly salty, greasy potato chips with a strong coffee.

She examined the new data, combined it with information gleaned from previous runs, then subjected the results to every analysis she could think of. After several hours, her eyes were bleary and the shapes on the screen blurred. Scared that she might pass out, Danielle waited for the haze in her head to disperse, then took a ride on the nightly shuttle from the campus. She reached the little house on Chadwick Drive too tired to do anything but go to sleep.

Two cups of strong coffee on the next morning made Danielle feel again like a human being. She reached Fitzgerald Hall uneventfully. A niggling sensation that she was missing something important stopped her at the stony stairs.

"What have I forgotten or overlooked?" she asked the gargoyle jutting over her head. The beastly effigy did not deign to respond. Pangs of apprehension, Danielle thought, were completely natural. It was Thursday. She had only a day left to organize the data and make the slides.

Hours passed quickly. Too soon Ben entered into their office, saying jubilantly, "Cookies time."

"Today's specials," he added, peering over Danielle's head, "high fructose corn syrup and caffeine."

"We should go," Chi said, intimating that Green expected them to attend the departmental colloquium.

"I really can't," Danielle said.

When the door closed, she pressed her knuckles to her forehead. With all the stress and agitation, it completely slipped her mind that she would have to demonstrate the model's shortcomings in the presence of Ben and Chi. Since neither of them knew where the idea of rotating universe came from, Danielle outlined on the first slide Gödel's non-expanding solution. The second slide posed a dilemma. Should she mention Lisitsin's attempts to write down Einstein equations? Was it better to make the presentation as impersonal and non-argumentative as possible, and go straight to the professors' latest suggestion?

Danielle drooped her head, closed her eyes, and for a moment savored the solitude.

"Isn't it strange that over half a century only two physicists have thought about universal rotation?" an anxious voice asked in her head.

Danielle jolted, eyes open wide and wild with horror.

Lisitsin must have checked that there were no other publications on universal rotation, she reasoned, trying to calm herself. Everyone does so before starting a new study.

"Lisitsin is atypical," the anxious voice mumbled. "He might have believed that only he could have such an idea."

Fear shot through Danielle, clinching her stomach, sending funny rings to circle in front of her eyes. Instinct chimed in, telling her to leave the mess to others and return to Thorboro.

Jon, she thought. If he knew that she was tempted to quit it all, he would have told her to get a grip on herself. She forced herself to think coherently. Lisitsin habitually dismissed her labor, but he probably had some regard for the work of prominent physicists. Mentally crossing her fingers, she accessed the Science Citation Index, and searched for titles with the words "universal rotation."

The search engine found no matches.

Danielle did the same with "rotating universe." Again, the search yielded no results.

She blessed the stars that Lisitsin, despite his conceit and capriciousness, was first and foremost a good physicist. To silence completely her worries, she left only "rotation" in the title field. The search engine uploaded a hundred of the most recent references. Danielle skimmed the first three pages, found nothing pertaining to cosmology, and decided to go back to the slides. A noisome recollection of Lisitsin jumping to conclusions after seeing Lei and Amanda together stopped Danielle in her tracks. Lisitsin, she reflected, could make a similar leap after a superficial, quick search.

This was a paranoid line of thought. Nevertheless, Danielle searched for papers which cited Gödel's paper on universal rotation. The result was a short list of articles, with a paper in *Nature* at the top.

"Inflation Can Solve the Rotation Problem," she read the title of the paper.

"What ROTATION PROBLEM?" a confounded voice squeaked in her head.

The paper was from 1983. Danielle read the abstract, but did not decipher what was the problem. Rising on unwilling feet, she dragged herself to the library, climbed the spiraling steps leading to the section of old periodicals, walked to aisles lined with volumes of *Nature*. She pulled volume 303 from the shelf. Without opening it, she went to a cluster of tables and slumped on the nearest chair. Finding the "rotation problem" was like opening a Russian doll - the paper in *Nature* cited an older paper, published in 1973, in *Cargèse Lectures in Physics*.

Danielle's face was bloodless by the time she started to read George Francis Rayner Ellis' lecture. The yellowing pages moved in and out of focus, but she registered that within the framework of General Relativity there could not be an expanding rotating universe. As she went over a general proof that made any simulation completely redundant, her head felt light and her mind was bizarrely detached. Then the page dimmed and she glided into the darkness of a spinning funnel...

When she was conscious again, Danielle was lying on the floor. She opened her eyes, flexed her fingers, and gently moved her head - everything seemed to work fine. She gingerly scrambled to her feet and sat on the chair she had slipped from. Her eyes looked at the open pages, at the proof that the professors' model could have never worked. After a short while, Danielle's legs were able to carry her weight. She took the volume to the main floor, made a copy of the paper for herself and another one for Green. His office was locked. Wary that she would collapse, she went to her office and dialed for a ride home.

It was half past nine when Danielle called Jonathan. No one responded at his office. She called to his apartment, waited until the answering machine started to drone. She slammed the receiver, then picked it up again to call his cell phone.

"Hallo," Jonathan's voice came muffed by a noisy background.

"Where are you?" Danielle shouted.

"At the Heidrun. Can barely hear you."

"What are you doing at a pub on a weekday? Are you done with the software?"

"No, we'll test it till last minute." Jonathan's voice was hardly distinguishable from other loud voices. "Roy took us to unwind after we wrapped the user interface."

"Nice," she said. "Really nice."

"Is everything okay with you?"

Danielle stared at the hardwood floor, wondering what to say when Jon was unlikely to hear half of it.

"Sure," she fired back in the hope that the curt reply would signal Jon to go somewhere quieter.

"Great. Take care. I'll call you tomorrow."

"Have fun," Danielle muttered, unable to bring herself to ruin his rare outing.

She tossed and turned in bed for hours without getting a wink of sleep. When she fell into a slumber, she was staggering on her feet, desperately looking for a way out of a labyrinth of aisles. Shelves stretched almost to the ceiling, but her eyes caught a faint glow coming from a distance. As she walked towards the source of light, Danielle glimpsed a man sitting by a table. Awash with relief, she hastened to greet Jonah. At the sound of feet, the silhouette turned, and she faced Lisitsin's derisive smile.

In the morning, Danielle gawked at her reflection in the mirror. Her face, she painfully observed, could not have looked worse if she had spent the night bingeing at the Heidrun pub. She made a strong coffee. A carefully applied concealer hid most of the dark shadows under her eyes. In the kitchen, she spooned jam and gulped coffee, then promised herself a breakfast at the

Hungry Boson right after she'd talk with Green.

"There is no reason to give a presentation," Danielle rehearsed her pitch while she ascended Fitzgerald Hall's stony stairs. Keep it simple and dignified, she told herself in front of Green's office. She took a deep breath and knocked on the closed door.

George Green paused the conversation he was having on the phone to say "come in." Seeing Danielle, he put his palm on the receiver.

"We'll talk at the pizza seminar," he said. Without waiting for a response, Green turned the armchair to face the Venetian blinds and resumed his conversation. Taken aback, Danielle wordlessly left the office. Her head was reeling. She passed Jonah Cobs without seeing him.

Cobs, on the other hand, noticed Danielle's distress. He kept seeing her gaunt face after he settled in his regular place at the section of old periodicals. Danielle's bewildered expression hovered in front of his eyes, even when they looked at equations describing intersecting aether currents.

Professor Jonah Cobs willed himself to focus on the equations, but the father of Gemma could not stave off the memory of Danielle sobbing between the aisles. It was none of his business what George had said that made Danielle look shaky and distraught, but nevertheless Jonah heaved a deep sigh. If one of the physics professors had made it his business to show a little compassion when Gemma had been lost and miserable, his daughter might not have snapped in her senior year.

We are too accustomed to self-confidence, Jonah reflected, heaving another deep sigh. He had encouraged Gemma to follow his footsteps, but he had not understood that a physics department, where everyone vied for recommendations and scholarships, was not a place for an idealistic and passionate young woman. Although Danielle was older and more seasoned than Gemma, Jonah deemed that a woman who looked for an old PRL and cried over what she had found was no match for George Green's impartial, unflinching rationality.

Unaware that anyone in Fitzgerald Hall was concerning himself with her woes, Danielle wavered whether to imply in front of Ben and Chi that universal rotation had been ruled out long ago. Deciding to present only the evidence from her simulations ("Green can chew on Ellis' paper after the seminar"), she feverishly worked to complete the slides. At quarter to twelve, she took a key from Amanda and unlocked the seminar room. Ten minutes later, Ben went in. Coming forward, he saw that she was going over the slides.

"You aren't rehearsing before talking to George?" he jeered. "Next thing, you will call him Dr. Green."

Danielle clicked to return to the first slide.

"Are you going to Montreal?" Ben asked.

"Probably not. What about you?"

Ben did not respond.

"Are you going to Montreal?" Ben asked when Chi joined them.

"If my poster is accepted. Do you know who else submitted a poster?"

They continued to discuss the forthcoming conference, leaving Danielle to mind her slides. Soon, the pizza delivery came, and the aroma of baked dough and the scent of oregano wafted all around. Famished after forgoing breakfast, Danielle impatiently waited for the professors.

"Let's start with the pizza before it gets cold," Green said, after he and Lisitsin took their place at the head of the table. "Then Danielle can enlighten us why her simulation takes so long."

Without responding to Green's remark, Danielle took a slice and sat at her usual place near Lisitsin. As she bit into the pizza, the smell of garlic powder hit her nostrils and made her nauseous. The tomato sauce left a pungent, acid aftertaste. Preferring that the greasy cheese would glue her stomach rather than stick to her teeth, Danielle swallowed it.

Others, she jealously noted, did not have such problems. Green and Chi ate while talking about simulations. Ben cheerfully pretended to listen to Lisitsin, who expounded on cultural monuments Ben should see on his very short stay in Paris. Provoked by Lisitsin's pretense to know everything, Danielle itched to toss Ellis' paper at his face. Instead, she took another bite from the pizza. It tasted even worse.

None of them cared how it felt to be singled out and treated like a failure, she resentfully thought. But for once, she could tell the professors that their ingenious model contradicted the rudiments of General Relativity. Then, if she had the bravado, she could explain to Lisitsin why his pet project amounted to "nonsense and rubbish." Seething with indignation, she could not sit silently. She got up and went to the front of the room.

"Can I start explaining why the simulation was going on indefinitely?" she asked.

Green turned his head, slightly cocked one eyebrow. Before Danielle could decide whether it was "yes" or "no," Cobs walked into the room. Every eye followed the old professor, except Danielle's. She stared blankly, unsure what to do.

"Excuse me for coming late," Jonah said, nodding to Danielle. He took a seat in front of the other participants. "Please, do go on."

"I haven't started yet," Danielle muttered. Feeling Green's questioning stare studying her, she shelved the mystery of Jonah's appearance to ponder on later.

"I'm going to speak about rotation," she opened. "Generally speaking, it occurs at every length and energy scale, from elementary particles to clusters of galaxies."

"This is not an introductory lecture," Green interrupted. "Can you begin with the model you have been studying?"

Danielle turned to her first slide. "Universal rotation was suggested by Kurt Gödel in the late 1940s. His equations..."

"Describe a static universe with a negative cosmological constant," Lisitsin ordered. Then, deeming that she was inadequate to give an articulate explanation, he began to expound Gödel's model.

By the time Lisitsin elaborated the ramifications of Gödel's model in closed universes, Danielle repented every second she had wasted on adoring his brilliance. Once again, Lisitsin kept flaunting his knowledge without explaining the model's drawbacks. When he halted at a possible set of solutions in closed Bianchi universes, Danielle flipped to the next slide. "Gödel himself pointed out the main problem," she said quickly. "His model is at odds with the observed universal expansion."

"I've shown Danielle many times that this is not an intrinsic problem of rotating universes," Lisitsin said, addressing Green. "More to the point, it does not exist in our model."

Irritated that Lisitsin butted in every sentence, Danielle said, "I followed your explanations and for a month struggled with a program that could never run properly." She flipped a slide to show the data gathered from the simulations, then looked expectantly at Green.

Some interest flickered in the slate-gray, shrewd eyes. Hoping to end the farce, Danielle weighed whether she should simply hand him Ellis' paper.

"And whose fault is that?" Lisitsin's deprecating voice demanded to know.

Chunks of pizza fought against the pull of gravity in Danielle's throat. Nauseous and momentarily speechless, she shot a baleful glance at Lisitsin. She made the mistake of putting up with his bullying when she had been enthralled by his genius. It would be unpardonable if she let him lash at her in front of others.

Willing herself to ignore Lisitsin, Danielle flipped several slides. "Look at the data," she said, pointing at a table which summarized the simulations' results.

There was silence. Green carefully examined the numbers.

"Is that your mathematical proof that the model is inconsistent?" Lisitsin's withering sarcasm left no doubt that her claim was beneath the usual "nonsense" and "rubbish."

"No." Danielle's cheeks flashed with heat. "It's an illustration that something in the model is fundamentally wrong."

Paying no attention to what she had said, Lisitsin began to denigrate her work. Green listened equably. Both professors discussed the next steps that should be taken, acting as if she was not present. A distasteful, sour taste filled Danielle's mouth, a lump in her throat grew and moved upwards. She averted her stare, to hide tears of humiliation.

Unsought for, her mother's PRL materialized in front of her eyes. It was followed by images from TIST's library - Jonathan, then a stranger, coming to look for a volume of Differential Geometry she had been studying from. The most important moments in her life, Danielle realized, were linked to physics. Mom loved it, and yet made such a sacrifice, Danielle thought, her heart aching.

Knowing that Love had forged that legacy, she forced herself to stand upright. She looked at Green and Lisitsin. They used her work, and yet, made her an outcast. Chi, she saw, was looking at her with concern. Nearby, Ben was twiddling his fingers, overtly enjoying her degradation. Whatever was going to happen to her post-doctorate, she was damned if she left the room defeated.

"If you can spare a few more minutes." Danielle paused. Feeling she was about to vomit the disgusting pizza, she skipped to the last slide. "Look at this," she said pointing at Ellis' results.

Green and Lisitsin looked at the equations. Both grasped what they read without any need for explanation. Queasy in the ominous silence, Danielle waited for Green to speak.

"Why didn't you show us that earlier?" Lisitsin asked, his temples pulsing with rage.

Danielle clinched her hands and prayed she would not retch. She darted a confused glance at Green, mutely asking him to break his silence. Nothing changed in his stony expression.

Hurt by Green's hardheartedness, Danielle turned to Chi and Ben. "Won't you appreciate that I've saved you months of fruitless work?" she asked.

Chi looked worried. Ben gloated openly. Neither uttered a word.

"Are you done?" Green asked, in that maddeningly equable tone of voice.

"Stupid bitch," Lisitsin squeezed through his teeth.

Without even looking at either professor, Danielle closed the slides and turned off her laptop. The presentation was over, and probably also her post-doctorate.

"Hmm." Someone harrumphed nearby.

How could she completely forget Jonah? Danielle felt his compassion and sensed that he was sorry to see her on the brink of losing control. Was he dubbed "the seer of the physics department" because his eyes bore through a person, seeing and knowing too much?

"I found Ellis' paper in a volume of *Cargèse Lectures* yesterday," she said quietly, speaking to Jonah. "It was from 1973."

Jonah looked at her ruefully, showing empathy but no surprise.

"Do you have a copy of the paper?" Green's cold and composed voice filled the room.

Danielle staggered to the top of the table to hand him a stapled photocopy. With every step, the bits of pizza rose in her throat, the sour taste intensified in her mouth. Focused only on not vomiting, she did not notice the meaningful look Jonah gave to Green. Ignoring murmurs and stares, she snatched her laptop and dashed out of the seminar room. She passed over puzzled Amanda without seeing her, pulled the door of the women's restroom. Holding the sink with both hands, Danielle threw up.

22

SPRINGTIME

The deluge of tears started as soon as Danielle shut the door of the little brick house: bitter tears of pain, smoldering tears of impotent rage, shameful tears encapsulating humiliation and failure – being right all along, showing that the model was inherently flawed, and getting nothing in return but disparaging taunts. She flung herself on the sofa and wept until her head threatened to implode. Emerald and sapphire specks flashed all around, amber lights twinkled in blackness. Then the tears and the pain drained away, and she slipped into oblivion.

When Danielle woke up, face pressed against the sofa, she was exhausted, sniffling, and shivering. The house was cold, but she could not bring herself to get up and turn on the heating, let alone to make a cup of hot tea. She curled, stared at the empty hearth and the shadows on the creamy walls.

Dusk was falling on the barren trees framed by the window when the phone rang. Danielle turned her throbbing head, found that any additional movement required too much effort, and waited for whoever was ringing to leave a message. The ringing stopped, but repeated half an hour later. She rose from the sofa, shakily picked up the receiver, and rasped, "Hello."

"Danielle?" Michelle asked. She had a niggling feeling that her daughter was in pain. "Can you hear me?"

"Mom?"

The sound of Danielle's hollow voice set up an alarm. "What happened, dearest?" Michelle asked. "Are you sick?"

Having no tears left, Danielle whimpered.

"Can you speak?" Michelle asked urgently, a note of panic

rising in her voice.

"Yes. I'm not sick, just a bit groggy. I didn't expect you to call tonight."

"If you are unwell, I won't keep you up. You'll tell me tomorrow about your presentation."

"It was a complete disaster," Danielle sniveled, then lapsed into muffled sobs.

"Problems at work are not the end of the world," Michelle said, palpably relieved that Danielle did not suffer from any physical harm. "Give yourself some leeway, let your mind rest, and you'll be able to work out what is wrong with your simulations."

"Even you assume that it's my fault," Danielle muttered, "but it's the other way round. I sorted out why the professors' model didn't work and showed that at the seminar."

"That should make you proud. Why do you feel wretched?"

"Proud?" Danielle spat the word. "Everything I worked for is going down the drain."

There was a short pause, then Michelle said, "I can't understand what you are talking about."

"I'm going to take the brunt of the professors' model's failure."

"You don't expect Green to fire you?" Michelle asked incredulously.

"Why not? I've shown that his and Lisitsin's model is worthless, and to add insult to injury, I did it in front of his group members and another professor. Do you expect Green to pat me on the back?"

"I doubt he'll resort to unethical means. Did he say anything about firing you?"

"Green said nothing, did nothing while Lisitsin denigrated my work and insulted me. As a matter of fact, my boss never lost his infallible, heartless calmness."

Despair permeated through Danielle's voice; it pierced Michelle's heart, tormented her mind and awakened memories of being alone and helpless, almost consumed by fear. Michelle wanted to scream and bring her girl back home, but she restrained her need to protect Danielle. Her daughters were past the age when motherly love could heal disillusionment or be a substitute for aspirations and dreams.

"Danielle," Michelle uttered tenderly, imbuing the name with love and acceptance.

"Mom," Danielle whispered, knowing that there would be no criticism, no veiled accusations.

"I won't give advice or inflict suggestions on you, but you'll tell me if you need anything." Michelle's voice choked. "If you can take some time off, do come home."

For Danielle, love that made no conditions and asked for nothing in return was a ray of hope in a surrounding sea of apathy. She opened her mouth, struggled to find the words.

"I'm grateful to have this option," she said at last, "but I can't go back to Thorboro. There is a contract I signed with the university and another one with my landlady. Green might sack me, but I've invested too much in this post to quit."

"At least take a couple of days to recuperate before you return to work," Michelle said. "Speak to Jonathan, daydream, try to figure out what you really want."

Jon's unconditional and unwavering love, Danielle thought.

"I'll take care of myself," she said aloud with as much reassurance as she could feign.

It was easier to speak about facing the consequences to her mother, than to get moving when every task seemed either too difficult or pointless. Chiding and challenging herself, Danielle managed to undress and get into the shower. She stood under the stream of hot water, cleansed all the traces of vomiting. Feeling better, she bent to lather her toes. Blood rushed into her head, iridescent sparks blinked in front of her eyes. Scared, she leaned on a wall and waited for the show to stop. By the time Danielle dressed, she was spent. She lay in the bed, gazed at the ceiling, and waited for Jonathan's call. When he called, they spoke very little - he was in the midst of work, and she was too tired to bring up what happened.

Danielle planned to tell Jonathan everything when he'd call on Saturday night, but when he did, it was to speak about Nickka's latest preparations for the beta. When he was finally done, she had no energy left to speak about the professors. On Sunday, he called in the early afternoon; to Danielle's surprise, their conversation did not start with the beta.

"Are you done, then?" she asked.

"No, but Roy pulled Tim, Paul and me out of quality control. We've started brainstorming the demo for the expo."

"I see," Danielle said. Jon's concerns shifted from the beta to the demo, but they still revolved around his responsibilities at Nickka. Considering his workload, Danielle reflected that he had enough on his plate without being told that her post-doctorate was in tatters, and that her stomach churned every time she thought about Green. Even if Jon knew, she reasoned, there was nothing he could do, except be supportive and encouraging on the phone.

"Before I forget," Jonathan said offhandedly. "My mother asked what dress you are going to wear at the wedding."

"What?"

"A dress. Can you buy something classy and understated that will blend in with DeWitts' other guests?"

"No," Danielle shouted. "I can't buy anything 'classy and understated.' Believe it or not, but I also have pressing concerns, other than accommodating your mother's whims."

"You don't have to bitch," Jonathan said impatiently. "I know that you have a hard time at work. On the other hand, it's not that demanding to spend a few hours on shopping. It might even cheer you up."

This suggestion obliterated any need to spare Jon from additional stress. Without mincing words, Danielle explained what "a hard time at work" really was.

"You worry too much," Jonathan said when she was done. "Green is too shrewd and calculating to terminate your contract straight after you found such a paper."

Danielle gaped at the receiver, amazed by Jonathan's impregnable logic. He saw beyond her misery, and struck directly at her boss's weakness.

"I think that you are right," she conceded. "Green is scrupulous about his reputation. But even if he bears with my presence for a few weeks, that doesn't change the situation, it only postpones the end of my career."

"It gives you time to apply to other universities, start afresh, faraway from Lisitsin."

"Which might be relevant if I were looking for a job in

programming. Cosmology is a small, tightly knit community. Who will consider my application after it becomes known that I lasted seven months in Green's group?"

"If you need to stay longer at King Solomon University, do it," Jonathan said.

"How exactly?" Danielle retorted.

"Swallow your hurt feelings and stop moping around, then think what unexpected results you might get."

"Haven't you listened to me?" she hissed. "The root of my problems is that I showed Green unexpected results."

"The problem was that you worshiped Lisitsin and mindlessly followed whatever he suggested. Now, it's up to you to convince Green to give you another chance."

"Why would he, after I contradicted him?" Danielle asked, remembering Green's unmasked disdain throughout her presentation. "Green would rather get rid of me, and hire someone who suits his requirements and expectations."

"If he's a good physicist, he appreciates you finding an inconsistency that evaded him and Lisitsin." Jonathan paused, as if to examine the options laid before Green, then added, "I see no reason why he won't extend your post if you come up with something promising."

"Jon, right now I don't know whether I want to work for Green. I can't pretend that nothing happened, let alone start looking for a new topic. And I don't see the point of pushing ahead with useless simulations."

"How can you give up when you want a career in physics and you have the aptitude for it?" Jonathan interrupted. "Every time you focus on research, you find something intriguing. Isn't it worth it to make the effort and show Green it's worthwhile to continue your post-doc?"

Jon did as he preached, Danielle thought. He wrestled with algorithms and software until he forged something that satisfied even him.

"'Something intriguing' sounds more like a magic bullet than physics," she said. "Trust me, very little intrigues Green."

"Do or do not, but don't whine," Jonathan paraphrased Yoda. "And before you start convincing yourself that it's impossible, remember that you've always found a solution when you were pressed."

A protest that he overestimated both her creativeness and her drive stuck in Danielle's mouth, as she realized that Jon was not only non-objective, but also blinded by love. Little tongues of joy danced in the wasteland of dejection, kindling a yearning to tell him about her reverie.

Yet confessions should have to wait. As much as she pined to hear Jon's tender words, it felt wrong mentioning love amid the current mess.

"Jon, what if regardless of what I do, Green won't extend my post and no other university will employ me?" she asked softly, hoping to hear that he would love her anyway.

"Then you will know it's time to switch to a profession that offers more than a handful of employment options," Jonathan replied.

* * *

Danielle tried to be rational, but when Monday morning broke over Hopeville, she lay in bed queasy and lumpish, her limbs lolling listlessly, her head reeling. A rumbling of a school bus, children's shrieks and rolling laughter cued her that it was time to be on her way to the campus.

It's better to face Green and be done with it, she tried to convince her unwilling body out of the bed. She dressed neatly, without fussing with clothes. A glance at her pinched reflection convinced Danielle to put on a little make-up.

The walk from Chadwick Drive to the campus stretched into an arduous journey, but at last she reached Fitzgerald Hall's familiar façade and halted to catch her breath before the stairs. The building loomed somber and overbearing; the gargoyle stared at her from the pediment.

"Don't expect me to reenact a Greek Tragedy," Danielle told the beast. Willing her reluctant legs to move up the stony stairs, she went into the building. The fluorescent lights at the entrance blinked ominously, as if warning against imminent danger. Ill-at-ease with her squeamishness, Danielle ordered herself to stop seeing omens everywhere.

She was ascending the steps to the second floor, when she heard a pair of familiar male voices carried from the hallway.

Blood drained from Danielle's face, her pulse beat widely. Instinct told her to flee, but the footsteps were too close for that. Forcing herself to move, she climbed the rest of the stairs.

Noticing Danielle, Green's face hardened, assuming a stony expression; his slate-gray eyes looked forward as if there was no one where she stood. Lisitsin swelled his chest, and lifted his pointed chin. His watery-blue eyes glinted belligerently.

"Good morning," Danielle mumbled.

Green passed by as if the space was vacant. Lisitsin scanned Danielle as he might do to a statue, twisted his lips into a derisive smile, and haughtily swaggered after his colleague. Mortified and nauseous, she trudged to the office, where Chi was assiduously checking papers handed in by Green's undergraduate students.

"Hi," Danielle said.

Chi turned his head. "Hi," he replied. "How are you?"

Wasn't the answer self-evident? Danielle restrained herself from being rude to the only person who, thus far, did not ignore her.

"I've just met Green and Lisitsin," she said. "Green pointedly took no notice of me."

"You didn't show him respect on Friday." Chi's meditative cadence suggested that he justified Green's conduct.

"Respect?" Danielle raised her voice. "How can I profess any respect after the pizza seminar?"

"Dr. Green pays us to check previously published papers," Chi said calmly.

"Sure, but that doesn't give him the right to be insolent or act as if I don't exist."

Chi shook his head and turned to the students' papers. Unable to tolerate his unquestioning acceptance of whatever Green did, Danielle blurted out, "I don't get it. Green swamps you with assignments that have nothing to do with research, and you do all that extra work without a single complaint."

"It isn't important," Chi said.

"Not important?" she repeated acerbically, unable to accept that someone as intelligent as Chi could be that submissive. "Is that why you go on like that?"

"My son is happy here, and we are expecting another child in

August," Chi said, smiling inscrutably at Lei's smiling photo. "So, I'm ready to work even harder."

"Oh," Danielle murmured. It had never occurred to her that Chi, encumbered with family demands and medical bills, could not afford taking a high moral stand, nor grumble about exploitation. She blushed crimson and turned to read her emails. She skimmed the news headlines and assorted gossip, then, more out of habit than curiosity, checked the state of the simulations. The runs generated a new crop of snapshots during the weekend. Ironically, when the data was not needed, all the programs were running smoothly.

Out of deference to Chi, Danielle killed the superfluous jobs that rotated the universe without expanding it. Then, to pass the time, she toyed with images of receding, spinning galaxies. Hours trailed without bringing any message. At five thirty, she decided that Green might as well sack her on the following day, said "bye" to Chi and left.

* * *

A week had passed after the pizza seminar, and Green still did not acknowledge Danielle's presence, except making a couple of public snubs at the astrophysics seminar and at the departmental colloquium. Dejected and distraught, she kept to her office, where the only stings came from Ben's cheery comments and snide remarks. Wary of giving Green any legitimate reason for firing her, Danielle came to work every morning, analyzed the accumulated data, arranged it in plots and tables, made little adjustments in the code, and caught up with simulations reported in published papers. She handled the calculations and other tasks automatically, using skills honed by habit. For the first time, her thoughts and emotions were completely detached from her research.

It took several more days before Danielle noticed that she did not have any insights or ideas since the pizza seminar. She forced herself to envision what she was doing, but her mind failed to conjure new images, or even summon older ones. Dreading that she was burned out and would not be able to create anymore, she grew even more subdued and depressed. The only place she went to was the Hungry Boson (Anne, who must have heard about the pizza seminar, showed her more sympathy and attention than before). The only subject that took her mind off her problems was the quickly approaching deadline of Nickka's beta.

On April 13th, Danielle sat in front of the monitor, too tense to think about anything unrelated to Jon. When Ben came to show off before he would fly to Paris and Corsica, Danielle left the office before she would snap and say something unpardonably offensive. She had a coffee and an éclair in mind, but standing under a bright blue sky dappled with scudding white clouds, she heard birds chirp, saw robins walk importantly on brownish ground. Unaware of her misery, spring wafted through the air – tender leaves extended from the tips of gnarled trees, buds swelled on grayish branches, little patches of green lawn sprouted in the sunniest spots. Danielle looked in wonderment at the first, hesitant blossoms, and decided against the confines of the old teashop. She rambled between Victorian edifices, mock-Gothics and rows of Greek Revivals, until she found herself staring at the monstrously slick bio-informatics tower. Why not? she thought, and headed toward the tallest building on the campus.

Mendel Hall's façade boldly proclaimed that it rolled in money and deserved every cent it had ever received. The main entrance had an oversized, transparent glass door, with a modernistic, slick handle. The enormous lobby had a ceiling two- or three-stories high. The decor was expensively minimalistic. Biology-themed posters and abstract artwork were hung on the walls.

Danielle registered a dozen or so matching armchairs scattered around low tables (few were occupied, mostly by youngish people working on laptops); a pair of sofas of the same style and color faced the glassy front wall. She darted curious glances at a group sitting on and around a sofa, then shifted her attention to the posters. Even the titles were incomprehensible. Unable to get the gist or pronounce what she read, Danielle turned to the gleaming nameplates on one of the inner walls. Mendel Hall, she read, housed bio-informatics, a genomics center, a center for computational biology, the biophysics department, and another bio-something she was clueless about. A glance at a nearby list of donors left her with an open mouth, the might of the contributing agencies, foundations, and corporations was staggering.

Fitzgerald Hall, in comparison to Mendel Hall, looked shabby and despondent. Its appearance bore witness to decline, or at least, to erosion of physics' former scientific glory. Danielle felt sadness tinged with shame. She wanted physics to thrive, its breakthroughs to draw attention, its discoveries to inspire more research and open new opportunities. Yet, engulfed by Mendel Hall's moneyed prominence, she knew that such wishes belonged to the times of her great-uncle Aaron Lichtfeld, or at most, to the days when Michelle had been a student.

The immaculate, glossy lobby attested that research needed funding, and that funding went almost exclusively to practical disciplines. Knowing that her time in Fitzgerald Hall was running out, Danielle mulled over Jonathan's words about showing resilience, about moving on if her aspirations turned out as unrealistic. Was it irresponsible to put off looking for a more down-to-earth field to work in? A jumble of protests whirred in Danielle's mind, interrupting any attempt to contemplate the idea. How could she discard the only profession she had seriously considered? How could she turn her back to the family heritage?

"I did my best," Danielle told the protesting voices, "but that didn't suffice to crack the enigma of dark energy." Jon was right. Whining and clinging to the past was as pointless as fretting about being isolated in Green's group.

Thinking about Jonathan, she pictured their lives. Her priorities quickly reshuffled; the protesting voices disappeared. She was willing to switch directions and start all over, if that would enable her to return to Thorboro to live again with Jon. Wondering whether there were post-doc openings in biophysics at TIST, Danielle looked at her watch. She wished the beta demonstration would soon be over.

Jonathan called Danielle's office shortly after three.

"It works, it flies," he said exultantly.

Thrilled by his elation, she listened to a description of how Nickka's staff had gathered in the company's largest room, how the presentation went under the watching eyes of the brass from California. Jon, she noted, sounded as if it was one of the happiest days in his life.

"I don't have the words to describe how happy I am for you," she said, without caring that Chi was also in the office, "but I'm ready to hop over on the first available flight to Thorboro."

"I want you here," Jonathan said.

Brimming with joy, Danielle whispered, "I love you."

"I love you too," Jonathan replied.

"So, shall I come to Thorboro tonight?" she suggested.

"On a second thought it isn't such a good idea. I'm flying to California a day after tomorrow, and there are several minor glitches we need to iron out before the demo."

"You aren't going to do that today?" Danielle asked.

"No, I'm going to sleep, then go to some sort of bonding activity Pilcher has planned."

"You are going to work overnight then?"

"Work and think about you," Jonathan said.

"I'll also think about you," Danielle whispered after the line disconnected. Daydreaming about her life with Jon, she picked up her mug and strolled to the kitchenette. Gazing into the thick steam rising from the kettle's spout, she envisioned Jon's proposal.

When Lisitsin went into the kitchenette and saw Danielle, he was taken aback. He deemed that George let Danielle to stew in her own juice, intending her to get the broad hint and resign. Yet, Danielle's face, which lately looked haggard and pale, was practically glowing. Her lips, Lisitsin noted, were curved into a sensual, expectant smile. Several explanations popped in Lisitsin's prolific mind, but only one caused him to scowl, then to estimate how many months had passed since he had seen Danielle running into the arms of a man. Being a through and through theoretician, Lisitsin ruminated over the time Danielle had been teary in his office, and considered other evidence of her raging hormones. Satisfied with the veracity of his idea, he thought about his daughter, who one day would graduate from a top college, marry well and bear his grandchildren.

"You should not drink much coffee," he sagely advised.

Danielle jerked, almost got scalded. She poured boiling water into her mug. "I'm fine," she muttered and scuttled to her office, too anxious to be away to notice Lisitsin's leering stare at her waistline.

Alone in the kitchenette, Lisitsin concluded that George needed to know that Danielle would cling to her job regardless of their discouragement. He smiled foxily, thinking about the reaction of his politically correct colleague when he finds out that his unwed post-doc is pregnant.

* * *

Even though Danielle had no inkling of what had passed between Lisitsin and Green, the week after the beta was quite stressful for her. First, Green called her to his office to inquire about the simulations she was running on the group's cluster. After learning that she was diligently doing her work, his pointed antagonism ebbed, and he acted as if the pizza seminar had never happened. She got new instructions, and although she could neither like nor respect her boss, Danielle was content to be accepted again in his group.

"Green's deeds show more decency and integrity than I've allowed," she said over the phone to her mother. "In fact, if my simulations will result in what he wants, he might extend my fellowship for another year."

"Is that what you want?" Michelle asked.

"I've been thinking about moving to the biophysics department at TIST," Danielle said. She paused, heard no reaction, and went on. "Actually, I saw on their homepage that two professors have grant money for post-docs with experience in computer simulations. I've started to read their papers, but so far made little progress. These papers are packed with weird biological terms and abbreviations alluding to methods I've never heard of."

Although Michelle cautioned her against overworking, Danielle did her best to improve the code and do whatever data analysis Green asked for, ASAP. Every night, she dedicated three to four hours to study rudimentary biology. As April drew to a close, she preferred to stay occupied. It was reassuring to build foundations for the future, and it took her mind off worrying about why Jon did not call yet, or panic because there was no news from Nickka's investors.

Jonathan sent an email when he arrived at Frankfurt.

"The hotel-room is fine," Danielle read. "Roy had his prep-talk in a bar, so we are jet-lagged and boozed. I Love U."

She smiled at the image of sleepy computer geeks staring at Roy's laptop instead of ogling at the females around them. "Enjoy the expo. I Love U 2," she wrote, and clicked on send. In seven more days Jon would be back in Thorboro. She kept daydreaming about their meeting.

* * *

The phone rang soon after dawn, while the moon and Venus still gleamed in a pale blue sky.

Picking up the receiver, Danielle heard Jonathan's voice. Alarmed, she asked, "What happened?"

"I thought you wouldn't mind waking up a bit earlier when you hear the news." Jonathan's voice vibrated with suppressed excitement. "We might have our first client."

"Someone from the expo?"

"No. A contact made by one of our investors after the beta. He told Ned Jones about Nickka's software. Ned has shown a strong interest in having the software tailored for his business."

"What does he do?"

"He is invested in banking security. If a deal comes through, it's going to be a pretty big job."

"That's great, but I won't congratulate you prematurely," Danielle said. Her heart pounded faster.

"The first step was to persuade Ned to meet with Roy. He and I will fly in a couple of hours back to San Francisco."

Danielle gazed stupidly at the morning star and wondered whether or not it was Thursday. "Doesn't the expo end tomorrow?" she asked.

"Paul and Tim will stay in Frankfurt. The meeting is scheduled for Friday, before Ned leaves to Wellington."

"Wellington? Is it in Canada?"

"New Zealand." Jonathan chuckled. "Don't worry, we won't relocate that far."

Somehow, the combination of "don't worry" and "relocate" sounded wrong.

"Jon," Danielle said. "When are you going to be back at Thorboro?"

"I don't know yet. Why?"

"I have been waiting to talk to you before I make some important decisions about the next year."

"I didn't ask you to put your life on hold." Jonathan's voice lost its ebullience. He sounded distant.

In Hopeville, Danielle watched the morning star fade away and swallowed her disappointment.

"I love you," she said. "I want to be a part of your life and you to be a part of mine."

"I love you too," Jonathan said. "When Roy told me about the meeting, I could barely wait to call you with the news."

It hurt that Jon did not understand what she said. Looking at the rising sun, Danielle regretted that she had never told him about her revelation.

"I want you," she said, "not phone calls and emails."

"You didn't complain when you were engrossed in physics or in a hurry to write a paper for PRL," came a resentful reply from Frankfurt. "You are needy now because you don't have something you care about to stimulate your mind."

The nasty cynicism struck Danielle like a punch in the stomach.

"Do you blame me for trying to prevent us from drifting apart?" she hissed.

"How can we drift apart when I love you regardless of what is happening with Nickka and of whatever you have done and will be doing?"

"Do you?" Danielle asked. Light filtering through the window spread fairy's magic across the room. She sensed Jon's presence, and murmured, "Are you asking me to come back?"

"Hmm, look," Jonathan sounded uncomfortable. "Love is necessary, but we don't live in Jane Austen's times, when a woman dropped everything once a man said 'I Love you.' Right now, you need to find your way and I need to consolidate mine."

Logic as sharp as a needle punctured Danielle's fairy-tale.

"You are not speaking to a bunch of software developers," she cattily observed. "And if you have ever read any of her novels, you would know that Austen's heroines never dismissed the importance of having a sustainable income. I wanted to discuss it face-to-face, but since we are unlikely to meet in the foreseeable future, I'm telling you now. I'm considering to apply for a post-doc in biophysics at TIST. Does that sound levelheaded enough for you?"

"Since when do you have any interest in biophysics?" Jonathan asked, then immediately added, "No, don't tell me, I don't have time to discuss it right now. Just don't make rash decisions and don't lower your aspirations on my behalf."

"Sure," Danielle said. "Have safe flights. I'll cross my fingers tomorrow for good luck."

She went back to the bed, got up again, put on the kettle, changed her mind before the water boiled. It was obvious that Jon did not understand how much she had changed, he did not realize she had learned to treasure love and trust much more than brilliant ideas and outstanding research. Unable to relax and needing to move while thinking, she dressed and left the house, meandered through the leafy neighborhood, where tulips started to bloom in flowerbeds, tricycles and bicycles were left on immaculate lawns, swings waited for children. A new yearning stirred – to have a place she and Jon could share.

She intended to treat herself to a strawberry tart and a large espresso, but ambling absentmindedly, Danielle found herself in front of Fitzgerald Hall. Raising her head to look at its somber façade, she saw the gargoyle's skeptical expression. That moment, Fitzgerald Hall moved, the ground spun under her feet. She grabbed the metallic rail without thinking.

Everything steadied quickly, except Danielle's shaky stomach. About to retch, she went slowly to the second floor, where she sidled into the women's restroom. Behind the closed door, she leaned over the sink and doused her chalky white face with cold water until it regained some color.

"Still having morning sickness?" Amanda's voice asked.

"Ah?" Danielle turned her head and stared bewildered at Amanda's amber pendant, which hung over a fawn-colored sweater.

"It usually passes after ten to twelve weeks," Amanda said compassionately.

"It does?" Danielle echoed, while she wondered what Amanda was talking about.

"The second trimester is the best time. You'll gain weight, but it will be distributed evenly all over you."

Danielle shifted her stare to the glistering tiles over the sink and racked her brain as to why Amanda was blabbering about trimesters and weight. Was Amanda pregnant? A sideways glance revealed a slightly rounder outline, but that might be the fault of Amanda's brightly colored sweater.

"How do you feel?" Danielle asked.

"Excellent." Amanda patted her pendant. "I'm just ending the ninth week. When is your due date?"

"Mine?" Danielle squeaked. "Why do you think that I'm pregnant?"

"Well, it's hardly a secret," Amanda's voice trailed off as she saw Danielle's shocked face.

Scrapping every bit of self-control she could muster, Danielle offered her congratulations. Amanda beamed at her and went to one of the toilets.

Who the hell started this rumor? Danielle frantically thought. Chi, Marjory, and the professors were, of course, beyond suspicion. Ben could have done it as a warped joke, but he was away at the summer school, and she doubted that the rumor had been circulating that long.

She recalled Lisitsin's warning against drinking coffee. "He couldn't," Danielle whispered, but when she replayed in her mind the scene in the kitchenette, she admitted that it was like Lisitsin to come up with a farfetched speculation. Nevertheless, it was unlikely that Lisitsin had discussed his idea with a secretary. Mulling over to whom he could have told such nonsense, Danielle came up with one name: Green.

So, was that why, all of a sudden Green started to appreciate what she was doing? What an idiot she was to attribute the change in his behavior to decency. Unable to control her growing agitation, Danielle shivered.

Amanda came nearby to wash her hands. "Are you sick?" she asked, warily backing a few steps.

"No, just a bit queasy." Danielle said in a hollowed, barely audible voice. "I'm going to be fine, but I need a few more minutes for myself."

"Feel well," Amanda said near the door.

Sure, Danielle bitterly thought. Did she look pregnant? Or had the professors jumped to the wrong conclusion just because she was a female suffering from nausea and dizziness?

"Why couldn't I see that Green belittled me from the beginning?" Danielle berated herself. She had been dazzled by his eminence and respectability. Now she felt betrayed. Her struggle to keep going after the accursed pizza seminar seemed pathetic. Her perseverance backfired, for Green despised her for sticking to the job. Even Amanda and Marjory must know that her work counted for nothing, that Green tolerated her only because he didn't want to smear his reputation in case she'd complain about discrimination against pregnant women.

Blood pounded in her temples, pain pierced her head. Danielle rubbed it, charging her hair with static. She felt desire to storm into Green's office, make such a scene that his precious name would be dragged in the *Hopeville Herald* and ridiculed in the *King's Monkey*. Picturing how Green would squirm, she happened to catch the sight of her own reflection. It looked disheveled, hair sticking in every direction. There was an unnatural, almost mad gleam in her eyes. The blatant vulgarity of her appearance brought Danielle to her senses.

Confronting Green might cause him a fleeting embarrassment, but he'd weather it without any material harm. No one in the venerable King Solomon University cared how professors treated their post-docs, at least not until the case had a potential to escalate into a Crawford-like scandal. She, on the other hand, would be branded as a spiteful bitch who could not come to terms with her failure.

"Why is it always a no-win situation for me?" Danielle asked her reflection.

In the silent restroom, it occurred to her that someone might get in and see how she looked. She found a comb in her backpack and tidied her hair, then pulled out her minimalistic make-up kit. Green's unwarranted and demeaning generosity might be of some use yet, she decided. It was unlikely he would object to her taking some time off.

Satisfied that her appearance was quite tolerable, Danielle strode to his office, knocked on the door.

"Come in," Green said.

She entered and closed the door. Standing in front of his desk, a wave of hatred washed Danielle's mind. Green was sitting on his imperious armchair, frowning like a successful physics professor who was unduly interrupted in the midst of his work. In his eyes, she was nothing but a nuisance. Wary of losing control, she quickly shifted her stare to the physics books stacked on the shelves, to familiar titles and authors. Agony extinguished anger. She ached to leave the physics she loved, the world she wished to belong to. A lump in throat heralded tears, which Danielle automatically tried to stop. Why bother? a thought flickered. Any demonstration of feeling was unpleasant to Green.

He lifted his graying head, his slate-gray eyes looked at Danielle indifferently.

Danielle forced herself to look at Green. Feeling nothing, she realized that she did not care anymore of what he thought. "I need to take a few days off," she said.

"Fine," Green answered, then turned his head to indicate that the interview ended.

She left his office, strode out of Fitzgerald Hall. After breakfast at a cafeteria on the campus, she whiled away the time until it was lunch period in her mother's high school. Then she phoned to Michelle.

"Mom, can I come tomorrow and spend the weekend with you and Dad?" Danielle asked.

"Of course, dearest. Come home."

23

MICHELLE'S STORY

The taxi hurtled up the street, leaving Danielle at the sidewalk. She picked up her bag, glanced at Michelle's Jeep and Joseph's Volvo, then walked towards a garden that encircled the parental home. By Hopeville's standards, the garden was of modest size and cluttered with too many plants. In Danielle's eyes, it was both quaint and unpretentious, a whimsical jumble of shapes and colors that perfectly reflected her mother's taste.

Mom always plants whatever she likes whenever it pleases her, Danielle mused, as she stopped to soak up the bloom on cherry trees, and to inhale the fragrant scent of blossoming lilac bushes. Many years ago, on the spot where trailing vines sprouted tender green stems, she had built a spaceship with Joyce and Julie. Touched by the memory, Danielle let the bag slip to the ground and rubbed her nose in tiny lilac flowers.

Life can go on harmonically even without cosmology, the plants seemed to say. Michelle has had many joys and delights, even though she sacrificed her physics career.

"What's so delightful to teach in a high-school?" a disgruntled voice groaned in Danielle's mind.

"It's far better than feeling damaged and reaching the brink of meltdown," retorted a voice tired of self-analysis and soul-searching.

All around the dusk was falling, adding depth to the trees and shades to colors. Danielle wanted to cry. She had wept in an aftermath of failing, but now it was worse. What Green had done tainted her entire physics odyssey.

"That wouldn't have happened if you were content with

getting a PhD and publishing a PRL," Lamentation whined righteously. "Aunt Sophie said many times that you would come to regret leaving Jon. Finally, you got your comeuppance for being a smart aleck and defying everyone."

That's a twisted outlook, Danielle thought. A post-doctorate in a good group was a stepping stone towards an academic career. And if she had not accepted Green's offer, she'd be accused of being a spineless coward.

"Going to Green's group was not your biggest mistake," hissed a venomous voice. "The root of your failure was your being unsatisfied with doing what others did. Your belief that you might shed light on the origins of dark energy bordered on hubris."

"Standing up to a pair of prissy professors is not hubris," Reason haughtily cut in. "Fate has nothing to do with ebbing creativity, blackouts, and headaches."

Danielle winced; for the blink of an eye, the venomous voice and Reason sounded like Lisitsin and Green.

"You all miss why Danielle failed," an oily voice intervened. "She muddled aspirations with delusions and mixed wishes with proper physics."

"You have been told to avoid taking risks with your research," Reason added.

"Especially a research which is over your head," hissed the venomous voice.

Fed up with the chorus, which was discussing her shortcomings since the previous day, Danielle ordered, "Enough!" She raised her head to look at the sky – the moon gleamed, stars feebly twinkled. She craned her neck, tilted her head, and tried hard to envision something her eyes did not see. She saw only the blackness of a Stygian firmament.

"The ability to conjure images will return if you make the right choice," a little voice muttered in the recess of Danielle's head.

"Don't heed to arcane, irrational drivel. Snap out of it," Reason commanded.

The little voice peeped from its deep-storage compartment, looked at Reason with pointed disgust, and said, "Hunches will reappear if you don't let fear shrink your mind."

Ignoring the voices, Danielle heaved her bag and went to the house. At the entrance door, she took a deep breath and rang the doorbell. A couple of minutes later, Joseph Meller opened the door. He took Danielle's bag and put it down, then embraced his daughter in a hearty hug.

"Good to see you," he said.

"It's good to be here." Danielle clasped her arms around her father's shoulders. "I missed you and Mom."

"Tired?"

"A little."

"How was your flight?"

"Smooth and surprisingly on time, but the ride in the taxi reminded me of Jon's driving."

A patter of footsteps heralded Michelle rushing from the kitchen. Joseph backed sideways to be out of her way.

"Mom," Danielle murmured when her mother's stretched arms tightly pressed her.

"It'll be all right," Michelle whispered, holding Danielle. Mother and daughter stood oblivious to everything else, until meaty smells oozing from the kitchen reminded Michelle that the veal might burn. She gently unfastened her arms, said, "Osso Buco," and hurried to the kitchen.

Danielle sniffed, then asked, "What's that?"

"Michelle is trying her hand at a new recipe," Joseph said. "Come to the living room."

Nothing here changes, Danielle observed as she followed her father. Everything she knew about her parents indicated that they had mutual respect and understanding, but it was always her mother who labored over the meals. In the living room Joseph sat in his favorite armchair, Danielle slumped onto the sofa. On the coffee table, beside a vase with fresh garden flowers, a medical journal laid open.

"How is Jonathan doing?" Joseph asked.

"I guess he is fine, but I don't really know. Jon said he'll email me after a meeting he and Roy will have with a potential investor."

"It's amazing how fast start-ups grow," Joseph said reflectively. "Twenty-somethings get salaries and bonuses our interns and residents can only dream of."

Bitterly aware of the ruination of her career prospects, Danielle didn't waste sympathy for physicians' relatively slow advance. "Any news from Joyce and Julie?" she asked.

"Both are cramming at Duke," Joseph said proudly. "Michelle asked them to come, but they couldn't."

It's going to be a gloomy dinner, Danielle mused, anticipating heavy silences interposed by her mother offering another helping and her father airing little escapades that interested no one. She thought he would comment on her sudden arrival, but he did not. Reckoning that it was pointless to postpone a conversation they would eventually have, Danielle asked, "Did Mom tell you what has happened at King Solomon?"

"Yes. She has been worried a lot about you since yesterday."

"I'm sorry, very sorry for upsetting Mom. I wasn't myself last night, thinking only of the termination of my post."

"Michelle did not say you were fired."

"I wasn't." Seeing no compassion on her father's face, Danielle said, "Green doesn't have the decency to do it. Anyway, I can't go on working for him."

"You are not forced to quit," Joseph said disapprovingly. "It's an unpleasant situation, but I'd have expected you to have more stamina."

Danielle scathingly thought about the tried and tested advice, "take a deep breath, grit your teeth, and work harder." Considering the damage it brought, this advice should come with a warning, "highly toxic, use at your own peril."

"I carried on with my work after being bullied at the pizza seminar," she said. "But I can't keep going when I know that I'm tolerated only because Green presumes that I'm pregnant."

"Can't or won't?" Joseph asked sharply. "Green might have continued your employment out of reasons you deem as unacceptable, but you actually don't know what were his reasons. Do you think it's romantic and noble to leave as a matter of principle?"

Danielle stared vacantly at the vase. After three decades in operating rooms, her father was too used to life-and-death situations to consider mental assaults that sapped one's capabilities. She couldn't tell him about the blankness she felt while attempting to envision cosmological scenarios, or even when she tried to focus on something more creative than technical calculations. Any mention of headaches or blackouts, and her father would usher her to neurologists.

"I see nothing 'noble and romantic' in leaving my profession, certainly not after working hard for ten years to become a physicist." Danielle paused. Her mouth was dry, she had difficulty talking. "I have tried over and over to get along with Green and Lisitsin, I did whatever they told me. Until yesterday I never asked nor expected any allowances or special consideration for being a woman. I got it unwarranted."

"Never wanting special attention isn't the issue," Joseph said. "Have you considered what you are going to do after handing your resignation?"

"I'm going to look for a job. I don't know where, but it'll be far away from King Solomon University."

"It's usually easier to get another offer while you are still working," Joseph said gently.

His voice brought back memories of a father who came to say goodnight, and to tell a bedtime story regardless of what had happened in the operating room. Maybe, Danielle reflected, he still saw her as a child in need of protection.

"I have no grounds to file a complaint, but what Green and Lisitsin have done sullies everything I aspired and worked for. It's not merely a matter of principle. By staying there, I'll knowingly let them negate what I've achieved so far."

Danielle stopped to check her father's reaction. Unable to discern any support in his pensive expression, she asked, "Did you also try to persuade Mom not to leave a promising career in physics when she gave birth to me?"

Joseph heard the bitterness in Danielle's voice. Looking at her face, he noted the unhealthy pallor of her skin, the gleam of raw pain in her eyes. "What you need right now is plenty of rest, and a change in nutrition," he said affectionately. "Why don't you ask Michelle for some chicken soup? She made it from scratch especially for you."

Accepting that her father loved her but did not understand her, Danielle followed his suggestion.

A pungent smell of bay leaves welcomed Danielle into the kitchen, where Michelle was stirring something over the stove.

Steam was rising from a big pot. In a large skillet, brownish chunks of meat sizzled. In a smaller pan, tomatoes floated in an oily mixture which smelled of onions and wine.

"Can I help?" Danielle asked, coming closer. The heavy aroma brought tears to her eyes.

"No, I'm almost done," Michelle said, turning to her daughter. She pointed at a shiny casserole dish, half filled with steamed vegetables. "The Osso Buco will be ready in about an hour and a half."

"I didn't want you to fuss on my account."

"I needed to occupy my hands." Michelle gave the mixture in the smaller pan a good stir. "Do you want a bowl of hot chicken soup before taking a bath?"

Danielle looked at the pot with the slowly simmering soup. "Mom," she said, propping her chin on Michelle shoulder. "A homemade chicken soup is not a remedy for every problem."

"Neither is ice cream," Michelle retorted. Seeing that her daughter was not hungry, Michelle said, "I bought some sea salts you may like to try. Use whatever appeals to you."

Ghosts of the past haunted Danielle in her former bedroom. Wary that they would soon communicate with the boisterous voices in her head, she unpacked as fast as she could, then made a quick retreat to the bathroom. Soon, the gurgle of running water filled the room, scents of lemongrass, lavender, jasmine, and orange blossom wafted from little bottles and unwrapped soaps. Sniffing luxuriously, Danielle soaked in bubbles. She was ready to enjoy normalcy and daydream about Jonathan.

"Why do you pretend that Dorian never told you about your destiny?" the small voice peeped in Danielle's head.

"Go away," she said. "I don't want to listen to you."

"Other voices don't speak when you are relaxed," the small voice earnestly explained. "I do, as I come from deep inside."

"With all due respect, I'd appreciate if you just return to wherever you have come from."

"It would be a mistake," the little voice warned. "You have to make decisions, but they depend on why you studied physics."

"I was curious, pigheaded and ambitious," Danielle retorted. "And you can keep silent, for none of that is currently relevant." To make her point, she dived under the bubbly water. The little voice did not speak after she reemerged.

Rosy and smelling like a bouquet of herbs, Danielle returned to the kitchen, where Michelle was still standing stooped over the burners. She ladled chicken soup and poured it into a smaller pot, while stirring its contents ferociously.

"Thanks for the soaps and the sea salts," Danielle said. "Can I help now?"

"Yes, take a bowl, bring it to me, and I'll pour you some chicken soup. The risotto requires constant stirring until the rice is half cooked."

Reckoning that her mother's intense stirring was due to nerves rather than following the recipe, Danielle accepted the soup without arguing.

"It's excellent," she said after a few spoonfuls. When it cooled a bit, she gulped the rest.

"Can you set the table and bring me a platter for Osso Buco? It's almost ready," Michelle said when Danielle put the bowl in the dishwasher. "Use the English china and don't forget to put on a vase with flowers."

Joseph, who was reading the medical journal in the living room, paid no attention to Danielle coming and going. When Michelle said the dinner was ready, he went to bring a bottle of wine, then joined the women.

"Is it good?" Michelle inquired after her husband and daughter took a couple of bites from the new dish.

"The veal is delicious," Joseph replied. "You can add it to your repertoire."

"And the risotto?" Michelle looked at the yellowish lumps scattered over Danielle's plate. "I might have stirred it too hard or put too much broth. Does it taste right for you?"

Danielle cast a dubious look at what tasted like a chicken-flavored rice pudding. "Are you asking me?" she asked.

"If I remember correctly, you praised risotto after returning from Italy."

"Hmm, yours is a bit different," Danielle muttered, recalling a risotto studded with shrimps, squid, and clams, "but it is mouthwatering."

The dinner proceeded pleasantly enough – good wine complemented the food, the conversation was sparse and unaffected.

Danielle cleared the table after they were done with the main course. Returning to the living room, she saw her parents looking at each other as if they were concluding a conversation they did not want to share with her.

"Would you like some tea?" Michelle asked. "I bought delicious looking almond cookies, and a lemon pie."

Joseph stood up and went behind his wife's chair. His hands began to massage Michelle's drooped shoulders. "Your mother wants to tell you something," he said to Danielle. "Later, I'll make tea for both of you."

Danielle looked at Michelle, who was staring glassily at the flowers from her garden. Joseph left the table, picked up his journal and sidled upstairs.

"Mom, do you want me to brew tea?" Danielle asked, when she could no longer bear the surreality of the silence. "Bring you anything?"

"No. Stay here."

"We can speak later or tomorrow. You must be exhausted doing all that cooking after a full day at school."

"I watched you when you were in the garden." Michelle's face was expressionless. "Do you still talk to the stars?"

"Mostly to myself," Danielle replied, unwilling to add to her mother's worries by mentioning the quarrelsome voices in her head.

"You have changed." Michelle's stare remained glassy, as if she was listening not to Danielle but to someone speaking in her head. "You learned to be afraid."

"The last couple of months were nerve-wracking. Being away from Jon added more stress."

Michelle shook her head. "I'm not speaking about nerves and anxiety. You had plenty of those before every major test. The fear I'm talking about is irrational."

It was unnerving that her poised and sensible mother sounded like the little voice in her head. Stifling her discomfort, Danielle took Michelle's hands. "You don't need to worry. I made a big mess, but I know what's really important and cherish it. I'm going to follow your steps, and focus on building a life with Jon."

Michelle paled as if she was seeing an apparition. "You don't know what I did." Her voice quivered. "Otherwise, you wouldn't want to emulate the decisions I made when you were born."

"It's okay, Mom," Danielle whispered. "You need to relax. Do you want me to call Dad?"

"On the evening before you were born, I stayed alone in the office. Everyone else was at a workshop at UNC Chapel Hill. I inserted corrections in my paper, intending to make it ready for submission before going on maternity leave." Michelle's voice grew thicker as memories trailed each other. "It was almost completed when I dozed off in front of my desk."

Danielle sat transfixed, yet eager to hear how she came into the world.

"I woke up wet, and it was dark all around. While I slept, a blizzard had started and there was a power failure in the building."

The distress in Michelle's voice permeated the living room; it carried urgency and panic, as if she was reliving what had happened twenty-eight years ago.

"When I found my way to the restroom, I discovered that my water had broken."

Trying to imagine the spreading of sticky wetness while Michelle grappled with the darkness, Danielle began sweating.

"Don't recount these ghostly hours, Mom. You told me about the blizzard and having difficulty reaching the hospital. Why torture yourself reliving it, when everything turned out well in the end?"

"I planned to tell you after you have a child." Michelle sighed. "Joe and I decided today that it cannot wait. You should know why I left physics."

"I know that you chose to care for me first and foremost. You gave me the best childhood a girl could want. When Joyce, Julie, and I grew up, we were the ones who got your best, and not a university."

"You make it sound so simple," Michelle said, "simple and reasonable."

"I'm sure that when we became older and more independent you felt frustration. Everyone would have preferred to have a fulfilling academic career rather than teaching the same old material to a new bunch of dopey teenagers every year."

"I've tried to do my best after you were born. But before that? I stayed to work in a half deserted building because everyone around me worked that way. It was irresponsible in my condition."

Although Danielle stared at the spring flowers, she saw the bleak whiteness of swirling snow, its relentless ferocity as it had slashed her and Jonathan. "TIST isn't that far from the hospital," she mumbled unconvincingly. "You could not foresee the blizzard and the power cut."

"I should have thought more about my baby than a paper," Michelle countered. "I'll make us some tea, and will be back in two minutes. Then I will tell you what happened, and you will listen without making comments."

It took a bit longer, but Michelle returned, carrying a tray with their teas, and a plate full of cookies and thin chocolate mints. Danielle drank hers gratefully, although it was scalding hot.

"It took hours until I reached the hospital. There was nothing I could do most of the time."

"Did Dad know that you were about to give birth?"

"Not until I was admitted into the hospital. I was on my own."

Danielle pictured a blizzard and darkness, a baby pushing to be born and amniotic fluid dripping, maybe mixed with blood. But she couldn't fathom the wrath of the forces threatening her mother. She could not envision Michelle's pain, fright and horror, only a paralyzing, encompassing fear. "I cannot imagine how you had the presence of mind to keep warm, to call the campus security. Most women..."

"Would not lose their mind, and would act instinctively to protect their unborn babies," Michelle said. Her mouth tried to smile, but her eyes were sad. "I prayed fervently, I begged that you'd be born alive and unscathed."

"Everyone would pray and hope," Danielle said. "You saved my life that night."

"I did all I could think of before I was in the hands of nurses and a physician." Michelle paused, took a deep breath. "Then a doctor put an oxygen mask over my nose and my mouth. He told me you were in distress."

"Mom, you..."

"I was told to breath and relax between contractions, but there was nothing I could do to protect you." Michelle voice was barely audible. "Then I did something..."

Everything Dorian had told her resurfaced in Danielle's mind. She wanted to stop her mother, to tell her that she already knew, but she did not dare to interrupt with words.

"I did as the doctor said, breathed and so on, but I couldn't relax nor wipe out what had happened. I made a vow that if you lived, I'd stay with you, and would never return to the paper or the university or any kind of scientific research."

"You gave up everything," Danielle whispered.

Michelle's hands held her daughter's. They sat silent, until Michelle finally asked, "Do you understand why I told you all these years that no one else was responsible for my decision?"

"Didn't you tell Dad?" Danielle blurted out. She regretted the question as soon as she uttered the words.

"I told Joe and my mother when they tried to persuade me to return to physics. Much later, when I decided to apply to a college for a teacher's certificate, my decision generated too much unwarranted advice. At some point, I realized that the only way to get peace and quiet was to tell Aunt Sophie and Natalie the truth."

Danielle only nodded. It was not the right time to tell her mother that Dorian was privy to her secret.

24

A NEW OPTION

Unable to sleep after her mother's revelation, Danielle stood by the window of her former bedroom and watched the star-studded darkness. The night stretched indefinitely, serene and secretive, teeming with possibilities. She waited for an omen, for a glimpse into a future, for an insight from her mother's story, on whose moral she could not stop pondering. In the dead of the night, nothing stirred. The voices in her head were silent, even the little voice from deep-down did not intervene in her contemplations.

Would she ever have become a physicist if her mother had not made that decision? The circumstances of her birth planted the seeds of interest in physics, but childish curiosity often fades away in adolescence, and it usually does not bud into a career. She worked hard, solved countless equations, but diligence and curiosity did not lead her to the right solution. Imagination and intuition - chill rippled through Danielle's spine as she thought about them. What were her chances to succeed in physics, when she lost a part of what made her a physicist?

The sun was high above tree tops when Danielle went downstairs. Michelle was sitting at the patio, a cup of coffee in her hand. Despite dark circles under Michelle's eyes, she looked composed and self-assured.

"Good morning," Danielle said. "Where is Dad?"

"He went to swim." Michelle stretched her arms to hold Danielle for a minute. "Take yourself something to eat and come here."

A wedge of lemon pie was not exactly what Michelle had in her mind, but she smiled indulgently at her daughter. "I thought we would go shopping today," she said brightly.

"Shopping?" Danielle grimaced at the suggestion. "You don't really want that nuisance. Shopping won't take my mind off what you told me, and I'm not particularly inclined to spend money when I'm about to resign."

"I have no doubt that you would rather ruminate over right choices all day, but we are not going to discuss my decisions nor what you should do."

"Why not?" Danielle asked, feeling let down. "I can use your advice before making crucial decisions. I have no one else to turn to."

"What about Jonathan?"

"Jon emailed me that nothing concrete turned out from the meeting with Jones, and that he'll stay in California while Roy works on persuading the brass that Nickka is a good investment. I prefer not to email him about Green."

"I think you should take a timeout to digest it all," Michelle said curtly, her tone of voice making it clear that she would not discuss any life-changing decisions. "Now, tell me what you are going to wear for Amos' wedding."

Rats, Danielle thought, knowing that she had nothing that would not affront Sarah's pretenses and Alice's snobbishness. Estimating the cost of an evening dress, she frowned. The little she had saved during the post-doc would be wiped out.

"I wouldn't worry about the money," Michelle suggested, reading correctly the cause behind her daughter's expression. "It'll be a gift from your father and me."

Heat flushed Danielle's cheeks. "You and Dad shouldn't bail me out," she said mutinously. "I don't want you to pay so that people won't see what a failure I am."

"Why not?" Michelle countered. "We can't prevent strangers from belittling your achievements, and neither Joe nor I can guide you in your profession. A nice dress won't solve any of these problems, but it will help you be comfortable among the wedding guests. So, why reject what we can easily afford?"

"I don't feel I deserve such generosity. You treat me like a Cinderella, while I've messed up like Antigone."

"Why won't you settle for something in between a fairy-tale and a Greek tragedy?" Michelle fondly suggested. "You might borrow some of your favorite heroine's outlook."

"Darcy proposed to Elizabeth Bennett twice," Danielle pointed out dryly. "She got everything she wanted by the age of twenty-one, without ever having to fight for his love."

Michelle sighed, then drank the rest of her coffee. "Let's go," she said unceremoniously when Danielle finished her pie.

It was an exhausting expedition. When Michelle and Danielle returned home early in the evening, their feet ached, but their mood was triumphant. To the lessons that Danielle had learned at King Solomon University, she added another one: when perseverance was combined with unwavering encouragement and an outrageous sum of money, it stood a good chance of resulting in a success.

"You should see the silk dress I'm going to wear at your brother's wedding," she emailed to Jonathan.

"Looking forward to see you with(out) the silk. Is that why you came to Thorboro?" he emailed back.

She stared at Jon's innocuous wording, feeling reluctance to write about the nasty speculations that tarnished the value of her work. Yet, it felt wrong to evade his question; if Jon really cared to know what had happened, he deserved a straight answer.

"If you want to know why," she wrote in reply, "call to my parents' number."

Jonathan called almost immediately. Danielle closed the door of her old room, and told him everything that had happened, except her blackouts and headaches.

"Can you be pregnant and not know it yet?" Jonathan asked.

"That's possible, but I've checked that I'm not."

There was a pause, then Jonathan spoke again. "What Amanda has said is hardly a proof," he noted.

"But it explains why Green has changed his attitude and accepted me again into his group. When I informed him about taking a vacation, he didn't make the slightest objection."

A laughter rumbled from the receiver.

"What is so funny about me remaining employed just because Green has decided that I'm pregnant?"

"The joke's on him. He is the one who forks out for your

paycheck."

Seeing that Jon did not grasp how degrading her situation was, Danielle said, "I've never tried to mislead him. If Green had bothered to ask me, I'd have told him the truth."

"By asking, he'd have risked your complaining about discrimination. Have you forgotten Crawford's scandal from a year ago?"

"I remember what Crawford said, and I think that he's prejudiced against women, if not outright misogynist. Green is neither, but somehow, his political correctness is meaner. I can't work for him, and I don't know what else I can do."

"As a first step, take all the time off you have. I'll persuade Roy that I should work from Thorboro."

Although Jon's advice did not solve her problem, it cheered Danielle that he might be back soon. On the following day, when Michelle urged her to get out of the house, Danielle called Lucy. To Danielle's surprise, Emily crawled in the child-proofed apartment, while Lucy poached and mashed fruits. After Emily was fed, they went to a nearby park. While the baby took a nap in the stroller, Danielle shared her thoughts about switching to biophysics. Lucy had no suggestions, but she gave Danielle a new perspective, speaking about her experiences as a mother working full-time.

On Monday morning, Danielle puttered around the house, feeling ill-at-ease to be the only one not at work. Finding little consolation in ice cream, she went to fetch one of the biology textbooks shelved in her sisters' room. All of them, she discovered, were as big as the behemoth *Gravitation;* none of them appealed to her. A tome devoted to the cell seemed the most relevant to biophysics. She pulled it out and began to read. After skimming through hundreds of pages, Danielle's only conclusion was that biologists found in a single cell more diversity and complexity than cosmologists pictured in the entire universe.

Humbled by the immensity of the field, she plowed through the undergraduate introductory course, taking notes as if she was a freshman. Her attempts to speed up the process ended up with headaches and blurred vision. She felt frustration at being so dense and slow, at being unable to make use of what she had learned in the last ten years. Reminding herself that she could not return to cosmology, Danielle forced herself to learn a new approach rather than dwell on former achievements.

* * *

Jonathan returned to Thorboro on Friday. He looked tired yet elated, but it was his evident desire to be with her that reassured Danielle about moving to his apartment. Waking up with him in the same bed, she felt that she finally was in a place where she belonged.

"I'm going to stay in Thorboro for the rest of May," he told Danielle when they breakfasted.

"How did you talk Roy into that?" she asked.

"It's not how but when. Our investors agreed to infuse enough money to keep Nickka afloat until the New Year."

This timely break seemed too good to be real, but a look at Jonathan's beaming face confirmed that Nickka's immediate future was secured. Embraced in his arms, Danielle's contentment morphed into sheer joy.

It did not take long before they established a routine that would have been very pleasant for both, if Danielle could forget her failure. Although they hardly spoke about her intended resignation, or discussed her plans to study biophysics at TIST, she felt self-conscious about the imbalance between their careers. At twenty-eight, her baby-steps in biology looked pathetic; she often felt completely worthless. Fortunately for them both, Jonathan did not care that Danielle did not measure up to his success. He appreciated that she put her mind into a direction more rewarding than cosmology and that she pushed herself to learn the basics in her new field rather than whined about being ill-treated. He was delighted when, on occasion, she was again cheerful and passionate. Having Jon behind her new aspirations, Danielle became more interested in what she was reading. She read the biology textbook while he was working; during the rest of the time, they went out, teased and bickered, quenched lust, or simply took pleasure in being in love.

Unwilling to interrupt the newly acquired togetherness, Danielle put off returning to Hopeville until May 14th. The little house did not welcome her. Its creamy walls, the sofa facing the living-room windows – all were reminders of how desperate she had been in the last few months. Restless and itching to leave Hopeville as soon as possible, she started to pack her belongings. That night, her sleep was fraught with dreams. She could not remember any of them in the morning, but her head reeled when she lumbered out of the bed.

Soon Danielle walked across the vividly green university campus, looking at the magnificent trees and stately old buildings. The sadness she felt was unexpected. Strangely, along with being disillusioned with the professors' work, she learned to like this venerable university and its traditions.

Fitzgerald Hall's looming façade brought a different reaction - she dreaded going inside. Even without lifting her eyes, Danielle felt the gargoyle's presence.

"I wish I didn't have to quit when I'm disgraced and defeated," she told the beast. "But I have no option except of handing Green my resignation."

The gargoyle looked at her skeptically. Wary that she would lose her balance, Danielle kept her eyes cast down while she ascended the stony stairs.

The second-floor corridor looked eerily deserted. The doors of Green's, Lisitsin's and Cobs' offices were closed. Reaching her office, Danielle found that it was locked. She looked around bewildered, and then slapped herself on the forehead. Everything about her post-doctorate must be cursed, or else she wouldn't have returned to Fitzgerald Hall when Green was attending a conference in Montreal. She hesitated before the door, wondered whether to go in and quietly remove her possessions from the office, then decided to find out first what forms one had to fill upon leaving the university. To Danielle's relief, Amanda was not in the secretaries' office.

"Good morning," Marjory said, as her eyes swiftly scanned Danielle's figure. "How are you?"

"Good morning," Danielle said as she tacked her belly inwards, to show that the pregnancy rumor was baseless. "I came to resign."

Marjory looked at the young woman in front of her desk, and mentally shook her head. Working for thirty years at King Solomon University's physics department, the secretary saw many career-related dramas, and inevitably, she toughened up to others' heartaches. Danielle's case, however, had a special claim. It was the first time in many years that Jonah, who told her how Danielle had rebutted Green's and Lisitsin's model at a pizza seminar, declared that someone was "an intuitive, natural physicist." Marjory was not a feminist, but she had respect for a woman who came from an undistinguished university, and yet could point to fallacies in the work of two of the department's most prominent professors. Moreover, Danielle impressed Jonah, who scarcely found anything worthy of praise in Fitzgerald Hall.

"Did you tell George?" Marjory asked politely.

"I intended to, but I forgot that he is at a conference."

Marjory stifled a smile, asked Danielle to sit down, then weighed what should be done.

The simplest course, Marjory thought, was to tell Danielle to wait for George's return. But Amanda being away for a checkup and an ultrasound-screening opened up an opportunity to find out discreetly if Danielle would consider a "might-be" option.

"Can I ask about your plans?" Marjory inquired, her placid intonation making the question sound emphatic and tactful rather than nosy.

"Hem, well. I thought..." Danielle's voice trailed off. It was too embarrassing to admit in front of Fitzgerald Hall's powerful secretary that she was about to leave cosmology. She clasped her hands so they wouldn't toy with anything and turned her eyes to little Kim's photos. "Well, actually..." Danielle swallowed, then said, "I intend to switch to biophysics."

Marjory's arched brows rose very slightly. "Have you been looking for a post-doctoral position?"

"No, not yet. It's a very different field, and I don't know anyone." Noticing Marjory's expression, Danielle blushed a little and shut her mouth.

Has any theoretical physicist wholly reconciled himself to leaving the field? Marjory cynically thought as she reassessed the situation. Since Danielle might be the helper Jonah needed, the most straightforward approach was to tell Danielle about the seer of the physics department, and then send her to seek Jonah at the section of old periodicals. Considering Danielle's lack of assertiveness, and Jonah's disinclination to speak about his work, Marjory looked for a middleman who was privy to what Jonah was working on, and also could explain to Danielle how to approach the most reclusive professor in the physics department. A self-satisfied smile spread over Marjory's face as she zeroed in on the right man.

"Do you know Isaac?" Marjory asked. "He was a graduate student here. He's a faculty member at the biophysics department."

"I spoke with him once," Danielle said, "but I don't think that he remembers me." She had not seen Isaac for months.

"You must network if you want to succeed," Marjory instructed. "Isaac can give you advice and answer your questions."

"Yes, I know," Danielle mumbled unconvincingly. Everyone could email a professor, but having no referrals or recommendations, what was the chance that he would also respond?

Perceiving that Danielle would dither when she should be putting herself forward, Marjory reached for the phone. "I'm calling him," she said to Danielle while dialing.

"Isaac? How are you?" Marjory's words wafted like a breeze of warm wind. "Laura is thriving, I have never expected her to be such a doting mother. I'll tell her... Yes, there is. Danielle Meller, George Green's post-doc is in my office right now... You remember her? Very good."

Danielle listened astounded; she pinched her thigh to convince herself that she was not hallucinating.

"I haven't spoken with Jonah... Yes... That is exactly what I was thinking... No, she hasn't... A lunch? Excellent... I'll tell her. Thank you Isaac. Goodbye."

"Isaac will meet you at King's Kitchen, at 1pm, a day after tomorrow," Marjory said to Danielle after she put down the receiver.

"I don't..."

"You will be fine," Marjory said, positive that she had done the right thing. Isaac would be able to decide what Danielle might be told about Jonah's lifework. Moreover, if Danielle was not interested in plunging into a research that had not borne fruits for a quarter of a century, Isaac could be very persuasive.

When Danielle left Fitzgerald Hall, her mind was in turmoil.

She sauntered across the campus, pondering on how her failed resignation turned out. By the time she found Mendel Hall's library, she aspired to be more than fine. Skimming Isaac's recent paper, she hoped he'd accept her to his group for some sort of semi-official internship.

Two days later, about ten minutes before the designated hour, Danielle stood near the King's Kitchen's entrance and watched for a redheaded man heading into the restaurant. When Isaac was a quarter of an hour late, she began to worry that he might not come.

"Hi," Isaac said when he saw Danielle.

"Hi," Danielle replied. She was miffed that he made her wait, but her annoyance quickly dissolved. Isaac's friendly cheerfulness, so unlike Green's sober pensiveness or Lisitsin's overbearing smugness, put her at ease.

They followed a waitress through an almost full restaurant. Isaac turned every few steps to nod, wave his hand, smile or say, "Hi." Danielle walked silently and listened to fragments of conversations carrying in the room. In the casual atmosphere of King's Kitchen, patrons who looked like university professors spoke about administrative and academic issues with more frankness and colorfulness than she was accustomed to. She wanted to belong, to be a part of their world; she knew that her chances were slim. Even if Isaac would be impressed by her PRL, he would not speak to her again after a phone-call to Green.

After they were seated at a vacant table for two, the waitress asked, "What would you like to drink?"

"Mineral water," Danielle said. Her mouth was dry.

"A pint of lager," Isaac ordered. He reclined on the chair, looking nonchalant yet friendly. "Bring it with the food."

"I appreciate you meeting me," Danielle said after the waitress had left.

"No problem." Isaac flashed a guileless smile. "You deserve a steak for shouting at George."

Danielle felt her muscles knot, her stomach becoming jittery with nerves. If Isaac knew about the pizza seminar, he might have also heard the nasty pregnancy rumors. She darted a furtive glance, saw that he was looking at the menu, and followed his example. As she read the long list of steaks, ribs, and hamburgers, she felt growing nausea.

"Queen's salad," Danielle said to the waitress who brought a bottle of cold water.

"Number 15 for me," Isaac ordered, "make it rare."

While Danielle gratefully gulped the icy cold water, Isaac entertained himself with fantasizing how she had yelled at Lisitsin that his model was rubbish and nonsense. She lacks confidence and self-possession, Isaac reflected. Just a couple of minutes ago, Danielle had looked ready to crawl under the table. Notwithstanding Marjory's delineation, he intended to find out with whom he would be dealing before making any suggestions or offers.

"So, you want to switch to biophysics," Isaac opened.

"Yes," Danielle said.

"Have you taken any courses in biology or biophysics?"

Danielle tried to think, while her mind conjured Green's cold disdain upon hearing a "no." For a moment or two she hesitated, then she said, "Not yet, but I'm studying on my own."

Noting that Isaac still looked friendly, she added, "I read your papers about protein transport in cells. I want to learn how your group handles that kind of simulations."

"Aspiring for the tenure track?"

"In the long run. First, I'd like to get a hands-on experience with simulations in biophysics. I don't expect to be paid straight away."

"Can I give you some unofficial advice?"

"Sure."

"If you ever want to be seriously considered for a tenured position, don't offer to work for free."

Surprised by such forthrightness, Danielle looked at Isaac's face. He had an open, slightly humorous countenance, which invited one to trust him.

"Would you consider me for a post in your group even though I don't have a recommendation from Green?" she asked.

Instead of saying that he had no money available or bringing up a similar excuse, Isaac chuckled. "Not having a recommendation from your boss is the best recommendation you can bring."

Hope raised her head, although Isaac did not say yes. A

waitress came with a lager before Isaac spoke, then a waiter brought a huge plate with a thick, scorched steak accentuated by steamed broccoli and baby carrots sautéed with pine-nuts. In his left hand, the waiter balanced a platter with a big green mound and a small bowl of sauce.

"Thank you," Danielle said to the waiter.

Isaac merely nodded, keeping his eyes on the steak. "Are you a vegan?" he asked.

"No."

He looked pityingly at Danielle's lunch. "A vegetarian?"

Danielle shook her head.

Paying her no further attention, he shoved aside the broccoli and the carrots, cut a piece of semi-raw meat, brought it between his nose and mouth, and sniffed it like a dog. The sight of red-brown juices splattering Isaac's plate ruined whatever was left of Danielle's appetite. Unable to look at how he devoured the bloody steak, she eyed her platter, then slowly disassembled the Queen's salad into small heaps of sliced cucumbers, a mixture of various lettuces, garden cress, grape tomatoes, stripes of yellow and red bell papers, rings of purple onions, and miscellaneous or unidentified veggies.

"The greens aren't good?" Isaac asked when he was halfway through.

Danielle forked a tomato and swallowed it. "They are excellent," she said.

Isaac cut another raw-looking piece of meat.

"Having read biophysics papers, you already know that it's a very different discipline from cosmology." He spoke very quietly, so that Danielle had to lean forward to hear every word. "A living cell has the capacity for self-replication. In some sense, that makes it more complex than what you perceive as the visible universe."

"I know." Danielle forked a few pieces of lettuce. "I don't expect biophysics to be easy after cosmology, but you and others have shown that changing fields is doable. I'm ready to work very hard."

"Everyone is," Isaac said. He took a gulp of beer. "When I left cosmology, the community buzzed and quibbled about a factor of two in the calculated age of the universe." Seeing disbelief on

Danielle's face, he smiled. "Back then, entire conferences were dedicated to this question."

"Cosmology made huge progress," she said loyally. "The discovery of dark energy was a major breakthrough."

Getting the answer he was looking for, Isaac leisurely finished his steak. "If you are stubborn and have the brains you can change fields," he said. "Yet, to speak frankly, I expect it will be harder for you than for many others."

Turning redder than Isaac's hair, Danielle reckoned that even Lisitsin wouldn't dare to be that blatant.

"Can I you ask something and get an equally candid answer?"

Isaac looked marginally interested. "Go ahead."

"Is it more difficult for me because I'm a woman who may start a family?" Danielle asked very quietly.

Intrigued that Danielle brought up a disadvantage others would have skirted at an interview, Isaac asked whether she had been at Karen Gould's talk.

"Yes, it was very inspiring," Danielle said automatically.

"You may be even more inspired to know that Karen has four children. The lore in the field says that she packed a stack of papers every time she went to a hospital. When Karen left with a newborn, she had read them all."

Understanding that she made a gross mistake, Danielle studiously stared at cress and lettuces. Isaac casually glanced sideways. The rush hour was over, but patrons lingered at neighboring tables.

"When I said it would be more difficult for you," he said, in the same quiet, almost whispering tone of voice, "I meant putting cosmology behind you. Biophysics is a hard and competitive field. You won't have time at nights and weekends to keep up with research on dark energy."

"I appreciate your warning," Danielle said defiantly, "but I don't plan to mix biophysics with anything." Seeing Isaac's skeptic expression, she elaborated, "My work on the dark energy problem was by no means a success. In fact, one of my reasons to switch to biophysics is that I have nothing to contribute to cosmology."

But she'll continue to think about dark energy, Isaac thought sardonically. He could wager on Danielle never succeeding in wholly immersing herself in another field.

"I was twenty four when I completed my PhD," he said, "brash and eager to work with Jonah Cobs on a new physics. Your boss took care that the department would not back me for fellowships." Grimacing as if he still felt a bitter aftertaste, Isaac emptied his beer. "I was angry after the departmental rejection, and also determined to have the freedom of a tenured professor. To ensure that I'd have better prospects at biophysics, I spent my post-doc in one of the top biology departments."

While Danielle perfectly understood how Isaac had felt receiving a rejection, she was at loss of why there was a bitter note in his voice. What did he have to complain about? As much as she could tell, everything turned well for Isaac.

"I didn't plan to leave theoretical physics for good," Isaac continued, "but during the post-doc I didn't have time for it. I wasn't especially worried. Jonah progressed slowly. I intended to catch up with his work after I'd return to King Solomon University. The first two or three years after I returned to King Solomon passed in a hectic whirl. I had to setup everything from scratch, build a group, scramble for results worth publishing. I did research, had endless grant proposals to write to deadlines, courses to plan and teach. I went to every conference I could give a talk at, having to network and establish myself."

Was that meant to dissuade her from wanting an academic career? Danielle wondered. Impatient to hear about her prospects in biophysics, she was not interested in Isaac's reminiscences.

"To make a long story short," Isaac concluded, "when I finally caught my breath, it was too late to work with Jonah."

"I'm sorry," Danielle muttered. Having nothing else to say, she started forking cucumbers.

"If my cautionary tale did not change your mind," Isaac paused to increase the effect, "you have an offer for a postdoctoral position in my group. I have money for a year, starting on September the first."

Danielle gasped. "Just like that?" she blurted out.

"Well, I read your PRL and I reckon that George was satisfied with your recommendations. You wouldn't last long in his group if you couldn't write neat code. If you managed to make head or tail of Lisitsin's ideas, you should be able to grasp rudimentary biology."

Danielle gaped at Isaac's ginger hair and willed herself not to contradict him. "Thank you," she said.

"While you think about it, bear in mind that if you really want to stay in physics, you have another option."

"Aha?" was all Danielle could say, while looking wide-eyed at Isaac.

"Have you considered working with Jonah Cobs?"

Rats, she thought. The idea was so ludicrous it could have competed with Sarah's admonition about her embarking on a managerial career.

"I assume that you speak hypothetically," Danielle said. "Cobs doesn't take graduate students and post-docs."

"You might be an exception."

"I don't think so. When I asked professor Cobs about his work a couple of months ago, he told me, very politely, to back off."

"Jonah rarely speaks about it, but he knows he won't be able to complete what he set himself to do before retirement. I and some of his former colleagues have argued for years that he needs someone competent to go over the material he has amassed and check his calculations."

Not me, Danielle thought. She had had her frustrations being Lisitsin's soundboard. She was not going to take a job which amounted to sorting out Jonah's papers and notebooks.

"Jonah isn't trustful, but he regards highly your integrity, and won't worry that you might appropriate his work," Isaac went on. "Luckily, he also praises your intuition and physical insight."

It was nice of Jonah to esteem her as a physicist, Danielle thought, but working for him did not chime with her interests. She did not intend to cling desperately to the past, but to find a job that would be a steppingstone to a new career. Knowing better than to voice such thoughts, she forked unidentified veggies.

"You won't even consider it," Isaac commented.

Choosing her words carefully, she said, "The little I know about Jonah's work is that it evolves around a quintessential substance which permeates the space and gives rise to physical bodies. This is a beautiful idea, and it might someday pose an alternative to the accepted physics, but I lack the necessary background in high-energy physics to assist him. The simplest grand-unified theories are over my head."

"Even better," Isaac said. "Jonah doesn't need or care about unification models. His aim is to derive all the fundamental forces from interactions between currents of an unique substance he dubs as aether."

"If anyone could achieve that, he'll get a Nobel Prize," Danielle said impetuously.

"And change the course of physics," Isaac stressed.

I had already borne the brunt of a failed promising idea, Danielle thought.

"The question is whether that's possible," she said coldly.

"I don't know, and I doubt that Jonah knows. Yet, considering his previous contributions to physics, it might be a big loss if his work won't be made accessible for the scrutiny of the physics community."

Danielle looked squarely at Isaac. Behind a face as innocent and cute as puppy's, she saw a tenured professor who expected others to be noble and self-sacrificing in pursuit of scientific progress.

"And what if nothing would come out of it?" she asked acerbically.

"Jonah's name has brought considerable money and prestige to the department, so securing funding for a year won't be a problem. Otherwise, it's a risk." Isaac's eyes dared Danielle to take it. Isaac's mouth said, "You have other options, including a post in my group."

"I cannot be held responsible for whatever happens to Jonah's work," Danielle answered the eyes.

"It's entirely up to you to make a decision." Isaac glanced at his watch, then gestured to a waiter, who arrived momentarily with their bill. Isaac pulled a departmental credit card and paid for their lunches. On the way out he stopped by one of the tables for a brief conversation. Danielle stood a few steps away.

"When shall I give you my answer?" she asked after they left King's Kitchen.

"Call me at the end of July if you want a postdoctoral

position in my group, or if Jonah won't take you." Isaac strode faster. "I have to go now. See you."

He crossed the road, and hurried into the campus. Dazed by a gazillion of conflicting thoughts, Danielle strode in the opposite direction towards Stateside Street and the Hungry Boson. She passed the teashop, walked to a fork, then turned into an alley, where a huge gray marble arch guarded the road to Fitzgerald Hall. The sight of the monument brought back the frisson of foreboding she had had seeing it for the first time. Was it an omen? A premonition about Jonah? A foresight about her floundered post-doctorate? Her gaze shifted from the hovering arch to the canopy of trees that stretched almost to Fitzgerald Hall. She thought about the gargoyle, then pulled her cell phone and called Jonathan.

"You won't believe it," Danielle said. Leaning on the gray marble, she recounted the meeting with Isaac.

25

LOVE AND OTHER THINGS

Sometimes Jonathan Lerner felt that if instead of a few days he had had a couple of weeks to sort out the most pressing issues, everything would turn out fine. He felt like that when he had to fly to San Francisco just after Danielle had gotten an offer that exceeded their most optimistic expectations. He felt like that when he returned to Thorboro and found that their nominal time together was in fact snippets, shared either too early in the morning or after a day at Nickka. Most days ended up in a rehearsal or some other wedding-related function to which Danielle was not invited. To Jonathan's surprise, Danielle bore his family's slights with admirable calmness. On the other hand, she seemed to spend inordinate amounts of time pondering whether she should help Jonah Cobs to wrap up his lifework.

"Did you sleep at all last night?" he asked Danielle one morning, when he came into the kitchen. She was nursing a coffee and mulling over something or daydreaming.

"Not much. How was Amos' bachelor's party?"

"He seemed to enjoy it."

Used to his morning gruffness, Danielle did not ask for details.

"Look at the bright side," she said. "It's behind you, and so is the rehearsal."

There was still the ceremony at Edva's town hall and the luncheon at the DeWitts' country club. Danielle wasn't invited, and knowing that everything about the wedding was emotionally charged, Jonathan had not insisted on including her in the party. The ceremony and the lunch would be attended only by the couple's parents, brothers, Amy's sister-in-law, and the couple's witnesses - Amy's best friends, Gwyneth and Brianna. Jonathan drew a line, however, threatening to be in California if Danielle would not be invited to the reception the DeWitts would be giving after the wedding.

"C'mon," Danielle said. "People who obsess when their software undergoes quality assurance trials should understand those who obsess about having their wedding run smoothly."

"We don't make our software other people's business," Jonathan grumbled. "Nor become so irrational that we won't have a party of thirteen."

Danielle smiled at Jon's belief that no one was affected by his work. "The wedding fervor is going to fade away by the end of the weekend," she said.

And then, I'm back to California, Jonathan thought. He made himself coffee and came to sit across the kitchen table.

"Have you made your mind up about accepting the post-doc at King Solomon University?" he asked.

"Not really," Danielle said. Since Jon usually avoided lengthy conversations at what he called "uncivilized hours," she asked, "Are you sure you're capable of serious discussion before noon?"

"Only half of my gray cells are asleep. The other half is wondering why you have such a hard time to accept an offer that could jumpstart your academic career."

"Haven't we had a similar discussion before I accepted Green's offer?" Danielle's voice was laced with irony. Once again, Jon did not ask her to stay in Thorboro.

"You shouldn't let what happened with Green and Lisitsin discourage you from having a career. You'll sell yourself short if you pass up the opportunity."

Danielle sighed inwardly. Not long ago, she had believed that advancement in a career was a measure of one's achievements. After the pizza seminar, she would never take for granted that one's achievements would be rewarded.

"People can adapt and make compromises, and yet they won't necessarily thrive in what is considered to be a promising field." She looked inquiringly at Jonathan. He drank his coffee silently, with no apparent intention of contradicting her. "One thing I learned at King Solomon University is that to succeed, one has to be perceived as outstanding. I tried to follow Green's idea of outstanding, to do what others do, only better. I couldn't mold myself this way. Isaac is by no means Green," Danielle hastened to say, "but taking the long view, I doubt whether I can fit into his idea of outstanding. In that sense, working with Cobs is my real opportunity, because the outstanding is about physics and not about me."

"I won't try to dissuade you from working with a subversive hermit," Jonathan said. "But what if his physics will turn out to be an irrelevant research no one cares about? Have you considered what will you do then?"

Jon did not criticize her, Danielle noted. In fact, he sounded almost rueful. Apparently, partying with a bunch of Amos' MBA friends made all branches of physics look equally pointless.

"I've thought about it," Danielle said. She also thought about her mother's sacrifice. It made no sense, but without Mom's unconditional love she might not be alive.

"You'll regret it if by age of thirty you won't have laid solid foundations for your career," Jonathan said.

"I probably will, but decisions aren't always rational. Sometimes, I'd rather risk failing again than regretting that I haven't helped Jonah as Isaac asked. I can't assess Jonah's work, but I don't want it to sink into oblivion because of me."

The words hovered in the quiet kitchen. They did not dangle any reward, but they opened Jonathan's eyes. He loved Danielle. Her curiosity and passion drew him, even though she craved to understand what could never affect anyone or anything. An academic career in physics would be a perfect match for her, Jonathan thought, but Danielle couldn't advance her career by turning her back to the physics she loved. Love, it dawned on Jonathan, transcended reason.

In his mind's eye, he saw Danielle standing on a bluff, watching the Pacific ocean. Despite the drizzle, her face looked enchanted, her eyes sparkled, full of life. He stood nearby, then came closer to hold her. Snuggling with each other, they faced the majestic entity, the luring abyss which started under their feet and stretched to the horizon. In his vision they were together indefinitely.

"A kiss for your thought," Danielle offered.

Jonathan rose from his chair and went to Danielle's. "It's a question," he said after their lips parted.

Danielle cocked her head and looked at Jonathan. "Yes?"

"Will you marry me?"

"Yes!!!" she said without stopping to think.

Jonathan stayed in the apartment to celebrate the new stage in their relationship, doing pretty much what they did before he proposed and Danielle accepted. When he finally went to work, rapturous and dazzled, Danielle sat down to daydream. Later, she called to invite herself to her parents' house.

Michelle, who was the first to hear about the engagement, looked as happy as if she was getting married. Joseph's congratulations were also expressed with unusual warmth and unreserved approval. Since he considered Jonathan a part of his family, Joseph did not feel obliged to hold his tongue.

"Most men propose with a ring," he commented.

"It was completely spontaneous," Danielle defended her fiancé.

"Spontaneous? Haven't you discussed marriage last May, before you went to Italy?"

"We did," Danielle said, her intonation implying *but who actually cares?*

At that, Joseph and Michelle exchanged broad smiles.

"Shall I call Richard and Sarah?" Joseph asked his wife.

"They don't know yet," Danielle replied. "We'll tell them after the wedding."

"You don't expect..." Joseph started, but a glance from his wife stopped him. If Danielle and Jonathan believed that their long-expected engagement could surprise anyone, Joseph did not want to spoil that particular delusion. Happily humming to himself, he went to chill a bottle of champagne.

* * *

Friday was Amos and Amy's wedding day. When Jonathan returned to his apartment after the luncheon (he politely declined Graham and Alice's invitation to stay at their house), a surprise waited for him at the living-room. Almost drooling, he closed the door.

"Do you like it?" Danielle asked, raising her arms and twirling in her new silk dress.

"You better take it off before I show you how much," Jonathan rasped.

Although they did not make it as early as Sarah had admonished, Jonathan and Danielle were among the first guests to walk on DeWitts' well-tended lawn. Glowing with happiness, Danielle congratulated her hosts without noticing how distinguished Graham looked, or how gracious Alice was on her daughter's wedding. Turning to congratulate Jonathan's parents, Danielle observed that her worries about a dress were a waste of time. Sarah was in flutter of delight, and cared to talk only about Amos and Amy. Richard, as usual, said very little, yet Danielle had not seen him that happy before.

Other guests trickled to the front lawn, waiters circulated with wines and cocktails, waitresses roved with trays full of bite-size canapés. Jonathan shook hands with friends, male relatives clapped on his back, older women smacked their painted lips in a mock kiss half-an-inch from his face. Danielle glided on his arm, beamed to whom she knew and smiled to those whom Jonathan introduced. It was effortless to appear lighthearted when she brimmed with happiness.

"One wedding brings another," commented Sarah's balding cousin when he hugged Danielle.

His wife harrumphed meaningfully and asked where were Amos and his bride.

Jonathan turned to the big house. Its formal entrance bloomed with flower arrangements. In twilight, it was dappled with pink and gold.

"They will come out soon," he said. "Right after a magic show which is about to start any moment."

A change in music cued other guests to look at the front door. It opened, but nothing happened. There where murmurs, ripples of anticipation, then a girl in a white dress ran out. Every eye followed her.

The girl held a bouquet of pink roses. She pointed the roses at a tree and it burst with light. Several people clapped. The girl ran to another tree, and repeated her magic. Clapping followed the girl's course between trees and shrubs.

"Cute, isn't it?" Jonathan whispered into Danielle's ear.

"She even looks like a fairy," Danielle whispered back. "Who is she?"

"Elizabeth, Amy's niece."

The clapping grew stronger as Elizabeth lighted two rows of lanterns. Completing her show, she ran to her grandmother.

"Look at the house," someone said nearby.

Over a hundred guests gasped almost simultaneously, seeing Amos and Amy holding hands in front of the colonnaded entrance. Illuminated by the rays of the sinking sun, Amy's traditional wedding dress brought to mind a princess from a fairy tale. Amy's radiance outshone the flashlights cameramen used to capture the moment.

"Wow," Danielle murmured, when Amos and Amy descended to the lawn and walked between the lanterns. She could not picture Amos as Prince Charming, but he looked as if his wishes came true.

Waiters served champagne, guests whispered, cameras flashed. Silence broke when Graham raised his flute. He made a toast for Amy and Amos. Some eyes teared. Others cheered. After the flutes were emptied, relatives and friends went to congratulate the young couple.

The rest of the evening was a credit to Alice and Fiona, to the schools which refined their tastes, to generations of bankers who had paid for those schools to instill proper upbringing. Watching the privileged, Danielle felt as little envy as they had interest in the universe surrounding them.

"Candles in the sky," Jonathan whispered when they sat at their table. The cloudless indigo sky above them was dotted with glittering stars.

The dinner was elegant (although not all the guests were so). The three-tiered wedding cake was an artist's creation.

After the cake, the music changed into a soft, lyrical melody; a bluish projector lit the dancing floor. Amos and Amy walked under the limelight. Awash with whimsical blue, their eyes locked together, they started to swirl to the tune of their song. Their motions were fluid and slow, their steps matched perfectly. Other projectors lighted up as the music rolled; by the time the song ended, Amy's dress was of the colors of a rainbow.

Graham and Alice joined the newlyweds on their second dance; Richard and Sarah followed to the dancing floor. Mesmerized, Danielle watched the three couples swirling. In her mind's eyes they were eddies in a sea of colors, all rotating in the same direction, like the progenitors of galaxies she had simulated not so long ago.

Let bygones be bygones, she told herself. That chapter was over. Besides, she was not supposed to think about physics at a wedding.

Other couples joined the dancers. Danielle noted that all pairs rotated in the same direction, which she deemed as pretty straightforward, for ninety percent of the population were right-handed. In the back of her mind, an idea sprang into existence.

"Do you want a piece of paper to jot your ideas?" Jonathan quietly asked.

"In this place? You'll find best-quality linen napkins, but no paper."

"If you can't write it down, do you want to dance?"

It felt good to follow the music, to rotate with Jonathan under the stars.

"How did you know I was thinking about cosmology?" Danielle whispered when the music ended.

Jonathan grinned. "Only two things bring out that gleam in your eyes."

Acknowledgments

This book was written over a period of ten years. I'm grateful to my family for giving me the support and encouragement I needed to go on and complete it.

I'm indebted to physicists who made their work on dark energy available through the arXiv. Thanks to NASA for allowing the use of images taken in space.

Special thanks to my father for inspiring my interest in physics, and for telling me about aether. Huge thanks to Alon and Ori for reading and commenting on the various drafts, for making editorial suggestions, and lastly for proof-reading the manuscript during the holidays. Without Michael my ramblings would have never become an actual book. He helped from the earliest stage, all these years, in too many ways to mention. So, thanks Michael for being who you are.

Made in the USA
Lexington, KY
02 June 2015